About the Authors

Annie O'Neil spent most of her childhood with a leg draped over the family rocking chair and a book in her hand. Novels, baking and writing too much teenage angst poetry ate up most of her youth. Now, Annie splits her time between corralling her husband into helping her with their cows, listening to audio books whilst weeding and spending some very happy hours at her computer writing.

Andrea Bolter has always been fascinated by matters of the heart. In fact, she's the one her girlfriends turn to for advice with their love lives. A city mouse, she lives in Los Angeles with her husband and daughter. She loves travel, rock n' roll, sitting at cafés, and watching romantic comedies she's already seen a hundred times. Say hi at andreabolter.com

Author **Ally Blake** loves strong hot coffee, fluffy white clouds, dancing in the car to a song she hasn't heard in ages, and the glide of a soft, dark pencil over really good notepaper. She also adores writing love stories. Having sold over four million copies of her books worldwide she is living the dream. Alongside one handsome husband, their three spectacular children, and too many animal companions to count, Ally lives and writes in the leafy western suburbs of Brisbane, Australia

Royal Rebels

Royal Rebels: Royal Weddings

ANNIE O'NEIL

ANDREA BOLTER

ALLY BLAKE

MILLS & BOON

First Published in Great Britain 2021
By Mills & Boon, an imprint of HarperCollins*Publishers* Ltd
1 London Bridge Street, London, SE1 9GF

www.harpercollins.co.uk

HarperCollins*Publishers*
1st Floor, Watermarque Building,
Ringsend Road, Dublin 4, Ireland

ISBN: 978-0-263-30021-5

MIX
Paper from responsible sources
FSC™ C007454

This book is produced from independently certified FSC™ paper to ensure responsible forest management.

For more information visit: www.harpercollins.co.uk/green

Printed and bound in Spain
by CPI, Barcelona

CLAIMING HIS PREGNANT PRINCESS

ANNIE O'NEIL

This book is dedicated to my great friend Jess. She had the most epic hen do in the history of hen parties and somehow we ended up in a three mile parade in the center of a town just outside of Venice. As you do, when you're dressed as a nun and the lawfully intended is dressed as a minx. I mean bride. Big love xx Annie O'

CHAPTER ONE

"DR. JESOLO! THERE'S a full waiting room!"

"*Si, pronto*, Teo!" Bea poked her head out of the curtained exam space and then repeated herself in English, just in case her Australian coworker hadn't understood. "On my way."

He nodded, screwed his nose up for a minute and gave her a funny look.

She hoped her pasted-on happy face simply looked like a case of first-day jitters.

Her new colleague didn't need to know she was fighting another wave of impossible-to-quench tears.

She swiped at her eyes again and forced herself to tune in to the various conversations happening in the exam areas surrounding hers.

English, Italian, French and German. Broken arms. Asthma attacks. Altitude sickness. They were all mingled together up here in Torpisi, and she was loving every moment of it. Or would be if she could get her eyes to dry and see another patient.

That was why this multilingual, brain-stretching trauma center suited her needs to a tee.

Hormones or history. It was always a toss-up as to which would unleash the next flood.

You can do this. You're a princess! Trained in the art of...of artifice.

At least work would give her poor over-wrung tear ducts a break.

The Clinica Torpisi catered to the needs of international tourists. Ones who didn't read the gossip rags. Adrenaline junkies, fun seekers and good old-fashioned holidaymakers kept the *clinica* operating on full steam over the summer—and probably more so in the winter, when the skiing crowd came in. It was the perfect place to hide in plain sight. And to create some much-needed distraction from her real-life problems.

Zurich, Lyon, Salzburg and even Milan were only a couple of hours' drive away, but the press still hadn't caught wind of the fact that she was up here in this magical Italian mountain hideaway.

Ha! Foiled again. Just the way she liked it. They'd had their pound of flesh after the wedding nightmare. Painting a picture of her as if she'd been abandoned at the altar... The cheek! She'd been made of fool of, perhaps, but *she'd* been the one to pull off her ring and walk away.

The press might have stolen what little dignity Bea had left, but she wouldn't let them take away her precious Italy. Especially now that returning to England was out of the question.

Her fingers pressed against her lips as the strong sting of emotion teased the back of her nose again.

Ugh. She'd tried her best to shake off those memories. The ones she'd kept locked away the day since she'd agreed to her mother's harebrained plan. What a fool she'd been!

She'd had a shot of living the perfect life and had ruined it in a vainglorious attempt to please her blue-blooded family. Power and position. It was all they'd wanted.

Well…they'd hit the tabloids, all right, just not in the way anyone had anticipated.

Hopefully the paparazzi were now too busy jetting around the globe trying to find "Italy's favorite playboy prince" to worry about *her* any longer.

Bea pulled the used paper off the exam table and stuffed it in the bin. It was her own fault this mess had blown up in her face. If she'd stayed strong, told her parents she was in love with someone else…

Inhale. Exhale.

That was in the past now. She'd made the wrong decision and now she was paying for it.

Bea took a quick scan of the room, then glanced in the mirror before heading out for her next patient, smiling ruefully as she went. Trust an Italian clinic in the middle of nowhere to have mirrors everywhere! She was willing to bet the hospital on the Austrian side of town didn't have a single one. Practical. Sensible. More her style. Maybe she should have tried to get a job there…

Her eyes flicked up to the heavens, then down again.

Quit second-guessing yourself! It's day one, and so far so good.

She forced herself to look square into the mirror at the "new" Bea.

No more Principessa Beatrice Vittoria di Jesolo, fiancée of Italy's favorite "Scoundrel Prince."

Her eyes narrowed as she recataloged those memories. Everything happened for a reason, and deep in her heart she knew marrying for tradition rather than for love would have been a huge mistake. Even if it would have made her mother happy.

A mirthless laugh leapt from her chest.

She was well and truly written out of the will now!

She shrugged her shoulders up and down, then gave her cheeks a quick pinch.

Saying goodbye to that life had been easy.

The hard part was living with herself after having let things go as far as they had.

"Dr. Jesolo?"

Bea started, and wagged her finger at herself in the mirror.

Self-pity wasn't going to help either. Work would.

"Si, sto arrivando!"

From today she was simply Dr. Bea Jesolo, trauma doctor to the fun-loving thrill seekers up here in Italy's beautiful Alpine region.

She tipped her head to the side. Now that she was a bit more used to it, she liked the pixie haircut. The gloss of platinum blond. It still caught her by surprise when she passed shop windows, but there were unexpected perks. It made her brown eyes look more like liquid shots of espresso than ever before. Not that she was on the market or anything. Just get up, work, go to bed and repeat. Which made the short, easy-to-style cut practical. Much better than the long tresses she'd grown especially for the wedding.

She gave a wayward strand a tweak, then made a silly face at herself when it bounced back out of place.

Undercover Princess.

That was this morning's newspaper headline. She'd seen it on the newsstand when she'd walked into work. There had been a picture of heaven knew who on the front page of Italy's most popular gossip magazine. A shadowy photo showing someone—no doubt a model wearing a wig—looking furtively over her shoulder as she was swept through airport security in Germany. Or was it Holland? Utrecht? Somewhere *she* wasn't.

Undercover Princess, indeed.

She pulled her stethoscope back into place around her neck and shrugged the headline away.

It was a damn sight better than the handful she'd seen before sneaking away to lick her wounds on her brother's ridiculous superyacht for six weeks, ducking and dodging the press among the Greek islands.

There were perks to having a privileged family. And, of course, pitfalls.

Abandoned by the Wolf!

Prince Picks Fair Maid over Princess!

Altar-cation for Italy's Heartbroken Princess.

Heartbroken? Ha! Hardly.

Love-Rat Prince Crumbles at the First Hurdle

That was getting closer. Or maybe:

Pregnant Principessa Prepares for First Solo as Mama.

Not that anyone knew *that* little bit of tabloid gold.

Doctor by day…

Her hand crept to her belly. Though she wasn't showing yet, she knew the little tiny bud of a baby was in there… just the size of an apple seed. Maybe a little more? Bigger, smaller… Either way she'd protect that blossoming life with every ounce of power she possessed. Hers and hers alone. How she'd go about living the rest of her life once the baby was born was a problem she hadn't yet sorted, but she'd get there. Because she didn't have much of a choice.

Bea swiped at her eyes, forced on a smile, then pulled open the curtain. Nothing like a patient to realign her focus.

"Leah Stokes?"

She scanned the room, bracing herself against the moment that someone recognized her, air straining against her lungs. Her shoulders dropped and she blew a breath slowly past her lips as all the patients looked up, shook their heads, then went back to their magazines and conversations. All except a young twentysomething woman, who was pushing herself up from her chair. She was kitted out in cycling gear and… *Oh. Ouch!*

"Looks like some serious road rash there." Bea's brow furrowed in sympathy and she quickly walked over to the woman and put her arm around her waist. "Lean on me. That's right. Just put your arm around my shoulder and let me take some of the weight."

"I don't think I can make it all the way." Leah drew in a sharp breath, tears beginning to trickle down her cheeks now that help was here.

"Can I get a hand?" Bea called out.

There were a couple of guys in rescue uniforms at the front desk. She called again to get their attention. When the closest one looked up, the blond…

Her breath caught in her throat.

He wasn't blond. His hair was hay colored—that was how she'd always remembered it… The color of British summertime.

A perfect complement to startling green eyes.

As their gazes grazed, then caught, Bea's heart stopped beating. Just…*froze.*

She'd know that face anywhere. It had been two long years. Two painfully long years of trying to convince herself she'd done the right thing, all the while knowing she hadn't.

Fate had intervened in saving her from a loveless marriage, but what was it doing *now*?

Taunting her with what she could never have?

She blinked and looked again.

Those green eyes would haunt her until the end of time.

Before she could stop herself she spoke the name she'd thought she'd never utter again.

"Jamie?"

For a moment Jamie thought he was hallucinating. It *couldn't* be her. Beatrice was meant to be on her honeymoon right now. That and *no one* called him Jamie.

He'd gone back to James the day she'd left. He'd changed a lot of things since then.

"Jamie, is that you?"

For a moment everything blurred into the background as he looked straight into the eyes of the woman he had once thought he would spend his life with.

Still the same dark, get-lost-in-them irises, but there was something new in them. Something...*wary*. No, that wasn't right. Something...fragile. Unsure. Things he'd never seen in them before.

Her hair was different. Still short, but... Why had she gone platinum? Her formerly chestnut-brown hair, silky soft, particularly when it brushed against... A shot of heat shunted through him as powerfully as it had the first time he'd touched it. Touched *her*.

Instinct took over. She was struggling with a patient. Before he could think better of it, he was on the other side of her, calling to his colleague to find a wheelchair.

"What's your name, love?" he asked the girl, who was whispering words of encouragement to herself in English.

"Leah," Beatrice answered for her. "Leah Stokes."

Jamie hid a flinch as the sound of Beatrice's voice lanced another memory he'd sealed tight. If he'd doubted for a second that this transformed woman—the blond hair, the uncharacteristically plain clothing, the slight shadows hinting at sleepless nights—was the love of his life, he knew it now. She had a husky, made-for-late-night-radio voice that was perfect for a doctor offering words as an immediate antidote for pain. Even better for a lover whispering sweet nothings in your ear.

"The exam table isn't far away. Instead of waiting shall we—" Beatrice began.

He nodded before she'd finished. Once-familiar routines returned to him with an ease he hadn't expected. The looks that made language unnecessary. The gestures the said everything. They'd done this particular move when he'd "popped in" accidentally on purpose to help out with her trauma training. Carried patients here and there. Practiced the weave of wrists and hands. Supported each other.

"On three?" The rush of memory and emotion almost blindsided him. He'd been a fool to let her go. Not to fight harder.

But a modern-day commoner versus a latter-day prince? There'd been no contest. He'd seen it in her eyes.

Like a fool, he looked up.

"One…two…"

He saw the words appear on her lips but could hardly hear them, such was the rush of blood charging around his head.

Never again.

That was what he'd told himself.

Never again would he let himself be so naive. So vulnerable. So in love.

As one they dipped, eyes glued to each other's, clasped one another's wrists and scooped up the patient between them, hardly feeling Leah's fingers as they pressed into their shoulders once she'd been lifted off the ground.

It definitely wasn't the way he'd imagined seeing Beatrice again. If ever.

"Just here on the exam table, *per favore*." Beatrice had shifted her gaze to her patient, her hands slipping to Leah's leg to ensure the abraded skin was kept clear of rubbing against the paper covering the table. "Thank you, Dr. Coutts."

Her dark brown eyes flitted back toward him before she returned her full attention to her patient, but in that micromoment he saw all that he needed to know. Seeing him had thrown her as off-kilter as it had him.

Whether it was a good thing or a bad thing was impossible to ascertain. At least he hadn't seen the thing he feared most: indifference. He would have packed his bags and left then and there. But something—the tiniest glimmer of something bright flickering in those espresso-rich eyes of hers—said it would be worth his while to stay.

Answers were answers, after all.

"I'll leave you to it, then," he said, tugging the curtain around the exam table, his eyes taking just a fraction of a second longer than necessary to search her hand for the ring. Jewelry had never been his thing, but that ridiculously huge, pink cushion-cut diamond ring—a family heirloom, she'd said—was etched in his mind's eye as clearly as the day she'd told him she was moving back to Italy. *Family*, she'd said. *Obligations. Tradition.*

He yanked the curtain shut, unable to move as he processed what he'd seen. Pleasure? Pain? Satisfaction that neither of them had succeeded in gaining what they'd sought?

A chilling numbness began to creep through his veins.

No sign of a ring.

Nothing.

Each and every one of her fingers was bare.

Bea's heart was thumping so hard behind her simple cotton top she was sure her patient could see it.

Even though she had taken longer than normal to put on her hygienic gloves, Leah would have had to be blind not to notice her fingers shaking.

Jamie Coutts.

The only man who'd laid full claim to her heart.

Why wasn't he in England?

Leaving Jamie had been the most painful thing she'd ever done. The betrayal she'd seen in his eyes would stay with her forever. Having to live with it was so much worse.

"Is everything all right?" Leah asked.

"Si, va bene." Bea gave her head a quick shake, pushed her hands between her knees to steady them and reminded herself to speak English. She had a patient. Rehashing the day she'd told the man she loved she was going to marry another would have to wait.

"Let's take a look at this leg of yours." Bea gave her hands a quick check. Jitter-free. *Good.* "Cycling, was it?"

"We were coming down one of the passes," Leah confirmed, her wince deepening as Bea began gently to press the blue pads of her gloved hands along the injury. "A car came up alongside me. I panicked and hit the verge too fast."

"A fall when you're wearing these clip shoes can be tough. It looks largely superficial. Not too much bleeding. But from the swelling on your knee it looks like you took quite a blow." Bea glanced up at her, "I'm just going to take your shoes off, all right? Do you feel like anything might be broken? Sprained?"

Leah shook her head. "It's hard to say. I think it's the road rash that hurts the most, but my knee *is* throbbing!"

"Did you get any ice on it straight after you fell? A cool pack?"

"No..." Leah tugged her fingers through her short tangle of hazel curls, loosening some meadow grass as she did so, before swiping at a few more tears. "The guys had all ridden ahead. Downhill pelotons freak me out—and I wasn't carrying a first-aid kit with me. A local couple saw me fall and brought me here."

Poor thing. Left to fend for herself.

It's not any fun, is it, amore*?*

Bea gave her a smile. "Trying to keep up with a peloton of adrenaline junkies is tough." She pushed herself back on the wheelie stool and looked in the supplies cart for the best dressings. "I don't think you've broken anything, but it's probably worth getting some X-rays just in case."

"But we've still got four more days of riding!" Leah protested, the streaks of dirt on her face disappearing in dark trickles as her tears increased. "Richard's going to think I'm such a weakling. This was meant to be the time I showed him I could keep up with the boys."

Bea took a quick glance at Leah's fingers. Bare, just like hers. "Boyfriend?" she chanced.

"Probably not for long. He's going to think I'm such a wimp!"

"With a road rash like that?" Bea protested with a smile. "This shows *exactly* how tough you are. I've had men in here with half the scraping *your* thigh has taken, howling like babies."

"Howling?" A smile teased at Leah's lips.

"Howling," Bea confirmed with a definitive nod.

She wouldn't mind tipping back her head and letting out a full-pelt she-wolf howl herself right now, but instead she told herself off in her mother's exacting tones. *Princesses don't howl. Princesses set an example.*

She screwed her lips to the right as she forced her attention back to Leah's leg. "*Mi scusi*, I can't see what I need to dress this leg of yours in here. I want to get some alginate and silver dressings for you."

"What are those?"

"They're both pretty amazing, actually. You should get some dressings to carry in your pack. There are derivatives from algae in one of them—really good for wounds like this. Ones that ooze."

Leah sucked in her breath after touching a spot on her thigh. "It's so disgusting."

"It's not pretty now, but it will definitely heal well. Once the dressing gets wet, it will begin to form a gel and absorb any liquid from the abrasion." She pressed her hands into her knees and put on her best I-know-it-stinks face. "Keeping the wound moist is essential to preventing scarring. The dressing I'm hoping to use contains silver. It's antibacterial, so it will keep the wound clean of infection." Bea tipped her head to catch Leah's eye before she rose. "Are you going to be all right for a few minutes while I get the supplies?"

Leah half nodded, her interest already diverted as she pulled her phone out of her bag and flicked on the camera app. "I'm going to send the guys some pictures. Give them a proper guilt trip for abandoning me."

"Back in a minute," Bea said unnecessarily as Leah snapped away.

No doubt the photos would be hitting all sorts of social media sites in seconds. She'd taken all those things off her *telefono* within hours of the wedding being called off. She'd even tried throwing the phone in a canal when some wily reporter had got hold of her number, but Francesca hadn't let her.

"Just put the thing on Mute or change your number," Fran had insisted. "*Use* us. Stay contactable. We want to help."

If only someone *could* help. But she and she alone had got herself into this mess.

Bea hurried into the supplies room before a fresh hit of tears glossed her eyes. She missed her best friend. Could really do with a Bea-and-Fran night on the sofa. A pizza. Box set. Bottle of wine—nope! Nix the wine. But… Oh… nix everything. Now that Fran had gone and fallen in love with Luca, and the pair of them were making a real go of the clinic at Mont di Mare, Bea would have to make do on her own. And stay busy. Extra busy. Any and all distractions were welcome.

She forced herself to focus on the shelves of supplies, desperate to remember why she'd gone to the room in the first place.

"Hello, Beatrice."

She froze at the sound of Jamie's voice. Then, despite every single one of her senses being on high alert, she smiled. How could she have forgotten it? That Northern English lilt of his accent. The liquid edge he added to the end of her name where Italians turned it into two harsher syllables. From his tongue her named sounded like sweet mountain water…

When she turned to face him, her smile dropped instantly. Jamie's expression told her everything she needed to know.

He wasn't letting bygones stay back in England, where she'd left him some seven-hundred-odd days ago. But who was counting? Numbers meant nothing when everything about his demeanor told her it was the witching hour. Time to confront the past she'd never been able to forget.

"Since when does Italy's most pampered princess get her own supplies?"

The comment held more rancor than Jamie had hoped to achieve. He'd been aiming for a casual "fancy meeting you here," but he'd actually nailed expressing the months of bitterness he'd been unable to shake since she'd left him. True, he hadn't put up much of a fight, but she had made it more than clear that her future was in Italy. With another man.

It had blindsided him. One minute they were more in love than he could imagine a couple ever being. The next, after that sudden solo trip to Venice, her heart had belonged to another.

He'd not thought her so fickle. It had been a harsh way to learn why they called love blind.

When their gazes connected the color dropped from Beatrice's face. A part of him hated eliciting this bleak reaction—another part was pleased to see he still had an effect on her.

Ashen faced with shaking palms wasn't what he'd been hoping for… Seeing her *at all* hadn't been what he'd been hoping for…but no matter how hard he tried, no matter how many corners he'd turned since he'd left England, he didn't seem to be able to shake her. This was either kismet or some sort of hellish purgatory. From the look on her face, it wasn't the former.

Self-loathing swept through him for lashing out at Beatrice. A woman who'd done little more than proactively pursue the life she wanted. Which was more than he could say for himself.

"What are you doing here, Beatrice? Aren't you meant to be on honeymoon? Or is this part of it? Dropping in to local clinics to grace us with your largesse before embarking on a shopping spree. Dubai, perhaps? Turkey? Shouldn't you be buying silver spoons for the long line of di Jesolos yet to come into the world?"

Jamie hated himself as the vitriol poured out of him. Hated himself even more as he watched Beatrice's full lips part only to say nothing, her features crumpling in disbelief as if he'd shivved her right then and there rather than simply pointed out everything the tabloids had been crowing about. The engagement. The impending wedding. The royal babies they were hoping would quickly follow the exotic and lengthy honeymoon.

A month ago he'd refused to read anymore. He'd endured enough.

He looked deep into her eyes, willing her to tell him something. Anything to ease the pain.

As quickly as the ire had flared up in him, it disappeared.

You're not this man. She must've had her reasons.

Jamie took a step forward, his natural instinct to put a hand on Beatrice's arm—to touch her, to apologize. As he closed the space between them the handful of gel packs and silver dressings she'd been holding dropped from her fingers. They knelt simultaneously to collect them, colliding with the inevitable head bump and mumbled apologies.

Crouching on the floor, each with a hand to their forehead, they stared at one another as if waiting for the other to pounce.

By God, she is beautiful.

"You've grown your hair," she said finally.

She was so close he could kiss her. Put his hand at the

nape of her neck as he'd done so many times before, draw her to him and…

She was talking about haircuts.

A haircut had been the last thing on his mind when she'd left. *Work.* Work had been all he'd had and he'd thrown himself so far into the deep end he'd been blind to everything else. Got too involved. So close he'd literally drained the blood from his own body to help ease the pain of his patient.

Elisa.

That poor little girl. They'd shared a rare blood type. Foolishly he'd thought that if he saved her life he might be able to save himself. In the end his boss had made him choose. Take a step back or leave.

So here he was in Italy, just when he'd thought he was beginning to see straight again, eye to eye with the woman who had all but sucked the marrow from his bones.

"It looks nice," Beatrice said, her finger indicating the hair he knew curled on and around his shirt collar. What was it she'd always called him? Hay head? Straw head? Something like that. Something that brought back too many memories of those perfect summer months they'd shared together.

He nodded his thanks. Blissful summers were a thing of the past. Now they were reduced to social niceties.

Fair enough. He glanced at his watch. The chopper would be leaving in five. He needed to press on.

"C'mon. Let's get these picked up. Get you back to your patient." No matter how deeply he'd been hurt, patients were the priority.

She reached forward, sucking in a sharp breath when their fingers brushed, each reaching for the same packet of dressings.

"I'm not made of poison, you know."

Beatrice's gaze shot up to meet his, those rich brown eyes of hers looking larger than ever. He couldn't tell if it was because she'd lost weight or because they were punctuated by twilight-blue shadows. Either way, she didn't look happy.

"No one knows who I am here," she bit out, her voice low and urgent as she clutched the supplies to her chest. "I would appreciate it if you could keep it that way."

A huff of disbelief emptied his chest of oxygen. Flaunting the family name was the reason she'd left him, and now she wanted to be *anonymous*?

She met his gaze as she finished scanning his uniform. "Since when do pediatricians wear high-octane rescue gear? I thought life in a children's ward was all the excitement you needed?"

"Snide comments were never your thing."

"Pushing boundaries was never *yours*."

Jamie's lungs strained against a deep breath, all the while keeping tight hold of the eye contact. He wanted her to see the man he'd become.

After a measured exhalation he let himself savor the pain of his teeth grating across his lower lip. He turned to leave, then changed his mind, throwing the words over his shoulder as if it were the most casual thing in the world to lacerate the woman he loved with words.

"People change, Dr. Jesolo. Some of us for the better."

Ten minutes later and the sting of his comment still hadn't worn off. Perhaps it never would.

And hiding in the staff room with her friendly Aussie colleague had only made things worse. He was a messenger with even more bad news.

Jamie Coutts was not just back in her life—he was her boss.

"Wait a minute, Teo." Bea held up a hand, hardly believing what she was hearing. "He's *what*?"

Teo Brandisi gave Bea a patient smile and handed her the cup of herbal tea he'd promised her hours earlier in the busy shift.

"The big boss man. The big kahuna. Mayor of medics."

"But *you* hired me."

"He was out in the field. He hands over the reins to me when he's away."

"But—"

"Quit trying to fight it, sweetheart. He's *le grand fromage*—all right? I wouldn't be working here without his approval, so if you've got a bone to pick with him, I'm recusing myself. He has my back. I have his. You got me?" Teo continued in his broad Australian accent.

Bea shook her head and waved her hands. "No, it's not that. I've nothing *against* Dr. Coutts."

Liar.

She cleared her throat, forcing herself to sound more neutral. "I just don't understand why he had to approve appointing *you* but not me."

"Foreign doctor." Teo pointed at himself. "We can't just swan in and take all the choice jobs. Even though he's English, he's been qualified to practice here for over a year."

He'd been in Italy for a year and she hadn't known.

Well...she'd done a whole lot of things *he* didn't know about, so fair was fair.

"My advice?" Teo was on a roll. "You have to suck up to people like James Coutts."

"James?"

"Yeah... Why?"

Teo scrunched up his nose and looked at her as if she was giving proof positive she was losing her marbles. Maybe she was. And if Jamie was James, and she'd shortened her name to Bea, then the only thing that was clear was that they were both trying to be someone new.

A reinvention game.

Only games were meant to be fun. And everything about seeing Jamie again was far from fun. Confronting what she'd done to him was going to be the hardest thing she'd ever done.

"Anyhoo..." Teo continued. "James has got the whole British-reserve thing going on big-time." A glint of admiration brightened his blue eyes. "The man's like an impenetrable fortress. Impossible to read. Well done!" He clapped her on the shoulder. "A gold star to Dr. Jesolo for getting under the Stone Man's skin!"

"The Stone Man?"

"Yeah. We all take bets on how many facial expressions he actually has. I'm going with three. Contemplative. Not happy. And his usual go-to face—Mr. Neutral. No reading that face. No way, no how."

Bea hid her face in the steam of her tea for a minute. Her kind, gentle Jamie was an impenetrable fortress? That wasn't like him. Then again...*she* was hardly the same. Why should *he* be?

"It's most likely a fluke. That or he doesn't like blondes?"

Teo gave her a sidelong glance as if he already knew the whole story. Could tell she was just making things up. Covering a truth she wasn't yet ready to divulge.

"Fair enough."

They stood in an awkward silence until Bea launched into a sudden interest in removing her herbal tea bag from her mug.

If Teo had known she was pregnant, she could have just blown the whole thing off as a bout of pregnancy brain. Not that she even knew if pregnancy brain hit this early. Sharp bouts of fatigue certainly had. And morning sickness. She'd never look at a hamburger the same way again! At least when she'd been on her brother's yacht she'd managed to fob off the nausea she'd felt as seasickness. Now that she was up here in the mountains she couldn't do that. It was meant to pass soon. And by the time her contract was up she'd be off to hide away the rest of her pregnancy somewhere else.

"So, on a day-to-day basis *you're* my boss?" She kept her eyes on her tea, wincing at the note of hope in her voice.

"Nope. Dr. James Coutts is your actual boss," Teo continued, after taking his shot of espresso down in one swift gulp.

Classic Italian. She would be amazed if he went back to Australia. He might be second generation in Australia, but the man had Italy in his bones.

"I step in when he's out on rescue calls, like today. The fact I was on duty when we held your interview was just a coincidence."

"So…he knew I was coming?"

The interview had been a week ago. Start date today. He'd had a whole week to come to terms with things and yet she was sure she'd seen shock in his eyes. The same shock of recognition that had reverberated through to her very core.

"He knew *someone* was coming, but he's been tied up training the emergency squads."

Her Jamie? Better-safe-than-sorry Jamie?

She'd always thought *she* was a solid rock until she'd met him. But no one had been more reliable, more sound than him.

"He's pretty good about not breathing down your neck." Teo pulled open a cupboard and began to look around for some biscuits. "And he lets staff make decisions in his absence. He's a really good guy, actually. Don't let the whole Dr. Impenetrable thing get to you."

Her lips thinned. Jamie was better than a good guy. He was the kindest man she'd ever met.

Strangely, it came as a relief to hear his bitterness seemed to be solely reserved for her. Deservedly so. How she could have dumped him just to make good on an antiquated match between her family and the Roldolfos was beyond her now. Family loyalty meant altogether different things when your blue-blooded mother was trying to uphold hundreds of years of tradition. Pass the princess baton…even if it came at her daughter's expense.

She heard Teo sigh and looked up to catch him lovingly gazing at a plate of homemade biscotti. Someone's grandmother's, no doubt. There was a lot of bragging about grandmothers up here. She missed hers. No doubt *she* would have had some wise words for the insane situation Bea was in now.

"Did you hear the crew earlier? Sounds like it was a pretty intense case," Teo continued, oblivious to the turmoil Bea was enduring.

"I didn't see any patients come down from the helipad." She shook her head in confusion.

"They dropped the patient off in Switzerland. A little kid. Five, maybe six years old—broke his leg. Compound fracture. Tib-fib job. Massive blood loss. The mother nearly lost the plot. She was attacking the staff, threatened to kill one of them if they didn't let her on the helicopt—"

"All right, all right." Bea held up a hand, feeling a swell of nausea rise and take hold as he painted the picture. "It's obvious someone's a bit jealous that *he* wasn't out on the rescue squad today."

"I'm on tomorrow." Teo gave his hands a quick excited rub. "You can sign up, too, if you like. We do it on rotation, because summers are so busy up here, but you'd probably have to do your first few with James. The man is a right daredevil when's he's wearing the old rescue gear. Biscotti?" He held out a plate filled with the oblong biscuits.

"*No, grazie.* Or, actually…" Maybe it would help settle her stomach. She took one of the crunchy biscuits and gave him a smile.

He gave the door frame a final pat and then was gone.

Bea sank into a nearby chair. As far as she was concerned, Teo could have all her emergency-rescue shifts. About eight weeks, two days and…she glanced at her watch…three hours ago she would have been all over them. High-octane rescues and first-class medical treatment? *Amazing* experiences.

Experiences she would have to miss now.

Compromising the tiny life inside her while the former love of her life looked on…

She let her head sink into her hands.

Clinica Torpisi wasn't going to be the healing hideaway she'd been hoping for.

More like hell on earth.

CHAPTER TWO

HE SAW HER across the piazza. Jamie wondered now, having adjusted to the platinum blond hair, how he hadn't noticed her instantly. He certainly had when she'd walked into Northern General. How could he not have when he'd entered the *clinica*?

Fathomless chocolate-brown eyes straight out of the Italian-nymph guidebook. Slender. The darkest chestnut hair he'd ever seen. Short, but thick enough to lose his hands in when he wanted to put his fingers against the nape of her soft, swan-like neck. Perfect raspberry-red lips. Olive skin. Carrying herself like royalty.

She was royalty.

He shook his head again.

Little wonder he hadn't recognized her straight off. He hadn't wanted to.

A bit of shock.

A splash of denial.

Hope, pain, love, despair… All those things and more made up the roiling ball of conflict burning in his heart. Most of all he just wanted to understand *why.*

He hitched his trousers onto his hips. She wasn't the only one who'd lost weight in the past couple of years.

Stop apportioning blame.

The closer he got, the more he wondered what the hell he was doing.

No. That wasn't true. Ripping off the bandage had become his modus operandi since she'd left. He might as well stick true to his course. Life wasn't sweet. Might as well get used to it.

"Mind if I join you?"

Beatrice started, as if her thoughts had been a thousand miles away. When she'd pulled him into focus he watched as she searched his face for signs of enmity. He couldn't say he blamed her. After his performance in the supplies room earlier in the day he'd hardly made a good show of the manners his mother had drilled into him.

"Please..." Beatrice pushed aside a small plate of antipasti and indicated the chair beside her. One from which he could enjoy the stunning lakeside view. One that would seat them side by side, where they wouldn't have to look into the other's eyes.

He sank into the chair, grateful for this reprieve from animosity. Perhaps a few hours apart had been what they'd each needed. Time to process.

"Is that a spritzer you're having?" He pointed at the bright orange drink on the table, the glass beaded with condensation as the final rays of sunlight disappeared behind the mountain peaks beyond the lake.

"No." She shook her head. "I never liked spritzers. Too..." Her nose crinkled as she sought the right word. "Aftertasty," she said finally, her lips tipping up into the first suggestion of a smile he'd seen. "Orange soda is my new guilty pleasure. I don't seem to be able to drink enough of it."

He was about to launch into the lecture he gave all his patients—too many fizzy drinks were bad for the bones, bad for the brain, bad for the body—but just seeing the tension release from the corners of her eyes as she lifted the glass, put her lips around the red and white stripes of the straw and drew in a cool draught made him swallow it.

He hadn't come here to deliver a lecture. He had questions. Thousands of questions.

A waiter swooped in, as they all did at this time of day, keen to get as many people as possible their drinks before the early-dining Americans began infiltrating the wide square in advance of the Europeans.

He and Beatrice both bit back smiles at the waiter's terse "Is that all for *signor*?" after he'd settled on a sparkling water.

"Going back to the clinic?" Beatrice asked.

"That obvious?"

"Mmm, 'fraid so." Beatrice looked out toward the square as she spoke. "It would be a glass of Gavi di Gavi if you were finished, wouldn't it? If..." She hesitated. "If memory serves me right."

He nodded. Surprised she'd remembered such a silly detail. Then again, there wasn't a single detail he'd forgotten about *her*. Maybe...

He rammed his knuckles into his thigh.

Maybe was for other people. He was all about sure things. And Beatrice wasn't one of them.

Jamie scrubbed a hand along his chin, then scraped his chair around on the stone cobbles until he faced her head-on.

"What are you doing here, Beatrice?"

"Well, that's a nice way to—" She stopped herself and lifted a hand so that he would give her a moment to think. Say what she really meant to.

Despite himself, he smiled. She'd always been that way. A thinker. Just like him. The more they'd learned about each other, the stronger the pull had been. Interns hadn't been meant to date residents—but try telling that to two people drawn to each other as magnetically as iron and nitrogen. Weighted and weightless. He'd felt both of those things when he'd been with her. Secure in himself as he'd never been before, and so damn happy he would have sworn his feet hadn't touched the ground after the first time he'd tasted those raspberry-ripe lips of hers.

"You *have* read the papers lately, haven't you?" Beatrice asked eventually.

"I have a hunch that world peace is a long way off, so I tend to steer clear of them." Jamie leant forward in his chair, elbows pressed to his knees. "C'mon, Beatrice. Quit throwing questions back at me. Why are you in Torpisi?"

She shook her head in disbelief. "You are the one person in the world I wish had read the tabloids and you *haven't*!" She threw her hands up in the air and gave a small isn't-the-world-ridiculous? laugh.

When their eyes met again there was kindness in hers. A tenderness reserved just for him that he might have lived on in a different time and place.

"I never got married."

She took another sip of her soft drink and looked away as casually as if she'd just told him the time. Or perhaps it was guilt that wouldn't let her meet his eye.

Jamie blinked a few times, his body utterly stationary, doing its best to ingest the news.

Despite his best efforts to remain neutral, something hardened in him. "Is this some sort of joke?"

She shook her head, seemingly confused about the question.

"Why did you do it?"

"Do what?" It was her turn to look bewildered.

"Oh, well…let's see, here, love. Quite a few things, now that I come to think of it."

He spread out his fingers and started ticking them off, his tone level, though his message was heated.

"Up and leave me for a man you didn't love. Ruin the future we'd planned together. All that to never even see it through?"

He pulled his fingers into tight fists and gave his thighs a quick drumming.

"Is this some sort of cruel game you're playing, Beatrice?"

He pushed back in his chair and rose, no longer sure he could even look her in the eye.

"If you're here to rub it in and make sure you made your impact, you can count me *out*."

"Jamie! Wait!"

Bea's voice sounded harsh to her own ears. As quickly as she'd reached out to stop Jamie from leaving she wished she'd rescinded the invitation, tightly wrapping her arms around herself to brace herself against the shards of ice coursing through her veins.

She'd betrayed too much by calling out to him. Jamie would know better than anyone that there had been pain in her voice. The ache of loss. But what was she going to do? Explain what a fool she'd been? That she'd gone and got herself pregnant at an IVF clinic in advance of her wedding so her family, the press and the whole of Italy could coo and smile over the Prince and the Principessa's "honeymoon baby"?

She was the only one in the world who knew that her fiancé—her *ex*-fiancé—was infertile, apart from a doctor whose silence had been bought. She was surprised he'd even told *her*. Perhaps their family get-togethers had begun to rely a bit too heavily on talk of children running around the palazzo, in order to cover up the obvious fact that neither of them were very much in love.

Their one joint decision: an IVF baby. Keeping it as quiet as possible. A private clinic. More paid-off doctors and nurses. An anonymous donor.

The less anyone knew, the easier it had been to go ahead with it.

Her sole investment in a relationship she had known would never claim her heart. A child… A child who had been meant to bring some light into her life.

Now it just filled her with fear. Confirmation that she'd been a fool to agree to the plan. She no longer had the support of her family and, worse, she would be a single mother in a world where it was already tough enough to survive on her own.

It hadn't felt that way when she'd been with Jamie. With him she'd felt…*invincible.*

Relief washed through her when Jamie sat down again, pressing his hips deeper into the chair, his back ramrod straight as he drained his water glass in one fluid draught before deigning to look her in the eye.

"I'm in trouble, Jamie."

As quickly as he'd tried to leave, Jamie pulled his chair up close, knees wide so they flanked hers, fingers spread as he cupped her face in both his broad hands, searching her eyes for information.

"Are you hurt? Did he hurt you?"

No, but I *hurt you.*

He used an index finger to swipe at a couple of errant locks of hair so his access to her eyes was unfettered. Against his better judgment—she could see that in his eyes—he traced his finger along the contour of her jawline, coming to a halt, as he had so many times before, before gently cradling the length of her neck as if he were about to lean in and kiss her.

It was like rediscovering her senses all over again. As if part of her had died the day she'd told him she was returning home to marry another man.

She blinked away the rising swell of tears.

Part of her *had* died that day. The part that believed in love conquering all. The part that believed in destiny.

"Beatrice," Jamie pressed. "Did he hurt you?"

I was a fool to have left you.

She shook her head, instantly feeling the loss of his touch when he dropped his hands, sat back in his chair and rammed them into his front pockets, as if trying to hide the fact that his long surgeon's fingers were balled into tight fists. For the second time in as many minutes. Twice as many times as she'd ever seen him make the gesture before.

He'd aged in the years since she'd seen him last. Nothing severe, as if he'd been sick or a decade had passed, but he *had* changed. His was a proper grown-up male face now, instead of holding the hints of youth she had sometimes seen at the hospital, when he'd caught her looking at him and smiled.

It felt like a million years ago. Hard to believe it was just two short years since he'd been thirty-three and she twenty-eight.

"Just a young lass, you are," he would say, and laugh whenever she whined about feeling old after a long shift. "Perfect for me," he'd say, before dropping a surreptitious kiss on her forehead in one of the busy hospital corridors. They'd been little moments in heaven. *Perfect.*

She closed her eyes against the memory, gave them a rub, then forced herself to confront the present. It was all of her own making, so she might as well see it for what it was. *Payback.*

A painful price she knew she had to pay when all she really wanted was for him to love her again as he once had.

Impossible.

Sun-tanned crinkles fanned out from Jamie's eyes, which she still wasn't quite brave enough to meet. The straw gold of his hair was interwoven with a few threads of silver. At the temples, mostly. More than she thought a man of thirty-five should have.

But what would she know? When she grew her dyed hair out again it might *all* be gray after the level of stress she'd endured these past few weeks. It was a wonder she hadn't lost the baby.

Her hands automatically crept to her stomach, one folding protectively over the other.

"Did he *hurt* you?" Jamie repeated, the air between them thick with untold truths.

"Only my pride," she conceded. "He didn't want me."

The explanation came out as false, too chirpy. She hadn't wanted Marco either. What she most likely really owed him was a thank-you letter.

"Can you believe it?" She put on a smile and grinned at the real love of her life, as if having her arranged marriage grind to a halt in front of some of Europe's most elite families had been the silliest thing to have happened to her in years.

"He should be shot."

"Jamie…" Bea shook her head. "Don't be—" She huffed out a lungful of frustration, then unfolded her arms from their tight cinch across her chest, visible proof she was trying her best to be honest with him. Open. Vulnerable. "*Mi scusi.* I'm sorry. I don't have any right to tell you what to feel."

"You're damn right you don't," he shot back, but with less venom than before.

Something in her gave. He deserved to vent whatever amount of spleen he needed to.

"Serves you right" was probably lurking there in his throat. Along with a bit of "now you know how it feels" followed by a splash of "what goes around comes around" as a chaser.

She deserved the venom—and more.

After a moment had passed, with each of them silently collecting their thoughts, Jamie reached across and took one of her hands in his, weaving their fingers together as naturally as if they'd never been apart.

A million tiny sparks lit up inside her. A sensation she'd never once felt with her ex-fiancé.

Obligation didn't elicit rushes of desire. She'd learned that the hard way.

"Talk to me, Beatrice."

His voice was gentle. Kind. His thumb rubbed along the back of her hand as his features softened, making it clear he was present—there just for her.

In that instant she felt he was back. The man she'd met and fallen in love with in the corridors of a busy inner-city hospital tucked way up in the North of England. Their entire worlds had been each other and medicine.

She vividly remembered the first time she'd seen him. So English! *Male.* He'd exuded…*capability.* So refreshing after a lifetime of worrying about etiquette and decorum and the thousands of other silly little things that had mattered to her mother and not one jot to her. Surviving finishing school had been down to Fran. Without her… She didn't even want to think about it.

She glanced up at Jamie. His eyes were steady…patient… She knew as well as he did that he would wait all evening if he needed to.

She lifted her gaze just in time to see the topmost arc of the sun disappear behind the mountain peaks.

"Maybe we could walk?" she suggested.

He nodded, unlacing his fingers from hers as he rose.

She curled one hand around the other in a ridiculous attempt to save the sensation.

He pointed toward the far end of the piazza. "Let's go out along the lake. Have you been to the promenade yet? Seen the boats?"

She shook her head. She'd had enough of boats and morning sickness over the past few weeks to last a lifetime. She agreed to the route anyway. It wasn't as if this was meant to be *easy*.

Every part of Jamie itched to reach out and touch Beatrice. Hold her hand. Put a protective arm around her shoulder. There was something incredibly fragile about her he wasn't sure he'd seen before. She was nursing something more than a chink in her pride. And all the rage he'd thought would come to the fore if he ever found himself in her orbit again… It was there, all right. It just wasn't ready to blow.

Instinct told him to take things slowly. And then start digging. A verbal attack would elicit nothing. As for a physical attack… If that man had laid one finger on her—

"How are you settling in here? Everyone at the clinic helping you get your bearings?"

Beatrice nodded enthusiastically. "I love it. All one day of it, that is."

He smiled at the note of genuine happiness in her voice. Excellent. The staff were making her feel at home. He fought the need to press her. To get her to spill everything. Explain how she'd found it so easy to break his heart.

"Your contract is…?"

"For the rest of the summer. I guess one of the early-summer staffers left before expected?"

"No." He shook his head. "She had a baby. Worked right up until her due date."

"Ah…"

Beatrice's gaze jumped from boat to boat moored along the quayside. Families and groups of friends were spilling out onto the promenade to find which restaurant they'd eat in tonight.

"I suppose she'll be coming back, then, after maternity leave. Although I did tell your colleague, Dr. Brandisi, that I would be happy to extend if the clinic loses any essential staff after the season ends."

"It waxes and wanes up here. There'll be a time when the summer wraps up where we hit a lull, and then ski season brings in another lot. It's usually all right with just the bare minimum of hands on deck."

Beatrice threw a quick smile his way, her lips still pressed tight, so he continued. "Mostly Italians to start, then Swiss, German, Austrian… A complete pick 'n' mix at the height of the season."

That was why he liked it. Nothing stayed the same. Change was the only thing keeping him afloat since he'd finally faced facts and left Northern General. Everything about that place had reminded him of Beatrice. And then, after Elisa… That had been the hardest time of death he'd ever had to call.

He swallowed and pushed his finger through a small pool of lake water on the square guard railing, visibly dividing it in two.

Everything leaves its mark. And nothing stays the same.

Those were the two lessons he'd learned after Beatrice had left. Now was the time to prove it.

He rubbed his hands together and belatedly returned

her smile. "So! What sort of cases have you had today? Anything juicy?"

They might as well play My Injuries Were Worse Than Yours until she was ready to talk.

The tension in Beatrice's shoulders eased and she relaxed into a proper smile. "Actually, all my cases have been really different to what I treated at home in Venice. With all the recreational sports up here I'm seeing all sorts of new things. It's made a great change."

He felt his jaw shift at the mention of "home." Home—for a few months at the end of their relationship, at least—had been their tiny little apartment, around the corner from the hospital. The one they'd vowed to stay in until they could afford one of the big, rambling stone homes on the outer reaches of the city. One of those houses that would fall apart if someone didn't give it some TLC. The kind of house where there'd be plenty of room for children to play. Not that they'd talked about the two boys and two girls they'd hoped to have one day. *Much.*

Let it go, Jamie. It was all just a pipe dream.

"Were you still working in trauma? When you came back to Italy?" he added.

"Off and on." She nodded. "But mostly I was working in a free clinic for refugees. So many people coming in on boats..."

"With all your language skills you must've been a real asset. Were you based in Venice?" He might as well try to visualize some sort of picture.

"Just outside. On the mainland." She stopped farther along the railing, where the view to the lake and the mountains beyond was unimpeded by boats, and drew in a deep breath, curling her fingers around the cool metal until her knuckles were pale.

The deepening colors of the early-evening sky rendered

the lake a dark blue—so dark it was hard to imagine how deep it might be. Fathomless.

"It was relentless. Working there. The poverty. The sickness. The number of lives lost all in the pursuit of a dream."

"Happiness?" he asked softly.

"Freedom."

When she turned to him the hit of connection was so powerful he almost stumbled. It was as if she was trying to tell him something. That her moving back to Italy had been a mistake? That she wished she could turn back time as much as he did?

"Do you miss it? Working at the refugee clinic?" he qualified.

If she was going to up and leave again, he had to know. Had to reassemble the wall he'd been building brick by brick around his heart only to have the foundations crumble to bits when she'd walked back into his life.

She turned her head, resting her chin on her shoulder, and looked at him.

"No." Her head shook a little. "I mean, it was obviously rewarding. But I don't miss being there. Venice…"

Something in him gave. His breath began filling his lungs a bit more deeply.

"What drew you up here to our little Alpine retreat?"

He leant against the railing, unsurprised to see her give him a sideways double take.

Nice one, Jamie. Super casual. Not.

"I used to come up here to one of my cousins' places. Skiing. The next valley over, actually," she corrected herself, then continued, her eyes softening into a faraway smile. "One year I brought Fran with me. Remember Francesca? My mad friend from America? I don't think you met her, but she was—" Beatrice stopped, the smile dropping from her eyes. “We saw each other recently. She’s getting married.”

“Ah.” Jamie nodded.

What was he meant to say to that? *Congratulations, I wish I was, too?* He elbowed the rancorous thoughts away and reharnessed himself to the light-banter variety of conversational tactics.

“Wasn’t there something about finishing school and a giggle-laden walk of shame before the term was out? Mussed-up white gloves or something?”

“We snuck away one day.” Beatrice feigned a gasp of horror. “Away from the ‘good’ set.”

“You mean the ‘crowned cotillion crowd’?” he asked without thinking twice.

Beatrice had been so contemptuous of them then. The group of titled friends and extended family who seemed to drift across Europe together in packs. Hunting down the next in place, the next big thing so they could put their mark on it, suck it dry, then leave. The exact type of person she’d left him for. *Oh, the irony.*

When he looked across to see if his comment had rankled he was surprised to see another small cynical smile in Beatrice’s dark eyes.

Huh. Maybe she’d softened. Saw things now she hadn’t before. Not that he and Beatrice had ever “hung with the crowd.” Nor any crowd, for that matter. They had been a self-contained unit.

It had never once occurred to him that she was keeping him at arm’s length from the affluent, titled set she’d grown up with. He’d never considered himself hung up on his low-income upbringing. The opposite, if anything. Proud. He was from a typical Northern family. Typical of his part of the North anyway. Father down the mines. Mother working as a dinner lady at the local primary school. Brother and sister had followed suit, but he'd been the so-called golden boy. Scholarships to private schools. Oxford University. An internship at London's most prestigious pediatric hospital before he'd returned to the part of the country he'd always called home.

Meeting and falling in love with Beatrice had just been part of the trajectory. *Local boy falls in love with princess.* Only that hadn't been the way it had played out at all. He hadn't known about Beatrice's past for—had it been a year? Maybe longer. Those two years at Northern General had been like living in a cocoon. Nestled up there in the part of the country he knew and loved best, hoping he'd spend each and every day of the rest of his life with Beatrice by his side.

He cleared his throat. "Sorry—you were saying about your friend?"

"*Si*—yes." Bea gave her head a shake, as if clearing away her own memories. "She's staying in Italy. Fallen in love with an Italian."

"Happens to the best of us."

Beatrice looked away.

He hadn't meant to say that. Not in that way. Not with anger lacing the words.

"It's a magical place up here. I'm glad I came," she said at last.

He nodded, turning to face the view. Despite the summer, snow still capped the high Alpine ridges soaring above the broad expanse of blue that was one of Europe's most beautiful high-altitude lakes.

"You know there's a little island out there?"

"Really? Uninhabited?"

"Quite the opposite. There's a group of monks. A small group living there… It's quite a beautiful retreat. Stone and wood. Simple rooms. Cells, they call them."

"Sounds more like a prison than a place of worship." Beatrice's eyebrows tugged together, but her expression was more curious than judgmental.

"No. The simplicity is its beauty. Gives you plenty of time to think."

He should know. He'd spent long enough in one of those cells, just staring at the stone walls until he could find a way to make sense of the world again. The friary was the reason he'd chosen to come here in the first place. He'd needed to hide away from the world for a while and atone for—he still didn't know what.

Failing himself?

Not fighting hard enough for Elisa's life?

Not fighting hard enough for Beatrice?

Those two years they'd spent together in England felt like a lifetime ago. He'd felt…*vital*—full of the joys of life. In his prime. When she'd told him she didn't want him anymore he'd just shut down. "Fine," he had said, and pointed toward the door. *What are you waiting for?*

He sure as hell hadn't found any answers when she'd taken him up on his offer.

And he was certain there hadn't been any when Elisa had died.

He'd found a modicum of peace when he'd gone out to that tiny island friary.

When one of the monks had fallen ill he'd brought him to the clinic here on the lakeside, had accepted the odd shift and found himself, bit by bit, coming back to life. Part of him wondered if the monk had been faking it. And when the clinic "just happened" to mention they needed full-time staff he'd thrown his hat into the ring. He'd been there almost a year now and—as strange as it sounded for a village several hundreds of years old—he felt a part of the place.

"They make some sort of famous Christmas cake—a

special sort of panettone. I'm surprised you haven't heard of it."

"The Friars of Torpisi!" Beatrice clapped her hands together, her eyes lighting up as the dots connected. "Of *course*. I had some last *Natale*."

Again that faraway look stole across her face.

What happened to you, my love?

Jamie scrubbed a hand through his hair before stuffing both hands into his pockets again.

Perhaps some questions were best left unanswered.

CHAPTER THREE

"How can you do that?" Bea asked, finally pressing herself into the entire point of the walk. Laying her cards on the table.

"Do what?"

Jamie glanced over at her, his green eyes actively searching her face while the rest of his body remained turned toward the lake.

"Be so forgiving."

"I hardly think I'm being *forgiving*. We've got to work together. It'd be a shame to lose a good doctor because of water under the bridge."

Jamie's hands disappeared behind his back. Whether he was crossing his fingers to cover the lie or polishing a fist to take it out on a wall later, she didn't know. Either way it was a hard hit to take.

Water under the bridge.

No chance of reconciliation. Not that she had done a single solitary thing to earn his love, much less earn it a second time.

Even so…would it be crazy to take it as an olive branch?

"So you're not going to fire me?"

He looked at her as if she'd gone mad. "Is that what you think this is about? I may be a lot of things, but I'm hardly a sadist, my love."

A surprised laugh escaped her throat. "I can think of a thousand other things you could call me besides—" She stopped, finding herself completely unable to repeat the words.

My love.

A thousand times she'd said them once. More. An infinity of moments she'd closed down all in the name of tradition.

"Why aren't you married?"

Shocked at the bluntness of his question, Bea froze as her mind raced for the right answer. The truth might push him away even further. Yank back his olive branch.

Just tell him. You owe him that much.

"The most immediate answer is that he was cheating on me."

Color flooded Jamie's face. The show of emotion meant more to her than she could say.

She continued before she could think better of it. "So I gave him back his ring and told him the wedding was off."

Jamie's shoulders broadened as he pressed himself to his full height. "He'd better have left the country if he knows what's good for him."

"He has." She had to laugh. "He's taken his new lover on *our* honeymoon."

"The tabloids must be loving that."

Jamie laughed, too, but she could see he was far from amused.

"I've been doing my best to avoid the tabloids."

"Probably just as well."

"Why? Have you heard something?"

"No, no." He held up his hands. "I hate those things as much as you do. They're…*toxic.*"

"You've got that right."

He leant against the railing, his back to the view, and

folded his arms across his chest. "You don't seem that upset for someone whose fiancé has ripped her future into tatters."

It's so much more complicated than I ever imagined it would be.

"I think you and I both know I never loved him."

There it was. The real truth. Whether or not it would make Jamie hate her more, or ultimately find a way to forgive her, only time would tell.

Jamie's jaw set hard. Long enough for her to wish she'd never said anything. Maybe it would have been better to pretend her ex had broken her heart. That there had been more of a reason than family obligation to her agreeing to the ridiculous marriage.

"Well, that's something anyway," Jamie said, holding his stance. Body taut, shoulders held back. He'd never hunched. Never shied away from anything.

Bea ran a finger along the railing, buying herself a bit of time before being truly honest. "For as long as I can remember my family and his were…were sort of *promised* to one another."

"The families, or you and their son?"

"Me and their son," she confirmed.

It sounded so clinical. Patriarchal. Hierarchal. Archaic. You name it. But that was what it had been. An arranged marriage cloaked in a foolish whirlwind of cocktail parties, whispered promises she'd hardly let herself believe—thank heavens—and her mother's long-sought joy. Her satisfaction that, finally, her daughter was behaving like a proper princess.

In other words, she'd taken one for the team.

"Your mother never really liked it that you came to England, did she? Worked in the A&E."

"Have you added mind reading to your skills list since I saw you last?"

Without even thinking about it she reached across and gave his forearm a squeeze. They'd always been like that. Touching one another. Confirming each cue—verbal or social—with a little hug, a little stroke on the cheek, a light brush of the fingers as they passed in a corridor too populated for them to get away with a proper kiss.

Jamie looked down, considered her hand for a minute, then looked back up into her eyes. "I always used to think I could read your mind, but after you left… Not so much."

She dropped her hand back to her side. "I could've handled that better."

"You could have stayed."

Tears leapt to her eyes, and for the first time since she'd laid eyes on him, Jamie didn't do a thing. No pad of his thumb wiping them away. No digging into one of his pockets for a fresh linen handkerchief. Just the set of his jaw growing tighter.

She *should* have stayed. Been true to her heart *and* his. Then she wouldn't be in this ludicrous position. Unmarried. Pregnant. Facing the future alone.

She nodded, letting the tears fall fat and unceremoniously down her cheeks, along and off her chin, darkening the light blue of her linen blouse. They were coming so thick and fast she didn't bother wiping them away.

"I thought I was doing the right thing. If I'd stayed with you—"

"If you'd stayed with me, *what*?" Jamie challenged. "What would have happened if you'd stayed with me? We would've got married? Perhaps had a child by now? Not be here in this—" He swept an arm out along the vista when his anger collapsed. "Well…this is pretty beautiful. I don't regret *this*."

Beatrice spread her hands across her face and wiped at the tears, laughing despite herself. "You always could see the best in everything."

"You brought that out in me."

"No." She shook his words away. "I don't deserve that. You were good at that before I met you. It's one of the things that made me fall in love with you."

Jamie gave her a sidelong glance. "And what was it exactly that changed how you felt? Did you see something you didn't like? Or something you liked more in *him*? Even though you weren't 'in love' with him."

He hadn't needed to put up air quotes as he spoke. His voice had said it all. The glint of opportunities lost sparked in his green eyes, which flared to show her time *hadn't* healed the wounds she knew she'd inflicted in the way she'd hoped it might.

"Oh, Jamie." Her voice was barely a whisper, and her heart was doing its very best to leap out of her throat.

He could have said a lot of things. Accused her of leaving for the money. For the opulent palazzos she would have lived in. The parties, the traveling, the haute couture she would have been pictured wearing in all the glossy magazines, at all the parties where people cared about those sorts of things. Palaces and pistes. Beaches and ballrooms. The list went on and on, but none of those would have been the answer.

"Why did you do it?" he asked again, his voice hoarse with emotion.

"A little girl trying to please her mother, I suppose," Bea whispered, her voice breaking as she spoke.

She didn't suppose. She knew it. She'd hashed and rehashed it on an endless loop these past few weeks. And the answers she had come up with were sobering. It wasn't entirely her mother's fault. Her family's fault. Even tradition wasn't to blame.

At the end of the day, all the blame lay solidly at her own feet. *She* was the one who had left the man she loved. Put on that white dress. All that ridiculous lace!

The waste.

The heartache.

Heartache she couldn't admit to because, as Jamie had so bluntly put it, their relationship was "water under the bridge." Even if all she wanted to do right now was drop to her knees and beg his forgiveness. Plead with him to believe that she'd never stopped loving him. That she would do anything to make things right again. But it was impossible.

When her ex-fiancé had made it more than clear that she'd be raising her child on her own she had vowed never to enter into a relationship again. Too painful. Too many pitfalls.

And now that the one man she would have made an exception for was in front of her it was like stabbing a dagger into her own heart. But her choice was made. She had to continue alone. Live with the pain. With what she'd done.

There was no way in the world she could ask Jamie to love her child. Raise it. Love it as his own. Not after what she'd done.

She cleared her throat and forced herself to look him straight in the eye. "I guess you could say I fell in line. Our families—the di Jesolos and the Rodolfos—have known each other forever. Generations. It's what our people *do*."

She sought Jamie's eyes for some sort of understanding. Anything to make her feel the tiniest bit better… Nothing. Just a blank expression as if she'd been listing cement prices. His lack of response was chilling.

When he finally spoke his voice bore the toneless disappointment of a judge on the brink of laying down a guilty verdict.

"Do you *really* believe this was entirely your family's doing? That you didn't play *any* role in it?"

Bea's hands flew to cover her chest, as if protecting her heart from his words.

"Well, not entirely, no—but surely you can understand how—"

"No. I can't." He held up his hand, putting an end to her appeal. "Maybe it's culture. Maybe it's class. But *my* family has done nothing but make sacrifices to ensure my life was better."

"And is that your guilt for their sacrifices talking? Or righteous indignation because I made my own sacrifice at the di Jesolo altar? A sacrifice for the greater good of *my* family!"

Bea hated herself for the cruel words. Jamie was the last person she should be lashing out at. The last person whose forgiveness she should expect.

She'd been a fool to think he might be the one to go to for compassion. For one of those unchecked, bear hugs he used to give. The hugs that had assured her everything would be all right.

She steeled herself and looked him in the eye again. Nothing. The shutters had dropped.

This summer was going to be a test.

Penance for the mistakes she'd made along the way.

And, in the end, perhaps proof that she'd be able to put up with anything once her baby was born.

If she could survive the arctic gaze shredding her nerves right now she could survive anything. Raise a baby on her own. Teach him or her right from wrong…ensure they lived the life they wanted to live.

Steeling herself against that remote gaze of his, she

turned to Jamie, matching his tone with a level of cool that took her by surprise. "Like you said, Jamie. People change."

Beatrice might as well have reached in and ripped his heart straight out of his chest.

Of *course* he'd bloody well changed!

Jamie set off with determined, long-legged strides after Beatrice, who had marched away, with quick, tight steps to start and then, when she hit the end of the promenade, stretched her legs into a run.

What did she expect? She'd *left* him. Yanked the world out from under his feet. Smashed his heart into bits. He'd been utterly dumbfounded when she'd left, had made it through each and every day since then through sheer force of will.

Eyes glued on that platinum blond head of hers, he pushed himself harder, even though he didn't have a clue what he was going to say when he reached her.

Tell her to leave.

Beg her to stay.

Either way, this *wasn't* how they were going to leave things. With her storming off in a huff because he wasn't rolling over and placating her ego. She'd left him once and he'd be damned if he was going to see the back of her again unless it was by mutual agreement.

Furious that he'd let things degenerate between them so quickly, Jamie reached out and grabbed Beatrice's elbow. The move threw her off balance, so he quickly stabilized her with both hands, holding her square in his arms. The two of them were breathing heavily, eyeing each other in anticipation of who would make the first move.

Before he could think better of it he cupped her chin in his hand, tipped her lips toward his and kissed her as if his life depended upon it. At this very moment, tasting her, feeling her respond to him as passionately as she was, sure as hell felt as if it did.

As suddenly as the moment began it was over. He wasn't sure who had pulled back first or if they'd simply needed to come up for air. Either way, he was sure of one thing. Beatrice was right. She hadn't left him because she didn't love him. It was still there. The spark. The fire.

Knowing that made the whole scenario worse.

If he couldn't count on her to stick with him through thick and thin there was little point in asking her to try again. No way would he be able to pick up the pieces a second time.

He stepped back and away from her, his hands scrubbing at the back of his head as if his fingers could reach in and reestablish the order he'd only just put into place.

"I shouldn't have done that."

Beatrice didn't say anything, pressing her fingers into her kiss-stung lips. Her eyes were wide, red rimmed with the tears she'd already shed.

"Let me walk you home." He stuffed his hands into his pockets to stop himself from pulling her into a hug, stroking her hair, whispering to her all those things a man told a woman when he knew she was hurting and wanted it to stop.

"Don't worry." She shook her head, took a quick scan of the piazza as if to regain her bearings. "It's been a long day. I'd like to walk home alone, if you don't mind."

It came out as almost a question. Just the merest hint of her genuinely caring if he *did*, in fact, mind.

"Do you want to make this work?" he asked instead. "The working-together thing?" he continued when she looked up at him, eyes as wide as saucers.

"I do." She nodded, her voice more solid than he'd heard it all day.

"Well, then… Looks like we'd both better get some rest. Tomorrow's going to be a long day."

And without a second glance he turned and walked away.

CHAPTER FOUR

"AM I ALLOWED to take showers with this on?"

Bea smiled. Since when were thirteen-year-old boys worried about *showers*?

"He means *go swimming*," his mother interjected, rubbing a hand through her son's sandy blond hair. "*Il est mon fils*. He's my son and he's like me," she translated, though they had been speaking French for most of the time Bea had been circling the colored fiberglass wrap onto the boy's arm. "He's addicted to the lake. My little minnow."

Guillaume squirmed and muttered something about not being so little anymore. Probably a teenage growth spurt and a lack of awareness of his new gangly limbs were the reason behind his fall. It also explained why rock climbing might not have been the best choice of activity.

Bea finished off the task with a smile, smoothing the last bit of blue wrap onto his arm. "Good thing you were wearing a helmet."

They all turned to look at the multicolored helmet, which had received an almighty dent in the boy's fall.

"You know, your cast is made out of the same thing as your helmet. It should keep your arm safe until you heal, but unfortunately it's not one hundred percent waterproof. I've put a waterproof liner in there, and I can get you a waterproof sheath—but it's not a perfect guarantee it will stay dry."

"I can pretty much guarantee, now that you've said that, Guillaume is going to be in that lake straightaway."

Bea laughed. "If you can bear it, hold off until tomorrow. You want it to dry properly and make sure everything's set. After that—" she looked at the mother "—the main goal is to make sure his skin stays clear of rashes or any other irritation. If you have a hair dryer, use the cool setting to dry inside the cast if it does get wet."

The mother and son looked at each other and laughed. "Marie is *never* going to let me borrow her hair dryer!"

"Perhaps if you asked nicely, instead of teasing her all the time." His mother gave him an elbow in the ribs.

"Older sister?"

Mother and son nodded as one.

Bea busied herself with tidying away the packaging from the wrap, wondering if she and *her* child would share moments like that. The relaxed camaraderie. So different from what she'd grown up with.

Clearing her throat, she banished the thought. She had to get through the pregnancy first.

"A vacuum cleaner works just as well."

"Ah!" Guillaume's mother laughed again. "If only my son weren't allergic to cleaning! I doubt he even knows there's a vacuum cleaner in our cottage."

Guillaume pretended not to hear, tapping away at his cast, examining the multiple colors his fingers were already turning in the wake of the break.

"I can't wait to show Marie my X-rays. She'll have to take back everything she said about me crying for nothing."

Bea pushed back on her wheeled stool as the boy's mother put her arm around her son's shoulder and pulled him in for a gentle hug. "It's all right to cry, *mon amour.* Strong men *should* show their feelings."

He wriggled in embarrassment, but didn't pull away.

Bea looked away again, fastidiously training her eyes on the paperwork.

It seemed every single thing in the universe was a little lesson, guiding her toward impending motherhood.

Moments like these would soon be in the pipeline for her. Trips to A&E. The frantic worry that her son or daughter would be all right. The relief, flooding through her when she was assured her child would be just fine. The love shining through it all.

"Let's get back to your *papa*, shall we, Guillaume? Show him your latest achievement."

The smile stayed on Bea's lips as she handed over the release papers, but inside, her heart had cinched tight.

That was the missing ingredient in her life. A father for her tiny little child.

Her fingers instinctively moved up to her lips, reliving that kiss. Even though it was a week ago now, in those few precious moments she'd thought maybe…just *maybe*…

"Is there anything else, Dr. Jesolo?"

Bea shook her head, unwilling to allow the wobble she knew she'd hear in her voice if she spoke.

Pointing the pair in the right direction, she curled her fingers around the cubicle curtain and tugged it shut, needing just a few seconds to compose herself. Another rush of tears. Another case of embedding the emotions of each of her patients straight into the fabric of her soul, of not being entirely able to retain her professional distance.

Hormones, no doubt.

All of a sudden Beatrice's eyes snapped wide-open. Was that really what she'd thought it was? Just the tiniest of flutters and yet…

Her hands slid instinctively across her belly… *Oh! Yes.* There it was again. Like having a butterfly inside her, but so much better.

Years of medical training told her it *couldn't* be what she thought it was. That precious little life letting her know that he or she was in there. It was far too soon to feel anything. There were all sorts of other possibilities. Medical explanations.

A need to pee. *Again.* An increase of blood flow to her womb, drawing her attention to the area. The fact that the low waistline of her skirt was becoming the tiniest bit more snug, despite weeks of morning sickness.

Either way, she believed the sensation *was* her tiny, precious baby letting her know he or she was alive in there.

"Can I get a hand here?"

Bea pulled her stethoscope around her neck and ran, not even bothering to take a swipe at the tears she didn't seem to be able to control. Happy or sad, they appeared on tap these days. Allergies, she told everyone.

Jamie.

Her focus was so complete as she ran to the triage area she hardly noticed that he had moved in alongside her as two gurneys were wheeled in by paramedics.

"Here." He handed her a disposable surgical gown. "Better put this on. Things might get messy."

"What's happened?" She saw Jamie's double take as she swept away the remnants of emotion before turning her full attention to the patients and the paramedic rattling off their status.

"Two women presenting with second- and third-degree burns."

"Where's my wife?" A man pushed through the swing doors, his eyes frantic with worry.

"She's here with us. Exactly where she needs to be." Jamie's solid voice assured the man.

"I *told* her not to use that kerosene stove. It didn't look safe. I *told* her it didn't look safe!"

Bea threw her attention to the woman on the gurney closest to her as she heard Jamie continuing to placate the man, convincing him to go back to the waiting room to be with his other children.

"Why are her clothes all wet?" she asked.

"When the stove exploded she jumped into the lake!" the woman's husband shouted over Jamie's shoulder.

"Second- and third-degree burns." Dr. Brandisi appeared on the other side of the gurney, his gloved hands at the back of his neck as he tied on his disposable gown. It was critical the wounds were kept as hygienic as possible. Infection was a burn victim's worst enemy. "We need to start cutting these clothes off."

Bea did her best to soothe the woman, although she was unable to run a hand across her brow as the flames had hit her forehead.

"What's your name, *amore*?"

"My sister!" The woman struggled to push herself up. "Is my sister here?"

"She's blistering. Only remove what isn't anywhere near the burns." Jamie's voice came through loud and clear as he took control of the team. "We need Brandisi and Bates with the sister. Her name's Jessica. Dr. Jesolo?" Jamie's eyes hit Bea's as she tied on a face mask. "This is Monica Tibbs. You're with me."

Bea nodded, not questioning his assignment for an instant. To do so would waste precious time. Just a rough glance told her that somewhere around thirty percent of Monica's body had taken a hit from the explosion. The damage was significant.

The calm with which Jamie approached the chaotic situation infused everyone with much needed focus. Collectively, they went to work. Instructions, low and urgent, flew from doctor to doctor, nurse to nurse.

Bea didn't have time or any need to worry about the fact that Jamie was now by her side, carefully cutting along the length of the woman's trouser leg. Pieces of cloth stuck to her skin. It was hard to look at. Essential to treat.

"Jessica's lost consciousness." Dr. Brandisi's voice rose above the rest. "Can we get a check on her stats, please?"

"Where's the oxygen? We need to get some oxygen."

"It's impossible to attach the monitor tabs."

"Use your fingers. The woman's still got pulse points."

The tension in the room ratcheted up another notch. After a moment of taut silence and furious concentration a nurse rattled off some numbers. The voices rose around Jessica's bed, then dropped just as suddenly.

"What's going on?" Monica whispered.

"Can we get an intubation kit?" Dr. Brandisi asked.

"Anyone clear on the ambient temperature? We don't want to add hypo to the symptoms." Jamie threw the question over his shoulder to the stand-by staff awaiting orders.

"They're doing everything they can for your sister," Beatrice told Monica, taking as much of the her top off as she was able to, steering clear of the burns. Thank goodness it was cotton. A synthetic top would have melted instantly. "Hypothermia can be a problem if the room's too cool and there's a large burn surface."

"I never should've suggested making pancakes! It was ridiculous!"

"There's soot in Jessica's airway."

"Better that than losing oxygen."

"She's not breathing?" Monica rasped, lifting the oxygen mask from her mouth, her throat losing its battle for moisture.

Bea looked across to Jamie. He nodded. She knew that nod. *Go ahead and be honest*, it said. *But do it with care.*

Bea ran her fingers as gently as she could against the unburnt skin of the woman's cheek. "This team of doctors are exactly who she needs to be with right now. Let us focus on you."

"Give me a moment." Dr. Brandisi silenced his team as they prepared to intubate Jessica. "All right—we're in. Let's get her into surgery, people."

As one, the team flicked switches, unlocked wheels, tugged rolling IV stands close and moved toward the swinging doors that led to the small surgical ward.

"Is my sister going to be all right?" Monica tried to sit up again, screaming when her exposed arm brushed against the side of the gurney. "Cut it off!" she pleaded, her one good hand clutching at Bea's surgical gown. "Please—cut it off if you have to, but make the pain stop!"

"We're doing everything we can. As soon as your IV is in, the pain will begin to ease." Bea turned to the nurse hanging up the bag of electrolyte fluid. "How much lidocaine do you have in there?"

The nurse told her she'd used the standard calculation.

"Ten milliliters to a five hundred milligram bag?"

The nurse nodded.

"There isn't any potassium in the bag, right?"

"No. We've heard about the risks. Even up here in the hinterlands."

Bea's eyes flicked to Jamie's at the comment. She hadn't been questioning the nurse—just making sure all the bases were covered.

She returned her attention to Monica. This wasn't the time to bicker about whose pool of knowledge was bigger, even if her specialty *had* been trauma. Malnutrition and respiratory infections had been her bread and butter at the charity clinic in Venice, but today she was going to have to draw on every ounce of experience she'd had at Northern General. And rely on Jamie. This was *his* turf. His call to make.

"I know it's difficult, Monica, but if you could lie back it will help with the pain." Her eyes flicked to Jamie. Which way would he want to go with this?

"Have you done the fluids calculation for the first twenty-four?" Jamie asked. He had removed all the clothing he could from Monica's side and begun checking her circumferential burns.

"Four mils multiplied by the patient's body weight by TBSA?" She winced. She hadn't meant it to sound like a question.

"You've got it." He didn't sound surprised. "Make sure fifty percent of that is fed through in the first eight hours, the rest infused over the last sixteen. Are you all right to oversee this?"

"Sure." Bea turned to the nurse and asked for extra bags of the electrolyte solutions essential for rehydrating the patient, along with giving her a request to monitor the urine output.

"I'm swabbing for microbiological contamination."

Jamie looked to Bea. Again, as if reading his mind, she knew what he was saying. *Brace your patient.* It would hurt, but Monica had been in a lake. They had to know what germs they'd be fighting.

After talking Monica through the pain of the swabs, Bea returned her attention to Jamie. If he was needed for other cases she should show she was on top of this. Or was he babysitting her? Making sure nothing else had changed about the woman he'd thought he'd known inside and out?

Either way, it just showed he was a good doctor. It wasn't anything to get bristly about.

"Warm water wash before dressing, and then what would you like?"

"We'll need a CBC and ABG, a check on urea and electrolytes." Jamie turned to the nurse. "Would you please get Monica's blood glucose levels, B-HCG and an albumin test?"

"What *is* all that? Am I going to live?" Monica's hoarse voice croaked up through the list of instructions.

"We're doing our best to get you through this," Bea replied.

She would have loved to say yes. Make assurances. But burns this big opened a patient up to multiple complications. The tests Jamie had ordered were only the beginning of weeks, if not months of treatment. The poor woman would no doubt need extensive time with multiple therapists as her body was healed from its devastating injuries. Luckily, it seemed most of hers were second-degree burns—unlike her sister, who seemed to have taken the bulk of the fireball's heat.

"We need to get some saline into her. And some blood. Her heart's going to need all the help it can get." Jamie nodded at Beatrice to get the IV. "Anyone ascertained a blood type?"

"O positive," answered a dark-haired nurse, Giulietta. "And her husband said she doesn't have any allergies. Do you want me to organize a transfusion?"

"Not just yet. Let's see how she goes with the rehydration solutions and lidocaine first. Dr. Jesolo, have you established the TBSA yet?"

Beatrice pulled a sterile needle from its packaging and

prepared to inject antibiotics into the fresh IV bag. "To me it looks like thirty percent. Maybe a little bit more."

He nodded. "Good." His eyes flicked to Giulietta. "Can we get a call in to the burns unit in Pisa? These two are going to need to be transferred as soon as they're stabilized."

"They're from the UK. Is it worth putting a call into a hospital there? A medevac?"

He shook his head. The hospitals in the UK were terrific, but time was a factor. "Let's get her stabilized and en route to Pisa for the time being. We'll call in a translator if necessary."

"Yes, Dr. Coutts."

Another nurse filled her spot as quickly as Giulietta left.

"I'm just going to check on Jessica—are you all right on your own?" He knew what the answer would be, but wanted to triple-check with Beatrice. There was something a bit fragile about her today. Something in direct contrast to the slight bloom he'd thought he could see in her cheeks when she'd come in this morning. He'd been a fool to cross the line as he had with that blasted kiss, but it was too late to wish it back now.

"We're going to be just fine here. Aren't we, Monica?"

Jamie watched as Beatrice bent close to her patient's lips, listening intently as a message was relayed.

When she looked up at him, there were tears in her eyes. "Could you let Jessica know that her sister loves her?"

"Of course." Jamie nodded somberly as he met Beatrice's gaze.

They both knew how severe these two cases were. How, even if their patients survived the blast, their lives would be changed forever.

"Straightaway."

From the moment he entered the operating theater he sensed something was wrong.

The instant he heard the words *hypovolemic shock*, his mind went into overdrive.

Jessica's extensive burns meant her body couldn't retain fluids—crucially, blood.

Dr. Brandisi gave Jamie a curt nod when he joined the table, tying on a fresh gown as he did so. "We can't get enough blood into her. Or saline fluids. Her heart's beginning to fail."

"Raise the feet, please." It was a last-ditch attempt to try to increase her circulation, but a quick glimpse at her heart rate and pulse were sure signs that there was little hope. The atmosphere in the room intensified.

"I don't suppose there are any peristaltic pumps hidden in a cupboard somewhere," he said to no one in particular. He knew as well as everyone else that there weren't, and rehydrating the patient was critical. Despite the fact they were a midsize clinic, they simply weren't equipped to deal with an injury of this nature.

"Negative," Teo replied needlessly, his expression grim. "The chopper is on its way. Potassium levels are too high. Can we try to get more fluids in her?"

"She's going into cardiac arrest."

"Kidneys are failing."

"Temperature's falling. Let's not add hypothermia to the list, people!"

Jamie scanned the woman's chest. The burns were too deep to consider using the standard defibrillation equipment. They could try for open-heart surgery, but they simply didn't have the means of getting enough blood into her body to warrant any success.

As the team worked with a feverish intensity, Jamie did what he had promised. Jessica's chances were fading with each passing moment, and he sure as hell wasn't going to let her die without hearing her sister's words. He knelt low beside her, gently holding each side of her head as he did so, and passed on the message of love.

All too quickly the team had exhausted every means of keeping Jessica alive.

"Do you want to call it?" Teo stood back from the operating table, angrily pulling his gloves off and throwing them in the bin. No one liked to lose a patient. No one liked to make the call.

Jamie glanced up at the digital clock as he pulled off his own gloves. "Time of death—"

"The helicopter's here. Are you ready?"

Beatrice burst through the doors of the operating theater holding a mask in front of her face, her eyes darting around the room until they landed on Jamie.

"Time of death," he repeated, with more feeling than he'd anticipated, "nine-oh-seven."

Beatrice dropped the mask, a flash of dismay darkening her features before she quickly composed herself. She gave Jamie a quick nod. "I'll let the staff know. I might hold off on telling the sister until her transfer is complete."

"As you see fit," Jamie agreed.

It was always a delicate balance. Family desperate for information. Taking it hard. Losing the will to survive. Monica's burns were severe, and she would need every ounce of fight she had left in her.

He nodded his thanks to the support team and went out through the back of the clinic for just a moment to recover. Regroup.

Behind the clinic was a small courtyard, paved with big slabs of mountain granite. One of the nurses kept the flower boxes bright with fresh blooms. They were a cheery, lively contrast to the hollow sensation that never failed to hit him whenever their efforts failed.

He heard the helicopter rotors begin their slow *phwamp, phwamp*, building up speed and ultimately taking off, banking to the south to head for the burns unit in Pisa.

His thoughts were with Monica's husband, still in Casualty with his children, where the nurses and doctors were tending to their minor injuries. His holiday up in the mountains turned into a living nightmare.

Jamie wouldn't have wished what they were going through on anyone.

It was a vivid reminder that no matter how difficult he'd found it to see Beatrice these past few days, she was *alive*. While they were obviously still stinging from their breakup, neither of them was going to have to deal with the physical traumas Monica would for the rest of her life.

The poor woman would have to focus with all the power of her being on the silver linings. Her children had escaped injury for the most part. Her husband was fine, dedicated to his family and their welfare. Monica would bear the scars of this day forever, but in her heart she would be eternally grateful for pulling through.

He looked up into the bright blue sky, dappled with a smattering of big cotton-ball clouds. He picked one and stared, squinting against the brightness of the morning sun as it rose at the far end of the lake.

So Beatrice had left him to do right by her family. She had never been a woman to take a decision lightly, so there must have been something deep within her, compelling her to choose to fall in and play the good daughter. *His* family had made sacrifices for him. Life-changing sacrifices so that he wouldn't have to. What if he had been put in a similar situation?

He closed his eyes and let the sun beat down on his face.

His family wouldn't have *had* a similar situation, but he knew that if push had come to shove he'd have laid his life on the line for any single member. It would be two-faced of him not to expect Beatrice to do the same.

At the time her decision had hurt as badly as if she'd stabbed him and left him for dead. But she'd never said she didn't love him. Never said she didn't care. And when he'd kissed her… The sensation had kept him up near enough half the night. He knew what he had felt—and it was about as close to love as he dared let himself believe.

He opened his eyes, surprised to feel a soft smile playing on his lips. Tough start to the day. But it had given him some much needed perspective. A way to get through the summer with his heart intact.

It was at moments like these that Bea felt overwhelmed by the beauty of the human spirit.

The day had been a long one and having heard at long last that Monica had arrived at the specialist burns unit and was receiving the best treatment she could get, Bea had felt the tightness in her chest loosen a bit. When the doctor changing shifts with her had mentioned the community's response to the accident she'd taken a walk down to the lake, and the sight that greeted her now set her heart aglow.

The lake was sparkling so brightly it looked as if it were inhabited by thousands of tiny stars, and out of respect for the family who had suffered such a heavy loss today holidaymakers and locals had joined forces, piling huge bouquets of flowers on the boat launch where the accident had taken place. As the sun set one by one people were releasing floating candles onto the lake. Hundreds of people had turned up. The overall effect—shimmery, magical, otherworldly—was healing.

"Quite a turnout."

A spray of goose bumps rippled up her arms. No need to turn around to guess the man behind the voice. But before she could think better of it Bea did turn, her body registering Jamie's presence and her brain still spinning to catch up, as if her skin remembered what it was like to be touched by him without a prompt.

Little wonder. When she'd agreed to the arranged marriage she had forced herself to preserve her time in England in a little memory bubble and hide it as far away as she could. How else would she have survived?

And now that she was pregnant… *Oh, Dio!* It was as if the bubble had been sliced open and her dream man had been put in front of her just in case she hadn't already known what she'd given up.

She was going to have to find a way to be stronger than this, better than this, when her child was born. There was no way her baby was going to suffer for her own madness-fueled mistake. Because it did boil down to just one. Leaving Jamie.

"Really good work today." Jamie tucked his chin down so that his eyes were on a level with hers. A move he'd once used to great effect to tug a smile out of her after a rough shift.

She swallowed before she answered, knowing those ever-ready tears would come if she spoke straightaway. "You, too." She went for a casual, buddy tone. "I'd almost forgotten how well we work together."

"I hadn't." He pushed up to his full height, eyes looking out upon the lake. "Look, do you see there, where the moonlight meets up with the candles? It's as if they're drawn to one another."

Unable to respond, she murmured an acknowledgment and looked back out at the lake.

Drawn to each other...

Just like the pair of them. She'd used to think their combined energies made them a force to be reckoned with. Now, with the situation she'd found herself in—correction, *put* herself in—she was a moth drawn to the flame. Falling in love with Jamie again would be all consuming. Something she wouldn't be able to come back from.

In a few months' time she would need to give all her energy to her child. Figure out how to pay the bills. Work. Breastfeed. Love. Laugh. Cry. All of it with one sole focus. Her newborn child.

So right here and now, opening up the heart she knew was near to bursting with love for the man she'd left behind wasn't an option.

They stood for a few moments in silence, gazing out at the lake. The area was crowded, and there wasn't much room. Someone trying to get a lakeside view caught Bea off balance, and despite her best attempts not to reach out to regain her balance her hands widened and found purchase on Jamie's chest. His arms automatically cinched around her back, creating a protective barrier by pulling her in close to his chest.

Bea was hit by a raft of sensations.

The scents she would have been unable to describe a fortnight earlier came to her now as clear as day. Cotton. Cedar. Spice and citrus.

The feel of the firm wall of chest her fingers hadn't been able to resist pressing into.

The memory of being able to tuck her head in that secure nook between his shoulder and chin, her forehead once getting a tickle when he'd experimented with growing a beard.

Despite herself, she laughed.

"What's so funny?" Jamie asked, pulling back to examine her.

"Do you remember when you wanted to grow a beard? It was wintertime, wasn't it?"

"Winter into spring," he answered, the memory lighting up his own eyes as he spoke. "That's why I ended up shaving it off." He scrubbed a hand along his bare chin. "That thing itched something crazy once the weather started warming up. What made you remember that?"

"Just popped into my head." A white lie. What else was she going to say? *Being this close to you made me want to nestle into your chest and relive some of the most perfect moments of my life?* Hardly.

"Memories are funny things." Jamie loosened his hold on her and then dropped his hands to his sides. "I've been having quite a few myself today."

Bea's forehead lifted, though it wasn't in surprise. How *could* he be immune to the fevered trips down memory lane she'd been tearing along from the moment she'd seen him again?

"Shall we?" Jamie tipped his head toward the square, where the crowd was less thick.

She shook her head. "I should probably be getting back to my apartment. I'm an early-to-bed sort of woman these days."

"No more double alarms?"

They both laughed at the memory and she shook her head. No. That had all changed.

"I'm up with the lark these days," she said, grateful for the reprieve from looking into Jamie's beautiful green eyes when he turned to forge a path through the crowd for the pair of them.

When they'd been together she'd slept like a log. So deeply she would turn off her alarm without even remembering having batted around in the dark to stop its beeping.

That had all changed when she'd returned to Italy. She'd

blamed it on the one-hour time difference knowing full well it was nerves. A permanent feeling of foreboding, as if she *knew* marrying Marco would never bring her the joy loving Jamie had.

She stared at his back as he worked his way steadily, gently through the crowd. If she'd been with him she would never have…

Ugh. Sigh.

She would never have done a lot of things.

Like agreeing to have an IVF "honeymoon baby." Marco had pushed her into it so that no one would know he was infertile. Completely incapable of providing the Rodolfos with the heir they craved.

Not that she'd ever jumped into bed with him to see if the doctors had been wrong.

And not that he'd protested.

Having this mystery baby had never been a question for her. It was hardly the child's fault she'd agreed to marry someone whose pedigree rendered him more playboy than prince.

The only relief she felt now was that the baby wasn't his. The way things stood, the child growing inside her belly was one hundred percent hers and hers alone.

"Time for a drink?" Jamie asked over his shoulder, as if sensing the discord furrowing her brow.

She shook her head. "I shouldn't really."

"I won't bite. Scout's honor." He turned, crossed his heart, then held up his fingers looking every bit the Boy Scout she knew he'd once been.

"Are you still in touch with your old den leader?"

"Dr. Finbar?" He shook his head. "Not for a while." His gaze shifted up and to the right as he made a calculation. "Must be a year or so before I left since I saw him.

I should've gone to see him before I up and went, but—" his gaze returned solidly to hers "—I wasn't at my best."

"I'm so sorry, Jamie. If I could have done anything—"

"No." He cut her off. "It wasn't you—it was a patient. Why I left."

Something in his tone told her that wasn't entirely true, but Jamie was allowed his privacy. His pride. He'd been the one left behind to pick up the pieces. To explain to everyone why she'd left after they'd seemed so perfectly happy with each other.

Being humiliated in front of the enormous crowd at her wedding had served her right. She wouldn't have been the slightest bit surprised to have learned Jamie had raised a glass at the news. A bit of schadenfreude for the embittered suitor.

"How is it you can even face me?" she asked, surprising herself as much as Jamie by the forthright question. "After what I did, I'm surprised you can even speak to me—let alone not hate me."

"Oh, my beauty. *Ma bella Beatrice…*" He pronounced it the Italian way, hitting each vowel and consonant as if he were drinking a fine wine. He stroked the backs of his fingers along the downy soft hairs of her cheek. "I could never hate you. I think I hated myself more than anyone."

A sad smile teased at the corners of his mouth. His lips were fuller than most men's. Sensual. She could have drowned in his kisses, and just the thought of never experiencing one again drew shadows across her heart.

"I can't imagine why you would feel that way. What would make you think so poorly of yourself?"

"Oh…" He clapped his hands together. "About a million reasons. Not putting up a better fight. Not—I don't know—challenging him to a duel? Confronting your parents? Showing them I was every bit as worthy as…"

He paused and swallowed down the name neither of them seemed able to say.

"Water under the bridge." The words rolled off his tongue as if he'd said them a thousand times before in a vain effort to convince himself it was true. "We're both grown-ups. We've moved on. Whatever happened, it happened for a reason, right?"

She shrugged and tried her best to smile, not really coming good on either gesture. The last thing Jamie was to her was water under the bridge. A moment of perfection embedded in her heart was more like it. "Sometimes I'm not so sure."

Jamie shook his head. A clear sign he didn't want her to plead with him. Beg him to try again as she so longed to do.

"We're on different paths now, Beatrice. But it doesn't mean we can't be on friendly terms for the length of your contract. So, what do you say?" He put out his hand in the space between them. "Truce? At the end of the summer you go your way, I go mine?"

A voice inside her head began screaming again and again. *No*, it cried. *No!* But a softer, more insistent voice told her that to do anything other than agree would be unfair. Cruel, even. He'd endured enough. And she didn't deserve him.

She and her baby would find another place, another way to be whole again.

She put her hand out and met his for a solid shake. "Truce."

CHAPTER FIVE

"IT DEFINITELY LOOKS worse than it is, Hamish." Bea took a step back from her patient and gave him an appraising look. "The stitches should cover the worst of it, but opting out of wearing a helmet while kayaking…? Not a good move."

"But no one else was!" Hamish gave his chest a thump with his fist. "Scotsmen are *hard*!"

"Doesn't make them smart. You could've been a trendsetter. Using what's *inside* your head instead of bashing the outside of it on a boulder!"

She tried to keep the admonishment gentle, but threw him a stern look as she tugged off her gloves and popped them in the bin. He had a pretty deep gash in his forehead, and if it hadn't been for one of his friends pulling him back up into the kayak and keeping a compress on it until they arrived at the clinic he might easily have died.

"You're going to have to keep the dressing dry *and*—" she wagged an admonishing finger at him "—you need to let your friends know one of them is going to have to stay with you at all times for the next two days. Concussion watch."

"*Ach, no!* I've still got another few days here!" The young man protested. "I've been saving for *months*!"

"You could very well have a concussion." Bea pressed

down on his shoulders when he tried to get up from the exam table and wobbled. "Any dizziness, nausea, headaches...all signs of a concussion."

"It's all right, Doc!" Her patient waved off her concerns and launched himself toward the curtains around the exam room.

"Hold on!" Bea ran the few steps toward him and tried to get under his arm to support him, but he pulled away and brought them both crashing to the ground.

Her instinct was to pull away. Protect her stomach. She knew the baby was still only teensy—tiny—but she'd already messed up her own life. She wasn't prepared to mess up the little innocent soul inside her.

Seconds later she felt a pair of hands pulling her up.

"Are you all right?"

Jamie's rich voice swept along her spine as she lurched into an upright position, far too aware of how close they were to one another. One arm was grazing against his chest. And her breasts. Ooh...that was a sensual trip down memory lane she didn't need to take. Especially with everything in her body on high alert.

Touch.

Sensation.

The pair of lips just millimeters away from her own. The bottom lip fuller than the top. Just perfect for nibbling. A bit of blond stubble around them, highlighting just how soft those lips were to touch in contrast to the tickle of his five-o'clock shadow...

"Beatrice?" She felt Jamie's grip tighten on her forearms. "Your patient is waiting."

Pregnancy brain be damned!

As quickly as she could, Bea wriggled out of Jamie's arms, unsure just how many precious moments she'd lost to daydreaming about his mouth. And kissing it.

Another shot of heat swirled around her belly. *Santo cielo!*

"*Si, Dottore.* I'm fine. *Grazie.*" He could play the white knight all he wanted, but she needed to prove to herself she could stand on her own two feet.

"Are you sure you're okay to treat this patient?"

He rocked back on his heels, his eyelids dropping to half-mast as if he were suddenly in doubt as to her skills as a physician. Desired effect or not, it slammed her back into the moment. She might be a lot of things, but she was no slouch as a doctor.

"*Si, Dottore.* If you'll excuse me? Hamish and I have to finish our discussion about concussions."

"I think I'll join you."

Her eyes flicked to his, searching them for more meaning than she could glean from his neutral tone.

"In case Mr.—" He leaned over her shoulder to glance at the patient assignment board, giving her another waft of undiluted alpha Jamie. "In case Mr. McGregor, here, decides to take matters into his own hands again."

Beatrice didn't know whether to be relieved or furious. Her lips were dangerously close to tipping into a scowl, but ever the professional, she put on a smile, reminding herself she probably would need an extra hand in case Hamish decided to flee the scene again. Concussions were no laughing matter.

"Now, Mr. McGregor—" Jamie gestured toward the exam table "—what do you say we take another look at you?"

He knew he sounded like an uptight by-the-letter diagnostician, but it had thrown him off his axis when he'd seen Beatrice hurtling through the curtains as if in a full-on rugby tackle.

His every instinct had been to protect her. When he'd

lifted her up and she'd pulled away from him as if he were made of kryptonite it had more than stung. It had riled him. Which meant he still cared—and that made the silent war he was waging with himself to treat Beatrice as he would treat anyone else even harder.

He had loved her with every pore in his body. And had spent every waking hour since she'd left trying to forget her.

Unsuccessfully, as was beginning to become wildly apparent.

Moving to Italy hadn't helped. The language, the food, the blasted snowcapped mountains were all reminders of her. He should have accepted the job in the Andes. He still could have had his snowcapped mountains, but also extra servings of beef charred on an enormous open fire and about twelve thousand miles between himself and his memories.

As if you could outrun something branded onto your soul…

"Just hold still for a moment," he heard himself saying, going through the examination by rote even as his mind played catch-up with life's strange twist of events. "I want to take a look at your eyes."

"I've already examined the cranial nerves," Beatrice said.

The exam area was small and she was close. Close enough for him to smell the sweet honey-and-flower scent that seemed to travel in her wake.

"Given that Mr. McGregor has had a *second* fall, I thought I'd just check again."

He felt a huff of air hit his neck. One that said, *Why are you treating me like a plebeian? You helped train me. You, of all the people in the world, should know I'm the best.*

Who knew a little puff of air could contain so much sentiment?

"I'm not going to have to pay for this twice, am I?" Hamish asked, leaning around Jamie as if the only real answer could come from Beatrice. He pulled out the pockets of his shorts to show they were empty.

"No. All part of the service." Jamie leaned in closer to the young man with his medical torch, taking note of Hamish's various pupil responses and all the while pretending not to hear Beatrice's sotto voce grumblings behind him.

Caveman this...

Entitled Englishman that...

To her credit, she was saying it all in Italian, so the Scotsman appeared none the wiser.

Despite the fact that her venom was directed straight at him—like verbal darts in his back—Jamie smiled.

If someone had treated *him* like this, he probably would have responded in the same way. Boorishly barging in and repeating what was a standard exam was straight out of the Cro-Magnon handbook. But he hadn't liked seeing the look of terror on her face as she hit the floor, curling in on herself as if protecting a small child in her arms. It had frightened him. And though he might have closed his heart to the idea of loving her again, he damn well wasn't going to see her hurt. Not on *his* watch.

"Right, Mr. McGregor! It looks as though Dr. Jesolo has done her best by you. What did you recommend in regard to follow-up?"

He turned to Beatrice, only to receive a full hit of Glaring Doctor. Arms crossed tightly over her chest. Foot tapping impatiently. One eyebrow imperiously arched as if in anticipation of another admonishment. Something told him not to laugh if he didn't want to turn that heated gaze to ice.

Through gritted teeth she began detailing what she'd presumably already run through with her patient. Rest. No kayaking or other contact sports—with or without a helmet—for at least forty-eight hours. A close watch by others on whether he was feeling nauseous, dizzy, light-headed, and some paracetamol—

"But no aspirin," Jamie interjected, suddenly feeling playful. They'd used to do this when they went on rounds together. See who could come up with the most obscure information on a case. Out-fact each other.

"I also made it clear to Mr. McGregor that if he loses consciousness, has any clear fluid leaking from his ears or nose, or feels unusually drowsy while awake, he should return immediately."

"Or has a seizure," Jamie couldn't help adding, knowing it would send that eyebrow of hers arcing just a little bit higher on her forehead.

"Or loses power in any part of his body. An arm or a leg, for example."

"And if he has a headache that worsens, that's a definite cause for concern."

"As is consuming any alcohol, engaging in stressful situations or losing eyesight."

This time he couldn't stop himself from smiling. She'd seen through him now. And was meeting him medical beat for beat.

"Perhaps he should also consider returning if he has problems speaking. Or understanding other people."

"You two are really freaking me out!" Hamish broke into this verbal one-upmanship. "Am I going to totally *die* or something?"

They turned to him as one and began apologizing. Jamie took the moment to recuse himself from any further involvement in the case, faking a pained look at the same time. "I've got to dash. Lovely to see Dr. Jesolo has given such thorough treatment. All the best for the rest of your holiday. Toodle-pip for now!"

He took two long-legged strides, yanked the curtain open and closed it behind him and then looked up to the invisible heavens.

Toodle-pip?

His family would have had a right old laugh at the antiquated expression. One usually used by Britain's upper crust—not a working-class family like his.

He gave his head a shake.

Beatrice.

She was the only one who could put him in a tailspin like this. Truce or no—he was going to have to continue to watch his back if he wanted to be in one piece by the end of the summer.

He shook his head again and headed toward the assignment board to find himself a patient.

Toodle-pip...

Teo looked at Beatrice and Jamie as if they'd both morphed into mountain goats.

"What do you mean, you're not coming? *Everyone* on the last shift is heading out to the piazza for the Midsummer Festa. I think the crew inside are even taking it in turns to run out and get a bite to eat before drinks this evening."

He flicked a thumb toward the main square, where it seemed the town's entire population was headed.

"Gotta meet my missus. She's eating for two and I want to make sure I get a look-in."

Jamie didn't miss the sideways glance Bea shot him from the other side of the doorway they were inhabiting.

Was it hearing about "the missus"? Or the news that she was pregnant that had caught Bea out?

"C'mon, guys!" Teo persisted. "What are you waiting for? Grub's up!"

"Would you like to go, Beatrice? Get a taste of mountain living?"

"I've been to quite a few *festas*," she answered noncommittally, giving an indecipherable shake of the head. Then added, "When I was younger."

It wasn't a yes. But it wasn't a no. From the impatience building on Teo's face it was obvious he was taking it personally.

Okay. Bull. Horns. Time to seize them and make a decision.

"All right, I'll go."

Jamie and Beatrice spoke simultaneously, turning to one another in wide-eyed horror, then just as quickly recovering with an about-face to Teo and swiftly pasted on smiles.

Teo shot wary looks from one to the other. "I'm going to head off, but I guess I'll see you both in the square?"

"The piazza—yes." Beatrice nodded, as if she'd been the one to suggest going to the Midsummer Festa in the first place. "I haven't had cherry *crostata* in years. Just the time of year for it."

Her voice might have sounded enthusiastic, but she didn't make even a hint of a move.

Nor did Jamie.

Again Teo's eyes flicked from one to the other. "So..." he drawled in his lazy Australian accent. "Are either of you planning on going to this brilliant festival anytime in the near future? Or are you going to wait until you can sneak in under the cover of darkness?"

Jamie laughed. Too heartily.

His guffaw sounded about as genuine as Beatrice's giggle.

Not one bit.

Trills of genuine laughter sounded on the streets beyond them. Then came the sound of an orchestra tuning up for the musical entertainment. An opera diva giving an initial run at her higher range.

Strangely, the collection of sounds and the general buzz of excitement reminded him of a night when the two of them had scraped together their small incomes and plumped for a getaway in Blackpool.

The classic seaside resort in Britain might not have been to everyone's taste—particularly a princess raised with all the finer things in life within hand's reach—but Beatrice had loved it. The over-the-top light displays. The dance halls. The bright pink candy floss.

The memory hit a spot he had once thought he would never be able to return to without a wave of acrimony following in its wake.

They might never be lovers again, but he had really meant it when he'd called a truce. Tonight he would simply be putting his theory to the test: bygones should be bygones.

"Right, Dr. Jesolo. Let's not keep poor Dr. Brandisi waiting any longer. He's obviously desperate to join his wife."

"Girlfriend," Teo corrected. "She's not made an honest man of me yet. Although—" he glanced at his watch "—the wedding's got to be by the end of the summer. The baby's due in October, and I want my child to have happily married parents when he's born."

Beside him, Jamie felt Bea stiffen. No great surprise when the words *happily* and *married* were bandied about, he supposed. Proof that money couldn't buy you happiness. Teo obviously had bundles of the latter, but not much money.

An idea popped into his head.

"How about at *Ferragosto*?"

"Aw, *mate*!" Teo feigned a few boxing jabs at Jamie. "That's *brilliant*. Alessandra will go nuts for that idea. A wedding *and* a festival for the price of one! What's not to love?"

Beatrice abruptly turned away. Wedding talk was probably not high on her agenda. A protective urge to steer the conversation in another direction took hold of him.

"Right!" Jamie clapped his hands, then rubbed them together. "Everyone's at their stations and ready for the next shift. I'm with Teo. Let's get a move on."

Jamie turned to Beatrice, his arm crooked, and a genuine smile began to form on his lips as she tentatively tucked her fingers around his elbow. He gave the tips of her fingers a pat. More akin to one a grandfather might give a granddaughter than a slighted ex-lover to a woman, but they were meant to be friends. And friends didn't caress, stroke or give one another unexpected passionate kisses that reawakened every part of the masculinity he hadn't tapped into in heaven knew how long…

"To the square?"

Beatrice nodded, her cheeks streaked with just a hint of a blush.

A hint of pride took hold in his chest. Though he knew it was best to keep things neutral, he couldn't help but enjoy having made an impact. Knowing he could still bring a touch of pink to those high, aristocratic cheekbones of hers.

"You're looking pretty as a picture tonight, Beatrice."

He meant it, too. Her short-cut hair accentuated the clean line of her jaw, and her dark brown eyes, always inquisitive, absorbed the flower displays already on show at the periphery of the square they were fast approaching. Her tongue darted out to lick her lips when they passed a *pasticceria*, its windows bursting with delectable pastries.

He didn't realize he was humming until Beatrice pulled back a little, her fingers still linked into the crook of his arm, and gave him a sidelong look.

He hadn't hummed since…

He knew exactly how long it had been.

"I'm still the same old me," Jamie said, when her expression remained bemused.

"Hmm…" Her lips tightened, then pushed into a moue before doing the little wiggly thing he'd used to be so familiar with. The telltale sign that she wasn't entirely sure of something.

"C'mon, Beatrice." He lowered his voice so Teo, who was talking away on his phone, wouldn't hear them. "Let's make the best of a—" He stopped, trying to find the best words.

"A bad situation?" Beatrice filled in the words he'd been about to say.

"An awkward one," Jamie parried.

She wasn't going to get away with making this harder than it already was. He'd endured more than enough angst on his own. Reliving those dark, lonely hours he'd fought and survived in front of her…? Not a chance in hell.

"Well—" she gave a quick laugh "—that's probably more accurate. But I have to confess I'm still reeling a bit." She changed the tone of her voice to mimic a film star of yesteryear. "Of all the clinics in all of Italy…" She trailed off, her dark eyes darting anywhere but up at his face.

A hit of defensiveness welled up within him. *He* had arrived here first. Well, not in Italy, but at the clinic.

"A clinic geared toward tourists was a good fit for me." *All things considered.*

"But an *Italian* clinic? I still haven't quite managed to figure out why they hired you."

"Thanks very much!" He feigned being affronted, knowing it wasn't what she meant. Even so, it felt a bit like she was drawing a line in the sand.

England—his turf. Italy—hers.

Well, too bad. It didn't work that way.

She laughed again, this time pulling her hand out of his arm to hold her hands up in protest. Though her hand hadn't been there long, his arm felt instantly cool at its absence.

"I didn't mean it that way. You know I think you're an amazing doctor."

Their gazes connected and he saw that she meant it. It would have been so easy to attach more meaning to the compliment. More sentiment. But that time had passed.

"I just meant I thought they would hire a fluent Italian speaker for the post."

"They did. Or near enough."

She turned to him, eyes wide with astonishment. "I didn't know that."

"There are a lot of things you don't know about me."

He swallowed the bitter words that might have followed. Some men might have done their very best to close off every last detail of a lover who'd chosen another path, but he had found it impossible. Their lives had been too interwoven. Beatrice's love of her home country had become as much a part of him as his Northern English heritage.

What was spring without stuffed zucchini flowers? Or winter without chestnuts? Scents, sights, smells—they had all vividly shifted when Beatrice had swept into his life like a refreshing spring breeze. Turning dull, dark England into a brighter landscape, only to plunge into darkness again when she left.

After a year of trying to block everything out but work, and then losing the young patient he'd grown far too close to, he'd needed that light again. And the closest he'd been able to get to rekindling that light had been to go to Italy.

"For starters," he began, by way of a gentler explanation, "you left your copy of *The Silver Spoon* behind."

"I thought you *hated* cooking!"

"Not anymore."

"But when we were together—" She stopped.

He wondered if she'd actually go there. Try to take him on a trip down memory lane neither of them seemed well equipped for. They'd effectively lived together during the second year they'd been together. Not officially—she'd still had her own apartment—but he doubted her roommate had ever seen her there. He couldn't remember a night when they hadn't fallen asleep, woven into each other's arms.

"I guess a lot of things have changed," Beatrice said finally. "Ah, *va bene*! Look at all the people!"

And just as quickly as they'd been held together by the invisible strands of the past, the strings had snapped with a hit of reality.

CHAPTER SIX

BEATRICE KNEW IT was feeble to duck out of the important conversation they should be having, but guiltily welcomed the approaching *festa*.

Exploring the past was too close to asking for a different future. One with Jamie in it. And she knew she couldn't go there. No matter how much it hurt, she'd have to pretend she was happy as could be with their collegial truce. There couldn't be anything more. She would never be able to forgive herself for what she'd done to him. The lies. The betrayal. If even the tiniest part of her thought Jamie could love her again…

She scrunched her eyes tight until she saw stars.

When she opened them again she saw an entirely different world from the quiet cobbled lanes they'd been walking through. Before them swirled a riot of color, music, laughter and scents that all but exploded in front of them when they rounded the corner into the teeming piazza.

"Looks like we've lost Teo to the crowds."

"Hunting down his fiancée, no doubt," Jamie said, scanning the sea of heads.

At six feet two inches, he was able to see across the top of most of the crowd. She'd always loved his height. Taken comfort in the fact that when she'd needed a hug he'd been able to rest his chin on top of her head, holding her close enough for her to hear the beat of his heart.

A shiver went through her—as if she'd just been in his embrace and then stepped away.

"Are you all right?" Jamie was already taking off his light linen jacket. "Here—put this on."

Without waiting for an answer he draped the coat over her shoulders.

How can you be so chivalrous?

The gesture was both cruel and kind. Kind because that was Jamie, through and through. Cruel in its vivid reminder of what she wouldn't have when her baby was born. Someone to look out for her. To care if she was hot or cold. Frightened or tired.

Another tremble juddered through her, despite the relative warmth of the night, though experience told her the high altitude would set a chill into the air soon enough. She tugged the lapels of his jacket over her shoulders and dipped her head to receive a deep hit of the scents she knew she'd never forget. Ink. Pine. Cotton.

Her shoulders shook against the fabric. The sorrow she'd carried with her all these years was being released in unforgiving waves, and icy tremors reminded her of the day she'd let such a good man go.

"Do you mind if we head over to the fire pits for a minute?"

"Not at all."

Jamie raised his arm as if he was about to drape it over her shoulders, as he would have when they'd been together. Then, his arm half-aloft, eyes blinking himself back to the present, he remembered otherwise and let it drop to his side.

Beatrice was half-tempted to slip her arms into the sleeves of Jamie's jacket and grab hold of his hand. It was how they'd first realized they'd felt the same way for each other. A surreptitious moment of holding hands in a crowd.

It had been a busy night in Jamie's village. It was actually more of a town, but it had a warm, strong sense of community. Unlike tonight, it had been properly cold—wintry, even. She'd been all zipped up in a thick parka, with a wooly hat on her head designed in some silly holiday theme. A Christmas pudding? She couldn't remember, but she knew it had made Jamie's green eyes light up every time he had turned to her.

"What was that thing we went to?" She didn't look up at him, but could tell he'd turned to look at her. "The one where I wore the funny hat?"

He laughed before he answered. A soft faraway laugh, hinting at the genuine warmth they'd shared.

"Bonfire Night. *Remember, remember...*"

"The fifth of November," she finished for him when he left off with a slight lift to his voice.

It came back to her now, in a wash of distinct memories. Much like this evening, people had filled the historic English town—all thick slabs of stone and austere houses lit up by an enormous pyre in the very center of the square. Music had echoed off the walls and the scents of mulled wine and frying doughnuts had permeated the air. Fairy lights had twinkled from just about anything that was stationary—even some members of the brass band.

But more than any of those things Beatrice remembered Jamie insisting she leave the hospital after a forty-eight-hour shift to come out and enjoy the spectacle. They hadn't kissed. They might not even have hugged. She knew her cheeks had flushed regularly when he'd looked at her, and on the rare occasions when their hands had brushed against each other's...it had been heavenly. Like fairy dust sparkles lighting her up from the inside.

"Do you remember when you were almost speared by those two lads wrestling in Viking helmets?"

"How could I forget?" Bea smiled at the memory for, as frightening as it had been, Jamie had scooped her out of the way, lifting her up and swinging her out of reach of the one-pint-too-many brawlers as if she'd been made of air. Heaven knew she'd felt as if she were walking on air for the rest of the night.

Against her better judgment she let her fingers drop from their too-tight hold on the lapels of Jamie's jacket and let her hands swing alongside her as they strolled past the detailed flower displays. Thousands of buds and petals were arranged in intricate designs. Some religious, others nods to the Midsummer Festa's pagan origins. Either way, they were beautiful.

"It was the first time I ever had a sparkler."

Jamie stopped and stared at her, mouth agape in disbelief. "What? At the ripe old age of—what were you then—twenty-five?"

"Twenty-six," she corrected.

"You always did look young for your age." He winked in an obvious bid to let her know he was teasing.

Trust Jamie to retain his sense of humor in the situation. If she'd been in his shoes? *Ugh.* She didn't know if she could have done it. Swiped the slate clean and tried to work together. She could see he really *was* trying, and knowing that made her feel even worse.

There has to be a day when the guilt ends. When I can make my peace with him.

Her eyes shot up to the sky, barely visible for all the light in the piazza, and she swallowed down the prayer, trying to make it a living, breathing part of her.

If she were going to raise her child she would have to find an inner peace.

"First time with a sparkler…" He shook his head again in wonder. "And there was me thinking you couldn't do *anything* new for a princess."

Bea's hopeful mood evaporated in an instant. She shot quick panicked looks around, fearful in case anyone had overheard, forgetting for a moment that nearly everyone within earshot wouldn't have the slightest clue who she was. The world's gossip magazine readers were looking for a brunette long-haired woman, grief stricken after those sensational altar revelations. Not a short-haired platinum blonde snuggling into her boyfriend's linen jacket.

Well, not *boyfriend*… But to an outsider up until about three seconds ago it might have looked that way.

"Too close to the bone with the princess comment?" Jamie asked, his expression unreadable.

No doubt it was a means of protecting his own feelings. Proof she couldn't help but hurt him when all he'd done was make a lighthearted comment.

Get over yourself! Prove to him you're the woman he once thought you were. Not the princess.

She held up two fingers and pinched them together to signify that, yes, unwittingly or not, his comment *had* stung a little bit.

"You know I never thought of myself that way."

She tried to shrug the moment away, but only ended up fighting the sharp sting of tears gathering high in her throat. She quickly turned away, feigning interest in a small stall selling exquisite posies of wildflowers.

"Signor!" She could hear the vendor appealing to Jamie. "Buy your beautiful woman a small bouquet. *Va bene.* It is midsummer. Without flowers in her hand, she is naked!"

Bea chanced a glance at Jamie, relieved to see he that was laughing. Trust an Italian to insist a woman was naked without flowers. Especially when he was walking with his ex-girlfriend and didn't know she was pregnant from an anonymous donor.

He didn't owe her anything. Least of all…

Wait… Was he…?

"*Per favore, solo uno mazzetto.* To bring a smile to her face again."

There he was again. Indefatigable. The sympathetic, generous man she'd fallen in love with.

Just the sound of Jamie's warm caramel voice—the rich, deep-chested tone he'd used to use when he was trying to coax a smile to her face when she'd had a rough day at the hospital—told her he was doing his best to mend fences.

How could she let him know he didn't owe her a thing?

Bea silently smiled her appreciation, watching as he dug a hand into his pocket, rattling around for some change only to come up empty-handed.

He turned to her, and just as she realized *she* must be the one in possession of his loose change he tugged her around via the lapels of his jacket so that she was square onto him. Achingly slowly, he purposefully slid his hands down the lapels, just skidding along the tops of her hypersensitive breasts, pausing when her breath caught, then continuing until each of his hands found purchase on the edge of a pocket. His fingers dipped into the squares of linen, moving assuredly inside them, grazing her hips as he felt for coins.

Everything inside her was alight with anticipation.

When their eyes met, she knew he had felt it, too. The same thing *she* had felt when their hands had shifted and glanced across each other's time and again on that long-ago Bonfire Night. The tension between them had built until it had been virtually unbearable, until at long last Jamie had finally taken charge of the situation and grasped her hand firmly in his.

And from the moment they had touched…

Fireworks.

"I've got a better idea about where to find supper."

Jamie could hardly believe what he was saying. It was the smooth line of an assured lover. A man confident that if he made a move, he'd win the girl.

Was that why he was doing this? Trying to win back his girl?

A harebrained idea, given how it had ended last time. With him throwing himself into work as if it were the only thing keeping him alive. Neglecting his family. His home. Not that he'd ever been one to be house-proud. But what Beatrice didn't know was that the house of their dreams was sitting as empty as the day he'd bought it. If she'd waited just one more day to tell him her news…

There were so many ifs.

Beatrice was looking up at him, thick lashes framing those perfect chocolate-pot-colored eyes of hers, posy held up to her nose, cheeks still flushed with the remains of a blush. Her lips were nestled among the flower petals and every bit as soft. *Perfection.*

A shot of heat seized his chest as the memory of that stolen kiss worked its way back into his blood flow. Beatrice had made him feel more alive than anyone else in the world and when she'd gone—

Was it foolish or wise to hold on to his pride? Resist what came so naturally?

"What's this idea, then?" she asked, twisting back and forth like a schoolgirl behind her fistful of flowers. "Or are you going to keep it a secret?"

Excitement—or maybe it was just the fairy lights—twinkled in her eyes. She'd always loved an adventure. He had no idea what she got up to in her spare time here.

Just went home, he imagined. He'd definitely not seen her in the square since the night he'd pulled her into his arms and reminded himself of everything he should have long forgotten.

She'd played with his heart.

And he'd lived to see another day.

What was that saying he'd learnt from one of the friars on the island?

He heard the monk's voice as clearly as he could now hear the diva launching into a beautiful aria by Puccini.

Che per vendetta mai non sanò piaga.

Revenge never healed a wound.

A renewed sense of purpose gripped his heart, then released it, repurposing the sensation into the first shot of pure happiness he'd felt in years. He would have to say goodbye to Beatrice at the end of the summer. That much was sure. But this time he would do it with his pride intact. His heart at rest.

"As we've lost Teo for the evening, we're going to be heading up on the chairlifts." Jamie gave her an appraising look as she gamely weighed up his proposal. "But first I think we'd better stop at one of these stalls. Get you a shawl. It might be a bit chillier where we're headed."

Beatrice's eyebrows rose. "Should I be worried? You're not going to lock me up in a cave or anything, are you?"

"That all depends," he countered, channeling the man he knew was buried somewhere deep in her heart.

"On..." Beatrice's smile was growing bigger. They'd done this dozens, if not scores of times before. Explored. Found new places to show each other. Watched the delight unfold.

"On how much you like cheese!"

Something flickered in her eyes. Indecision? A hint of reserve? That wasn't like her. To hold back.

Just as quickly it was gone.

"As long as there's plenty of hard cheese. It's my favorite these days."

"Not 'the gooier the better'?"

She shook her head and ran a fingertip along one of the flower buds in her posy before dropping it to her side. "No. I'm all about good old hard Italian cheeses these days. I'll leave the gooey ones to the French."

"All right, then." He offered her his arm again. "I see slivers of pecorino and shavings of parmigiana in your future."

He pressed his hand on top of Beatrice's when she tucked it back into the inner crook of his elbow—with greater comfort than earlier in the evening, he noticed.

A shard of warning sounded in his mind.

This is only temporary. This is putting the past to rest. If you can do this without kissing her, you can do anything.

By the time they got to the stall selling locally woven cashmere scarves, Bea was beginning to feel as if she'd stepped back in time.

Jamie was the very embodiment of… Well…*himself.* She knew it seemed ridiculous, but the man she'd fallen in love with was right here beside her, as if nothing had happened, no hearts had been broken… As if their lives had carried on as one.

And it felt so right. *Real*, even.

Would it be tempting fate if she just allowed herself one night of pure happiness?

"Here—what do you think of this one?" Jamie tugged a beautiful evergreen wrap from the midst of one of the piles. In one fluid move he unfurled the downy, soft cashmere and swirled it around her shoulders.

She brushed her cheek against the fabric, reveling in

how silky it felt against her skin. There were fine threads of cream and mixed pastel colors woven throughout the scarf, giving it a greater depth…almost as if it were a wildflower meadow in the midst of an evergreen glade, seen from afar.

Jamie lifted a corner of the scarf and tested it along his own cheek. “Does it do the trick?”

A whirl of heat swirled around her as a vivid memory of Jamie lifting her fingers first to his cheek and then to his lips for a light kiss. Something he'd be doing right now if she hadn't bowed to her mother's wishes…

The tiny slice of space between them filled with warmth—the exchange of body heat melding them from two bodies into one—But there was another body. A tiny little baby she would love with all her heart.

A wash of longing poured through her so powerfully she almost lost her balance. If that baby was Jamie's…

She began to dig inanely through her handbag for her wallet. “It's perfect.”

“Trade you for my coat?” Jamie was already handing a couple of notes to the vendor.

“You don't have to do that.”

Why *was* he doing this? Each act of selflessness on his part only served to compound the ache of longing she felt for him. How was she ever going to channel the willpower to leave?

“Of course I do,” he countered taking his change and helping Bea slip his jacket from her shoulders and rearrange the wrap.

The wrap was beautiful but, ridiculous as it seemed, just those handful of minutes wearing his jacket had felt heaven-sent.

“Jamie, honestly. You don't owe me a thing.”

If anything, she owed him… Well, she owed him the

truth for one thing, but since his knowing she still loved him would probably only make things worse, keeping her lips sealed was her self-assigned atonement.

"A beautiful woman deserves beautiful things. I never bought you beautiful things before."

"I never wanted *things*," she chided softly. "You know that."

He nodded. "Even so…"

His eyes flicked away, as if something else had caught his attention, but it was more likely for the same reason she found herself unable to hold eye contact with him for more than a few seconds at a time.

Too painful. Too perfect.

Two years ago the most natural thing for her to do would have been to go up on tiptoe. Give him a kiss. Swipe at his nose with her finger and tip his forehead to hers. The time they'd spent just breathing each other in…*otherworldly.*

She tugged at the edges of her sundress, fighting the instinctive urge to give her belly one of the protective strokes she so often found herself doing these days. A harsh reminder that she was still keeping secrets from Jamie.

Holding back this precious information was almost physically painful. Because Jamie had once been her port of call for all her thoughts. No editing. No filter. The only person in the world she'd been able to be herself with. None of the frippery and trappings that went with being a princess.

Her brother had cornered the royal market for their family. Why hadn't her mother been content just to let her go?

"Look at these tomatoes!"

She smiled, grateful for the change of tack as Jamie steered her toward a table groaning under a mountain of tomatoes bigger than both her fists joined together.

Beautiful deep reds, oranges and yellows. There were

even some green tiger-striped fruits, all piled up in a magnificent display of the summer's early harvest.

"The North of Italy is far more generous than the North of England. My mother wouldn't believe her eyes!"

"My mother wouldn't know what a whole tomato looked like!" Bea shot back.

Both of them laughed, then said as one, *"La donna è mobile!"*

Woman—in this case her mother—was a fickle thing to be sure.

Jamie had heard more than enough stories of Beatrice's mother only deigning to recognize food if it was on a plate at a Michelin-starred restaurant. Deconstructed this… Reimagined that… If it wasn't à la mode, it wasn't in her mother's sphere of what existed in the world.

But she'd never been fickle about her choice for Bea's intended. Her daughter would marry a prince. Such lofty heights for her white-coated daughter, more content in one-use-only surgical scrubs than a ball gown.

"And those peaches. They're the size of a house! They'd fill up the fruit bowl nicely."

Jamie pointed toward another vendor handing out slices of golden fruit dripping with summer sweetness. In true Italian style he was peeling them, then giving slice after juicy slice to wide-eyed passers-by.

Though she was tempted, the Italian in her had to insist upon being a purist.

"As you may recall, any *true* Italian would know these are from the South. Sicilian peaches are… Mmm…" A soft breeze carried a waft of perfumed air her way and suddenly she was ravenous. A pregnancy craving? Or just good old-fashioned hunger? She forced herself to regroup. "Their presence here is near enough sacrilege!"

"Like mayonnaise on chips?" Jamie parried, happily

accepting a slice of freshly peeled peach from the farmer and making a big show of enjoying the sweet fruit, rubbing his belly to great effect as he swallowed it down.

"Che schifo!" Bea shuddered away the thought of gooey mayonnaise. "*Anyone* who knows how to eat a chip properly knows it's salt and vinegar if eaten with fish—but only by the seaside—or tomato ketchup if eaten with a hamburger."

Jamie smiled as she recited by rote the "training session" he'd given her. Bea had never eaten a chip in her life. She'd been astonished to hear they'd been a menu staple in his house when he was growing up.

"A man needs to keep up his strength when he goes down the mines..."

Jamie's father had been deadly serious when he'd told her that. Right before sending his wife a saucy wink as he picked up a jug and near enough drowned his potatoes in the thick pool of shiny gravy Jamie's mother had magicked up from the small joint of beef she'd prepared.

That had been a heavenly afternoon.

One of only two times she'd met his parents.

Once it had been just in passing…it might have been that Bonfire Night. Near enough every house had emptied into the town square that night. And, of course, when they'd gone over for traditional Sunday lunch.

Not one ounce of shame had crossed Jamie's features when he brought her to the humble two-up two-down brick house in the middle of a seemingly endless swathe of similar homes. Ironic, considering she'd been too mortified even to consider taking him to her parents' palazzo.

One of the most lavish in the whole of Venice, It was her mother's work, of course. Her father would have been content with simpler furnishings. Less gilding. More wood. Less ostentation. More comfort. He often said a happy wife meant a happy life. It had been the spirit with which she thought she'd approach her arranged marriage. A happy husband meant…

Hmm… Maybe that was the problem.

Nothing really rhymed with husband.

James, on the other hand…

Blame. Shame. Tame. Flame.

She bit down on the inside of her cheek. Maybe that wasn't such a good comparison.

"C'mon—over here, you. No wandering off just yet. You're not getting away that easily." Jamie turned to her, a broad smile on his lips, a second slice of peach pinched gently between his thumb and index finger. "Why not try living dangerously?"

When their gazes connected it was as if he'd flicked a switch, blurring everything around them. All Bea was aware of was the light shining in Jamie's forest green eyes. The tempting slice of peach he was holding between them. His lips just beyond. Lips she knew would taste of peach juice and pure male strength…

He was a rock. He'd been *her* rock. And from the moment she'd left him she had felt more adrift in the world than at any other time in her life.

He slipped the slice of fruit between her parted lips, and for just one incredibly sensual moment her tongue and lips connected with his fingertip. The old Bea would have drawn it into her mouth, given it a swirl with her tongue, grasped the rest of his hand in hers so that she could taste the drops of peach juice on each of his fingertips. She would have met his gaze without a blink of shame, her body growing warm with desire as each second passed.

But she had no claim on him now. No right even to think the decadently sexual thoughts, let alone act on them.

As if reading her mind—or perhaps reminding her of

where she stood—Jamie turned away, accepted an antiseptic wipe from the peach vendor, swiped his hands clean of the moment and threw it in the bin.

He turned back to her and smiled, as if they'd just been discussing the weather. "And how did little Beatrice become so au fait with the fruits and vegetables of the world?"

"My…my father, of course." She stumbled awkwardly over the words, and most likely failed miserably to cover the ache of longing she felt for him by adding a jaunty elbow in the ribs. "You know that."

"Yes, I do." Jamie nodded, his lower lip jutting out for a moment, her comment having clearly hit an invisible target. "And there are a lot of things I don't know."

In equal parts Bea felt consumed by a wash of guilt and the powerful urge to tell him everything.

About the pregnancy.

About the separate bedrooms she'd insisted upon prior to agreeing to move into her ex-fiancé's palazzo because something in her just hadn't been ready to give herself to him physically.

The relief when her best friend had blown the whistle at the wedding.

The first full breath of air she had drawn after the wedding dress had dropped from her shoulders, then her hips, and plummeted to the floor in a huge flounce of silk and tulle. Part of her had wanted to shred it to pieces. The other half had just wanted to leave. Which was precisely what she'd done.

Only that time it hadn't hurt at all. Not even close to the searing pain she'd felt when she'd left Jamie.

With Marco, she had felt backed into a corner. Trapped by ancestral duty. Or perhaps, more accurately, by the little girl hoping, for once, to win her mother's approval. The more she thought about it, the more astonishing it was that Jamie had been able to rise above it now. Not just treating her civilly, but pretty much acting as if nothing had happened.

No. She gave her head a shake, knowing she hadn't pinned it down right. Jamie was better than ordinary old "civil." He was treating her with respect. Grace. Chivalry.

"All right, there?" Jamie bent down as he spoke.

Another reminder of his thoughtfulness. Her ex-fiancé wouldn't have noticed if she'd fallen silent, talked too much or even started dancing like a chimpanzee.

She nodded, doing her best to focus on Jamie's hand as he pointed out the small passageway across the square. If she turned to him now he'd see tears in her eyes.

"You feeling up to plunging through the crowds?"

"*Si.* Absolutely." Her voice sounded bright. Too bright. But it would have to do.

Being with Jamie… It was like being whole again.

But he was the one thing she would have to learn to live without.

A few minutes of weaving through the crowd later, they turned onto a small road with lighter foot traffic than the square.

"You sure you're still up for this? It may take an hour or two." Jamie turned and gave Beatrice a smile.

Her reaction was a bit delayed. As if her thoughts had been somewhere else entirely.

"Oh…" She tugged her new wrap around her shoulders a bit more snugly. Protectively. "An hour or two of cheese? Hmm… Let me think…"

Her hips swiveled back and forth beneath the light cotton of her dress. It was too easy to picture her long, slender legs beneath the fabric. The gentle curve and jut of her hip bones. His hands swooping along the smooth expanse of her belly before he slid them along the length of her thighs…

A tug of desire eclipsed his pragmatism. The number of times he'd pulled her to him, snuggled her slender hips between his own, fitted her to him as if they'd been made for each other…and then teased her away, holding her at arm's length, reminding her of the long shifts at the hospital they each had in store.

"We have all the time in the world to make love," he'd murmured into her ear, again and again.

Now he knew it hadn't been enough. A lifetime of Beatrice wouldn't have sated his desire for her. And he'd only had those two precious years.

"You know…you're right." He did a quick about-face, no longer able to go through with the charade of being "just friends."

She looked up at him, startled.

"About what?"

"It'll take too long. The chairlift and all. I'm not even certain they'll be open with the Midsummer Festa."

"What?"

"The *enoteca*. I've been up there a few times when I've needed a break from the clinic. A glass of wine… A bit of cheese and bread… It's lovely."

And it was. But going up there with Beatrice the way he was feeling… Chances were he'd tell her how he really felt. And he couldn't let her have access to that part of his heart. Not anymore.

"It was a silly idea in the first place. There's plenty to eat here. And you said yourself you weren't in the mood for gooey cheese. Um…what if we…" He looked past her to the square—busier now than when they'd left it, if such a thing was possible.

"Actually, Jamie…"

He knew that tone. The polite one. The well-mannered Principessa backing out of an awkward situation.

"I'm feeling a bit tired. Perhaps I'll just head off. We can go to the *enoteca* another time. Rain check?"

When he looked back at Beatrice she appeared to him as if through an entirely new prism…fragile. Delicate. Two things he'd never imagined her to be.

Feminine, yes. But for every ounce of grace and beauty she possessed he'd always thought of her as having a solid core of fierce intellect and passion. More than enough to stand on her own two feet.

"I'm happy to walk you back to your apartment. You're not too far from the clinic?"

"*Si*, an apartment in one of the *baita*." She held up her hand in the stop position and took a step away from him. "Don't worry about walking me. There's a little café downstairs. I'll grab something there. I could do with a quiet stroll."

Guilt swept through him. He wanted to pull her to him, wanted to push her away. "I don't mind, honestly."

From the look she shot him it was pretty easy to tell *she* did.

Hell. There wasn't exactly a guidebook on how to deal with the love of your life reappearing just when you thought you'd pulled yourself together.

"Thanks for the wrap." She threw the words over her shoulder, smoothing her hand along the fine cashmere, her feet already picking up speed. "It's really beautiful. *Buonanotte.*"

He said the same words as he spun in the opposite direction, felt the hard lines of a man trying to keep his head above water returning to his face.

It wouldn't be a *good* night. He felt it in his bones. It would be restless. His pillow would bear the brunt of his frustration.

He shifted course, taking a sharp turn into a *calle* that would deposit him at the only place he could burn off this excess energy for the greater good. *Work.*

Sure, it hadn't worked out well at Northern General, but one of the reasons he'd chosen a clinic for tourists was the limited chance of getting attached. People were in, out, referred, transferred, never to be seen again. Only rarely did they see a patient twice. Enough times to start caring? Just about never.

He gave his hands a quick rub, forcing the doctor back into this man he'd not seen for a while. Peach slices? Cashmere wraps? Those were things lovers shared. Not platonic colleagues.

He steered his thoughts away from the glow he'd seen in Beatrice's eyes when he'd slipped the peach between her gently parted lips. There were bound to be people who enjoyed a bit too much high-altitude revelry on a night like tonight. Sprains, dehydration, the occasional fallout from a silly brawl over the last piece of prosciutto… They would keep him busy. The staff at the clinic wouldn't think anything of him showing up to relieve them for an hour or so.

A huge boom sounded not too far-off. He looked up to the sky, his eyes adjusting to the darkness and then the explosion of colored lights.

Instantly he dropped his gaze and sought out Beatrice's pixie cut. She should be seeing this. They should be watching it together. Hands brushing. Shots of heat igniting his every nerve ending as if he was discovering what it meant to be a man for the very first time.

He looked up into the sky one last time then turned back toward the clinic with a shrug.

Fireworks.

They weren't all they were cracked up to be.

CHAPTER SEVEN

Bea knew she should be at home, but restless sleep was worse than a bit of focused work, right? Just the idea of going back to her lonely apartment, with its plain single bed, and no green-eyed pediatricians lying in wait to pull up the covers and have a good snuggle…

"Are you sure you're happy to cover for me?" Rhianna handed over a stethoscope, not even waiting for an answer.

"You said a couple of hours, right?"

She smiled as Rhianna turned her Irish brogue up another notch and launched into an assurance that, with heaven as her witness, she'd be back before Cinderella had a blessed thing to be worried about.

Bea pursed her lips and gave them a little wriggle. The fairy-tale princess reference wasn't lost on her, but a quick glance to Rhianna, who was busy slicking on a fresh layer of lip gloss and lavishing her lashes with a thick coat of mascara showed she was being silly.

Stop being so sensitive!

Bea sat down on the long wooden bench and undid the straps of her sandals to change them for her sneakers, surprised to see her feet were a tiny bit swollen. Pregnancy symptom? Her mind raced through all the worst-case scenarios swollen feet at this point in a pregnancy might mean, then gave her head a sharp shake.

Probably just too much walking in flat sandals and having all her hopes and dreams plummet to the soles of her feet. Or something like that anyway.

"Ooh!" She put on a cockney accent and repeated something she'd heard a teenager say the other day as she gave her feet a rub. "My dogs are *barking*!"

"Hold on, there." Rhianna ducked her head down so she was level with Beatrice's eyes. Quite the feat now she'd popped on impossibly high cork-heeled sandals. "Is that you backing out already?" She swiftly pulled out her mobile phone and held it at arm's length. "Am I going to have to send a text to the lads and tell them no?"

"The lads?" Beatrice raised her eyebrows. She'd heard of a few summer romances beginning to blossom among the collection of seasonal staff, but…*lads*?

"Sure!" A blush appeared on Rhianna's cream and freckled complexion. "There's a whole squad of 'em over here—from Denmark, I think. They're all blond and rugged, and I'm sure half of 'em are called Thor."

"Thor?" Beatrice intoned drily.

"Or Erik." Rhianna struck what she guessed was meant to be a Viking pose, waved away Bea's disbelief, then adroitly twisted one of the male doctors' shaving mirrors to her advantage, lowering her eyelids to half-mast to receive a whoosh of eyeshadow as she continued her story. "They're up here on some sort of epic paragliding trip, or some such. One of them was in earlier today. He had a right old bash on his thigh from where he'd landed on some gravel instead of the meadow he'd been aiming for."

She gave a swift eye roll. Clearly the injury hadn't stood in the way of a bit of flirtation.

"Either way, they're all down at the piazza and looking mad keen for some company, if you get my drift. A couple of the chalet girls and I are going to play Eeny-Meeny-

Miny-Mo!" Her eyebrows did a swift little jig as a naughty grin appeared on her lips. "I'll tell you what, Dr. Jesolo. They're a right handsome bunch of lads. If there's any left over, I'll be sure to keep one for you when I come back in."

Despite herself, Bea laughed. She'd never really been that boy crazy, but she certainly remembered the giddy feeling of looking forward to a night out…the swirls of frisson…the nineteen trips to her wardrobe to make sure she'd put on just the right skirt or blouse or dress, only to turn away from the mirror and start all over again.

With Jamie it had never really been like that, it had just been…*easy.* Sure, she'd wanted to look her best, her sexiest, her most desirable, but he'd always had a remarkable way of making her feel beautiful. Even at the end of a day's long shift, when her hair had been all topsy-turvy, her makeup long gone and the shadows under her eyes had predicted a need for lots of sleep.

Quickly she finished tying her shoe and pressed herself up from the bench.

A bit too quickly as a hit of dizziness swamped her.

"Whoa! You all right there, girl?" Rhianna swooped in and steadied her. "You've not been out on the lash, have you?"

"No." Bea shrugged herself away from her colleague, trying her best not to look ungrateful. "Just got up a bit too quickly, that's all."

"Would you like me to get you some water or anything? A wee lie-down before I head off?"

"No." Bea shook her head firmly. "Absolutely not. Off you go. Have a good night, all right?"

Rhianna tipped her head to the side, her multicolored eye shadow on full display as she gave Bea a sidelong glance. "You're absolutely sure?"

"Absolutely sure about what?"

Both women turned sharply as the door to the locker room swung open.

Bea's heart swooped, then cinched tight.

One glimpse into those familiar green eyes told her she might be better off saying no.

"Dr. Jesolo here's a lifesaver!" Rhianna jumped in.

"Oh?"

If she'd thought Jamie had flinched at the sight of her he was showing no signs of any discomfort now. Just the cool reserve of a man who…

Wait a minute.

"Aren't you meant to be off tonight?" Rhianna veered off topic. "*And* you?" She wheeled around, her index finger wiggling away as if she were divining water instead of looking for answers. "What are the two of you doing here when the whole of Torpisi is out celebrating the longest day of the year?"

Collectively they reacted as a huge boom of fireworks sounded in the distance. Well, not Jamie. He was still frozen in the doorway, as if someone had sucked every last inch of joy out of him. *Terrific.* No guessing that her turning up for a few hours of burying her head in the sand had ruined his own plan to do the exact same thing.

Great minds…*per carita*!

Rhianna was the first to recover, pulling a sky blue pashmina out of her locker and swirling it around her shoulders. "Dr. Jesolo—this is your last chance. I'm telling you it's good *craic* out there."

"Craic?" Nice to have a reason to look away from Jamie. She hadn't known how powerful his not-happy glare was before.

A shard of guilt pierced through his skull. *Because you didn't bother to stick around.*

"Sure, you know good *craic* when you see it, Bea. A party. A good time—fun."

She took a quick glance between the two of them, clearly immune to the thick band of what-the-heck-are-you-doing-here? thrumming between them.

"What with Dr. Coutts being here when I guess he doesn't have to be they can spare you, sure? This is grand. You don't have to cover me at all—right, Dr. Coutts? You're all right here, aren't you? Happy to let the lovely ladies go out for a wee bit of gallivanting?"

Rhianna looked up to Jamie, seemingly undaunted by his unchanged expression. And then, just like that, it brightened.

"What a delightful idea." He unleashed a warm smile on Rhianna. One of those smiles Bea had used to get when she'd suggested they either stay on at the hospital for a couple of extra hours, just to talk through some cases, or go to bed early.

Ouch.

"Don't let me stand in the way of some gallivanting. Just the thing for a pair of young maidens on Midsummer Day."

"That's exactly what I was saying." Rhianna turned to Bea, arms crossed over her generous bosom with an I-told-you-so expression on her face. "C'mon, girl. What's the point of being up here in this rural idyll if you don't run into the arms of a Viking?"

"Oh, it's Vikings tonight, is it, Rhianna?" Jamie dropped her a playful wink, clearly no stranger to the young doctor's quest for a summer romance. Or seven. "Please. Feel free to go, Dr. Jesolo. We've got more than enough staff. Unless you were hoping for an early night?"

Bea opened her mouth to protest, then clamped it tight shut again. Where she should have felt a sting of hurt that Jamie was trying to get rid of her, she decided to take up the gauntlet from another direction. She wasn't the only one who'd told a fib in order to burn off some energy at the clinic.

"Actually, I was really looking forward to a few hours here. Special research on a—" she quickly sought a reason from the ether "—on a dissertation I'm writing."

"A dissertation?" Disbelief oozed from Rhianna's response. "What are you wasting time writing a dissertation on when you could be having fun? Isn't that the point of working up here?"

Bea's gaze flicked from Rhianna to Jamie. No way was she getting cornered into going out for a bit of *fun*!

Um...wait a minute.

"Dr. Coutts?" A nurse stuck her head in the doorway. "We've got someone I think you should see right away."

"I'll go." Bea pulled on her white coat, ignoring Rhianna's plaintive sigh and mumblings about leading horses to water—or something like that anyway—and swept past Jamie.

But not before getting a full lungful of Northern-British sexpot disguised as a surly doctor. *Humph!* She'd have to start holding her breath when she passed him from now on.

"I'm pretty certain *I* was the doctor requested."

Jamie was matching Beatrice step for step as she hotfooted it toward the waiting room.

"It doesn't matter, really," the nurse said, jogging a bit to keep up with the pair of them. "It's a lady. Midthirties, I'm guessing. She's presenting with severe gastrointestinal pain. I just thought—"

"I'll get it."

Jamie and Beatrice spoke in tandem, each with a hand on the swinging doors leading to the waiting room, their eyes blazing with undisguised sparks of frustration.

"What shall I tell the patient?" asked the befuddled nurse.

"Tell her I'll see her."

Again they spoke as one.

And then, as quickly as the fire had flared between them it shape-shifted into laughter at the ridiculousness of it all.

"You go ahead." Jamie swept a hand in the direction of the waiting room.

"No, really, I'm fine—"

A scream of pain roared past the double doors, jarring them out of their increasingly ridiculous standoff.

"Two heads are better than one?"

Jamie enjoyed the spark of recognition in Beatrice's eyes at his roundabout invitation to join him. It had been his oft-used excuse for pulling her into a consultation back at Northern General.

The adage still held true, and immediately dissolved any tension between them.

When they pushed into the room a flame-haired woman was staggering from a chair, one hand clamped to her back, one clutching her stomach. "Please help me! I can't stand it any longer!"

"Right you are, madam—oops!" Jamie swept under one of her arms, only just stopping her from falling to the ground.

"I want to lie down!" the woman howled. "Or crawl. Or *something*. Just make it stop!"

From her accent he could tell she was North American. There was a wedding ring on her finger. The flesh was puffed up around it. It looked like swelling. Water retention?

A quick glimpse down and he saw shiny white tennis shoes on her feet. The American tourist telltale. Not

Canadian, then. He'd keep his maple syrup and moose jokes to himself.

"She had some of those cheese-stuffed flowers." A rusty-haired man with the most remarkable sky blue eyes rushed over from the desk, where he had been filling out some paperwork. "Marilee, honey, I *told* you not to try the flowers. They're probably hallucinogenic."

"Do you mean the pumpkin flowers?" Beatrice asked gently.

"Jesse, I'm going to *kill* you for making me try those things—ooh! Make. It. *Stop!*" She doubled over again and her husband tucked himself under her other arm.

"Those are the ones," Jesse said, sending quick looks to Jamie and Beatrice, his gaze taking on a dreamy aspect as he continued to speak. "They were deep-fried. Filled with some sort of soft cheese and a truffled honey. We were at the *enoteca.* The one up at the top of the chairlift. Have you been there?"

He looked at Beatrice, who shook her head and gave him a rueful smile before looking behind her—presumably for a wheelchair.

"I'll tell you… I thought they were delicious. I'm Joseph, by the way, though Marilee here calls me Jesse. Her very own Jesse James," he continued with a laugh, giving a quick squeeze to Beatrice's arm, seemingly oblivious to his wife's pain. He let go to shoot a pair of invisible revolvers, only just catching his wife as she stumbled and unleashed another despairing howl.

"I'll get a wheelchair," Beatrice said in a low voice to Jamie.

Jamie nodded, then stopped her with a hand on her elbow as she turned to go. "Make it a gurney." He glanced around until he found the nurse who'd signed the woman in. "Name?"

"Marilee James."

"All right, Marilee. We're just going to get you—oops! Easy, there, I've got you. Over this way, love."

Beatrice had magicked a gurney out of the ether and was already pushing it through the waiting room door.

"Now, if I can just get my colleague to..." He flicked his eyes from Bea to Marilee, which, true to form, Beatrice understood as "Come over here and help me get her up on the gurney because the husband's not much use."

After a handful of awkward maneuvers, the sturdy but fit-looking woman was up and on the gurney.

"Mrs. James—"

"Call me Marilee. I can't stand the formal stuff... *Ooo-eee...* It hurts. Do you think it was the clams, Jesse?" She reached back and grabbed her husband's hand as he tried to keep up with the moving gurney, squeezing it until it was white. "We should never have had seafood up here in the mountains. This is *not* the vacation of my dreams you promised!"

"I know, my little cherry pie. But we'll get it right. I'm sure they have loads of medication they can give you here for the pain." He shot anxious looks in Jamie's direction as he pulled the gurney.

They did. But only if they knew what was going on.

"Have you been sick at all? Vomiting, diarrhea?" Jamie tipped his head toward an open exam area. "Let's get her in there for an abdominal exam. Can you call up to X-ray? We might need a—"

Marilee's scream drowned out his instructions to Beatrice, who stood, calm as she always was in a crisis. He could almost see the medical terminology whizzing past her eyes as her mind did its usual high-speed race through possible prognoses.

"She hasn't been sick," said Jessie. "Not at all. And we

only had the clams about half an hour ago. Lovely, they were. All sorts of garlic and some kinda green thingy. A little chopped-up herb."

"Appendicitis?"

Jamie threw the word softly to Beatrice, who nodded one of those could-be nods and then parried with a whispered "Spleen?"

"No, it wasn't that. Something more like parsley, but Italian-style. Mountain grass?" Jesse looked to his wife, who answered him with an I-don't-know glare.

"Are you having any trouble passing wind, Mrs.—Marilee?"

As if to prove she wasn't, the woman rolled to the side and rather dramatically passed a healthy gust of wind.

Beatrice turned to Jamie and rather spectacularly managed a straight face as she said, "Perhaps passing wind isn't the trouble after all. Can you tell us where the feeling is most acute, Marilee?"

She put a hand on the woman's belly, doing her best to work around the fact Marilee seemed unable to remain stationary for more than a few seconds.

"My back!" Marilee plunged a hand behind her and then quickly grabbed one of Jamie's hands and one of Beatrice's and dragged them to the center of her belly, pulling her knees up to her stomach as she did so. "Oh, my sweet blazes. It's wet. I feel *wet*! Am I bleeding?"

Jamie shot Beatrice a worried look. This was more than a case of gastroenteritis.

"Pseudocyesis?" Beatrice whispered, tucking her shoulders down and dropping a quick shrug.

False pregnancy was a far reach, but…

"Psuedo *what*? Don't bother whispering. Little Bat Ears, my Jesse calls me." Marilee tightened her grip on Jamie's hand.

"That's right, my little sugar pie." Jesse beamed from the far end of the gurney, his eyes suddenly widening. "Oh, my blue-blooded ancestors! Marilee, your dress is all wet."

"Marilee?" Jamie quickly untucked his hand from hers, seeing the situation for what it was in an instant. "Why didn't you tell us you were pregnant?"

"Uh..." Jesse held up his hands—minus the invisible pistols this time—and started backing up. "Hang on there a minute, Doc. My Marilee may be a lot of things. But pregnant is most certainly *not* one of them."

Marilee pushed herself up on her elbows and shot wild-eyed looks between each doctor, her cheeks pinkening as the rest of her face paled.

"Let's get you lying back down here—all right, Marilee." Jamie moved to the side of the gurney, gently pressing on the woman's shoulders and only losing eye contact to indicate to Beatrice that she should do a vaginal exam.

Beatrice quickly shifted down to the foot of the gurney, snapping on a pair of gloves as she went, and deftly blocked Jesse's view.

After a surreptitious glimpse, and the most infinitesimal of nods to Jamie to tell him that he'd made the right call, she turned to Mr. Jesse James and began to guide him to a chair adjacent to his wife's gurney.

Jamie replaced Beatrice, barely containing his astonishment at what he saw. Thank goodness Beatrice had stayed behind. He'd need someone who could keep their head on their shoulders for this one.

"How're your midwifery skills, Dr. Jesolo?"

"All right." Beatrice threw a look over her shoulder as she gowned up.

Jamie grinned. "That's good. Because Mrs. James is crowning."

"What the heck are you people on about?" Marilee cut in. "I just ate some funny cheesy flowers, is all!"

"Marilee, I think you'd better lie back and ask your husband if you can hold his hand." Jamie kept his voice as calm as possible. "It looks like the pair of you are about to become parents."

He shot a look over to Beatrice, who was popping on a fresh pair of gloves and unfurling a disposable surgical gown.

"Doctor?" Bea held out the gown for him.

He swiftly stepped into the gown and for one brief moment their gazes caught and meshed as if they were back at Northern General. Madly in love. Meeting challenge after challenge with dexterity and skill.

And that was when she knew she had never—not for one second—stopped loving him.

"There is no chance at all there is a baby inside me," Marilee was busy explaining. "We've been married over eighteen years. Exchanged rings the first day we were legal, then spent the next seventeen trying to have a baby. Isn't that right, Jesse? Then last year we decided to give up. It was just going to be you and me. Why, I think the last time we—"

She stopped midsentence and reached out for her husband's hand.

"Do you remember the last time *before* the last time? Not last night's last time, but the *other* last time?"

"Sugar bean, I don't know what you're talking about—unless you mean the last time we—oh… Do you mean… the whipped cream night?"

"Mmm-hmm… Thanksgiving?" She teased the memory up a bit more, her voice dipping an octave, to a lower, more sultry tone, saying something about pumpkin pie and cinnamon-hot spices before lurching back up with a sharply pitched gasp.

As hard as she tried, Bea couldn't contain the crazy feeling of sisterhood she felt with Marilee. Against all the odds, the American woman was going to have a child!

She'd be doing the same in a few months' time. Granted, she'd be on her own—Jamie wouldn't be there, asking if she'd eaten bad clams, and there would be the press to contend with eventually because she wouldn't be able to hide away forever—but…a *baby*! The explosive joy of it warmed her chest and recharged her, as if she'd just woken up from a perfect night's sleep.

"You're going to be all right, Marilee. If you thought about this for seventeen years, you'll have read a fair few books on what to expect."

Wide-eyed, Marilee looked up, panting through a hit of pain and doing her best to nod.

"I've read 'em all. And nearly each one of them mentioned getting painkillers. That's all I was hoping for when we came stumbling in here. Just a couple of pills to take the edge off and then we were going to get back for the rest of the fireworks—weren't we, honey bun?"

"Sure were, sugar bee. Now, look what you've done! Thrown everything all off-kilter. We're going to miss the grand finale."

"I think you two are going to have one exciting grand finale of your own to the evening," Jamie said. "You're fully dilated, Marilee. This baby's going to be here in the next few minutes."

Bea glanced across at him, enjoying the warmth of his smile. She knew he loved babies every bit as much as she did. He hadn't been the least bit shy about telling her he hoped to be a father to a fleet of little ones.

It wouldn't be fair to ask...

"Dr. Coutts, are you sure you're seeing everything straight? Are you *positive* it's a baby?"

Bea had to stem a rush of emotion as Marilee's voice caught and grew jagged as she well and truly began to take on board how enormous a turn her life was about to take.

"How could you not have known?" Jesse threw up his hands. "I thought you were meant to throw up or go off your favorite foods or something?"

"I most certainly did no such thing," Marilee shot back indignantly, then went quiet. "Or did I…? I can't remember. Maybe after those oysters on Valentine's Day, but… Jesse James!" She threw the argument back at her husband. "How could *you* not have noticed? Aren't men supposed to be fine-tuned to a woman's breasts getting bigger or something?"

She shot Bea a glance to garner some support for her argument. The best Bea could come up with was a who-knows? face. This was her first surprise pregnancy. She'd certainly heard about them, but… Well, everything about her own pregnancy had been planned down to the microsecond.

Not so much a surprise as a secret… Even if her ex-fiancé had held out until the wedding, he probably would have run for the hills once the baby was born. Perhaps his infertility was nature's way of stating the obvious. The man wasn't meant to be a father. Just as well, he'd hit the road before they'd had to worry about divorce proceedings.

Bea smiled as Marilee grabbed her, then tightened her grip on her hand, pulling her in for a stage-whispered "At least he knows it's his."

"How could I not, my little sugar plum pie? That Thanksgiving dinner was the best…" He looked up to the sky, swiped at the beads of sweat accruing on his forehead. "That was a real doozy."

"I sure do love you, Jesse." Marilee's eyes filled with tears.

"I love you, too, Marilee. There isn't a single other woman on the planet I would have a child with just when I thought we'd have the whole rest of our lives to play."

"You mean—" Marilee's eyes widened. "I guess this *does* take the cliff-jumping trip to Mexico off the agenda for a while."

"We'll get through it, Marilee." Jesse tipped his head down and dropped a kiss on his wife's forehead. "We always do."

As the scene unfolded Bea was finding it harder to keep a check on her emotions. Her family wasn't one of those so-called traditional European families—lavishing each other with kisses and bear hugs and the smother-love Italian mothers in particular were renowned for. Jamie's was. Open arms. Broad, unaffected smiles. Unfettered affection…

All the light she'd felt about her own pregnancy abruptly disappeared into a deep pool of fears.

She'd be a single mother.

Alone.

Her mother was the last person on earth she'd go to for advice. Her nanny would be a better source of wisdom than—

No!

She was going to do this.

But it's scary.

She had to do this.

All on your own.

Bea took a surreptitious glance at the couple, now reaching for each other's hands, trying to grasp the magnitude of what was happening to them, and felt a pure bolt of envy rocket through her.

She could have had this. Maybe not the surprise labor part—but she could have had this with Jamie. She hadn't been sure, but something had told her Jamie had wanted to ask her to marry him. They'd walked past that beautiful old stone house, paused and daydreamed enough times. It would have needed so much work…

"Here you are, Jesse. Why don't you keep your wife's forehead cool with this cloth? And, Marilee? Perhaps we should get a pillow under your head, there."

Bea huffed out a sigh, trying her best to disguise it as a reaction to the misstep she took as she turned away, no longer able to remain neutral as the couple began to shed tears of joy as the news sank in.

She'd misstepped, all right.

In so many ways.

She was—what was it now?—ten weeks along and not one person had noticed a single change in her. Not that there was anything dramatic this early on, but even so… Her breasts were a bit bigger than when she'd first found out. And though she hated to admit it, she was going to have to do some internet-shopping pretty quickly to get some bigger pants.

Bea glanced at Jamie, quietly, deftly at work, sliding a pair of stirrups down from the end of the multipurpose gurney. She knew it was crazy to look to him for reactions to this pregnancy that had clearly taken this pair by surprise, but she couldn't help wondering what Jamie would think if he found out *she* was pregnant. Keeping it secret had seemed the best thing at the time. The wisest thing. If he were to know, would he—

No. No, he wouldn't. And, no, you shouldn't, Bea silently chastised herself, before realigning her focus to Marilee.

"How about slipping your feet in these, love?" Jamie eased her tennis shoes off, then carefully slipped each foot into a stirrup.

Marilee grinned and giggled at the instruction, and then quickly her features crumpled in agony as another contraction hit. It was a sign for Bea not to get hopeful. She wasn't pregnant with Jamie's baby. And that simple fact made a world of difference.

"You've got a lot to answer for, Jesse James," Marilee hollered, in between biting down on her lip and doing her best to mimic Bea as she started to show her how to control her breath.

"Nice and steady, there, Marilee." She glanced across at Jamie, who gave her a nod. "You ready to start pushing?"

Sweat was trickling from the poor woman's brow. This was a lot of information to take in at once. A dream vacation turning into a—a dream baby? It was definitely the last souvenir the couple had anticipated bringing home from their European journey.

"Shall I get that cloth back in the cool water for you, Jesse?"

"You can get my wife some drugs, is what you can do," Jesse asserted, as if he'd been recalling a TV medical drama and remembering it was *his* turn to demand an epidural.

Jamie, having spread a paper cloth over Marilee's knees, was taking another look. "I'm afraid we're a bit too far along for any painkillers."

"We?" Marilee barked, trying once again to elbow herself up to a seated position. "We are talking about *me*, and *I* think it is high time you gave me some!"

"Breathe. Remember to breathe, Marilee. Just a couple more pushes and we're there."

Jamie ducked behind the blue paper towel, his hand already on the crowning head of the little one. Beatrice had wrapped her hands around Marilee's and was breathing along with her, murmuring words of encouragement.

Every bit of him longed to look across at those dark brown eyes of hers. Share a complicit smile. Revel in all that was yet to come for these soon-to-be-parents. But today was yet another vivid reminder that none of that would be coming for *him*. Falling in love again would be a big enough miracle, let alone having a family with someone who wasn't Beatrice.

"It stings! Really, *really* stings!" Marilee managed through her deep breaths.

"That's a normal sensation to feel. Especially without any painkillers." Jamie put up a hand to stop Marilee's knees from catching his head in a clamp. Given the madness of the situation, it probably would be fitting.

"Can't you give her *anything*?" Jesse was throwing panicked looks between him and his wife, whose face was scrunching up as she bore down for another push. "Gas? Ether? Knock her out with something? I can't stand to see my little sweet honey bear in so much pain!"

"Oh, no—we wouldn't want her to go to sleep now..." Jamie's jaw tensed as he cupped one hand beneath the baby's emerging head.

"Why the hell not? She's in *agony*!"

Jamie's own features tightened as Marilee's scream of primal pain reached epic proportions. Within seconds he was helping the rest of the little form wriggle free, uncoiling the tiniest bit of umbilical cord from its foot, tipping it back to prevent any blood or amniotic fluid from going into his lungs.

And, yes, Beatrice was there, as if he'd summoned her out loud. The same rhythm. The same ability to read his mind. No matter what chaos reigned between the pair of them on a personal level, he knew he could rely on her to be one hundred percent professional.

She gave the baby's mouth and nose a quick suction with a bulb syringe, and then, with the umbilical cord still attached, he reached across and laid the now-crying child on his mother's stomach.

"And miss the birth of your son…"

The Jameses gasped in disbelief, their eyes clouding with tears as they took in the sight of their red-haired son.

"Jesse Junior," Jesse whispered, tickling the tip of his son's teensy nose with his index finger.

"Jesse Walton Junior," Marilee added with an equally starry-eyed expression, her finger teasing at the clutch of fingers making up her son's miniature fist.

"J. W. Junior. My little boy."

As the couple carried on with their cooing, Jamie quickly clamped the umbilical cord, while Beatrice gave the baby a bit of a wipe to clear some of the vernix from his skin. Jamie could hear her agreeing, that, yes, he was the cutest baby she'd ever seen and, no, she'd never been through anything like this before. Yes, she *did* think he weighed enough, and he *was* long enough. She answered all the questions as calmly as if she'd done this a thousand times before, and as joyfully as if she'd never before experienced the magic of seeing a newborn.

He delivered the placenta and made sure his patient was clear of any cuts or tears.

"Not a one?" Jesse exclaimed, all the while giving his wife the thumbs-up. "That's my girl!"

Bea magicked the baby away to weigh and measure him, and put a little tag on his wrist—even though they had no obstetrics ward in the small clinic, so he would most likely be their only newborn tonight and there was no one to mix him up with.

A hit of longing struck him so suddenly when Beatrice reentered the exam area, holding the swaddled baby in her arms, that he had to turn away. She would see right through him.

Pulling in a draught of air, he swallowed back the sharp sting of emotion. That micromoment couldn't have been more pronounced. He could have sliced each second into a hundred frames. A glimpse into what fatherhood would feel like. Pride. Unchecked love. A bit of fear as to whether he would be able to do the best by his child—and its mother…

He forced himself to turn around again, only to clash and connect again with Beatrice's dark-eyed gaze. She hadn't moved. Had frozen on the spot as if the moment had been as laden with emotion for her as it had for him.

He felt as if his chest was being crushed, and his heart was barely able to provide the simple pumping action required to keep him alive… Because without Beatrice in his life…

Jesse was walking across the room to retrieve his son. Jamie barely noticed when he elbowed him out of the way.

"Now, you just hand that little whippersnapper over here, Dr. Jesolo. Daddy and Mommy are going to take care of him now."

Bea looked up, her dark lashes beaded with tears, her sole focus on Jamie.

"So…" Jesse looked between the pair of them, "What about the two of you, huh?"

Jamie cleared his throat, tore his gaze away from Beatrice, forcing himself to face reality. "What *about* us?"

"When are you two going to have a child?" Marilee

joined in, arms extended toward her husband to regain possession of her newborn.

Jamie hadn't meant to laugh. The idea had been far from ridiculous at one point in their lives. But now? *No.* Children weren't on the menu.

He glanced across at Beatrice, who had backed up against the curtain, her expression stricken as if the question had caught her completely off guard.

Marilee's brow crinkled. "You're obviously together, or you wouldn't have been shooting all those doe-eyed looks at one another when the baby came out, wouldja?"

"Oh, no." Beatrice pulled the curtain back and took another step away from Jamie. "We're not… We're not a couple."

"No!" Jamie shook his head and popped on a smile, as if people were always honing in on the fact that he was just pals with the woman who had smashed his heart into smithereens.

I messed that up a long time ago.

"If you'll excuse me? I'm just going to get a vitamin-K jab for your little one."

When the Jameses raised their eyebrows in alarm he assured them it was standard practice. Nothing to worry about.

When he headed out into the corridor there was no sign of Beatrice.

Being with her, watching her hold that tiny child in her arms was as close a glimpse as he'd get to believing he and Beatrice could start again.

Yes, they had history. And there was a part of him that wasn't sure he'd entirely forgiven her for leaving. Or forgiven himself for breaking his Hippocratic oath by getting too close to his patients. Too emotionally involved.

Which was exactly what he was doing right now. Superimposing someone else's emotions onto his own hollowed-out heart.

He might be able to forgive Beatrice for leaving, but how would he ever be able to trust that she wouldn't do it again? Pick up and leave when her mother unearthed another prince or far-off royal for her to wed in order to uphold the di Jesolo name?

More important… He needed to stop pointing the finger of blame.

He'd had a chance to fight for his true love and he hadn't done it. Had just stood back and watched it happen.

He *deserved* this. Deserved the searing heartache. The bleak, unfulfilling future as a bachelor… The single bed. The sleepless nights. All in a vainglorious attempt to escape the wretched truth.

He had let her go.

Let her walk out of his life as if she hadn't meant a thing.

It wasn't his place to forgive. He saw that now. It was hers.

CHAPTER EIGHT

"AT LAST!" TEO pulled his head in from the window. "This must be the first day without rain in—what?—a fortnight?"

"Something like that. It's not been the best of summers, has it?"

Jamie gave Teo a clap on the shoulder, before turning around and nearly careening into Beatrice as she went out to the waiting room to fetch a patient.

"Apologies!" He raised his hands and backed off, trying his best to ignore her sidelong look as she slipped through the swinging doors, leaving a trail of fresh linen and honey in her wake.

They might have called a truce, but polite chitchat wasn't making working with Beatrice any easier. If anything, the surprise-baby night had only made him more aware of just how singular a woman she was. An amazing doctor. Kind and generous. Calm in a crisis. Quieter than he remembered her being back in England, when her laughter had been able to bring a room to life. Still every bit as beautiful.

It didn't help that she had taken to life in the village as naturally as dewdrops to a flower petal. She had well and truly blossomed in the past few weeks. There was a lovely pink bloom to her cheeks, and a…a softness about her that complemented her slender figure.

He scribbled out a prescription for a patient he'd just seen—a regular at the clinic owing to his severe asthma, who'd had the temerity to scrunch his face up when he saw Jamie was going to be the doctor and asked for Beatrice instead.

"Such a lovely young woman. Don't you think so, Dr. Coutts?"

The cheek! He'd been there for a year and had yet to have *anyone* request him. Then again…he hadn't exactly been himself. Before or after she'd arrived. And no doubt he'd be a right old curmudgeon when she left. There was no winning at this game.

"Dr. Coutts?" Rhianna held out a tablet to him so he could check another patient's stats.

Jamie started. He'd been staring at Beatrice. *Again.*

"Yes…good." He scanned the stats. "I think she's good to go. Can you give her a couple of extra ice packs for the journey back to the campsite?"

"Will do." Rhianna nodded with a smile. "And Dr. Coutts…?"

Jamie turned away from staring at the platinum blond pixie cut, astonished at how short his attention span was. "Yes—sorry?"

"It's good to see you in—" her eyes traveled over toward Bea "—in such good spirits."

She gave her eyebrows a little happy jig and tossed him a knowing wink as she rejoined the mother and teenage daughter trying out new crutches in the wake of a freshly sprained ankle.

Jamie gave his face a scrub. Was he that transparent? He knew he hadn't been able to hide it at Northern General. Hadn't felt any need. He'd been in love.

He tried shrugging it off. Just because Rhianna was having a torrid summer romance with one of the adventure-tour-group guides it didn't mean every single person in the clinic needed to be floating on air. Someone had to keep his feet firmly grounded. He was *British*! Made of stern stuff. He could make it through the summer without falling in love again. As sure as the sun would hit the horizon every day of the week, he could keep himself emotionally off-limits.

He forced himself to focus on the patients board until, a few minutes later, he found himself unable to drown out the sound of a crying baby.

He turned and saw a mother handing her infant over to Beatrice, who expertly tucked the baby into her hands using *his* "magic trick." The special hold he'd been taught by his mentor that never failed to stop a baby from crying.

Fold the right and then left arm across the child's chest, use an index finger to prop up the little chin and tip the child to a forty-five-degree angle. Place your other hand along its nappy and rock it. A bit like a baby jig, but gently. Slowly. And in… That's right… In just a few seconds a smiley, relaxed baby.

He vividly remembered teaching Beatrice the technique. The light in her eyes when she'd had a success on her first try.

Beatrice looked up, perhaps feeling the weight of his gaze upon her?

And when their eyes met…

Lightning strike.

It never failed to amaze him.

Bea's gaze dropped to the child for just a moment before she returned it to meet his eyes, and in that instant of reconnection he saw something in her he hadn't seen before. Was it—longing for a *child*?

As quickly as their gazes had clicked and meshed, Beatrice's attention was straight back on the mother, discussing the reason for their visit. A rash on the infant's leg, from the looks of things.

"Dr. Coutts?" A nurse was holding out a phone for him as Beatrice disappeared behind the curtain of her cubicle. "You've got a call from 118."

His pulse quickened. The Italian mountain-rescue team.

"This is Dr. Coutts. What's the situation?"

He listened silently as the caller detailed an accident. An accident involving a school group on holiday from England. A massive landslide. A bus. Crushed roof.

Regular medics were en route in the helicopter, but they needed ground crews because of the number of children involved. The fire department was on their way, too, but they needed more medical personnel. Did they have anyone free?

He glanced up at the clock. It was late afternoon. They'd have a few hours of daylight left, and they were precious.

"We've got another shift coming in a couple of hours. For now I can get together a team of three or four. More to follow."

It would have to do.

He quickly called one of the ambulance drivers on the radio to come and meet them at the clinic entrance.

When he turned around Beatrice was waving off her patients—a happy mother and a giggling baby.

"Dr. Jesolo, can you suit up for an emergency rescue?"

If she wasn't keen to participate, she didn't let it show. Just nodded and headed off to the supplies area. A true professional.

"Dr. Brandisi?" He flicked his thumb in the direction Beatrice was heading. "Suit up. We've got a long night ahead."

Teo gave him a quick, grim nod, finished up with his patient and the pair of them headed off to change.

"Steel yourself," Jamie warned Teo—the most anxious and excited father-to-be he had ever encountered. "This one's full of children."

"Children?" Bea had caught the end of Jamie's warning as she tugged on a red jumpsuit. "What age?"

"A group of eight-year-olds, I think. Hiking holiday. Wilderness skills or something. About twenty-plus counsellors and a few parents."

Jamie's expression was flinty. A sure sign that he was steeling himself from the inside out for the worst-case scenario.

If there was any time she needed to keep her emotions at bay, it was now. Carrying a precious life inside her had not only ramped up her hormones, it had opened up her heart in a way she hadn't imagined possible. As if carrying a child herself had made her a proxy mother to every other child she encountered until she could hold her own beautiful baby in her arms.

"Fatalities?"

Jamie gave a sharp nod. "Definitely the driver. Thrown through the front window on impact. Lacerate carotid." He huffed out a tight breath. "We should get an update on our way up there. Have you all got your run bags?"

Teo shouldered his large emergency travel bag and picked up Bea's bag with his free hand.

"Don't worry—I can get that." She didn't want special treatment. Not yet anyway.

Teo gave her a look. One that said she hadn't been hiding her pregnancy symptoms as well as she thought she had. "I'll carry it to the ambo. When we get there you're on your own. But call me if you need anything. No heavy lifting, all right?"

She glanced across at Jamie, relieved to see he was

busy rattling through a list of medications they'd require in addition to what was already on the emergency vehicle.

"Is he..." Teo began, eyes gone double wide with disbelief.

"No!" Bea shushed him as quickly as she could. "Just—I need this job, all right?"

She pulled her fingers across her lips in a zip-it-up-pal move, but not in time to stop Jamie catching the end of it.

The vertical furrows between his eyes deepened. "Everything all right with you two? This is going to be intense. We don't have time for any disputes between colleagues."

"No, mate." Teo stepped forward, all business. "We're all good here. Just trying to be chivalrous and it got Dr. Jesolo's dander up a bit—didn't it, Bea?"

He turned and gave her a complicit wink. He'd be quiet. *For now.*

Which was just as well because she knew the coming hours were going to be tough.

The minutes of their ride to the accident ticked past in a merciless silence. Each doctor was shoring up their emotional and mental reserves as information began trickling in on the ambulance driver's radio.

Bea felt as though mere seconds had passed when the ambulance lurched to a stop and they opened up the back.

Cars were already backed up along the narrow mountain route—the only way to the summer resort at the foot of the Alpine glacier. And up beyond there was some hastily put-up emergency tape.

Bea could see the fire crew already on-site, and heard the loud, shrill screech of metal on metal reverberating against the exposed chunk of the mountainside laid bare by the devastating landslide.

Each shouldering their emergency packs, the three doctors took off at a steady jog to reach the overturned bus, precariously hanging to the cliffside. When they arrived, Jamie led them to the head of the 118 team.

"Dr. Coutts, good to have you on-site." The man stepped forward and gave him a quick handshake. "We've got to shoot off with two of the most critically injured patients. Will you be all right taking charge?"

Jamie nodded. "Anything in place yet?"

"Only the triage sites. I'll leave assignments up to you. We've kicked off with START." He glanced over at the helicopter, its rotors already beginning to whirr into action.

"START?" Bea looked to Jamie. She wasn't familiar with the acronym.

"Simple triage and rapid treatment." He nodded across to a lay-by near the bus, where large plastic ground cloths in bright colors had been laid out. "Red, yellow, green and black. Critical, observation, minor or walking wounded, and expectant."

"Expectant?" Bea gave a little stomp of frustration. What a time for her English to be failing her.

"Deceased or expected to die," Jamie said, his green eyes following a pair of fire crew members carrying an adult-sized body bag over to the black tarp. He looked back to Bea, concern tightening his features. "It's harsh, but essential if we're going to get to those who require critical care."

"I'll help with the crew tagging up at the bus—all right, Doc?" Teo took off at a run when he received Jamie's okay.

"Let us know if you need a hand," he called after him, and then placed a solid hand on Bea's shoulder. "Are you up to this? Do you want me to get someone else on board?"

"No. Absolutely not."

She shook her head clear of the fog of information overload. No matter how distant he'd been over the past few weeks, she took strength from his touch now. From knowing he was there. If she ever wanted anyone at an emergency situation it would be Jamie. The calm at the eye of any storm.

"Where would you like me?"

"Are you up for the critically wounded? I'll be there. Working between you and Teo."

She nodded. Despite everything, she knew she flourished at work with Jamie by her side.

"Let's get to it."

"I need an extra pair of hands over here!"

Jamie called across to Beatrice, who was downgrading a child she had resuscitated to the yellow crew. Another life saved.

"What have you got?" She was there in an instant.

He glanced across at her as she knelt on the other side of the young boy he was tending to, relieved to see the hesitation he'd noticed in her when they'd arrived had completely vanished. She was one hundred percent focused now. Exactly what the situation warranted.

And then she saw it. The long shaft of thin metal impaling the boy in the lower part of his chest. She glanced up at the boy's face, her eyes widening, then quickly regrouped into a smile as she felt the boy's gaze on her.

"Well, look at what you've gone and done!" Beatrice chided the boy teasingly, her eyes not leaving his for an instant.

"It's pretty cool, isn't it?" the boy answered.

"This is Ryan." Jamie pulled a hard plastic brace out of his case. "He's got quite a few ideas about his own treatment, but first I think we need to slip a neck brace on him. What do you say, Ryan?"

The boy began to nod in agreement, then winced.

"Easy, *amore*," Beatrice cautioned. "I love your enthusiasm, but how about we keep all responses verbal rather than physical?" She held eye contact with the boy until she'd received an okay and a smile. "And is this little bit of extra equipment coming or going?" Her eyes shot to the small blood stain slowly spreading out from the wound on the front of his T-shirt. Ryan had yet to spot it.

"It's one of the tent poles," Ryan volunteered shakily. "I was holding the tent kit in my seat so I could be ready to set up camp."

"You sound like me when I was in the Scouts." Jamie smiled at the memory of his escapades in the woods. When being a child was all that he'd had to worry about.

"I'm not a Scout," Ryan corrected. "I'm a wilderness expert! If my leg's broken, we can pull out this tent pole and break it in two and then use it as a splint. And if it grows too dark, I can start a fire with my flint stone. It's here in my pocket."

He began moving his hand toward his jeans pocket.

"Hold on there, pal. No need for fires just yet. Your leg's looking all right. Let's just try to stay as still as possible, okay, Ryan?" Jamie laughed at the boy. "As much as I'd like to take it out, I think Dr. Jesolo will agree with me that the tent pole is probably holding more together than ripping it apart."

Beatrice gave an affirmative nod. A surge of energy heated his chest. This was what it had been like in "the good old days." A real team. Better than that. A dynamic duo.

"What would happen if you took it out?" Ryan asked after giving a disappointed sigh.

"Well..." Jamie rocked his weight back on his heels. He always had to play things carefully with his pediatric patients. Kids were smart. They liked information and they could tell when he was holding back. Then again, they were *kids* and as enthused as Ryan was, terrifying him with details about bleeding out wasn't the object of the game.

"What do you say we leave it in place until we get you to a proper OR? That way if there's any blood loss they'll be able to sort you out straightaway. In the meantime we're going to hook you up to an IV to get some fluids and a bit of pain relief running around your system. How does that sound?"

"Cool! I've always wanted to see what it was like in an operating theater. Especially if I'm arriving in a helicopter!"

"Are you planning to be a doctor?" Beatrice asked, while Jamie began cutting away the youngster's shirt so he could get a better look.

He laughed along with her when Ryan announced that he planned to set up his own clinic in the woods to treat both humans *and* bears.

"Oops! Try your best not to move, *amore*."

Ryan's breathing shifted as they laughed, quickly becoming labored, indicating that the pole might have nicked one of his lungs. Pneumothoraxes could be fatal. But they didn't have to be.

Jamie did a quick run of stats. "Blood pressure is stable. Pulse is high."

"Not surprising, given then circumstances. When is the next helicopter due?" Beatrice asked, giving him a quick glance before they both turned to look up at the darkening sky. Dusk was just beginning to set in, and getting as many of the children out of the bus before the sun set was crucial.

"When do I get to ride in a helicopt—ow! It hurts."

"I know, mate. We're going to get you something for the pain." He looked across at Beatrice. "We can't use topical numbing agents. Can you hold on to the pole while I check if it's a through and through?"

"Me?" Ryan asked in disbelief.

"No, *amore*. I'll do that," said Beatrice. "You just concentrate on staying still. I know it's tough, but you're doing so well."

Beatrice gave Jamie a nod, indicating that she was ready, quickly folding the trauma pads he handed her in half and then placing them on either side of the metal rod.

"How many more pads do you need?"

"Are you pulling it out?" Ryan's voice was straining against the pain now.

"Not yet, Ryan." Jamie ran a hand along the boy's creased brow. "We're just seeing how far this bad boy has penetrated."

"A couple more pads, please." Beatrice held out a hand. "That should be enough to stabilize the rod up to the halfway point. Enough to turn him over and check for the through and through."

Jamie quickly handed her the extra folded dressing pads, which she laid crossways to the layer below, gently pressing on them as Jamie slipped both his hands under the boy's side and ducked to take a quick look.

"No." He shook his head, lowering the boy as carefully as he could back to the ground. "It didn't come through."

"Aw..." Ryan lifted his hand to the tent pole but Jamie quickly trapped the small fingers in his own, pressing them firmly to the ground. He couldn't help but laugh. "Were you hoping for a through and through, pal?"

"A little..." Ryan tried lifting himself up again, and instantly started gasping for air.

"I'm just going to put this oxygen mask on you, Ryan. It should help your breathing." Beatrice lowered her voice and continued to speak, ducking her head away from

Ryan's eye line to Jamie's as she did so. "Do you think the pole could've cracked any ribs on entry?"

"Tough to tell at this point. Best thing we can do is stabilize him as much as possible and get him to a hospital."

Jamie tugged his medical kit closer. He'd need to pull out the works on this one.

"Ryan?" A mother's frantic tones broke through the hum of voices. With so many children injured and receiving treatment, only a mother would be calling for one boy in particular. *"Ryan!"*

The calls began to fade as quickly as they'd risen. From the sounds of it she'd made a quick scan of the medical triage site and, having missed her son, was now working her way back toward the crash site.

Jamie pressed down on the boy's shoulders, knowing he would want to respond if it *was* his parent.

"Mum?" Ryan fought for breath to say it again—scream it—but found himself fighting for breath. Tears sprang to his eyes as he whispered, "I want my mum!"

"I know you do, mate. We'll get her, but you've got to stay put—all right?" He looked up to Beatrice. "Can you find her? Ryan? C'mon. Stay with us, mate. Can you tell me what your surname is?"

"Cooper…" Ryan's voice was barely audible as the blood began to drain from his face.

"There's swelling of the subcutaneous tissues," Beatrice said quietly.

"I'm going to have to put in a chest tube."

"Thoracotomy?" she asked.

"Needle decompression. Are you all right to find the mother?"

If he acted fast, he could get it done and restore the boy's oxygen flow. It would be less frightening for the mother to see her son with a needle and a valve in his chest than gasping for breath.

"Absolutely. I'll check on the helicopter, as well."

The low-altitude trip to the hospital might necessitate a chest drain, as well. He'd wait for Beatrice to return to put that in.

Jamie nodded his thanks, noticing as she rose, how her hands slid protectively to her stomach. It was the second or third time that day he'd seen her repeat the gesture. He wondered if she'd hurt herself—got a cut or scrape in all the frantic lifting and carrying of children from the bus to the triage tarps. Adrenaline ran so high during incidents like these it was easy enough to get injured while trying to help those in need.

She was gone before he could ask. Jamie shook his head, turning to his medical kit to rake through his supplies. It was hardly the time to speculate on things that weren't critical medical issues. Then again, maybe his not paying attention was what had lost him Beatrice's affections in the first place.

But his not paying attention now could cost this child his life.

Jamie blinkered his vision so it was on Ryan, forcing himself to drown out all of the other stimuli whirling around them. The sirens, the crying children, the screech and scream of the fire department's Jaws of Life still extracting children from the seats that had virtually fallen like dominoes in on each other.

The fact they'd only lost the driver so far was little short of divine intervention. Three children had already been flown out to a large hospital near Milan. Ryan was the last critical case they had here. The yellow team were busy with a lot of cuts, sprains and a few broken bones. The compound fractures had already been sent off by ambulance. So it was just him and Ryan right now on helicopter watch.

He pulled on a fresh pair of gloves, and by touch located the second intercostal space on Ryan's chest. Using his other hand, he swiped at the area with an iodine-based swab, then deftly inserted a large-bore needle just above the boy's third rib. Holding the needle perpendicular to Ryan's chest, he leaned in, listening for the telltale hissing sound of air escaping.

A sigh of relief huffed out of his own chest at the noise, and he quickly set to removing the needle, leaving the catheter in place while opening the cannula to air.

"Ryan? *Ryan!*"

Jamie looked up from securing the final piece of tape to see a woman running at full speed toward him, calling out her son's name.

Beatrice was just behind her, one hand on her belly as it had been before and the other on her back. When her eyes met Jamie's she stopped cold, her hands dropping to her sides, her expression completely horrified.

As quickly as he'd registered her dismay, it disappeared, and Beatrice joined the woman who had dropped to her knees beside her son and began answering the inevitable flood of queries, her hand slowly, but somehow inevitably, creeping to the small of her back.

A thousand questions were running through Jamie's mind and they should have all be about his patient. But every single thought in his head was building up to one shocking realization.

Beatrice was pregnant.

"The helicopter is on its way back." Bea braved looking into Jamie's eyes. "They think it'll be here in ten, maybe fifteen, minutes." Flinching at the wobble in her voice, she just prayed no one else noticed it.

"Right."

The monosyllabic answer was all the proof Bea needed.

Jamie knew. She'd seen it in his eyes. He knew she was carrying a child.

She'd been doing her best to hide the intense cramping that had hit her throughout the afternoon, but this latest bout of running must have exacerbated things. Fear suddenly gripped her. Her concentration on the injured children had been so intense she hadn't bothered connecting the dots.

She was twelve weeks pregnant now. Still within that window where miscarriage was, for many women, a constant worry. She'd never been pregnant before, so had no idea how her body would respond to pregnancy. So far it had been the typical symptoms: tender breasts, nausea and sharp hits of fatigue. She'd been careful. Or so she'd thought. Keeping her shifts at the clinic to a minimum, but regular enough so as not to raise any alarms.

"I think you will need to go with Ryan."

She only just heard Jamie through the roar of her thoughts.

"No." She shook her head solidly. "Absolutely not. His mother should go with him. There's not much room on the chopper."

"Which is why *you* should go. Mrs. Cooper…"

Bea watched as Jamie did what he did best. Calmed. Soothed.

"We can get you transported down to the hospital so that you'll be there in good time to meet him coming out of surgery."

"Oh, no…" Mrs. Cooper began shaking her head, too

worried to take on the looks shooting between Jamie and Bea.

Why couldn't he just stay out of this?

"I absolutely *insist* that Mrs. Cooper flies with her son to the hospital," Bea finally interjected as she and Jamie tossed the subject back and forth over Ryan's supine form. No need for the eight-year-old to have a battle over his transport reach epic proportions when all he needed was to hear his mum's voice and the uplifting whir of a helicopter on approach.

"Excuse us for a moment," Jamie said, giving Mrs. Cooper's arm a quick squeeze before rising and tipping his head toward a clearing a few meters away from the triage site. He stopped there and turned to face Bea, his expression deadly serious. "You need to go to the hospital."

"What makes you think that?" She knew she was buying time, but telling Jamie she was pregnant because of a ridiculous cover-up of her ex-fiancé's infertility now...? It would be madness.

Suddenly the shame of it all—the full impact of just how far she had gone to keep the family name golden—hit her like a ton of bricks. Had she really thought she could keep her pregnancy secret? And why should she?

Having this baby was the one good thing that had come out of that mess and yet here she was again—hiding the truth despite her vow to do otherwise.

Bea blinked, certain she could hear Jamie replying to her question, but all his words were beginning to blur. A swell of nausea began to swirl and rise from her belly as a sharp pain gripped and seized her. She reached out. Her thoughts were muddled. No matter how many times she blinked, her vision was blurring. And as the swell of sensations reached critical mass, darkness fell.

CHAPTER NINE

BEA HEARD THE beeping first.

A heart-rate monitor. She shifted. The sensation of wires sliding along her bare skin brought her to a higher level of alertness. They were taped on. She could feel it now. High up on the exposed skin near her clavicle. On her belly… She wiggled her left hand. There was a clip on her finger.

The heart rate was her own.

Panic seized her and she squeezed her eyes tight shut against the dark thoughts.

Please let my baby be alive!

Not yet ready to open her eyes and face what might be a dark reality, she listened acutely, forcing herself to mark the cadence of the small pips indicating her heart rate.

After a swift rush of high beeps the sounds leveled to a steady rhythm. Faster than normal, but not surprising under the circumstances. She was pregnant. Her heart rate was *meant* to be elevated. Her heart was pumping more blood—an ever-increasing amount as the baby grew—through her womb, her body, her heart.

Beep. Beep. Beep.

Like the beats of a metronome, the heart monitor was telling her she was stable. But all her thoughts were for her child.

Another layer of awareness prickled to attention when she heard light footsteps and the sound of a door opening. Then the sound of Jamie's voice. His wonderful, caramel-rich voice. Assuring a nurse in English that Beatrice must have just had low blood sugar or not enough sleep. He was sure that there wasn't anything to be worried about. Not yet anyway. Best to leave her to rest for a while. In private.

She heard the nurse leave but not Jamie.

For a few blissful moments her thoughts took on a dreamlike quality. She was together with him. They were going to have a child together. Be a family.

Everything in her relaxed, then just as quickly tensed as the click of the door reminded her that they were in the Torpisi Clinic. She was pregnant by a stranger. Her secret was now public.

She swallowed. This was the moment she'd been dreading most. The judgment, the disappointment and ultimately the indifference she was sure she would see in Jamie's eyes.

Her pulse quickened as she heard him approach, tug a wheeled stool across to her bedside. She felt his touch before her eyes fluttered open to see his handsome face.

His hand was lifting to tease away the tendrils of hair no doubt gone completely haywire over her forehead when he noticed she was awake. He pulled his hand away and pushed back from the side of the bed—as if he'd been caught trying to steal a kiss and she were Sleeping Beauty.

If only things were so simple.

Her fingers twitched. Aching to reach out to him. To hold his hand. Feel the warmth of his touch. The desire was urgent. Insatiable. Her hands began to move toward her stomach when fear gripped her. She wasn't ready to go there yet.

"How are you feeling?" Jamie asked from the other side

of the room, where he was briskly washing his hands as if scrubbing them with antiseptic would erase everything he'd been thinking or feeling.

She'd heard that tone so many times before. The caring doctor. The doctor who was there to help, but was keeping his emotions in check because he had to.

He shook the water off his hands and turned to her as he toweled them dry.

She parted her lips to speak, surprised at how dry they were. "Thirsty..." she managed, before closing her lids against the deep green of Jamie's eyes.

"Here." He elevated her bed with the electronic toggle. "I've got some water for you."

He handed her the glass, holding the base of it as she took a sip and then braved a glance at him.

Jamie knew. He knew she was pregnant. Why else would he have had her put in a private room? Hooked up monitors to her belly? And yet he still had room in his heart to be kind. Gentle. Caring for her in a moment that was making it more than clear that she'd chosen another over him.

She ached to blurt out the real story. Tell him it wasn't what he thought. Tell him she'd loved him all along. But to explain the whole ill-conceived story would only diminish what he must already be thinking of her. *Very little.*

She'd seen it in his eyes as the weeks had passed. That famed cool British reserve coming to his rescue time and time again. Just when she'd thought they'd be able to try out a fledgling friendship... *Slam!* Down had gone the shutters, crushing her hope that...that what? She could turn back time and have him back again?

Even the tiny part of her that was still a dreamer didn't stretch *that* far.

"Does your…?" Jamie stopped, swallowed, then began again. "Does he know?"

Bea nodded her head—yes. It was the single blessing she had in this scenario. That man would never be able to lay claim to her child.

But would any other man?

Would Jamie?

"How long have you known?"

She sucked in a deep breath. That was a much harder question to answer. Obviously the treatment had given her more than a ballpark date, but something in her had lit up within days—too early for a test but she had just *known*.

"A couple of months. More…" She was past telling white lies now. All she wanted to know was that her baby was going to be all right.

Just tell him.

Tell him everything.

"I'm guessing you fainted because of lack of food. A bit of dehydration. Sometimes a low iron count can contribute. Have you been taking supplements?"

She nodded. She had. Of course she had. Everything had been done by the book except reducing stress and making sure she always had a snack in hand. But it wasn't as if anyone had anticipated the bus crash. She'd just have to be more careful in the future.

Jamie crossed the room again and tugged open a drawer. He pulled out a little bag of almonds and held them up. "You should keep some snacks on you. At all times. Nuts, cheese, apples… There are all sorts of healthy tidbits you can keep without much bother. It's a bit early, but have you been tested for gestational diabetes?"

Shamefully, she hadn't. Whenever she thought about the baby she thought about the absurd mess she was in, and went right back to not thinking about it.

"I must've been out a long time," she said finally. "To get back here and not even notice."

"You were." Jamie nodded, his brows cinching together as if he were trying to piece together the bits of puzzle he'd only just been handed. "We got you into an ambulance straightaway. Sometimes when low blood pressure and a handful of other factors collide, fainting is the body's way of rebooting itself. Though it's not like *you* need explanations about what's happening..."

"I'm human as well as a doctor," she said softly. "It's always good to have reminders. An outside eye."

To have you.

Jamie let the words hang there between them without responding.

Bea pressed her back teeth together. It was time to face facts. She was still wearing the khaki pedal pushers she'd had on earlier. There was no telltale wetness between her legs that might indicate that things had gone horribly wrong.

"I didn't take the place of any of the children?"

"No." Jamie sat down on the stool he'd pulled up to Bea's bedside, his eyes on the monitors as he answered. "Most of the children were treated on-site. Those who needed extra care, like Ryan, were flown to Milan. It's easier to get blood supplies there, specialized surgeons, that sort of thing..."

Beatrice couldn't help it. Now that she knew she hadn't elbowed some poor child out of critical transport to a hospital, she blurted out the question she hadn't yet dared to ask. "Is the baby all right?"

"A full exam hasn't been done yet, but if it's miscarriage you're worried about, you can rest easy. I've listened for a heartbeat. Your baby is alive and well."

He sat down on the stool he'd pulled up to her bedside

so that they were at eye level. He ran his finger along the rim of her water glass.

Beatrice watched as that finger, long and assured, wound its way along the glass's edge, skidding up and over the area where her lips had touched it. Whether it was a conscious act or not, it stung.

And yet…he had kissed her. Although it was so long ago now it almost felt like a dream.

"Right!" He clapped his hands together. A bit loudly for the small exam room, but it wasn't as if they were having the most casual of exchanges. "How about we take a look together, then?"

Of all the moments Jamie had imagined having with Beatrice, it had never been this.

Giving her an ultrasound scan for a baby that wasn't his.

"Let's get some more water in you. If you can get this whole glass down, we'll be able to see it—your baby—better."

She nodded and started drinking.

He turned to get the screen in place, gather the equipment, willing the years of medical training he'd gone through to kick into action. Enable him to take an emotional step back as he once again turned toward the woman he'd thought he would one day call his wife and apply gel to her belly.

Now that she had unbuttoned her top and shifted her trousers down below her womb, he could see the gentle bump beginning to form. Fighting the urge to reach out and touch it, to lay his fingers wide along the expanse of the soft bulge, Jamie forced himself to rerun the past few weeks like a film on fast-forward.

All the bits of discordant information were coming together now.

Beatrice looking beautifully aglow one moment…gray or near green the next.

The light shadows below her eyes he knew he'd seen more than once… He'd written them off as postwedding stress, but now that he knew she was pregnant…

Everything was out of whack.

"I'm just going to put some gel on."

"It's going to feel cold."

They spoke simultaneously, then laughed. One of those awkward laughs when the jolt of connection reminded a soul just how distanced they'd become from the person they loved. Jamie looked away before he could double-check, but he was fairly certain Beatrice was fighting back tears.

Everything in him longed to pull her into his arms. Comfort her. Hold her. Touch her. Kiss her as he had on that very first day. But how could he now that she was pregnant with *that man's* baby?

Ba-bum. Ba-bum. Ba-bum.

"You hear that?" He kept his eyes solidly on the screen, but despite the strongest will in the universe he felt emotion well up inside him. Beatrice was going to have a child. A beautiful…

"I'm just taking some measurements, here."

"Twelve weeks," she volunteered through the fingers she was pressing to her lips. "It's been about twelve weeks."

The date put the baby's conception date somewhere right around the wedding date. Too close for it to have been a shotgun wedding.

He swallowed away the grim thought. Beatrice might have left him for another man, but he knew in his heart that she never would have cheated on him. On anyone. This child would be Marco's.

"The measurements look good. The baby's about seventy millimeters. A good length."

"Tall?"

"Not overly—but you're tall. The baby's bound to inherit some of your traits."

Her ex-fiancé was tall, as well. Not that he'd spent any time reading the tabloids. Not much anyway.

"Oh, Jamie. Look!" Beatrice's gaze was all unicorns and rainbows as she gazed upon the screen. "She's perfect."

"Or he," Jamie added. It was still a bit early to tell. Maybe two more months. The tail end of Beatrice's contract.

Beatrice was taking no notice of him, waving to the baby. "Hi, there, little girl," she kept repeating. Then to Jamie, more solidly, "She's a little girl. I can tell."

She lifted her hands and moved to caress her belly, only to remember the gel. She pulled them back, accidentally knocking Jamie's arm away from her stomach, and the image dropped from the screen.

"Oh, no! Bring it back! Sorry—please. *Per favore.* Just one more look."

When he turned to look at Beatrice both her hands were covering her mouth, and the tears were trickling freely down and along her cheeks as she took in the fully formed image of her child. All the tiny infant's organs were up and running at this point. Muscles, limbs and bones were in place. Beatrice was showing all the telltale signs of a parent who didn't care one way or the other if a child was a boy or a girl. She was just a mother, thrilled to discover her baby was healthy.

"Do you have plans to tell the father how the baby is doing?"

He didn't know who was more shocked by the question. Himself or Beatrice.

* * *

"I—" Bea looked to the black-and-white image on the screen again, then back to Jamie. "He doesn't want anything to do with the child."

"He—he *what*?"

"He didn't—*ugh*!" She scrubbed her hands through her hair. "When I called off the wedding he told me I could do what I liked with the baby."

Saying it out loud made her shiver at the coldness of his words. It was a *life*!

"But—" Jamie shook his head, visibly trying to put the facts in order. "What a coward." Disdain took over where disbelief had creased his features.

"We did it so it would appear to be a honeymoon baby."

The look of pure disbelief was back. Jamie shot it at her and it made her raise her hands to protest, then drop them as if anvils had suddenly fallen into them. "Calling the wedding off wasn't a scenario I had envisioned having to prepare for."

Jamie shook his head, obviously at a total loss for words. She didn't blame him. If she was hearing the same thing from a friend… Well, if it was a friend in similar shoes, from a similar background… She'd heard worse. *Much* worse.

"I know this isn't how things are normally done—"

"Certainly not where *I'm* from," Jamie intoned.

A surge of indignation shot through her. "That's not fair. I've never judged where you've come from. Not in that way."

"You must've judged it to an extent. Decided it—decided *I*—wasn't good enough for you."

All the words drained from Bea's arsenal. "Is that what you think?"

"I think a lot of things, Beatrice, and not one of them

involves you getting yourself knocked up by someone who doesn't have the backbone to step up and give a name to his child."

Bea was still reeling from his turn of phrase. "Knocked up?"

It sounded so coarse. Crude, even, the way he'd put it. She might have stooped low to a lot of things, but she had done everything for a reason.

"How dare you? I did this—all of this—for my *family*. Obligation. Duty…" One of her hands pounded into her open one as she continued. "That's how one 'steps up' in a family like *mine*."

For a mother like hers, you upheld tradition. Even when it came at a price.

Jamie took a final glimpse at the image on the screen, then turned to her, his expression an active tempest. The calm of his voice was so still and steady it almost frightened her.

"Beatrice, I don't think I should be involved in this any longer. Perhaps you can find a local obstetrician…?"

"No." She reached out to Jamie as he dropped the scanning wand on the tray next to the monitor and turned away from her. "If the press find out about this they'll have a field day."

"I'm afraid that's really not my concern."

The words landed in her chest like daggers.

"But you—" She stopped herself when she saw his shoulders stiffen and he took another step away from her.

She had no right to ask him for his help.

"This isn't my battle to fight," he said finally, after he'd cleaned his hands and thrown away the paper towels.

He was right. Of course he was right. But something deep inside her wanted to fight this out until there wasn't the tiniest shred of possibility.

Now that he knew everything…

But he didn't know everything. That was the point.

And wasn't his strong reaction because he was feeling the same things she was? Being together. Working together. Having a scan of her baby—

Screech!

Okay. Deep breath. She knew she must be coming across as an absolute screwball now, but the Jamie she knew and loved—

She still loved him. And when you loved someone…did you let them go free or fight?

You fought until there was no choice but to let him go.

"Why did you kiss me?" Bea pushed herself up and looked him straight in the eye. She had to know. Had he felt anything close to the full-on fireworks display she had when their lips had touched for the first time in two years…? Had he felt the magic when physical sensation had melded with powerful emotions and those two forces had joined together?

It had been pure seraphic bliss.

Jamie didn't seem to be taking the same rose-tinted journey down memory lane that she was. Thunder and lightning crashed across his features, rendering his face implacable.

"Everything was different then! I wouldn't have kissed you if I'd known."

"What? So it was all right to kiss me when you thought I was just a runaway bride?"

"You're going to be a *mother*." He turned away to yank some more paper towels from the dispenser.

"It's not what you think."

"Really?" Jamie wheeled on her, eyes flaring with indignation. "Because I don't believe you have the remotest idea what I'm thinking."

"I have a rough idea," she whispered, no longer able to hold his gaze.

Everything in her longed to run away from this moment. Find another village, another country, another continent to hide away in. But hiding could only last so long. She had a truth to face up to, and until she did she didn't deserve to be a mother, let alone have an ounce of Jamie's respect.

If the last few weeks had taught her anything, it was that hiding the truth from Jamie—no matter how hard she tried—was an impossibility. He was the beacon that drew it from her. Demanded it of her. He was her true north and she owed him an honest answer.

She stretched her arms out toward him, knowing he wouldn't fall into them as she ached for him to do, but at least the gesture would speak a thousand words she couldn't voice.

Jamie shook his head, refusing to move any closer.

"How can you have even the slightest idea of what I am thinking, Beatrice? Your life… You've made decisions that took away any right to know what I'm thinking."

"Those decisions had nothing to do with how I felt about you, though."

"How could they not?" He spread his arms out wide and looked around the room, as if there were a crowd assembled in a courtroom. A jury keen to pass judgment one way or the other. "You *left* me, Beatrice. Left me to marry another man. Now, I'm sorry it didn't pan out the way you envisioned it, but you're pregnant by another man and, like it or not, he's going to be part of your future."

"But I'm *not*."

Jamie gave his head a sharp shake, his hands latching onto his hips. "What do you mean you're not? We saw the baby. Alive and kicking." He pointed to the scan where the black-and-white image remained. "Whose is it if not his?"

"I don't know."

Bea's chest nearly exploded with relief. She'd said it. Said it and it nothing had happened. Well, nothing yet anyway, because Jamie's jaw was twitching and she knew what *that* meant. He had something to say, but he was going to wait until he was ready so that whatever it was would come out with surgical precision.

Before he leapt to any other conclusions she began explaining. She told him everything. About her ex-fiancé's infertility. The high expectations for a honeymoon baby. The demand for a male heir to the Rodolfo name. Their agreement for her to have the IVF treatment. The moment she'd walked away after discovering his infidelity.

Despite the gravity of the situation, she burst out laughing. "Isn't it hilarious that she's going to be a girl?"

"We're not going to know that for another eight weeks."

"We?"

The word hung between them like an offer of something more.

Everything in him fought to return Beatrice's smile.

We.

Two little letters.

Far too much history.

Though she didn't move, he heard the word again.

It ran over and over in his mind, as if he was trying to extract every ounce of meaning he could from the moment.

Her voice was full of hope. *Hell!* He could see it in her beautiful brown eyes. Trace it through the flush pinking up her cheeks, its heat adding even more red to her full lips.

But what was she asking of him? To forget the past? Forget that she had chosen her family and another man over him? The thought riled him.

Family, eh?

That wasn't how family worked where *he* came from.

After all his family had done for him—the sacrifices they had made—he would have a hard time telling them where to go if they didn't approve of the woman he loved. Maybe…

No. This was an entirely different scenario now. Perhaps Beatrice was good old-fashioned scared. He was a familiar entity, and she didn't want to go through this alone. But another man's child? A stranger's?

The way this whole crazy story was unfurling, Jamie couldn't help but think Beatrice was a stranger to him now. The woman he'd known wouldn't have done any of those things. It was time she owned up to her behavior. Accepted some responsibility.

"I think you should try to find the father," he said finally, after the silence became unbearable.

Beatrice threw him an odd look. "He's anonymous."

"What?" Confusion rained through him like nails. "Did aliens come down to earth, abduct the Beatrice I knew and once truly loved and replace her with *you*?"

She stared at him for a moment. As if processing the accusations. The facts. But he knew it wasn't as if any of this rang true with the woman he'd once known. The time he'd spent with Beatrice had definitely been a fairy tale compared to this nightmare.

Beatrice sat up in the bed, pulling her shirt closer around herself even though the monitors were all still attached. She reached unsuccessfully for a blanket at the foot of the bed, and for one not very nice second Jamie felt like picking it up and throwing it over her. Just hiding her away from sight.

"The treatment was anonymous."

He blinked and forced himself to pull her back into focus. Her eyebrows tugged together, then lifted, her expression changing into something a bit brighter. "I did stipulate that, whoever he was, he must have at least a drop of English heritage."

The words slammed him in the chest and sucked out the oxygen when he heard himself echoing Beatrice. "English?"

"English," Bea repeated, her eyes solidly on his as she gave a wicked little laugh. "That was my little secret at the clinic. No one knows—well, now you know...but no one else knows." She gave her stomach a reassuring pat and pulled her top down close, as if to warm it.

If possible, the atmosphere in the small exam room flexed and then strained against the swirl of information Jamie was trying to make sense of.

A flash of a future that might have been his slammed into his solar plexus. *He* should be the one fathering that little boy or girl growing in Beatrice's womb. *He* should be the one to soothe it, rock it to sleep while his wife caught up on her sleep. He should be the one to tickle its nose, read stories in the middle of the night even though he or she wouldn't be ready yet to hear about Treasure Island or Cinderella. Holding the tiny infant in his arms.

The tug of longing he felt in his chest near enough suffocated him. The harsh reality was that it *wasn't* his child. And it wasn't his future to dream about.

"Your fi—how did he become infertile?"

Bea's shoulders lifted and collapsed in a deep sigh. "I'd love to make a joke about Italian men and tight underwear, but it's a bit more complicated than that."

"He didn't—he wasn't unsafe with you, was he? Did he hurt you at all?"

Jamie fought the urge to go to her, pull her into his arms, instead channeling all his energy into tightening his fingers along the counter's edge—as if pressing the blood out of himself would make her revelations hurt less.

Why hadn't he done more to keep her by his side?

You just let her go.

"No." Beatrice shook her head, her upper lip curling a bit, as if she were reliving an unpleasant memory. "We never consummated our relationship. For a number of reasons."

Her features changed, as if even saying the words was akin to tasting the most sour of fruits.

As quickly as she'd sunk into a sigh she sat up tall, charged with an invisible shot of energy. "I need to get out of here."

She tugged off the monitor tabs and turned her back to Jamie. Shirt buttoned and tucked into her trousers, after a quick swipe and clean of the gel that had so recently helped give them access to that little baby inside her, she turned to him with a renewed sense of purpose flaring in her dark eyes.

"Jamie, listen. My cousin has offered me the use of his chalet in the next valley over. It's blissful. I went there once in the winter season. I have a couple of days scheduled off. Is there any chance I could convince you to come with me? Let me explain everything. Give you a chance to ask all the questions you must have."

A knock sounded on the door. The nurse called in and said that she had an update about a couple of the children who had been flown to Milan and one who was here at the clinic.

Jamie wanted more than anything to ignore it. To go to this "blissful" chalet and start asking the pileup of questions jamming in his throat. See if there was even the tiniest sliver of hope that they could start something new.

But he wasn't there yet. Couldn't pair the woman he'd

loved with the one in front of him—drowning him in a flood of off-key information.

"Sorry." He pulled a fresh white coat off of the back of the door. "Duty calls."

An hour, later Bea felt ready. Refreshed after a restorative walk along the lakeshore and a power nap that seemed to have supercharged her.

She was ready to fight for her baby. *And* for her man.

When Jamie stepped out of the back door of the clinic he looked exhausted. More tired than she'd ever seen him. And she knew it had nothing to do with work. The second their gazes connected, she knew her battle to win him over was already lost.

"Shouldn't you be at home? Resting?"

The words in another context, another tone would have been soothing. Caring even. But at the sound of the brittle tone they'd been delivered in all the impassioned reasons to try again Bea had planned to stack at his feet like Christmas presents were swept away.

"I thought I'd come in and do a couple of hours. Relieve anyone who was at the crash site."

"I think it's best if you don't." Jamie squared his stance to hers. "I know your contract runs until the end of the summer—early September, wasn't it?"

She nodded, her tongue weighted to the bottom of her mouth with disbelief. *He was going to fire her.*

Not wanting to hear what was coming next, she shook her fingers in a wide just-stop gesture that anyone with half a brain could have read.

And yet he continued, as if purging a poison from his own body.

"I think it's best if you don't come in anymore. I'm sure

we'll be able to get through the next few days with relief staff. Until we can get someone permanent in."

He spoke as if in a trance. The words coming out in the dull, staccato tones of an automaton. As if his hollowed-out heart would never know the joy of love again.

Part of her wanted to rush to him. Take her hand and press it to his chest, feel for the beat of his heart. She knew it was there. Knew blood pumped through his veins the same as hers. And yet…

This Jamie frightened her.

This Jamie was saying goodbye.

"If you've left anything, I'll get someone to bring it by. I presume you'll stay in town overnight?"

Her shoulders slumped with defeat as she watched his cool gaze drop to her lips, then to the dip of her clavicle. The swoop of bone and flesh he'd used to trace with the pad of his thumb before dipping his head to press hot kisses into the hollow at the base of her throat.

Heat clashed with icy cold as the sensation of his gaze and the memory of his touch collided.

She shut her eyes against the memory, willing herself to focus on the child she was carrying. The love she and Jamie had once shared. And when she opened her eyes again…willing to bare her soul to him for one last shot at being together…he was gone.

CHAPTER TEN

BEA PULLED THE covers around her shoulders, not quite ready to admit that it was morning even though the sun was already peeking through the shutters she could never bring herself to close.

Bah! Who needed another sunny day when it was raining inside her head?

Pragmatism told her that her behavior was bordering on depression.

Her heart said otherwise.

She'd laid it on the line. As good as reached into her own chest and handed Jamie her heart with a ribbon and bow on it and a little tag attached. *Take me.*

She pulled the sheet up and over her head and gave a small groan. She'd already cried as many tears as her body would allow. Cried until she'd fallen asleep. And even then it had been restless, fraught with terrifying dreams. Darkness. Unseen dangers. Cliff edges. Racing vehicles. Natural disasters. Anything and everything she'd ever been frightened of gathered together in a dream to lure her into the most harrowing of chases for survival.

Well…

She cracked an eye open and let the morning sounds of the town register.

She'd survived.

Just.

There was a part of her that still wanted to curse Jamie. Scream at him for not standing by her at this time of crazy, urgent need. The other half of her knew she had no right. All of this was a nightmare of her own making.

All of it save her inability to stop loving him.

It was time to let go. She knew it now.

No matter how cruel his looks, how callous his words, she knew she would love Jamie until the end of time. It was as if the first time she'd met him, he'd lit a single candle in the center of her heart. A pure flame that had refused—no matter what she had thrown at it—to be extinguished.

True love could never die.

But perhaps it could change form.

The harsh, unforgiving speeches she would normally be giving herself were impossible to drum up.

Had she…? Was this her first step in forgiving herself?

Her hands slipped to her belly. The only way she could go on was to forgive herself for all she had done. Everything—no matter how insane it had seemed—had been done with love in her heart.

Had it landed her in the deep end?

Most definitely.

Would she make it to the other side?

A smile tweaked at the edges of her lips.

Of course she would.

No matter how down she felt, it was time to find the reserves of strength lying somewhere deep within her and protect and care for the baby she was carrying on her own.

The phone rang and she let out a groan. Anyone who knew her would hear that her throat had been rasped raw with sobbing the night away. Maybe she should call in sick.

A fresh bloom of tears clouded her eyes.

There was no work.

She'd been unceremoniously fired.

Sighing, she batted her hand about on the bedside table until she hit the phone and pulled it under the covers.

"Pronto?"

"Don't go out this morning."

Bea sat straight up in bed, pulling the covers around her as if they would shield her from whatever news he was about to spill.

"Jamie?" She knew it was him, but the message he was conveying wasn't computing at all.

"The press. They're all around your *baita*. The clinic, too. They got a photo."

"Photo?" She shook her head, the information still not entirely registering.

"Of you… Me. Your hand on your belly."

She shook her head again, willing her brain to play along. Sort everything into the right place.

"When?"

One-word responses seemed to be all she was capable of this morning.

"Yesterday at the accident scene. There was press everywhere."

Her fingers flew to her mouth. Of *course* there had been. She'd been so engrossed in work she hadn't even thought to consider…

The accident scene came back to her in vivid snapshots.

Emergency tape cordoning off the onlookers… Had there been photographers among the crowd? Mobile phones?

Definitely.

The flash of cameras as they lost the light?

Paparazzi at a crash site?

Or a keen-eyed tourist trying to make some extra money.

Had anyone called out her name?

She shook her head again. It was so hard to remember.

Helicopters flying in and out.

One helicopter hovering… Something a medical chopper would never do… *Press.*

A man on a motorcycle, trying to talk his way past the *polizia di stato* overseeing the slow flow of traffic trickling down the mountainside past the crash site. He'd had a camera, long lensed, resting on his thigh…and then she'd stumbled.

She squeezed her eyes tight against the memory.

"Beatrice?" Jamie's caramel-rich voice was edged with worry. "Are you still there?"

"*Si*—yes." A logjam of words caught in her throat, and in the end all she achieved was a cry for help. "I—I'm not sure what to do."

"I know what you're *not* going to do…" And in a steady, assured voice, Jamie began detailing how to get out of this outrageous predicament.

She let his voice do what it always did. Pour down her insides like warm caramel, pooling at the base of her spine where it turned molten. Fiery. A lava-hot core of resolve.

Bea swung her legs out of bed, pressing her toes against the cool wooden planks of her apartment, taking strength from his assured tone that she would be fine.

"Close your shutters. Take a nice shower. Put on a loose-fitting dress. Find a hat. If you don't have one, I'll bring one."

"You'll bring one? What are you talking about?"

"I'm coming over. Don't open your door to anyone but me."

"Jamie, what are you talking about? I thought—"

I thought you wanted me out of your life.

"Never mind what I thought. I can't have my patients' welfares compromised because of the press outside."

Ah.

The patients. Of course.

"I'm going to drive up to the back door. Your landlord will let me in. Don't even be tempted to leave your apartment until you're certain it's me."

"It's really not your concern."

"It is now," he bit back, his voice as grim as she'd ever heard it. "You made it my concern the second you stepped into my clinic."

He was lashing out. She knew that. He'd never asked for everything she'd brought in her wake.

Her eyes worked their way over to the suitcases she'd already packed, the clothes she'd set out to make an early departure, before the full impact of Jamie's demand that she leave had kept her cemented to her bed.

She would leave on her own. No matter how hard it would be not to fight for the man she loved with all her heart, the life she'd thought they could share together, she would leave so *he* could survive.

"I'll get a taxi." She flicked an app open on her *telefono.* "There's a train leaving in a half an hour. I'll be on it. Just—" She swallowed back the tears stinging her raw throat. "It's really okay."

"It really *isn't,* Beatrice."

Why was he making this more difficult than he had to? For both of them?

"I've already spoken to the local police about an escort. Do you know the fastest way to your cousin's chalet? The one you mentioned yesterday? I can get some security in place before we arrive if you let me know what the address is."

"Wait! *We?*"

Leaving on her own was going to be harrowing enough. She'd just made the tiniest of baby steps toward making peace with herself and already it was torn to shreds. *Deep breath in...*

"Jamie. Surely I can get past a couple of paparazzi on my own? I know I'm no pro, but I have managed a few in my time."

"Beatrice, there are *dozens* of them."

Jamie's words crystalized in her brain as he spoke… then froze icy cold as he continued.

"Even more here at the clinic. You're trapped."

The phone clattered to the floor as her hands instinctively wove around her belly, protecting the tiny life inside. The fist-sized baby she'd vowed to take care of no matter what.

Something fierce and powerful rose within her. A mother's elemental chemistry at work, protecting what she and she alone could give life to. This was *her* battle. And hers alone.

She scooped the phone from the floor, took swift strides to the windows and pulled the shutters closed against the invasive glare of the tabloid press. There was an underground garage she could leave through. Calls she could make.

Part of her felt like striding out in front of them all, holding a press conference, pouring her heart out so the world would know once and for all that being a princess was far from living "less than a whisper away from heaven," as one of the tabloids had put it right before her disastrous wedding.

"I got myself into this mess. Thank you for your help."

She parted her lips again to wish him well in life, but stopped herself because the only words she knew would come tumbling out if she continued would be the three most beautiful and yet cuttingly painful words of all…

I love you.

She held the phone away from her ear and with great remorse pressed the little red symbol that would end the call. Then swiftly, through the blur of tears now flowing freely down her cheeks, she deleted the number.

It felt like cutting off a limb. But at long last she felt pride at her decision. A long-awaited fragment of self-respect that she knew would only continue to grow.

Jamie stared at the phone with an equal mix of terror and fury churning through his veins.

She'd hung up on him.

He was trying to *help*!

Surely she could see he was trying to help.

He stuffed the phone into his pocket, his gaze snagging on the tabloid newspaper in front of him. The picture took up nearly three quarters of the page. Beatrice was front and center. She was wearing the regulation emergency-care jumpsuit, so it wasn't obvious she was pregnant. Even now he knew it was still difficult to tell. There was a soft arc where he'd scanned her belly yesterday, but nothing so pronounced it was obvious. And yet…

He shook his head, willing himself not to relive the moment where he'd first laid eyes on the child growing inside Beatrice's womb. *Useless.* No matter what he did—eyes open, closed, half-mast—none of it worked. He could still see that baby—still feel the thread of empathy… *No.* It wasn't empathy. He'd seen hundreds of babies inside hundreds of wombs in the course of his medical career, and held even more in his arms as a pediatrician.

But he'd never felt for any of them what he'd felt for this one.

Love.

Electricity crackled through him as the thought took shape and grew.

Of *course* he loved the child.

Because he loved Beatrice.

It was why he hadn't been able to sleep. Why everything, despite being in the full bloom of summer, had seemed gray, dull and lifeless since he'd all but kicked her out of the clinic. Of his life.

It explained his ridiculous knight in shining armor attempt. By telephone.

The memory curdled when he tried to give it a softer edge.

It had been little less than cowardly.

He had given himself a way out by ringing Beatrice from the safety of his office, instead of elbowing his way past all those ridiculous camera-wielding journalists. Beatrice was right to have hung up on him. They were photographers—not armed snipers lying in wait to kill anyone.

Though they *were* stealing her right to live her life the way she chose. Just as he'd done by rejecting the baby she was going to bring into the world.

She wasn't mad. Or foolish. She was brave. Loving. Selfless, even, to bring a child created in such calculated circumstances into the world and love it as if she *hadn't* lost everything in the process.

A fire started in his gut. Beatrice shouldn't have to do this. Hide away from the press. Sneak out of her shuttered apartment under the cover of darkness or hidden behind another disguise. Be fired for being—what?—the love of his life?

So she was pregnant because of an attempt to do the right thing by a family so interwoven in the traditions of the past that she'd agreed out of loyalty?

He knew loyalty.

He showed it to his patients. He gave it willingly to his own family. Would lay down his life for them.

He glanced at the newspaper again.

Mystery Knight in Shining Armor for Venice's Runaway Principessa!

Hardly pithy, but no one needed to read the wordy headline to understand the one thing that photo showed.

He was in love with Beatrice.

It was there for all the world to see.

She was reaching out as the darkness of her faint began to consume her, and the expression on Jamie's face as he stretched out his arms to catch her was one of the harrowing anxiety of a man who would lose a part of himself if he lost her.

There was no chance Bea was going to risk another set of heartbroken-princess headlines.

Jilted Again!

Always the Fiancée...Never the Bride!

Destined to be Alone...Forever.

Well, screw that!

If she was going to leave, she was going to leave with her head held high.

One long shower, a session in front of the mirror and a bit of prevarication over the blue dress that flattered her olive skin or the green that definitely showed her small baby bump later...and she was ready to go.

Her heart rate accelerated as the elevator doors opened to the wide foyer on the ground floor of her apartment block…the last open space before she opened the doors to the world…

"Jamie?"

She looked over her shoulder, as if half expecting the press to jump out of some invisible closet and scream "Surprise!" All the while snapping away, taking photos of her looking shocked. But there was no one. No one except for Jamie, standing there as handsome as ever, blond hair curling over the edges of his shirt collar, green eyes holding her in their steady gaze.

Her gut instinct was to run to him, throw herself into his arms and weep with relief that she wouldn't have to go through any sort of charade with the press. The other instinct? The other instinct was hopping mad that he was there at all.

Wasn't *he* the one who had pointed the way to the exit yesterday?

Wasn't *he* the one who had refused to consider trying again?

Wasn't *he* the one to whom she had lost her heart all those years ago and against whom no one else would compare? *Ever.*

She put one foot in front of the other and made her way across the foyer, through the doors and out onto the street, Jamie keeping pace with her the entire time. He swept out in front of her, down the steps and toward his car.

"Madame..." He opened the passenger door of his dark blue 4x4—a typical rugged Alpine doc vehicle. "Your carriage awaits."

Bea stayed rooted to the spot. *No way.* She wasn't going to let her heart go on this crazy merry-go-round ride again.

She'd been through enough emotional joyrides and not a single one of them had been fun.

"What did you do?" she heard herself ask in a voice that didn't sound natural.

Jamie had the grace to look the tiniest bit bashful before he admitted, "I told them you'd left the clinic and were headed to Milan. Something about going to a hospital ward..."

The edges of her lips twitched. But he didn't deserve to win her smile. Not yet anyway.

"What type of ward?" she asked, her fingers still retaining their firm grip on the handles of her wheeled luggage.

"A maternity ward," he answered, the twinkle in his green eyes flashing bright.

The tiniest glimmer of hope formed in her chest.

"Oh, really? And what is it exactly I'm meant to be doing there?"

"I don't think you'll be doing *anything* there," he answered, his voice growing thick with emotion. He tipped his head toward the car. "What do you say we get you out of here? Before they figure out someone might've given them duff information."

Her hand swept to her belly. She couldn't do this again. Not if he was just offering her a ride to so-called freedom. It would just be a few days in a holding pattern until she came up with a new plan. A new place to hide away.

That wasn't how she was going to face life anymore. She was a handful of months away from being a single mother. It was time to stand on her own two feet. Even so...he *was* looking terribly earnest. It would be rude not to ask what his plan was.

Wouldn't it?

She gave her hair an unnecessary shake and showed him her haughtiest look.

"What exactly are you proposing, Jamie?"

"I'm proposing we get out of here," he said, taking a determined step toward her. "I'm proposing you consider forgiving me for acting like a boor."

Bea shivered despite the warm summer breeze as he took yet another step. Only a handful of stairs stood between them. She had a chance. A chance to turn around… flee. Escape with a bit of her heart intact.

Her fingers pressed against the warm curve of her belly.

"I'm also proposing," he continued, taking the steps in a few swift, long-legged strides and pulling her hands into his, "that we get out of here before any straggling paparazzi come by. C'mon!"

He tipped his head toward the car and reached either side of her to pick up her bags. She caught a warm hit of evergreen and…honey? Candle wax? She'd never been able to put a finger on it, but the scent had always been Jamie.

She would accept the ride and then she would say goodbye.

Loving a stranger's baby was a big ask. Just knowing he'd forgiven her, knowing she could leave with true peace between them, stilled her restless heart.

He dropped her a wink. "C'mon. I know a girl who has a cousin who has a chalet somewhere out there in the wilderness. Let's get out of here."

Jamie knew the only way to stop himself from popping the question on the torturously long thirty-minute car ride was to fill the car with opera. Beatrice loved listening to the beautiful arias of Puccini, so he scanned his phone's music library until he found the file he'd been unable to delete when she'd left.

Even catching a glimpse of it had been like swallowing bile up until today. But today? Seeing it there on his phone was like receiving a hit of much-needed sunshine on a rainy day.

As if he'd called up to the heavens and ordered it the clouds shifted away one by one until, when at long last they reached the hidden-away chalet, the sky was a beautiful clear blue and the sun shone brightly down on the broad spread of mountain meadows surrounding the estate.

Beatrice gave him the code for the gate, and when they drew up to the house she turned to him, her face taut with nerves. "You'd probably be best just leaving me here. I'll be all right."

"I am not doing any such thing, Beatrice di Jesolo."

He was out of the car before she could stop him and around at her side, opening the door and pulling her hands into his as he dropped to one knee.

"I was hoping not to do this next to the footwell of a beat-up 4x4, but if there's one thing I've learned this summer it's that waiting is a bad idea when it comes to you."

Beatrice's brow crinkled. "What do you mean?"

"I was a first-class idiot, Beatrice. Two years ago when you left I should've put up a fight. Proved I was the man for you. Maybe I wasn't. But I've grown a lot since then."

A dark sigh left his chest, leaving the bright hope of possibility in its wake.

"And I hope you will believe me when I say I've grown the most since you've come back into my life."

"What is it you're saying, Jamie?"

"I'm saying I love you. I'm saying I want to marry you. I've *always* wanted to marry you. I'm saying I want to be a father to the child you're carrying and any other babies you and I might create as we live out our lives of wedded bliss."

He pulled her hands into his and dropped kisses on each of them.

"We've missed too much time together, Beatrice.

Time I don't want to risk losing again. Please say you'll marry me?"

He looked straight into her eyes, praying that what was beating in her heart was the same fiery, undying passion beating in his own.

"Beatrice di Jesolo, will you do me the honor of becoming my wife?"

For one heart-stopping moment a crease of distress flashed across her features, before dissolving into the most beautiful smile he'd ever seen.

"You're absolutely sure?"

"Positively."

"My family is insane."

"Mine is *too* sane," he countered. "It'll make a nice balance."

"Your mother-in-law will be a very…uniquely challenging woman," she said warningly.

"I've been told I have a way with the ladies." He dropped a wink and rose to his feet so he could look her square in the face. "I'll win her over."

Beatrice's eyebrows lifted. "You have to win the bride over first."

"So it's a yes?"

"This *is* what you want?" she asked. "Mystery baby and all?"

She gently pulled her hands from his and swept them along the small swell beneath her cotton dress.

"Mystery baby and all," he replied, more solidly than he could even have imagined. He meant it. He wanted this baby. To love it. To raise it. To read stories to it while it was still in the womb and for every day after. "You are the love of my life, Beatrice. I can't let you get away again."

Tears popped inito her eyes as she nodded her understanding. "*Si, amore*. It's a yes."

He didn't need to hear another word. Whooping with joy, he swung her around before pulling her into his arms for a kiss that was long overdue.

Sweet, sensual, loving, impassioned… The kiss embodied it all.

When at long last they broke apart, heads tipped together as if any more space between them was an impossibility, he whispered to her again, "I love you, Beatrice."

"I love you, too, Jamie. Forever and a day."

EPILOGUE

BEA PUSHED THE shutters back so that the morning sun could flood into the bedroom, barely able to contain her fizz of expectation. January in Britain had never seemed so beautiful. Frost still covered the fields beyond the house—just as Jamie had described when he'd told her about the single winter he'd spent here on his own, with only the wood burner for company.

Well, a lot had changed since then.

A knock sounded at her bedroom door, and before she could cross to answer it Fran's face appeared in the door frame, wreathed in smiles.

"And how is the happy bride-to-be?"

"Happy!" Bea said, laughing as she spoke, feeling another jolt of enthusiasm crackling through her veins. She beckoned Francesca in and twirled around. "What do you think?"

"Beautiful!" Fran's fingers flew to her lips as emotion stemmed anything else she'd planned to say. "Jamie's going to go wild with desire when he sees you!"

"Hardly!" Bea swatted at the air between them, allowing herself a little twist and twirl to show off the A-line cap-sleeved dress she still couldn't believe she fitted into. "Eight and a half months pregnant, swollen feet and chubby cheeked is *not* how I was expecting to walk down the aisle."

"Oh, don't be silly," Francesca parried, flopping onto the old-fashioned bed with an added bounce or two. "You tried it the other way and that was clearly not singular enough for you. Surely your mother—"

"Uh-uh! No, you don't!" Bea feigned horror as she turned to her hodgepodge of a dressing table, pulled together from a packing box and a precariously balanced mirror she'd found in the attic a couple of hours earlier.

She lowered herself onto the packing crate in front of it, ensuring she swept the short train of champagne-colored fabric to the side as she found purchase on the slats. Her mother would be having an absolute hissy fit if she could see her right now.

"We already tried it her way, and the reason you're here and not her is because I thought I could rely on you not to go all Principessa royal this, royal that on me. We both know that is *not* a recipe for success."

"I don't know..." Fran pushed herself up from the bed and wandered over to stand behind her friend, their gazes connecting in the mirror. "It worked out pretty well for Luca and me."

"You and Luca have an entire village at your disposal!"

Fran's musical laugh filled the room. "It was a great day, wasn't it?"

"Amazing. Enough glamor to tide my mother over until my brother decides to get married."

"*Pfft!* Hardly!" Fran rolled her eyes. "I suppose Dad *did* go a bit over-the-top with the catering, didn't he?"

"You should see what *my* father brought over. His suitcase was full of food and nothing else!" Bea's hand swept across the arc of her swollen tummy. "*Oof!* I think this baby girl is going to be part focaccia and part wedding cake if the past few weeks are anything to go by! Italian made, that's for sure!"

Fran took up a lock of Bea's hair and started weaving it into an intricate plait along her hairline. "You're still convinced it's going to be a girl?"

"She," Bea answered solidly. "I'm sure of it."

"I thought you weren't going to find out?"

"We haven't, but… You should know by now—a mother can sense things."

Fran stepped to Bea's side and put her hands on her own growing belly. "It's madness, isn't it? The two of us pregnant at the same time?"

"Jamie would say it's the world proving to us that we can show our mothers how it's *really* done."

"Jamie would say anything to make sure you're here with him in this beautiful home, about to embark on a beautiful life together." Fran grinned, returning to her role as wedding hairdresser. "It's so great the hospital is only a fifteen-minute drive away."

"Mmm…" Bea nodded. "Great for work and great for when my water breaks!"

"I can't believe how much your hair has grown. It's *so* beautiful now." Fran pulled an apologetic face in the mirror and rapidly covered. "I mean the platinum thing was good for a while, but—"

"Well, you're not supposed to dye it when you're pregnant, are you? And it wasn't really *me*," Bea said, pulling a face in the mirror. "A lot of things weren't me over the past couple of years, but now…?"

She looked around the huge old high-ceilinged room, its corners stacked with boxes yet to be unpacked. Only the antique bed and the cradle beside it—lying in wait for its little occupant to make an entrance—were already made up and ready for use.

"Now I'm finally at home."

Jamie glanced at his watch again, his brow crinkling further when Luca gave a rich, throaty laugh.

"Relax!" He clapped an arm around the nervous groom. "I thought the whole point of having your wedding at your house was so you could enjoy yourself!"

"It would be *completely* enjoyable if my bride would ever—" Whatever else he'd been going to say vanished. There, at the doorway to their centuries-old sitting room, was an angel.

Beatrice had never looked so beautiful. Her dark hair had been magicked into an intricate updo. Miniscule little plaits and curls of mahogany hair outlined her perfect face. Lips full and pinkened with emotion rather than lipstick. He knew she hadn't put on a lick of makeup since she and her mother had agreed to disagree on "the true aesthetic of a princess." The swoop and swell of her stomach made his heart skip a beat.

A husband and a father all in the space of a month.

The celebrant they had chosen for their simple ceremony cleared his throat, and Beatrice's father jumped up from the armchair where he'd been making friends with Francesca and Luca's latest canine companion.

"Beatrice! *Amore...*" He raised a fist to his mouth to stem a sob. "You look beautiful," he added in English as he reached out his arm for her to take.

There was only a handful of steps to take from the doorway to just in front of the French windows, looking out onto the sprawling back garden and the farmers' fields beyond, but with each step Beatrice took Jamie felt his heart pound with greater conviction and pride than he thought he had ever felt before.

When Beatrice's father dropped a kiss onto his daughter's cheek and passed her hand over to Jamie's he whispered something in Italian—clearly meant for his future son-in-law's hearing. Jamie's mind was too scrambled to translate it perfectly, but he got the gist. *Take care of my little girl.*

He gave him a nod. There was nothing that would stop him from loving and protecting the woman by his side ever again.

Time took on an otherworldly quality, and it seemed that just a few moments later Jamie was pulling his beautiful wife in to him with one hand, while the other tipped her chin up so he could seal their wedding vows with a kiss.

When at last they broke apart he swept the tears of joy from her cheeks as the tiniest wedding party in history applauded their brand-new union.

"Are you ready to start your life as Mrs. Coutts?" he asked before they stepped away from the "altar."

"Only if you're ready to go and get the car keys," she replied, both her hands swooping over the rich arc of champagne fabric swaddling her belly as she sucked in a sharp intake of breath.

"Are you…?" Jamie looked at the other faces in the room, each as wide-eyed as he was. "Do you mean we…?"

Beatrice nodded, the smile on her face near enough reaching from ear to ear. "A husband *and* a father. All on the same day!"

Jamie ran a few steps toward the Victorian-tiled foyer for the keys, then doubled back to his brand-new wife and took her hand in his, forcing himself to take a steadier pace as they walked to the door.

He barked out orders to Fran to get Beatrice's shawl, to

Beatrice's bemused father to find the prepacked suitcase and to Luca to grab the wedding cake.

"You planned this, didn't you?" he whispered into his wife's ear. "The best wedding present of all."

She answered with a kiss, and by the time they had broken apart everyone had whirled into action and it were in place to head off to the hospital for an entirely new escapade as husband and wife.

"Mrs. Coutts?" Jamie swept open the door and scooped up his wife. "I know this isn't the doorway you were expecting to go through after we were married, but are you ready for the next stage of our adventure?"

"With you by my side?" she asked, nestling into the crook between his chin and shoulder. "Every day for the rest of my life."

* * * * *

[illegible] and [illegible] a great [illegible] everything [illegible]

"You glanced [illegible] about [illegible]," he [illegible] that his [illegible] wedding [illegible]."

She [illegible] back [illegible] by [illegible] whistle into action [illegible] to the [illegible] round.

[illegible] work [illegible] his [illegible] after [illegible] back [illegible] for the [illegible] adventure."

"What [illegible]," he asked [illegible] at my life."

THE ITALIAN'S RUNAWAY PRINCESS

ANDREA BOLTER

For Ellen

CHAPTER ONE

HER ROYAL HIGHNESS Princess Luciana de la Isla de Izerote finally inhaled the warm air of Florence, Italy. The secret journey from her home, an island near the coast of Spain, had been difficult. At last she was under the Tuscan sun, the yellow glow much different from the seascape she was used to. But the liberation she expected to feel as she took her first breath of freedom was hardly as she'd hoped.

As a matter of fact, Luciana was starting to feel afraid being alone. She was short of breath from walking too fast away from the encounter at the jewelry store, where she had been unsuccessful in converting a palace ruby into a typical tourist's spending money. Worse still, three teenage boys seemed to be following her. Swiveling her head enough to take a look at them behind her, she saw they were scruffy and wore shabby T-shirts and track pants. These unexpected companions made her entire escape plan seem not only reckless, but like it was about to become dangerous.

"*Bambolina*, let us see your necklace," one of the boys called out as they closed the distance between themselves and the princess. "We'll buy your jewel."

Luciana hastened her pace. She'd arrived in Florence

to have an adventure before she lived the rest of her life in royal duty. The escapade didn't include being chased by thugs who might be trying to steal the jewelry she'd brought with her to sell as a way to finance her trip, given that she had no actual money of her own. The princess quickened to almost a run as her hand clutched the ruby pendant that hung from a heavy chain. Her sense of direction turned all around, she didn't even know where she was headed.

The boys behind her may or may not have seen that she had other pieces of jewelry in the purse that hung from a long leather strap on one of her shoulders, crossing her body and slapping against her at the opposite hip as she rushed away from them. She might have been able to run faster had she not also been toting a wheeled suitcase that contained her belongings for her three weeks as a Florentine tourist. After which time, she'd return to Izerote. And to her obligations, including her arranged marriage to King Agustin de la Isla de Menocita, the widower thirty years her senior from a neighboring island.

Princess Luciana had thought about this getaway for a long time, plotting exactly how she'd make her way to Florence and how she'd finance the travels. What she hadn't counted on was how problematic it would be to sell jewelry. Having had no experience, she didn't know that the shops would require paperwork and authentication.

After she'd made it from the island to her first stop in Barcelona, she'd needed the first installment of cash for the train tickets to Florence and to buy some food. One jeweler had directed her to another of less repute, and he to another still, until she'd sold an amethyst cocktail ring for far less than its worth.

She knew little about city streets, having spent most

of her life behind the palace walls of Izerote. Leaving only to attend official engagements and social functions accompanied by palace security, she was always safely sequestered in private cars, boats and planes. That was exactly why she'd come to Florence, the place she'd fallen in love with through art, books and movies. To experience being a simple tourist, to wander here and there without an itinerary or bodyguards, was to be a once-in-a-lifetime dream.

Having trouble selling the jewelry and now being followed just after she'd arrived was turning it into a nightmare.

"Bella." One of the boys hurried even closer to her, his use of the endearment for *beautiful* sounding like a snake's hiss that terrified her.

"Signorina. *Carina. Tesoro...*" Another bounced around to the other side of her, trying every name he could think of to get her to stop and address him directly.

With a yank on her suitcase, she began to run faster, heart racing. She thought about calling out for help to the first person she saw, but she didn't want to attract attention to herself. Her tiny island country was not well-known to most the world, but nonetheless, if questioned, she was a princess and it would appear odd that she was alone on the streets of central Florence. No one knew she was here, and she wanted to keep it that way.

Turning a corner, the boys chased after her and one pulled on the strap of her purse.

"Stop. Leave me alone," Luciana cried out and broke free.

A part of her fully expected her father King Mario's security team to have outwitted her already, to know exactly where she was and to direct unseen bodyguards to arrive at any moment to whisk her back to Izerote without letting her have the grand escapade she'd planned. With these boys harassing her, she almost wished they would.

Thinking quickly, she worked in front of her stomach to block the boys' view as she removed the rest of the jewels from her purse and held them tightly in her free hand. If they managed to steal her purse, at least they would find it empty.

"You give us that purse, right now," one of the boys jeered in a threatening tone.

"Get away from me," Luciana shouted. She looked to see if anyone else was behind her, her suitcase wobbling. As she turned back around, she tripped over something on the ground and crashed right into…

The broad shoulders and chest of a man. Specifically, her face slammed directly into the center of the man's muscular chest. As she approximated where her nose hit into him, she estimated just how tall a man he was. Six foot three, at least. Her head involuntarily turned a bit sideways so that her cheek could replace her nose as she pressed against him. Because that exact spot was solid, warm, smelled like clean laundry, and she quite liked it. Although she knew she needed to bend her neck back in order to see the face of the man she'd crushed into, something in her resisted the idea and she simply wanted to nuzzle her face into his rock-hard chest for the foreseeable future.

"Hello," a voice from somewhere inside the man's body crawled into her. "Do you need help?" His very deep timbre completely enveloped her in muscles and sounds. He could be yet another foe, but it didn't feel that way.

One thing she knew for sure was that it was not the

chest of King Agustin de la Isla de Menocita, the man she was to marry in three weeks. Not only was King Agustin much smaller in stature than the man she pressed into, her fiancé spoke in a voice high and clipped. Nothing like the smooth-as-cappuccino voice of the man her cheek was touching.

"These boys are trying to steal my purse." Princess Luciana spoke into the good-smelling man's chest, knowing that he'd be able to hear her even though her mouth was far lower than his ear. She clutched her jewels so tightly that her fingernails cut into her palms.

His response was to do what every fiber in her being had actually hoped he would since she bumped into him. He placed both of his long arms around her and pulled her into a tight hold, encircling her in the most complete way. *"Mia amata—"* he used the words of a lover "—you're so late. I was running to the train station to find you."

Realizing that he was pretending to be with her as a way to shake off these would-be criminals, Luciana knew enough to play along. "I stopped at the jewelry store."

"Can I do something for you gentlemen?" The pretend lover turned his attention to the thugs. The boys seemed to be taking stock of the situation now that the good-smelling man had arrived on the scene. Without answering, they lingered awhile longer. "I repeat, can I do something for you?" the man with the gigantic strong arms around the princess shouted in a voice menacing enough to scare them.

Luciana craned her neck so that she could look up to see the man's face. As if the mere feel of his chest and tone of his voice wasn't enough, she now stared at one of the most handsome men she had ever seen.

Pale skin served to draw extra attention to the sparkling light blue eyes. He had high cheekbones, a full red mouth and a head full of beautiful golden curls, like a subject in a painting from the Renaissance, an era when Florence was abuzz with intellectual, scientific and creative discovery. A time in history that was one of the reasons Luciana had wanted to explore this important city.

"Oh, no, signore," said one of the boys behind her.

"We were taking a walk on this lovely day," another singsonged.

Only after they scattered away did the man with the lavish blond curls let go of Luciana. They looked directly into each other's eyes for the first time. She thought she might have been struck by a bolt of lightning, but the sunny skies rendered that unlikely.

The blue-eyed man then began to disentangle the long purse strap that had become twisted around Luciana's arm after the boys tried to pull it away from her. The strap was so mangled it became a puzzle to unravel it, and he gave his full attention to the task. Finally, he gingerly placed the strap back on her shoulder and the purse fell naturally across her opposite hip as intended.

The care this total stranger was extending to her was surprising. And also a first for Princess Luciana. Commoners were not permitted to touch her, except on occasions of handshakes during official processionals through the streets or when meeting military heroes, and under close supervision. But certainly nothing involving a gorgeous man with enormous hands putting his arms around her or arranging a purse onto her body.

Only then did Luciana remember what she held in her still tightly closed fist. "Oh, my gosh, I'd forgotten that I'd been holding my jewels all of this time. I thought surely those boys were going to tear my purse off me, so I grabbed the contents."

"Why are you carrying such valuables in a flimsy purse on a city street?"

"It's a long story."

The princess opened her purse and placed her jewels in a zipped pocket inside. As the man with the gigantic hands said, it was absurd that she'd let the few palace jewels, which she had chosen as sacrificial lambs to buy her this voyage of freedom, be tossed around in a thin pouch of leather not properly protected. That was only one of the possibly crazy decisions she had made.

There was no turning back now.

"Thank you." She bowed her head to the Renaissance painting of a man on the street. "You saved me from danger and harm."

"That's me. A regular Prince Charming."

Her Royal Highness Princess Luciana de la Isla de Izerote had never wished harder that words were true.

"May I show you to your destination?" asked the handsome savior after the thugs were long gone from view.

"All right," Luciana answered although she didn't know what her destination was. Which, as she was zooming to Italy through Spain and France on high-speed trains, felt like a marvelous relief. To be able to go wherever she wanted, whenever she wanted. Not to be bound by a schedule or accompanied by an entourage. Now, the unfamiliarity of all that liberty had her frightened.

"By the way, I'm Gio. Giovanni Grassi. And you are…?" He took hold of Luciana's suitcase handle and gave it a tug.

"Luci…" She left it at that, the nickname her mother

used to call her when she was a small child. A name she hadn't heard in years. It was fitting that she thought of her mother now, who had died without ever fulfilling her own quest for the bit of autonomy that Luciana hoped to have.

"It's a pleasure to meet you, Luci."

She wasn't sure that she should be letting this man she didn't know pull her suitcase. What if he ran away with it? Or what if he was luring her into some kind of trap so that he could steal her jewels for himself?

Princess Luciana sensed that he meant well. After all, no one had forced him to come to her aid as he did. And she couldn't just continue standing on the street now that those threatening boys had been chased off. She'd lost all sense of direction, not that she knew where she was going in the first place. Had she been able to sell the ruby, she would have returned to the train station to look for a tourist bureau that could help her find accommodations. That could still be her plan. But now she wasn't comfortable walking alone with the jewels.

So they began forward, Gio's grip on her suitcase keeping its wheels cooperating under his control. Princess Luciana caught a reflection of herself in the glass of a shop window. In the commotion of her arrival, her failure at the jewelry store near the train station and the threat from those boys, she'd completely forgotten that she wore a wig in disguise. While Izerote was not a famous island and her monarchy had not made her a recognizable face throughout the world, she knew there was a good chance that her father would send someone looking for her. Even though she had left him a note promising to return in three weeks to marry King Agustin as planned. If the cloak she donned could help throw any operatives of King Mario's off her track, it was well worthwhile. Plus, she liked the idea of having a new appearance.

Gone were the long girlish locks of hair that spent many evenings as a showplace for the family tiaras. Now the thick brown strands that fell halfway down her back were bound and tucked under a blond wig she'd bought in Barcelona. The wig was cut into a lob, a term the princess knew from idly flipping through fashion magazines was the hip description for a long bob.

The surprisingly realistic-looking hairstyle fell in sleek sheets to the tops of her shoulders where it curled under just a bit. Every move she made caused the lob to give a slight swish that Luciana found chic. The hair made her feel like a woman on the go. Which was quite unlike the fussy preplanned existence she had always known. Although her *let's see what happens* attitude, so out of character, had almost led her into hazard.

"Where to, signorina?"

The scare of those boys had been an immediate awakening to the perils she needed to look out for, and she didn't know what she should tell Gio Grassi. Yes, his beautiful crystal-blue eyes seemed trustworthy, but outward appearances told her nothing.

Nonetheless, she had to start somewhere.

"I don't know, Gio. I find myself arriving in Florence with less money than I had planned. Would you know of a reasonably priced hotel?"

"No, actually, I'm sorry I don't. I grew up here in Florence but I've spent many years traveling for business. I no longer know the city."

Disappointment rung through her. Barcelona had been quite an eye-opener once she discovered that the jeweler to whom she had intended to sell the first of her lot was unwilling to buy what Luciana referred to as her *estate pieces* without proof of ownership and certifications. She'd made up a story about the jewels belonging to her recently deceased grandmother.

At her begging, that jeweler put her in touch with another jeweler who refused her and sent her to yet another, this one located in a downtrodden part of town. He gave her far less than she had estimated for the first piece. She knew now that this trip would have to be on more of a budget than she'd originally envisioned.

That didn't matter. At least she was here.

"I'll need to sell more of my jewels."

"More of them? Does that mean you have already sold some?"

Yes, but she didn't need to tell that to Gio.

"I had tried at a shop near the train station. That's where those boys began following me."

"Florence is a big city with people both opulent and poor, honest and not. You should watch out at every turn."

Luciana was already learning that the hard way. But as they turned a corner into a piazza, a public square, her troubles receded and the widest of smiles swept across her face. Here it was. The Florence she'd seen in movies and travel websites, and read about in books. Firenze, the central city of Tuscany, with its centuries of trade and finance, art and medicine, religion and politics.

People moved across the piazza in every different direction. Fashionable girls giggled as they snapped selfies of themselves. A tour group of older travelers dutifully stopped so that their guide could point out landmarks. Four men stood in front of a shop arguing, their loud voices and hand gestures marking them as uniquely Italian. A flock of children chased pigeons, their overjoyed faces bursting with surprise every time one of the birds made an unexpected escape. Two lovers sat close on a bench while they shared a fresh orange, the woman holding the peel in her hand.

Every which way, people wove in between each other to get to where they were going. It was everything the princess had imagined it would be, alive and magnificent under the autumn of the Tuscan sky. She placed her hand over her mouth as she took it all in.

This was what Luciana came to see. To be a part of this city that had always held her fascination, if only for a stolen moment of her lifetime. She drew in a slow breath. The air wasn't as thick and pure as it was in pristine Izerote. Florence had a particular fragrance, one she suspected it had for centuries.

It smelled like free will.

Which she had never inhaled before.

As if the panorama of all these people and their doings and their businesses and their architecture and their dogs wasn't enough, Luciana stood witnessing it in the company of a chivalrous, and she had to acknowledge gorgeous, Italian man.

For the first time she took notice of what Giovanni Grassi was wearing. A tweed blazer with a pink button-down shirt and tan tie, jeans with a brown belt and brown oxford shoes. All of impeccable quality. He looked perhaps like a young professor, the type schoolgirls would giggle around but loved to gape at as he explained the important trigonometry equation on a chalkboard behind him. Reluctant hottie. That was the moniker the celebrity websites used for his type.

Hottie, for sure. Reluctant, she didn't know yet.

"Ah yes, Firenze," Gio chimed in. "There's nowhere

like it in the world. Some things change, others remain the same as they have for centuries."

Nothing ever changed in Izerote, Luciana reflected. It lagged far behind the rest of the world in technology and culture and commerce. Her father, King Mario, and his father before him were not forward-thinking rulers like some royal families were. The price they'd paid for the lack of progress was steep, as many residents or their adult children were leaving the island.

However, Princess Luciana was not in Florence to solve the issues of her island, although she didn't doubt that in this great city of thought and industry many dilemmas of the world had been debated.

"Here's my situation, Gio," Luciana started, not knowing what to do about her predicament. One way or another, this trip would come to an end. Either she'd have her three weeks here before she returned to Izerote to marry King Agustin and produce his heirs. Or her father would send someone to hunt after her and her visit would be cut short. Either way, now was all there was, so she had better make every second count. "I have no money. That's why I need to sell some of my jewels, in order to pay for a hotel room."

"Sell your jewels. That sounds so positively archaic. You may have noticed this is *modern day* where people pay for goods and services with credit cards or through apps on their phone," he said with a cute chuckle that sent a tingle down her spine. What a strange reaction she was having to this total stranger.

She couldn't explain to him that while she did carry credit cards, she couldn't use them because they were traceable. That's why she needed to obtain cash for the trip. "I know, it does sound rather medieval."

"Have you traveled forward in time? What era are you from?"

"You have no idea how right you are."

"Are you running from something?"

"You could say that."

"A mystery woman."

"You could say that, too."

"All right, Signorina Luci, if that's really your name. For how long do you need a hotel room?"

"Three weeks," she answered with ease. Because it was exactly three weeks and one day until she was to marry. Three weeks. That's how long she hoped to stay in Florence. If she had her druthers, she'd stay until the last possible minute and arrive back in Izerote just in time to be pinned into her wedding gown. The gown that had already been chosen for her, a chaste lacy puffball with a high neck and long sleeves that was as tight and confining as her impending marriage. Nothing like what she'd wear if the choice was up to her. If, for example, she was to be getting married of her own volition to a tall attractive man with sparkling blue eyes and golden curly hair.

"Three weeks," he repeated. "And how much do you expect to garner from the sale of those jewels?"

Nowhere near what she thought she might, Luciana mused. So, realistically, considering the price she'd fetched in Barcelona, she quoted Gio a figure. Still unsure if she should be confiding her financial woes to him.

"Twenty-one nights…"

"Twenty-one," she confirmed knowing that she wouldn't need a hotel room in Florence on the twenty-second, after her wedding. She winced at the thought of her wedding night and what would be expected of her from King Agustin, a widower who presumably had more experience in the matrimonial bed than she did. Hopefully he'd be patient and compassionate toward her when the time came.

"Then here is how much you'd have to spend each day." Gio performed a mental calculation and gave her a number that was far less than the rate of the hotels she had been looking at online.

"Do you think I could get a hotel room for that price? It doesn't need to be fancy, only clean."

"Luci, for that money I don't think you could find anything suitable, clean or safe."

He glanced at his watch.

It wasn't right to detain this man any longer, despite the fear that was returning in her.

"I'll figure something out. Thank you again for your assistance."

"You're quite welcome. Enjoy Florence," Gio said and then turned to walk away.

Prompted by his departure, a couple of tears smarted Luciana's eyes as she blinked them back. Which was ridiculous. She'd come to experience Florence alone. Gio had simply lent a hand to a damsel in distress. He was a stranger, now on his merry way as was appropriate.

After a few steps, he stopped and pivoted back.

"What are you planning to do?"

"I don't know. If you could point me in the direction of the train station, I'll go back there."

"I can try to find you a hotel. Let's get off the street. Come with me."

"Oh. No. I'll be fine."

He furrowed his brow. "Very well, then. Goodbye, Luci."

"Goodbye."

But when he walked away again, anxiety gripped Luciana's chest. Those boys had really scared her. And not having the cash she needed was a huge problem. She hadn't pictured herself alone and lost on the street.

"Gio," she blurted out, quickly catching up with him. "Thank you. I would appreciate your help."

Gio stopped in front of a large building with double doors made of oak, each bearing a brass doorknob. Although the structure was hundreds of years old, the fob entry system was proof it had been updated. When the tiny red light on the mechanism turned to green, Gio opened the door and held it wide for Luci to enter. Pulling her suitcase in with him, he then closed the door behind him. He led her through the stone tunnel passageway that kept the inner property well secluded from the busy streets of Florence.

The tunnel was a short distance, allowing Gio to see the sunshine that met it at the other end. He and his brother, Dante, used to play all sorts of games in this tunnel when they were kids.

"Where are we?" Luci asked with understandable trepidation.

"My home," Gio said as they came into the light of the central courtyard.

"Your home?" Luci began to take in the surroundings.

"My family's home. No one is here right now, but yes, this is where I grew up."

Up until a few days ago, Gio hadn't been home in many months. As the president of research, development and project management for his family's company, Grasstech, the world's largest manufacturer of computer components, Gio spent his life traveling among the company's operations centers all over the world. He touched down in Florence for crucial in-person meetings or for family occasions, but was then soon boarding a plane to his next destination.

"This is so beautiful," Luci exclaimed as she did a slow 360-degree turnaround in the inner courtyard of the villa compound.

"It's been in our family for six generations."

Indeed, Villa Grassi was a special place. It wasn't a showy high-tech complex befitting the Grassi family's standing in the computer science world. Instead the property retained its old-world charms, thanks to Gio's mother, although with plenty of modern conveniences. The villa comprised several stone buildings, all painted in a mustardy yellow color accented by the red terra-cotta roofs and wood trim.

"You live here?" Luci asked, still taking in the details of the central garden.

Mamma mia, but this young woman was pretty. Not just pretty, really, although Gio struggled for the right word to describe her. *Soulful*, maybe. There was depth in her light brown eyes. They were eyes with questions, eyes that longed. The dark, thick eyebrows that crowned those lovely pools served to set off their radiance even more. The sleek blond hair read as stylish, not that Gio knew much about fashion. Her petite frame was dressed with polish in her black skirt and gray blazer.

Why did this upscale-looking young woman have only jewels and no money? Something was quite off here, which Gio found suspicious. He would forever keep up his guard after the disastrous mistake he'd made in Hong Kong by trusting the wrong person. People weren't always who they said they were.

It seemed all but impossible that this woman in front of him could have somehow staged the incident with the boys on the street so that she could bump into him. That she had known where he was coming from and where he was headed. However, he'd learned the hard way that some people would say or do anything to get what they were after. Danger came in all shapes and sizes.

"I didn't understand what you said. Do you live here?"

"Not since childhood," he answered, still sizing her up. "But now I am home, so it seems."

The two-story main house anchored the buildings. Five steps led to the front door, constructed of the same oak as the door to the street. He looked up to the second-floor window that was his boyhood bedroom. Like all the windows, the sill was adorned with boxes holding plants in bright reds, oranges and yellows befitting the fall season. Beside it was the window in his brother Dante's bedroom. Late at night they'd tie up sheets to hold on to and swing into each other's bedrooms like Tarzan. Gio smiled at the antics of his daredevil brother, who hadn't changed a bit even as an adult.

In the courtyard, a cast-stone fountain gurgled with water, surrounded by the benches where his grandparents used to spend their afternoons. His grandfather would good-naturedly yell at Gio and Dante to slow down as they played their racing games in the tunnel. Their grandmother, content to sit for hours with her needlework, would ply the boys with blood orange juice from their fruit trees to drink, the color of which was still Gio's favorite hue in the world.

"We use the cottages now." Gio pointed to the two outbuildings beside the house, both of which had entrances that faced the courtyard.

"You said *we*. Who is we?"

"My brother, Dante, and I. And other relatives who come to stay. My parents still live in the big house when they're here, but we have a vineyard and winery in the countryside where they spend most of their time now that they've retired." His father had built Grasstech from a small purveyor of computer central processing units, known as CPU chips, into the multibillion-dollar conglomerate it was today. "Dante is working with our affiliates in India, now that..."

Gio was glad he stopped himself. Luci didn't need to know that Dante had failed at helming the company, which was why Gio had returned to Florence to do just that. Oversharing information had gotten him into trouble in the past, some of which he still needed to find a way to clean up.

In the silence of stopping himself, he focused on Luci's attentive face. There was something utterly enchanting about her, with that long stately neck and those curious eyes. She was much shorter than he had noticed at first. Of course, with him so tall, almost everyone was petite to him. Her bowed pink lips complemented her porcelain skin. Her posture was so straight and that throat so graceful she could pass for a noblewoman or a young duchess. Yet she had an inner spunk that made the thought of her as a stuffy royal thoroughly implausible.

Good heavens! Women should be the last thing on Gio's mind now that he'd returned home with a to-do list a mile long. And it was a woman who had got the company into trouble in the first place. He would be staying far away from them.

"That's the Duomo!" Luci pointed to the top of the dome visible in the distance past the villa walls. Florence's cathedral was one of the most identifiable sights in the city.

"Have you been inside?"

Her enthusiasm was contagious.

"No. I'm looking forward to seeing it. This is my first time in Florence. You rescued me just as I arrived."

A little wiggle traveled between his shoulder blades when she said the word *rescued.*

Now that he had, in fact, rescued her, what was he going to do with her? He'd find her a hotel. But some of Grasstech's investors were in town for dinner and he needed to get dressed, so it had to be quick. He wasn't looking forward to all their chitchat that bored him to tears. Nothing of substance was ever discussed at these things. Plus they'd all be bringing their stodgy spouses. The wives would ask why a nice young man like him didn't have a wife or a girlfriend.

With enough on his mind already, Luci's problems couldn't become his. Yet she'd been so shaken by those nasty boys following her, she finally accepted his offer of help.

She readjusted her purse on her shoulder, the one that contained her jewels. "May I ask you, Gio, would there be *any* hotel at *any* price that you could recommend for the night? I'll have to reevaluate my budget, but I do need somewhere for tonight."

He could give it a try. Pulling his phone out of his jacket pocket, he punched in a hotel search, hoping he'd recognize the names of some that were reputable.

"Yes," he spoke after calling one. "Do you have any rooms available for tonight? I see. *Grazie.*"

He phoned another. "Have you a room tonight? No? *Grazie.*" After three more, his patience was up.

"That's all right, Gio," Luci said, although the quaver in her voice belied her words. "I'll find somewhere."

With her obvious lack of street savvy? What if some other criminals tried to take advantage of her like the boys did with the jewelry? He might not know this vulnerable young woman, but a gentleman was a gentleman and he could not send her away alone.

"Why don't you stay here tonight?" Gio voiced the thought that had been bubbling up, despite raising caution. "I'm staying in this one." He pointed to one of the side-by-side cottages. "Why don't you sleep in the other?" He hoped that suggestion wouldn't prove to be a mistake, but he couldn't think of what else to do. He'd station her here, and the staff at his office could help get her situated tomorrow.

"Oh, no, I couldn't." Luci quickly shook her head with a side-to-side motion. "It wouldn't be right."

He put his hand over his heart in mock insult. "What do you take me for? I assure you I offer only to fulfill my quota of rescuing beautiful maidens from the mean streets of Florence."

Was he *flirting* with her?

"How are you doing so far?"

"I'm desperately behind. You'd be helping me out."

She looked at him with a bite to her lip. He knew she was deciding on his merits versus his potential risks.

"I'll only consent if you let me repay you in some way."

The idea quickly fell from his lips. "I have a very dull dinner with some investors to attend tonight. They will have no doubt chosen the poshest restaurant in Florence with a continental menu that manages to avoid anything authentically Italian. They'll pick an impressive bottle of wine chosen for its price and torture the sommelier as they swirl it around in their glasses pretending to know something about the vintage. They'll discuss the weather and the latest political scandal in Italy, and it will make watching paint dry sound compelling. Would you like to join me?"

"With an invitation like that, how could I possibly refuse?" Luci answered with a huge smile that shot straight into Gio's heart. He returned the grin.

Once he'd extended the invitation to dinner, it suddenly sounded like a marvelous idea. She was far more interesting than the blah-blah-blah he'd have to exchange with the investors. Rightly, they'd save any substantial conversation for boardroom conferences.

Why shouldn't he have a pleasant evening with an attractive woman? He knew he'd never take it any further than that. It was just dinner. And bringing her with him was better than leaving her alone on his property tonight. He'd get her out of the villa in the morning.

"It's set then? Pick you up right here?" He gestured to the fountain.

"I have a cocktail-length dress. Will that be sufficient?"

"And obviously you can accessorize." He pointed to the purse with all of the jewels. "You'll be the toast of the town."

"I hope not." Luci's eyes opened in alarm.

"I was only joking. See you at eight."

CHAPTER TWO

"THANK YOU, VIGGO." Gio acknowledged his driver as he parked the car in front of the villa. Viggo quickly got out of his seat and dashed around to the passenger side to open the door for Luciana and Gio. After Gio helped her out of the car, she straightened the skirt of the pale blue dress she'd worn to dinner with him and his investors.

It was her little secret that she'd chosen the dress to complement the color of her handsome companion's eyes. Of course, the color of Her Royal Highness Princess Luciana's dress for the evening was the least of her secrets. Nonetheless, with her cool blond wig, silver shoes and diamond earrings, she felt like a woman who had been on a real date with a real man, as opposed to a shielded virgin locked in a stone tower. Gio had quickly become part of her grand adventure.

"Do we have to go in?" Luciana touched Gio's jacket sleeve as he reached in his pocket for his fob entry to the wooden exterior door.

"Would you like to walk?"

"I'd love to."

Driving from the restaurant after the dinner, Luciana was agog as they drove past landmarks she wanted to visit while she was here. The incredible piazzas, historic churches, marketplaces, museums and neighborhoods she'd seen only as an armchair traveler in the solitude of her palace sitting room. While she'd traveled to many places in the world for ceremonies and royal engagements, she'd never seen them as a tourist, able to meander and linger, and appreciate anything that caught her fancy. She could hardly wait to get started.

"Let's walk this way." Gio gently placed his hand on the small of her back to direct her away from the villa door. Her awareness arched to meet his touch.

"Thank you for accompanying me to dinner. As I mentioned, I generally leave the finessing of investors to my brother, Dante, now that our father has retired."

"And Dante was unable to attend tonight?"

"Dante is spending some time at our offices in Mumbai. We have restructured the company and I will now serve as CEO."

"What did you do before?"

"Product development. Which is where my heart is. You'd find me happier trying to make an AGP bus that can carry graphics faster than anything else on the market than you would seeing me in a conference room."

"AGP?"

"Accelerated graphics port."

"Of course," she joked. "How would I not know that?"

"But now I'll do what needs to be done for the company. Actually, I welcome the opportunity to do things my way. To get them right."

"Are things not right?"

"Look at those two." Gio pointed to two dogs on leashes across the street that barked at and sniffed each other with great interest.

Ah, Luci noted, she had asked too snoopy a question

about Gio's work and he'd changed the subject. Her inner Princess Luciana should have known better than to pry, in spite of her curiosity to know more about him.

She hoped to recover with, "Your investors were a lovely group of people. I saw photos on many a smartphone of grandchildren performing in school plays and rosebushes that had yielded prizewinners."

The princess was only too used to smiling and taking interest in the lives of total strangers. In fairness, she was always quite honored that people she met wanted to share details about their lives with her. Meeting people was one of the things she did like about royal life. But not as much as she liked this, walking in the open air with Gio, and not a handler or schedule in sight.

"Enough about me," he said as they continued after watching the dogs perform mating rituals. "What do you do for a living?"

"I'm a teacher," Luciana fibbed. That was what she would be if she could. Royal duties combined with her father's outdated ways kept her ambition from coming to fruition. "I spend most of my days talking to four-year-olds."

"A teacher? I never would have figured you for that."

"Why not?"

"You're very—" he searched for the right word "—elegant. The way you handled yourself at dinner was distinguished. Well, there we go when we stereotype or pigeonhole anyone. My apologies."

If he only knew. How badly she didn't want to always have to be elegant. How her father raised her in a very old-fashioned monarchy she didn't question, where Luciana had been groomed her whole life to make appearances. To never share anything of herself, her hopes, her likes. To be only in the service of the crown. While she led a life of luxury and privilege for which she was grateful, her heart ached for more.

Perhaps she'd be content if the man she was to marry wasn't so much older and who, in the handful of meetings she'd had with him, hadn't talked to her as if she were already his possession. Maybe her life would be sublime if she was to wed a bold and good-humored man like say, just for example, Gio.

She blushed at her own thought as she noted the shadows the night sky cast onto Gio's defined cheekbones.

"*Bellissima*, what is a teacher doing traveling alone with only a bag full of jewels to pay her way?"

As she had learned in her years of training, restraint was always the best policy, so rather than answer him, she occupied herself taking in the light of the moon and how it played against not only Gio's face but also the architecture of this great ancient city.

"Where are you from, Luci?" Gio pressed.

"Spain," she simplified.

She had a flush of concern that she was out late at night in a foreign country with a man she'd only just met. Half of her considered the potential danger, but the other half wanted to throw caution to the wind and grab as many experiences as she could out of this trip to Florence. Including this unexpected interlude with a beguiling man.

"Your Italian is flawless."

"I studied for many years."

Indeed, Princess Luciana had always been fascinated with Italian history, art and literature, especially the Renaissance period when Florence was the center of Europe. It was a thrill to finally use the language she had practiced so diligently. While she had been to Rome for royal occasions and adored it, the City of Lilies had always held her interest.

About a year ago, her father, King Mario, had informed her that she would be marrying widower King Agustin of the neighboring island Menocita. She didn't protest, always wanting to please her father after her mother had died.

Izerote was racked with problems. Because theirs was a tiny country with limited development, unemployment had become a crisis. As the current generation had grown, many households sent their offspring away for higher education or to seek jobs in Spain or the rest of the world. Without careers on the island for future generations, the population would continue to shrink.

On Menocita, King Agustin's father had brought tourism to their shores. Exclusive resorts along with family-friendly water sports and vacation rentals had turned the island into a year-round paradise that created thousands of jobs for the inhabitants. After King Agustin's wife died, he'd decided to find another island to merge with to create the same tourism and bring larger prosperity to his family name. When the proposal of marriage to his daughter came to King Mario, he could not refuse. In turn, Princess Luciana could not let her father or her subjects down, so she had no option but to agree to it.

Yes, a future she wouldn't have chosen for herself was looming. But at least she'd always have this. Florence. This journey of self-discovery and of making a single dream come true.

Luciana did feel badly that she had left her father a note saying only that she would return to Izerote to marry King Agustin, but that she was going to do this one thing before she did. She had previously begged him to let her, just once, leave the island without attendants, limousines and security details. It was a liberty she needed to know, if even for a short time. It was something she longed for, a wanderlust she wasn't able to silence. King Mario, an overly protective man especially after her mother was killed in a car accident in Madrid, denied her. And not wanting to cause him anymore grief, she acquiesced—until she could no longer.

She thought back to the trip to Paris King Mario did plan for Luciana and a cousin her age. When they were there, clothing stores were closed to the public so that they could shop alone, never paying for anything. When the girls walked down the boulevards, bodyguards trailed only a few paces behind. An entire hotel floor was rented despite their needing only two rooms. They visited a museum after midnight, fully staffed for just the two of them. While Luciana did appreciate her father's efforts, it was hardly what she'd had in mind.

With the wedding imminent, Princess Luciana's heart, her soul, the very essence of her being, insisted that she break away from the protocol that had been drilled into her. And drove her to do something completely for herself, as reckless as it was. So, she escaped the palace walls and her role as the perfect daughter and princess, leaving no hint of where she was going. She bought no tickets for her transportation, brought along no phone where her location could be traced. As drastic a step as it was to take palace jewels to sell, she hadn't been able to think of another way.

Three weeks that belonged only to her wasn't so very much to ask for.

After her walk with Gio and their return to his villa,

Luciana was tired. She'd face the issues of the jewels and finding a suitable place to stay tomorrow. For tonight, she was eternally grateful for his generosity.

They lingered at the halfway point between her guest cottage and his.

"I can't thank you enough for this."

"My pleasure, Luci. Thank you for accompanying me to the dinner." He crossed an arm over his waist and bowed forward to her in an exaggerated posture of formality that might have been funny if she was a different person.

"Did you sleep well?" Gio called up to Luci as she stepped out onto the small Juliet balcony of the guest cottage, wrapping her hands around the wrought iron railing. Properly known as a *balconet*, it wasn't large enough for a chair or table. It was meant for enjoying the view of the courtyard below and to peer out beyond the villa's walls. When Shakespeare included the architectural feature in his romantic tragedy, the nickname stuck.

It took considerable effort for Gio to pretend not to notice how the transparent fabric of the flowing white nightgown Luci wore hid nothing of her lovely curves underneath. But the sudden twitch in his core told the truth.

He placed the pot of coffee he was holding onto the small glass table near the fountain. "Would you like to join me for breakfast?"

"How magical to wake up and smell all of these flowers," Luci said with a sweeping arm surveying the courtyard's garden. "The lavender is so sweet."

The same view was available from Gio's bedroom, as the two cottages were identical. He had risen early and let himself into the main house to find some breakfast.

He glanced up to Luci again. It was actually nothing short of surreal that a beautiful woman stood on the balcony of his guesthouse in Florence, albeit that her status there was temporary. Surreal even that he was back home, as most of his adult life thus far had been spent living away. The idea of staying in one place might take some getting used to. "Come down and have some coffee."

Luci accepted the bid with, "Just give me a few minutes to get dressed."

An unfamiliar voice inside Gio wanted to beg her to come down as she was, so fetching did she look in her cotton gauze. But decorum won out.

Always buried in work, he had not been alone with a woman in quite a while. In spite of the fact that this unexpected maiden with the blond hair and the big brown eyes had landed in his lap yesterday, this was a very important morning. Which was why he'd chosen to wake at dawn, go for a run, shower and dress, all the while leaving himself enough time to have a relaxed breakfast.

Today was his first official day as CEO of Grasstech.

He stepped into his cottage to gather a laptop and some briefings he had been looking over and brought them out to the courtyard so he was ready to leave after breakfast. The two cottages were small but sufficient with a sitting room on the first floor, and a bedroom and bathroom upstairs. They were decorated in yellow, black and gold with expensive, but simple, furnishings. Gio's mother had told him that she'd recently redone the guest quarters and looked forward to his seeing them. Later, he'd ring her at the vineyard to offer his compliments.

Such coziness was unfamiliar to him. President of research, development and project management, Gio Grassi was accustomed to traversing the world, and preferred the anonymity of hotels. Sleek, modern hotel rooms looked no different to him whether he was in Cape Town or Seoul or Dallas. Hotels perfectly suited the life he had been leading. Everything at his disposal and on his own time clock.

When he was lost in concentration on a new project it could be hours, sometimes even days, that would pass while he was surrounded by computer parts and algorithms. He lived immersed in a technological world most people had no understanding of. Where he laid his head to rest was of little concern to him. Until now, when his entire lifestyle was about to change.

Gio hopped up the five steps from the courtyard to the main house to fetch the rolls and fruit the housekeeper had left for him. When he brought them to the outdoor table, Luci was coming out her front door, suitcase and purse in tow. In the morning sun, her eyes caught glints of light.

"Is something wrong?" she asked in reaction to his expression.

"Please, sit." He pulled out a chair for her to take her place at the table.

After coffee was poured and rolls were bitten into, Luci asked, "You're going to the Grasstech office today?"

"Yes. I've got to go be the boss man now," Gio said with a titter belying his mixed feelings on the transition. On one hand he was relieved to be taking full control of Grasstech and knew he would fine-tune operations and move the company even further forward. Yet the other side of him rather dreaded becoming the face of the empire. He'd made a mistake that had cost the company dearly and he had a lot of mopping up to do. In trusting his ex-girlfriend, Francesca, there were now leaked company secrets to contend with and a press ready to bring that information public.

"Thank you so much for your hospitality. I'll leave right after breakfast, so don't let me add to your troubles."

"Have we settled where you are going?" he asked with a quick glance at his watch. As strangely intriguing as this domestic scene was, he had a million other things on his mind. He wouldn't be finding out who this lovely Luci in front of him truly was. Not only didn't he have time for a woman in his life, he couldn't buy the story that she was a teacher. There was more going on with her than met the eye, and that was something he hadn't any business getting involved in.

"That's kind of you to consider my lodging something *we* are concerned about, but I'll figure it out on my own."

"Of course." But he couldn't leave it at that. Her mysterious identity notwithstanding, Gio's mother had taught him to be chivalrous, and after hearing yesterday about Luci's budget issues he wasn't going to have her traipsing alone around Florence looking for a cheap hotel that might not be safe.

"I'll have someone at my office look into hotels for you." The sooner he squared her safely away, the less he'd fret about it later.

"I couldn't impose like that."

"It's no imposition."

"Thank you but…it wouldn't be…"

If he let her go, he'd be distracted all day worrying if she was okay. And he needed his concentration today. "Why don't you go out and see some sights? We'll meet later and I can complain to you about my workday."

A giggle escaped from her, which brought a lovable little blush to her cheeks.

She had been an utterly flawless dinner date last night, charming his investors by laughing at their unfunny jokes and asking questions about their families to get them talking about themselves. Gio despised making small talk. Luci, who had appeared poised and almost regal in her blue silk dress, knew exactly how to field the evening, which took the pressure off him. He could return the favor. After that, she'd be out of his life and on with her holiday.

"It's settled, then. Why don't you leave your luggage here?" Gio stood and gathered up his things, having been alerted on his phone that his driver was here. "Where can my driver drop you?"

"I'll just wander out on my own."

He escorted her to the street. "See you here at six."

Gio's driver, Viggo, delivered him to the street-level glass doors of the Grasstech headquarters. The family kept a much larger campus of offices outside the city, but this central Florence location was where the company's important decisions were still made. Gio passed through to the main reception area where a few employees were congregating.

"Hello, Mr. Grassi," one greeted.

"Good morning, sir," another followed.

"Welcome, Mr. Grassi."

While he generally interacted with everyone he met on a first-name basis, he quite approved of the employees here addressing him formally at first. It was important to establish sole authority immediately.

That had been part of the problem with his brother in the top seat. While he admired Dante as being more of a people person than he was—his brother had become a sort of brand ambassador for their company—

Gio doubted he elicited much respect among the staff. Because, unfortunately, Dante spent more time being photographed with a different woman on his arm each evening at social functions than he did overseeing the company's operations. Whereas Gio understood the ins and outs of Grasstech's stronghold in the tech world and had specific plans on how to increase their dominance against the competition.

While Dante had been happy to use the press to his advantage, the media were actually Gio's first challenge of the day.

As he made his way down the corridor to the corner office that was originally his father's, Gio was aware of a pretty assistant in step beside him. Although she was an attractive young woman, Gio found his mind immediately flashed back to Luci's gracious smile as she engaged the older ladies last night with a discussion of favorite holiday memories. Something about Luci had gotten under his skin. Which he needed to put a stop to right away. The last thing he wanted to be embroiled with was a woman, especially now that deceitful Francesca was the cause of his most pressing problem.

"What can I get you, Mr. Grassi?" the assistant asked as she escorted him into his office.

"A large bottle of cold water. And send in Samuele, thank you."

"Yes, sir."

"Mio amico." Samuele di Nofri greeted Gio with a bear hug and affirmation of their lifelong friendship. The older man was Grasstech's director of operations and had been working with the company since the day Gio's father conceived of it. "Finally, we have you back in Firenze."

"Sit." Gio gestured to one of the leather chairs that faced his sleek steel desk.

"It was like yesterday that you were a boy, sitting at one of those desktop computers we used to keep here." Samuele pointed to a wall where a row of clunky old computers used to be lined up. Before everyone had laptops that weighed less than a cup of coffee. "Six years old and you would sit for hours writing code."

"Technology has come a long way since then."

"Grazie al cielo." Samuele kissed two fingers and lifted them to the sky.

"Although then, we didn't worry as much about security and hacking. Now look what I caused the company to have to deal with."

"It happens."

Yes, Gio's early proclivity for computers had led him to eventually receive multiple degrees from Stanford University in California's Silicon Valley. Then after years of apprenticeship in Tokyo, he emerged as one of the world's most respected component designers.

What Gio's education and experience hadn't taught him was how to look out for Francesca and her kind. With her eight-foot-long legs and her crimson red lips, she was a skilled and practiced seductress. She had set her sights on the workaholic techie Grassi brother and had not relented until she'd got what she wanted. Which was not his heart.

No, what Francesca wanted were secrets about Grasstech's new memory modules that were destined to take drop-in compatibility wider than the industry had seen before. So while Gio was conceiving, designing, testing and troubleshooting, Francesca had done what she did best.

Francesca Nefando, who had been hired to run analytic reports, was actually a world-class hacker. In a tight skirt and high heels.

"Fine, Samuele, you say it happens." Gio grimaced at the memory of the day he found out his proprietary DIMMs, dual inline memory modules, were being developed by a rival company with information only an insider could know. Samuele's kindly eyes tried to offer some comfort. "But now that the industry press has found out, Grasstech could look weak in the field."

"That's why the board of directors tell me that they want you to issue a statement to the media. Because you are taking over as the CEO, they see this as an opportunity to solidify your name as the trailblazer of the company. That alone will help deflect the breach."

"Me? We have public relations people for this."

"Yes. But put it in your own words, Gio. It will sound authentic and announce your personal style of leadership."

He watched Samuele's mouth form words, but Gio was having a hard time actually listening. Because his blood was boiling thinking back to the strategy Francesca had designed to seduce him. Once he'd begun to trust her, she'd started to ask questions that required long nights of huddling together over a laptop in bed, her auburn hair almost sickly sweet from the gardenia-scented shampoo she used.

Francesca had taught him a lesson he would never forget. He would never let anyone get that close to him again. But, weirdly, his thoughts meandered back to Luci this morning, so seemingly harmless as she stood on the balcony in her nightgown.

"What should I say in the press release? That I let a woman get the best of me?"

"No, Gio. Mull it over. You'll come up with something."

"Samuele, before you go. Can you look for a room at a decent hotel for about three weeks?"

Samuele regarded him quizzically.

"One of our investors isn't happy with where he's staying."

Gio took a deep breath. He had a full schedule and a multibillion-dollar company to run. So why was he already looking forward to seeing Luci again tonight?

"Drop us here," Gio instructed Viggo as the car approached the Piazza della Signoria. It had been ages since the piazza had been his destination. If he'd seen it at all during the past few years, it had been because he was merely crossing through to get to a meeting at an office or restaurant. Viggo let him and Luci out of the back seat.

Gio had decided to take her out. They'd have dinner in one of the *osterias* whose piazza-facing patios would still be warm enough in the autumn evening.

"Oh, my gosh." Luci brought her hand over her mouth in genuine reverence as she took in the piazza. He could appreciate her sentiment, as it was one of Florence's most dramatic sights. In fact, historically, it had been the meeting place for all of Tuscany.

"There's the Fontana di Neptuno!" The marble-and-bronze Fountain of Neptune. "I've seen it in pictures so many times, I can't believe I'm finally here."

Luci's enthusiasm lightened Gio's mood after a long hard day of putting out administrative fire after fire in the remains of mistakes that Dante had made while he was at the helm. Mostly, though, he was still strategizing about the Francesca fiasco and its aftermath.

Still, he reiterated to himself that one of his goals when returning to Florence was to slow his pace a little and to enjoy relaxing pursuits. He worked too much; even his father thought so. A night out on the town with pretty Luci was just what the doctor ordered. Even though he had sworn never to get close to a woman again, it was only one evening. Okay, there was last night, too, but it was not as if he was going to devote his life to her.

Although when he presented a bent elbow for her to slip her arm through, he felt an unfamiliar lump at the bottom of his throat when she did so.

"Here is one of the fake *David*s." She pointed to the replica of Michelangelo's masterpiece. "The original used to stand in this place but was moved to the Galleria dell'Accademia to protect it."

"You'll want to visit there."

"There's another replica of *David* in the Piazzale Michelangelo. The views of the city are supposed to be astounding from there."

"They are."

"And this is the Loggia dei Lanzi." The outdoor gallery of sculptures in the piazza.

"You've certainly studied up on the city. That way is the Uffizi Gallery—" he pointed a finger "—which, of course, you'll want to explore." One of the world's finest museums.

"Oh, yes." Her squeeze on his arm sent pricks of energy through his muscles.

"I can find a professional guide for you if you'd like."

"No. Thanks. I spend too much time already with guides and companions as it is."

"I take it you mean the children you teach? That's a cute way of describing them."

"Right." Luci's voice rose. "It does seem like they are the ones leading the way most of the time."

At the restaurant he'd chosen, Gio asked the hostess to seat them outside facing the piazza. It was about as fine a night as could be with the dusk and the statues, Luci's face aglow with the breadth of it all.

"We'll have the prosciutto with melon, the mushroom risotto and the grilled *branzino*," he instructed the waiter. Gio was hungry so he ordered for them without consulting the menu.

"Is that all right?" He turned to Luci.

"Yes. Thank you for asking."

"And we'll have a bottle of the Pallovana Frascati," Gio finished the order.

After the waiter returned with the Frascati, Luci asked, "You haven't told me anything about your first day yet. How did everything go?"

As they sipped their wine and took advantage of the superlative people-watching their vantage point on the piazza offered, he filled her in on reacquainting himself with staff and about some restructuring he was intending.

"My biggest problem is how to handle the information about a hack we experienced recently when the design for a product was obtained and sold to a competitor." The information about the hack was to soon be public knowledge, so he wasn't disclosing any secrets by talking to Luci about it.

"Has it been in the news?"

"Not officially. I know there's talk in the industry."

"Will you speak to the press about it?" That was exactly what Samuele had been urging this morning.

"I suppose I ought to before trade gossips do."

"So, should you issue a press statement?"

The waiter delivered plates with paper-thin slices of pink prosciutto draped across wedges of ripe orange melon.

"Grazie." Gio acknowledged the arrival and returned his attention to Luci.

"It was my own personal security that was weak in order for the hack to have happened. I gave clearance to someone I shouldn't have." Gio didn't want to tell Luci about Francesca specifically, so he kept it general.

"You don't want the company to appear compromised in the press," Luci said with her fork dangling in the air.

"Exactly. I'd like to think it was a grave mistake on my part but that, in general, our safeguards are very good. Nothing like that had ever happened before and hopefully never will again."

"Do you have any new products that are about to launch?"

"Why do you ask?" The question came out sharply. But here it was. This young lady who called herself a teacher from Spain could be, right under his nose, trying to get proprietary information from him under the guise of dinner conversation. That was how these charmers worked, wasn't it?

"I'm sorry, did I offend you?"

"Are you interested in computer science?" he baited, paying attention to every word.

"Not especially." She took a sip of her wine. "I was going to make a suggestion about your press release. Pardon me if I was being intrusive."

"Go on." He rubbed his chin as he continued to study her.

"What if you wrote a statement that wasn't strictly about the hack but was a *state of the company* address now that you've taken over? Then you can mention the leak and what security measures you're putting in place. But sandwich it in between news about the company's latest accomplishments."

"That's a great suggestion," Gio exclaimed. He thought immediately of the achievements he would like to announce, and that in the context of a report on the company they wouldn't come across as showboating. Indeed, his new peripheral component interconnect, PCI, was revolutionary.

Gio toasted Luci. As they clinked their wineglasses together it was as if they touched each other, a powerful sensation that traveled from his fingertips all the way up his arm to his heart.

They made it through the next two courses of their meal talking a mile a minute. Luci asked so many interesting questions about computers and listened patiently to techie mumbo jumbo that she surely didn't understand. Gio didn't reveal anything about his designs, and by the time dinner was over, his spy theory had lost steam. Luci was wonderful company.

The conversation continued as they stood in the courtyard of the villa under the night sky. "The random access memory, or RAM, is temporary," he finished the explanation he was giving her in the car.

"Your work is interesting."

The scent of the flowers in bloom permeated the garden.

Silence fell upon them.

The air between them stilled.

Her mood changed.

She'd spent dinner asking him about work and had avoided talking about herself. He looked into her eyes to coax her on but she said nothing. She definitely harbored a secret, although he was now convinced it had nothing to do with him.

"Something is wrong?"

"Thank you again for your generosity."

It was as if the entire city was quietly holding its breath.

"You didn't tell me about your day. What sights did you see?"

With her head slightly bowed, she peered up at him through her eyelashes. "I'm embarrassed to tell you that I got completely lost. I was planning to visit the Piazza della Repubblica, but I ended up just sort of circling in a big loop. It was all beautiful, but I didn't see anything I had intended to."

Florence wasn't the easiest city to maneuver if you didn't know it, with streets jutting out from its many piazzas. Still, in this day and age, with all of the online resources and apps, a person should be able to find their way.

"You didn't use maps or tourist sites on your phone?"

She waited a beat before admitting, "I don't have a phone. I didn't bring one on the trip."

"*Bellissima*, is that even safe?"

"I wanted to unplug," she quickly responded, "to truly be a wanderer without any trappings of real life. Besides..."

"Yes?" he prompted. Unplugging wasn't something he'd ever experienced, as his life revolved around being so very plugged in. Although it was something he needed to learn to do a little of.

"I'm not sure I should have come to Florence at all."

Gio stood firm and pierced his eyes into hers. "I can

tell that you've come to Florence to lose yourself. That you're hiding something. Or hiding from something."

Luci scrunched her forehead. As if she was making a decision.

Then she reached to her head to run her fingers through her blond hair. Her hand moved farther and farther back until, with a tug, she lifted the blond hair completely off her head.

It was a wig! And from under the wig an avalanche of long brown waves cascaded down far past her shoulders.

"First of all, my name is not Luci. It's Luciana. I am Her Royal Highness Princess Luciana de la Isla de Izerote."

CHAPTER THREE

"*BRAVA.*" GIO USED two fingers to mime tipping an imaginary hat toward Luci, or rather Princess Luciana. "That's quite a coup, a princess in disguise."

"You wouldn't believe it."

"Try me," he clipped. Luciana knew he would be upset to learn that she had pretended to be someone she wasn't, the deception made so much worse by the burn of the company hack he'd spoken of. He was quite sensitive during dinner when she'd asked about his upcoming products, as if he was suspicious of her and had been all along.

Now his jaw pulsed as he stood drilling into her with his big blue eyes, demanding an explanation.

"You've been so kind to me, Gio," she began constructing an apology. "I didn't expect to have a problem with selling my jewels. Then those boys were harassing me on the street and you came to my aid. And now you've given me this beautiful evening."

"You have an interesting way of showing your appreciation," he continued in a voice so low and tight she wasn't sure how the sounds were even escaping his throat.

Luciana fingered through the wig she held in her hand. The strands felt so fake despite how much she had liked wearing it. How silly it all seemed now, that she had tried to convince Gio she was a schoolteacher on a holiday. She supposed she had been trying that out on herself, a description of a woman and a life she could only imagine about.

"I'm so sorry. When I was sharing what I've learned about handling the media, you knew a schoolteacher wouldn't have any experience with that. I wanted to tell you the truth right then. I just didn't know how. I was trying to keep my identity hidden so that I could have just one anonymous adventure. I've never been on my own."

"I see."

"It's like what you're going through right now, having to transition from being a private to a public person. I've been in the palace my entire life. Although Izerote is not known to the rest of the world, on my own island I am under constant scrutiny."

Gio's expression slowly remolded from accusatory to something else, like he was truly listening to her.

"I'll just pack up my things and be out of your way." She turned from him to return to the cottage he'd been generous enough to let her stay in. She'd gather up as quickly as she could.

Over her shoulder she added, "Even though I have no right to, may I ask you one more favor? Could you not tell anyone about this? I would be eternally grateful if you forgot you ever met me."

As she swerved away, his big hand grabbed her arm.

"I didn't say you had to leave." Gio's voice kept its deep baritone but he didn't sound as angry anymore. "Please, Princess Luciana de la Isla de Izerote. Let me make us a cup of tea. I have to admit I'm intrigued. I've never hosted a real-life princess before. Let alone a runaway."

"I'm not made of fairy dust. Despite popular folklore."

If this had been a fairy tale, Gio Grassi could be her handsome prince. His armor would glisten as he swept her off her feet and hoisted her onto his proud white horse. Where they'd gallop away into the sunset to their kingdoms where marriages were conjured from love, not strategy.

"I'm dreading my entry into public life," Gio said. "So I do understand your desire for anonymity."

"That means a lot to me."

"You look quite different with your long and natural hair."

Luciana supposed she did. With her hair the same as she'd worn it her entire life she felt younger, like she was still a schoolgirl. How her father saw her.

"I actually love the wig," she confessed. "It's fashionable instead of how I usually look, stuck in time, born and bred to wear a tiara. What do you think?"

"Obviously, you should wear your hair however you want to."

His words stunned her. When was the last time anyone told her she should look however she wanted? Never.

"Shall we have tea?"

"Okay."

"I'll be right back."

As Gio went up to the main house, Luciana sighed with enormous relief. She couldn't have kept her identity a secret from him for a second longer. At first she thought he was so angry he was going to throw her out on the spot. Thank goodness his reaction changed. What a persuasive man he was. Her eyelids fluttered when he said she should do whatever she wanted with her hair.

Why couldn't she be marrying a compelling and progressive man like him? Why must she wed someone with a closed mind who had already told her that becoming pregnant was the first and only job he expected her to devote herself to? She did want children, but in all honesty, she dreaded the thought of giving her virginity to a man she would never love. That seemed a service past what was a reasonable expectation of any person.

"All right, Princess," Gio announced when he brought out two cups of tea and invited her to sit at the glass table in the courtyard where they'd had breakfast early that morning. "I want to hear all about this. How and why did you get yourself off your tiny island and all the way to Tuscany?"

Luciana took a sip from the steaming cup and then began to tell the story of what she'd been planning for months.

How she held no money, having no cause to ever pay for anything herself. That she did have credit cards but if she used them her whereabouts could be located. So she'd decided she would use a few precious stones to finance this expedition she was compelled to take. About how she carefully spread out on her bed all the palace jewels that had been worn by her mother, her grandmother, her great-grandmother and her lineage even before them.

Many were one-of-a-kind pieces crafted by the finest jewelry makers in the world and gifted to the royal family. Most of them were ornate and overdone, not at all pieces she would have chosen for herself. Yet she understood their legacy and importance. They would be passed down to her own children someday, either to a daughter or a daughter-in-law.

Returning those to the palace vaults, Luciana kept only a few plainer pieces whose stones would bring her enough money. They were everyday pieces that would never be missed.

The princess had also been keeping a careful watch on the schedule of supply boats that arrived regularly to bring goods onto the island. After reviewing her chart, she confirmed that one arrived at four o'clock every morning. Formulating her scheme, she'd creep outside the palace walls, avoiding security cameras and passing undetected through the pitch-dark of the wee hours to the shore. Finding a covering from which to spy, she'd timed the boatmen unloading their cargo and wheeling it through the service entrance of the palace. For at least ten minutes during the unloading process, the boat was unattended.

Gio put his elbows on the table between them, engrossed in her tale.

On the chosen night, Princess Luciana donned her darkest clothes, slid out the prepacked suitcase from under her bed and placed the jewels into a purse. She left a note on her desk for her father, climbed over the terrace off her sitting room and scurried her way to the dock in the darkness. Once on the boat, she'd covered herself in tarps and sailcloth. Shuddering with fear as she heard the crew return to the boat, she'd all but held her breath as they pulled away from the shores of Izerote.

When the boat touched land in Barcelona, she'd waited for the crew to disembark and then, having no idea what would greet her once she was on deck, was able to dash away from the dock unnoticed. Although she didn't get the money she expected for the sale of the first jewel, she'd had enough to board a train, and transferred from one train to another to another through France until she'd reached Florence.

"I'm astonished," Gio said as he leaned back in his chair.

Replaying the getaway in her mind, Luciana was just as shocked as Gio that she had pulled it off. Not just the actual escape, which was something out of a spy story. But that she'd had the will and the courage to do it. To take something for herself that every cell in her body was starving for. That she would have spent a lifetime regretting it if she hadn't.

Maybe a little piece of this was also a tribute to her mother, who Luciana knew was never happy under the confines of her tiara. Her mother's eyes had died long before the car accident took her life.

"One question," Gio mused. "Why did you come to Florence for specifically three weeks? Do you turn into a pumpkin after that?"

"Worse. I'm getting married."

"You're set to marry a man you don't love?"

"I must wed King Agustin of Menocita, an island near ours. It's my duty to my subjects. Izerote is a land of unspoiled green hills and clear blue waters. But our population has been shrinking over the last couple of generations. With globalization, the people of Izerote want more in their lives than what our island has to offer. Families send their children off to the great universities of Europe and the United States where technology is up-to-date and there are job opportunities."

Gio raked a hand through his curls as he listened attentively. They nursed the cups of tea he had prepared. He'd met a couple of royals in his life at social functions but never with any intimacy other than a handshake. He did remember that he got a standoffish vibe from them, as if they were separate from the rest of the world. Princess Luciana, Luci, was not like that at all, and from her he sensed a benevolence he almost never felt with anyone. If he hadn't known, he might indeed believe that she spent her days as a teacher among the needs and simple concerns of toddlers.

"How is it that marrying King Agustin will be good for your subjects?"

"Menocita was heading toward the same fate as Izerote until about thirty years ago when Agustin's father decided the island would become a tourist destination in order to create jobs and attract visitors. And it worked well. They built lavish beach resorts and all the ensuing industries, which have brought prosperity to the island. Although now their waters are polluted and they have to ship garbage out by the boatloads."

"King Agustin and your father want to do the same in Izerote."

"Yes." Luciana took a demure sip from her cup of tea. Those sensual bow-shaped lips had held him captive as she told him her story. He loved her upright posture as she sat on the chair opposite him while they talked. The moon glow, plus a couple of garden lights, cast perfect shadows of light and dark across her stunning face. She'd worn a simple dark green dress to dinner tonight, very modest with its high neckline and below-the-knee length. Last night for the dinner with his investors, it was a stiff-fabric light blue dress, quite formal. He wondered if princesses were ever allowed to dress in casual clothes.

Really, though, it was the sight of her in that sheer nightgown on the Juliet balcony this morning that he couldn't get off his mind. It made him want to run barefoot through a forest with her, crown or not.

"Agustin's wife died when they were quite young. He must remarry and bear children."

"You're being traded for a couple of hotels on the beach?"

Luciana laughed out loud, the dulcet tones carrying into the foggy air of the late night. "Yes." She continued to giggle so sincerely, it made Gio smile. "I love the way you phrased that."

"It's true."

"And what's sadder," Luciana added with a snicker, "is that I dislike Agustin, what little I know of him. He's stern and humorless."

Princess Luciana was not like any of the women he'd known before. First of all, with Grasstech's position as the world leader in its field, Giovanni Grassi and Dante Grassi were two eligible bachelors of accomplishment and wealth. With that, they attracted women who tried to glam onto them for a taste of the luxury life. That's exactly what Her Royal Highness Princess Luciana was running away from.

Many a woman like Francesca had crossed Gio's path. Dante's, too. The women who gravitated toward the Grassi brothers were nothing like their mother, the down-to-earth woman who was grateful for all of the blessings she and their family had. Noemi Grassi didn't have a phony bone in her body, and raised her sons to be the same.

Yet Gio and Dante were magnets for women who pretended they were one thing but were really another. Francesca being the state-of-the-art, and most costly, example. After her deception, Gio made a firm decision never to trust a woman ever again. It was ironic that now he was sitting across from a woman most definitely out to deceive, yet her reasoning was understandable. And he appreciated that she had come clean to him. In a strange way, now he thought of himself as her confidant. Partner in crime.

"I do have to marry him. The wedding is set. Invitations were sent long ago. The dinner menu has been selected. An ugly dress has been created. In fact, it was that horrible dress that pushed me into this trip. Once I saw myself all bound up in that lace like it was ropes of bondage, I decided it was now or never to claim something for myself."

"What if you didn't go back after the three weeks?"

"I have to. I owe it to my father. I'll be surprised if I even get the three weeks. I don't doubt that he has already contacted palace security and blueprints are being drawn up as to how to find me."

Gio winced when he thought of how that must be for her. Essentially a prisoner of her crown. Not permitted to be the schoolteacher she said she wanted to be. Not able to choose who, and if, she wanted for her husband. Bound by obligation to put the throne first, and herself second.

"How would anyone find you after that careful escape you executed?"

"You have no idea the lengths my father would go to." Luciana licked her top lip. "But in my letter to him I promised that I would stay safe and return, and remain in service to our people all the days of my life."

Gio would be in service to his family for the rest of his life, too. Although not unwillingly. However, he would have preferred to stay in the vocation that he loved. To create new products, to get lost in the mathematics, in the scientific discovery of hypothesis and proof. Now he would stand as the voice and face of the Grasstech empire. Analyze operations. Maintain a dedicated and productive staff. Make decisions about expansions and new territories. He would do it, with authority and justice, even if he had a tad of reluctance. Whatever his family needed, he would deliver.

While Luciana had an arranged union that she was loathe to undertake but must, Gio would trudge his road alone. In his parents, he witnessed the kind of love and partnership that dreams were made of. His parents were romantic, with genuine well-wishes and support for each other every day of their lives. Most important, they were friends who trusted each other completely. Gio never expected to see any of that in his lifetime.

Yet for reasons he didn't quite grasp, it bothered Gio that Luciana belonged to another. No one should be forced to live out their days with someone they didn't love. It was wrong.

Gio's phone buzzed in his pocket. He read Samuele's text out loud. "Not a decent hotel room to be had, with several large business conventions in town."

Luciana's face fell.

"Why don't you stay here while you are in Florence? You see I have room." What else could he do but take her in? If this was to be her one big hurrah before a life devoted to what others wanted for her, the least he could do was watch over her and try to keep her safe. Yes, because she was a princess. Yes, because she was a sheltered young woman who might not know how to avoid the menaces that anyone faced when traveling alone. And yes, because there was something special about her that had touched his heart.

Of course it didn't make sense, his urge to take her into his arms and kiss away any past and future. To bear her burdens. To take away everything other than this courtyard and the moon and the moment.

"And I can show you around a bit." Getting off the computer and out among the human race would be good for him. And would make him a better leader, too. He needed to take the long view of his well-being now that he was the company's CEO.

Gio didn't know what was prompting him to get so involved in this young woman's trip to Florence. Maybe it was only that he spent so much time alone, it was a breath of fresh air to talk and walk with Luciana. And he sensed that she needed him. Which felt strangely good. But after learning the hard way from Francesca that he couldn't trust anyone, it was essential not to get close. There was something so virtuous and sweet-natured about Luciana, it would be easy to forget that vow. Fortunately, she'd be in his life for only a short time.

"Hello, Viggo." Gio's driver met Luciana in front of the villa. After he'd secured her into the car and pulled away she asked, "Where are we going?"

"Signor Gio asked me to leave it as a surprise."

When Luciana had woken up this morning and stepped out onto the Juliet balcony of her room, Gio was nowhere to be seen. Which she had to admit was more than a little disappointing. The day before, she'd relished such a lovely breakfast with her handsome host. She was hoping for a repeat.

From the balcony, she had looked down on the courtyard and eyed a tray set with a coffee thermos and what looked like a plate of food under a cloth napkin. After a shower, she dressed and made her way downstairs.

Upon closer inspection of the tray, Luciana found that

it also held a single pink rose in a vase. Which made her heart skip a beat. She'd been given hundreds of elaborate flower arrangements and bouquets, whether at ceremonial processionals or formal introductions or sent to the palace. Yet she couldn't think of a flower she'd seen in her life that was as charming as that one rose on her breakfast tray. Because she knew it had come from Gio, and the mere fact that he had thought to include it brought a swell to her chest.

It wasn't merely out of respect for her title that he'd had the thought. Was it simply the gesture of a man who was innately hospitable? Or a man who appreciated the beauty of nature and thought to adorn the tray with a stem picked from the villa's garden? Or was it something else entirely? A time-honored gentlemanly practice of a man giving a flower to a woman as an act of romance?

Surprising herself with that thought, Luciana swallowed hard as she touched the velvety petals of the rose. Gio wasn't wooing her. And romance was never in the picture for Princess Luciana de la Isla de Izerote. Her parents and grandparents, and all the royal couples throughout Izerote's history, were beholden to the monarchy. Each and every one of the marriages had been carefully considered during meetings around a table between the male elders.

Some of the women in her lineage got lucky. Stories were passed down about her great-grandmother meeting her great-grandfather. At first, they clashed. He was a traditional man who concerned himself with laws and war. Whereas her great-grandmother was a nurturer, wanting to improve the lives of the poorest citizens of the island and a great lover of animals. It seemed they'd have nothing in common, and her great-grandmother grew quite sad.

Within a few years, three children were born. Luciana's great-grandfather fell in love with his children and their carefree pursuits of play and pleasure. Through those children, he and her great-grandmother fell in love with each other, some six years after they walked down the aisle at their wedding to each other as complete strangers.

It was important for Luciana to hope for the best. Maybe she'd find a camaraderie with Agustin. Or she'd uncover a good side of him. They might even become friends. She doubted she'd fall in love like her great-grandmother had in her arranged marriage. But romantic love wasn't necessary. The merger between the two islands was what mattered.

Luciana pulled back the napkin on the tray to see the same breakfast of rolls and fruit that she and Gio had lingered over the day before.

She thought of her grandmother and mother. They hadn't fared as well as her great-grandmother in their marriages to domineering men who did not allow their wives any independence or private pursuits. She remembered her mother's blank stare, that of a woman who was only going through the motions of her day. Although she knew her mother had loved her for the eleven years they'd shared together, even as a young girl Luciana could sense that something was wrong. Her mother fulfilled her obligations, but the deep corrosive peeling in her gut was too high a price to pay.

Harsh King Agustin had already informed Luciana that he expected her to begin producing heirs immediately and, in as many words, told her that a condition of his agreement with her father was the promise of her complete obedience. The thought of reporting to him as a servant was repulsive. Hopefully, in time, he'd come to see her more as a partner.

He would never set her heart on fire. Agustin would never on a whim present his wife with a single pink rose. Still, they'd find a coexistence she would come to terms with.

Luciana lifted the rose out of the vase and brought it to her nose to fully immerse herself in its lovely scent, the sweetness of the gesture and, most important, the man who had presented it to her. How they had sat here last night drinking herbal tea until the wee hours. She'd shared the story of her journey after assuming that she'd never tell it, that it would be a secret she'd take to her grave. Gio was so easy to talk to and listened attentively to everything she said rather than simply waiting for her to go silent so that he could resume talking like all of the other men she knew. They talked and talked and talked until they could barely keep their heads up.

After revealing her true identity to him, she assumed he would want her to leave his villa. Instead, after the shock, he seemed to understand her predicament. The backward ways of Izerote infuriated him. He was willing in his own small way to aid her on her voyage of discovery by offering her a safe haven.

Frankly overwhelmed by the incidents with the jewelry and the boys chasing after her and the lack of available hotel rooms, his kindly invitation was a relief she gratefully agreed to.

There was one other matter, too. The idea of spending time in Florence with a handsome, intelligent and free-thinking man was simply too exciting to pass up. What a thrilling ride this had already become!

As she sat down to eat her breakfast, she wondered what time Gio had left this morning, as it was still early. He'd left a note.

Viggo will pick you up at five o'clock to meet me for more of your sightseeing tour. Casual dress. Until then, Gio.

Now as Luciana was being driven through the streets of Florence to meet him, she kept replaying that *until then* salutation on the note. There was something incredibly alluring about those words.

She spent the entire ride trying to talk herself out of those thoughts. Certainly there would never be anything amorous between her and Gio. It was just an isolated girl's fantasies starting to spin out of control. She was about to be married, she was in Florence for three weeks and Gio was going through a transition, as well. He'd already declared that he was single and planned on staying that way. She felt guilty and wrong even having those thoughts about him.

But Gio had no idea what he'd done. Last night, she had satisfied a years-old yearning to visit the Piazza della Signoria, to sit in that storied square in the evening air. A scene she never could have imagined she'd be sharing with a man. One like him, no less. With his imposing six-foot-three-inch height and slim muscular build. The most bewitching eyes, blue as the midday sky. And that fascinating tousle of blond curls that she could convince herself wanted to have her fingers thread through them.

Something she knew wasn't the case and wouldn't be in a million years.

Although it was nothing she could have planned, the evening was infinitesimally better in his company. Unfortunately, it was an evening so perfect it made her wish. And there was no place for wishes in the life of Her Royal Highness Princess Luciana de la Isla de Izerote.

Viggo pulled the car over to the curb and Gio appeared to open her door and hold out an arm for her to take hold of. *"Buonasera."*

"Where are we going?" Luciana eagerly inquired, not used to surprises. That was another part of life as a princess. There was no spontaneity. Ever. A royal's life was plotted and protected from any intrusion that might throw off the organization. Plans were very important. People had to be notified, schedules had to be coordinated, itineraries had to be created. This rigidity was, of course, necessary to keep the palace running smoothly. "Your driver wouldn't tell me."

"Tonight, I'll show you one of my favorite pleasures from my adolescence. After dinner, we'll walk along the Arno River."

Luciana looked down at her dress shoes. They were made for appearances at children's charities, not for treading the streets of an ancient city.

Observing her hesitation, he said, "In my note, I suggested that you dress casual."

"This is as casual as I get." In fact, when the princess assessed the few outfits she had brought in search of the least formal, the best she'd come up with was a skirt that hit her midcalf paired with a lightweight jacket.

After nicking a suitcase for the trip from the palace storage room, she'd filled it with the only clothes she had. Dresses that were suitable for diplomatic luncheons and others for garden brunches. A few cocktail dresses for dinner. Luciana did not even own one pair of slacks. A princess worth her salt would never be caught wearing them.

"I see," Gio said as his mind shuffled through a thought.

"I'm curious about you." She gestured at his outfit. "This is the second time I've seen you in a jacket and tie with jeans. That's acceptable in your business?"

"I own fine bespoke suits. But yes, I work in jeans."

Obviously, she couldn't mention just how good he looked in said ensemble. This was a man who had a personal style and didn't care what anyone thought of it. He was unlike anyone she'd ever met before.

"I think we ought to buy you some jeans right now."

"Oh, no, I couldn't."

"So you'd stow away on a boat in the middle of the night, sell your family's jewels, sleep on trains to get to Italy, but you won't wear a pair of jeans?"

They both laughed. For Luciana, it was laugh or cry, and she'd done her fair share of the latter.

"You're an interesting study in contradictions," Gio pressed on. "Come on, I know of a shop near here."

He was going to take her shopping for casual clothes? Appearances were a big deal to royalty. They weren't supposed to look like commoners. The strict manner of dress garnered respect. She was again wearing the blond wig disguise, half assuming that operatives of her father were searching for her. The hair was enough of a change.

Yet she wasn't representing Izerote here in Florence. No one knew who she was other than Gio. Her heart began to beat double time. Walking the streets of Florence, both of them in jeans like a typical couple on a holiday? Simple denim was taking on a larger meaning. Maybe she really was pulling off the one thing she thought she'd never be entitled to. To know, just for a short moment in time.

Freedom.

Gio crooked his arm like he had last night, encouraging her to follow where he led. Silvery flashes almost dizzied her as she slipped her arm into his, opening her palm flat against the taut muscles of his biceps.

"Let's go, Princess."

CHAPTER FOUR

"I'VE NEVER BEEN in a shop like this," Luciana gushed when she and Gio stepped in off the street. Pinching herself, because she was surely living out a fantasy, in a busy boutique that sold everyday clothes to Florentine women, not tourists. It was as if she had inhabited someone else's body.

"You've never been to a clothing shop?"

"Not like this. Clothes are generally sent to the palace. Occasionally, we go to Paris or Milan to visit a designer's atelier. The building is cleared out and, of course, I'm accompanied by style associates, palace dressers and at least three bodyguards. I don't think I've ever in my life trolled through a rack of clothes on a sales floor."

"Have at it, Princess."

"Can I ask you a favor?" she whispered.

"Certainly."

"Will you call me Luci, like you did when I first introduced myself to you? I'm sure it's not anything anyone else would understand, but I love the idea of just having a regular first name without all of the pomp."

Gio's eyes smiled into hers, producing a hot whoosh that flowed right through her. It wasn't a sensation she was familiar with and, frankly, it was terrifying. Of all things, what she most wanted to do was kiss him. Right on that gorgeous mouth of his. She'd never kissed a man on the lips. Nor was she going to now, but apparently when in Florence in the company of the most unexpected of tour guides, a girl could imagine almost anything.

"Shop, Luci." Had he somehow read her thoughts, because he redirected her to their purpose in the store? He knew as well as she did that they could never kiss. Ever since she'd met him a mere two days ago, she'd already had to mentally repeat to herself a hundred times that this extraordinary man had landed in her life, but that it would be for only three weeks and then never again. She was about to be married and that was that.

Now, to the matter at hand.

Luci surveyed the shop in action. The customers were mostly women, a few with bored men obediently accompanying them. A couple of the women combed the racks with great seriousness, methodically considering every item as they moved down the aisle. Perhaps they were on the hunt for something in a particular size or color. That was another thing Luciana had never practiced, as the size and color of her clothes were always preselected for her.

Some of the shoppers had items draped over one arm as they worked through the offerings with their other. Another behavior Luciana had never known. Servants and handmaidens were always at the ready in the princess's life, lest she ever have the need to lift a finger.

The store carried a range from what she assumed would be office attire, to resort wear, to casual clothes.

"There are the jeans." Gio looked up from his phone and pointed her to a display case that held dozens of pairs folded onto shelves. He tugged her by the hand and led her to the assortment. One stack held the darkest of blues, azure as the midnight ocean. Others were a lighter wash. Others still had tears at the knees, a lived-in look that Luciana had never really understood when she saw it on fashion websites. The jeans styles were listed, as well. There was boot cut, straight leg, skinny and something called boyfriend.

With Gio holding her hand, seeing the word *boyfriend* spelled out in front of her made her lungs drain of air.

"Everything okay?" Gio perceived the change in her face.

"Actually, I don't think I should do this. I'm only here temporarily. I can make do with what I brought."

"Don't you want some comfortable clothes to explore the city in? If you're concerned about the cost, I accept diamonds."

This time his humor was not well received, as Princess Luciana was beginning to feel very uneasy. "I'm not comfortable doing this."

"Your subjects aren't here. No one knows you in Florence. Didn't you say you'd always wanted to wear a pair of jeans?"

As she'd told Gio on the walk to the shop, she'd had one meeting with a pair of jeans. A princess from a neighboring island, one with less old-fashioned ways, had come to Izerote to attend a diplomatic function. Luciana explained her predicament and begged the other princess to leave the pair of jeans she had brought along. Within twenty-four hours, a palace housekeeper had found the jeans in Luciana's closet, assumed that a laborer had accidentally left them behind and promptly discarded them. Luciana never even had a chance to put them on.

"I suppose I could try a pair on."

"That's right."

"What do you think boyfriend jeans are?"

Gio summoned over a saleswoman who explained the relaxed fit of the boyfriend cut. While he tended to business, she assisted Luciana in finding a couple of sizes that were likely to fit, and showed her into the changing room. It was yet another first for her to take off her clothes alongside other shoppers, each woman separated only by a privacy curtain.

She knew perfectly well that both girls and women the world over would have their own fantasies fulfilled if they got to try on Princess Luciana's ball gowns and tiaras. Yet the sound of metal against metal that the zipper made as Luciana pulled up the jeans gave her a special joy. Biting her lip, she allowed her eyes to slowly move up toward the mirror until she could get a good view of herself.

Wow. For the first time she could ever recall, she saw herself as just a young woman. Who might have borrowed her boyfriend's jeans, which fit loose around the hips and seat as they were intended to. She loved the heaviness of the denim, understanding why jeans were popularized by cowboys and miners.

But she couldn't traipse all over Florence in jeans! They were too unceremonious. Even if no one else knew she was a princess, she'd know. About to take them off and at least treasure the memory of being in this shop on this day, she decided to show them to Gio.

"Luci!" Gio nodded his approval as she exited the dressing room to model for him. She knew there wasn't anything particularly flattering about the jeans, but she wanted him to see her like a normal girl, wanted to keep them on for just a little bit longer. *"Bravissima."*

"Do they look good?" she asked in a quiet voice.

"Turn around."

Turn around? Gio Grassi, tech wizard and almost complete stranger, had just ordered Her Royal Highness Princess Luciana de la Isla de Izerote to circle around in a pair of jeans so he could examine her behind in them?

But that didn't stop her from obeying his command. And deriving a wicked satisfaction from doing so.

"Well?" she challenged.

"You look like a city girl on the go. What do *you* think?"

"They're so comfortable. And the fabric is so weighty. It makes me feel like…like my own person."

"We'll buy two pairs. You'll need tops and shoes, as well."

"No. I can't. It's not right. Trying them on was enough."

The princess glanced outside through the store window and noticed that there were two men in black suits standing near the entrance. Both wore earpieces that they spoke into. For a moment, she panicked that they were palace security from Izerote. That her father had already located her whereabouts and she was moments from being whisked back home.

If that was to happen, she steeled herself, darned if she wasn't going to first do some of what she came to Florence for.

"Thank you, Gio. I would love to buy these clothes."

"And don't worry. You're not getting anything for free. When we go to dinner, I'm going to need you to earn your keep."

Gio was happy to see that the rooftop restaurant he remembered atop a five-story building along the Arno River was still in business. With a view of the river and its many bridges, including the famous Ponte Vecchio, the trattoria was one of those secret-treasure restaurants that Florentines hoped no tourist would ever discover. Thankfully, it remained a low-key family establishment with an easygoing dress code.

Because now Her Royal Highness Princess Luciana, who had looked so dignified in the silken dinner dresses she'd worn the last two nights, was unfussy and relaxed in her new jeans, flat shoes and a T-shirt. She fit in fine with the young mothers out with girlfriends, and city workers, who unwound from their busy days with a glass of prosecco at the restaurant. Surely, no one would mistake her for nobility.

"Oh, my. This view is splendid."

As Gio took it in, he agreed. The red-roofed buildings, one after the next, lined the banks of the river and its stone bridges. Firenze was truly like nowhere else. Although it did occur to him that the sight of Luciana's face, with the sweet mouth and enthusiastic eyes as she took in the vista, was as stunning as the view itself.

At the office, he'd spent the day swamped with work. And could have put in several more hours. So he'd almost regretted having promised to take Luciana out tonight. Even though he had offered, he didn't really have time to play tour guide and rearrange his schedule. This was why he shouldn't spend time alone with women. The pheromones, or whatever it was they gave off, clouded his judgment. And he had a feeling that Luciana's pheromones had particular powers.

It had been entertaining helping her shop for those jeans. He shared her agony in buying them, though, knowing they represented more than a bit of cloth to her. In fact, his jaw tensed at the fact that something as simple as selecting her own clothes was an exception to her, not the norm.

The river glistened below as twilight was beginning to sweep the sky above, the open air taking on darkness. This was Gio's third dinner with Luciana. Considering he hadn't had dinner alone with a woman even once in the past few months, that was quite a record.

Lately, he'd been spending time immersed in development of some new biometric products. Generally when mealtimes rolled around he would ask for something to be brought in, as he was far too engrossed in his work to be bothered with leaving his desk. Or the whole team would go out for a late-night meal where beers and spicy food were eagerly consumed amid plenty of noise and clamor. He had no objection to either, although Luciana's lips, which appeared so pink in the softness of dusk, made him doubt that more pleasing company had ever existed.

Gio ordered wine and nibbles.

"You mentioned needing my help," Luciana said as she tore her eyes away from the river.

"Yes. I appreciated the suggestion you gave me about writing that press statement. To sandwich the hacking incident in between more positive news about the business. I hope the net effect was to put the matter in perspective."

"Do you think it did?"

"Somewhat. But the tech world is calling for details about the hack. Although fortunately no metadata was leaked, top secret information was breached. As leaders in the field, Grasstech always comes forward with information that could assist the entire industry."

"So you want to reveal more about what happened?"

Even though Luciana was involved in her own kind of deception, he held no ill feelings toward her like he did for Francesca, who'd misled him for her own personal gain.

Still, he had to remember never to tell Luciana anything truly confidential.

"Grasstech's advisers are pushing for this idea that I do an interview with the leading computer industry security magazine and talk about the hack from a strictly technological standpoint."

"Getting out in front of it rather than having the press snoop around is probably a good idea."

"And I have a live-stream chat scheduled with the computer science department at a local university. As you noted about my daily uniform—" he gestured down the length of his chest and then leg "—sitting bent over a computer all day, I don't give much thought to what I'm wearing. I put on a tie as a nod to my authority."

An appetizing plate of grilled vegetables and another of cheeses was delivered to the table. Both Luciana and Gio reached for a morsel.

"Are you suggesting we switch roles now? You've put me in jeans and now you want my help becoming camera ready?"

"Exactly."

"Ironic."

She smiled one of her bashful grins, as if she was sharing a joke only with herself. He supposed that the last thing she'd expected to be doing in Florence was giving public relations lessons to a techie billionaire.

"I'm all ears."

"All right, I've got an easy one for you. Take the jacket you have on right now, for example." She pointed to the blazer he wore tonight atop his starched shirt and Milanese tie. "Button it."

Gio followed her instructions.

"Now sit up very straight. Then reach behind you and tug down at the waist so that the shoulders stiffen back farther than they normally would."

Again, he did as she suggested.

Luciana approved.

"Now you have sharp, crisp lines. Very authoritative. And you can get the photographer or assistant to clip the jacket in back so it stays that way."

"I'll use that. Thank you."

This was a competent, and even confident, young woman. What a shame that her position wouldn't allow her to pursue whatever ambition she had. Gio could hardly imagine being held back intellectually. That might be a fate worse than death. Fortunately with the encouragement of his loving parents, he'd found the calling he loved in the computer sciences. Even if he had to turn to more administrative matters, he would still keep his hand in the product design he was so apt at.

"Could we have cappuccinos?" Luci asked.

"Certainly." Gio chuckled. The princess wanted a cappuccino while most of the women he'd ever known wanted far more. His money. Or his reputation. Or his secrets.

"What's funny?"

For an instant he looked at the woman sitting across from him as Luci, whom he was out with for an ordinary dinner date like many others around them in the restaurant. Where people came to talk about their days, or the tomorrows ahead of them. Where they didn't just eat a meal, but shared a human experience. They connected.

Would he ever make space for a personal life? His constant travel had been a deterrent to any long-term liaison. That was how he professed to want it, but was that really true? Or was he hiding from having to learn how to share himself with another, how to meet the demands of a relationship without diminishing his work?

There had been women here and there. If he was being honest, it was only to satiate bodily desires. Then he met Francesca. And became transfixed by her prowess of tech smarts combined with the looks of a film noir movie star from the 1940s in her dark clothes and red lips. Not unlike those old movies, it turned out she was a spy in disguise.

Gio had been duped. Perhaps his childhood was too idyllic, with parents who taught him to value honesty and candor. Trust. It was what he expected of others. Which proved to be a mistake he'd never make twice.

Peering left to right, he knew that no one in the restaurant would have any idea that Luciana was a princess. So while his pretty dinner companion had revealed her true identity to him, she still attempted to fool the city of Florence and Gio would remember a hard-learned lesson. Never let anyone get to him again.

After their delicious dinner, Luciana and Gio took a long walk along the banks of the Arno. He told her the name of each of the bridges that linked the two sides of the city. As they walked over the Ponte alla Carraia, they stopped to lean over the parapet and could make out the outlines of their reflections in the glistening waters.

They were silent for a spell in the glow of the night, after a dinner filled with interesting conversation. About the possibilities of technology. About the advances in communication, scientific research and the globalization of business. But also about the dangers of piracy and impostors on social media. The sharing of ideas made Luciana think of the great minds that had passed through this city over the centuries.

Although Her Royal Highness often sat in on meetings where matters such as improving the technology on the island were discussed, she was rarely asked her opinion. Plus, the conferences never motivated her father to take any action, and the island remained hopelessly behind the rest of the world. She wished futilely that she could bring some of Gio's heightened thinking and know-how back with her when she returned. But she'd be far too busy regrouping from her trip here, begging her father's forgiveness and marching toward her wedding day.

Still leaning over the side of the bridge, Luciana judged her image reflected in the water. She was wearing the straight blond shoulder-length wig that disguised her long and thick brown curls. Between the hair and the jeans—and, of course, Gio—her time in Florence couldn't be more different from what it was on the island. She recalled a cute expression she'd read in a magazine: people referring to a situation with the acronym YOLO. *You only live once.*

After listening to the quiet swish of the river in the dark of night, Luciana was ready to talk some more.

"You're so lucky that you developed that genuine interest in technology without your parents forcing you to follow into the company if you didn't want to."

"I am at that. My parents told Dante and I that they'd never want to sell the business but that if we decided to pursue something else, they'd let others run Grasstech."

"Your parents sound like wise people."

"You say you'd like to be a teacher. Why aren't you allowed any vocation outside of the monarchy? Plenty of members of royal families have careers."

"None of the women in my family have, and my father won't permit it. For heaven's sake, I'm not even supposed to be wearing jeans!"

She couldn't blame everything on her father. Always wanting to please him and not cause him any more pain after her mother died, Luciana had often kept her mouth shut when she should have spoken up. And so outdated customs perpetuated.

"I couldn't bear the lack of liberty."

"This is the only existence I've ever known. I don't mean to sound critical. Of course, to be royalty is an unparalleled honor and I have many experiences few other people do. It's just that all we ever do in Izerote, really, is walk in place. I fear the world is passing my people by."

"Hence, the tourism that your fiancé will bring."

Luciana cringed at hearing Gio say the word *fiancé*. Somehow it sounded even more undesirable coming out of *his* mouth.

The princess had never been allowed to date. If she had, Gio was exactly the type of man she would have gravitated toward. An intellectual. An iconoclast. Someone without walls to his imagination. Who was determined, and knew how to achieve his goals. A man who was receptive, fair, considerate and could have a laugh at the world.

What was she doing? She didn't even really know this man and suddenly she was able to list his attributes? *While you're at it, Luci, don't forget drop-dead sexy!*

In fantasy, she could envision him as the perfect man and even make him hers. But in real life, he could be in a relationship. Married, even. He could have a girlfriend, a wife and even children in Hong Kong or Mumbai or any of the other places he mentioned working from recently.

Perhaps they were waiting for him to get everything settled in Florence before he sent for them.

Somehow, she didn't think so. It sounded as if he'd come to distrust the people around him. Probably even more so after that hack. As a matter of fact, he could be running some kind of charade of his own and she'd never be the wiser. She'd be smart not to forget that Gio Grassi was merely an unexpected addition to what was already a dream, but definitely one that she would wake up from.

Once again, she had to remind herself to remain optimistic about her future. Duty had its own rewards even if it was sometimes hard to see it that way.

Gio gently nudged her arm with his elbow, sensing that sadness was beginning to take her over. She half smiled in return.

"It won't be so bad," he said softly. "It sounds as if you love children. Even if you can't be a teacher, at least you will soon have some of your own."

"Yes, but what will I be birthing them into? The isolation of the palace?"

"They'll have you. You'll teach them to understand a larger world."

Luciana's eyes blinked back tears. Everything Gio said was so supportive. And she was so aware of not wanting to give the impression that she was ungrateful. Yet she burned inside for more to her life. To challenge her brain, to stretch her soul, even to explore her body.

There was a wedding night to come when her virginity would be taken for the purpose of breeding. Yet she knew that marital relations could involve more than the obligation to her monarchy.

From reading novels and watching movies, she could fathom carnal longings. She'd had vibrations in her body that hinted at pleasure, that even promised ecstasy. The way her breath had stuttered when Gio had placed his palm on the small of her back as he'd ushered her into the restaurant this evening. The way he always offered the crook of his arm for her to take, which forced her body to brush against his, making her swoon a bit each time.

She'd implored herself to shut down those reactions to him. They were highly improper.

However, the battle was being lost.

Standing on the bridge with him right now, she could hardly contain herself. She wanted him to grab hold of her, to take her into his arms with a male urgency that was savage. That knew her not as a princess but as a woman made of flesh and blood.

Not willing to settle any longer for only the reflection of him in the river's water, she turned to face him and he followed suit. She gazed into his eyes that shone like stars in the night.

As if reading her mind, he bent down toward her face and softly kissed her lips. His touch might have been light but a thousand sensations shimmered down her body, waking every inch of her.

Not willing to stop there, she stood up on her tiptoes to bring her lips to his a second time. She felt her softness melt against his firm mouth to share another stolen kiss. Knowing that she should back away, she instead opened her mouth slightly, to know the kind of kiss she'd read about in books and seen in movies. A lover's kiss, only for him. Which joined them and made her wish it was forever.

Her knees went weak.

As hard as it was, she finally pulled apart from him.

He reached to twirl a lock of her hair in his hand. And

then abruptly let it drop from his fingers. “I forgot you were wearing a wig.”

“It looks real but it’s artificial to the touch.”

“I shouldn’t have kissed you. I’m terribly sorry.”

“I wanted you to. I kissed you in return.” They looked at each other in anticipation. Of what? “It can’t happen again.”

“I know.”

Their eyes locked for what might have been minutes or it might have been hours.

Finally, they had to break their gaze and returned to looking down into the river.

“Do you dislike my wig?”

“I’ll admit I was shocked when you removed it to show me your natural hair.”

“It’s as if I’m someone else when I wear it.” Someone who would kiss a man she was so attracted to she might have burst out of her skin if she didn’t. “I like it.”

“You should keep wearing it, then, Luci. You should do whatever you want to do.”

Those were words Luciana heard so seldom she could hardly make sense of them. Do what she wanted to do? Right now what she was dying to do was to kiss this amazing man again. In this most romantic of places. Under the dark skies and atop this ancient bridge.

However, she’d settle for wearing the new clothes and the wig, playing a game of reverse dress-up.

And she’d savor having heard Gio utter words she never expected to hear.

You should do whatever you want to do.

CHAPTER FIVE

PRINCESS LUCIANA LINGERED across the street from the hair salon for the longest time. Watching the activity, she observed as women entered through its heavy glass door. Other women exited, and Luciana found herself imagining what their hair might have looked like earlier that morning. How many were just getting a trim of the style they had been wearing for a long time, a hairdo that their family and friends and coworkers were quite used to? Or were some experimenting with entirely new haircuts and colors, reinventing themselves from the hair down? Would they go home to compliments from their partners, or would their kids make fun of Mommy's new look?

Were the women leaving the shop happy with their new hair, or would they look in the mirror later in the day and bemoan that they had made a terrible mistake? Would they seek consolation from their sister or best friend, who would convince them that it would grow out soon enough?

Luciana thought she could stand there all day and contemplate the women of Florence, their lives and their loves. And their hair.

Luci would dash across the street, bound through the salon door and declare exactly how she wanted her hair done. Luciana wasn't so bold. When she did finally cross the street, it was slow and tentative, half of her not believing that her arm was actually pulling the handle of the door. In one fell swoop she opened it, hunching over a bit so that no one would see as she quickly yanked the blond wig off her head and stuffed it into her jacket pocket. Her own long curls fell down all around her face.

"May I help you?" a receptionist at the front desk greeted her. She'd obviously not seen the princess's slick move to remove her wig. The dark-haired woman, with a pen in one hand and a phone in the arch of her shoulder, juggled many activities.

"I'd like to get a haircut and color," Luciana murmured tentatively above the pounding electronic music and echoing chatter in the modern shop. It was designed with beige furnishings and bamboo trees presumably to give it a Zen sort of look that was totally incongruous with the decibel level of noise.

"Say it again, sweetheart," the receptionist requested.

"Cut and color, please," Luciana said a little louder.

"I have Gabriel available."

The woman pushed a button on a console. Luciana flipped through one of the hairstyle books on the counter and chose a photo of a cut that looked exactly like the wig she'd been wearing. Within a few minutes a slim young man with bleached white hair and many bracelets on one arm approached. Luci thought him very fashionable and excitedly told her inner Luciana not to be frightened. This was a good idea.

"*Carina!* Gorgeous face," Gabriel said as he took Luciana by the hand and brought her to his salon chair, fourth in the line of eight along the long wall. The chairs were white leather with a silver-studded pattern around the edges that, ironically, made them resemble thrones. A bite to the lip helped Luci hold back a giggle. Each throne faced a large mirror and shelves that held combs, scissors and other tools of the trade. "Take a seat. We'll talk before we cut."

"That's a relief."

Gabriel lifted her mane of hair and wove it in his fingers. "Healthy. Thick and glossy. But kind of like a child, long without a style, right?"

"Yes!" Luci exclaimed. "I have had my long hair as it is for my entire life." Just as her mother had worn her own long hair. Natural, perhaps brushed back from her face with a headband or arranged to complement a tiara.

"We need something modern," Gabriel said as he examined all of Luciana's hair, "and chic, right?"

"I'll show you," she piped up and showed him the photo from the salon book. "This."

"Blond. Shoulder length. Yes, this will look splendid on you." With a quick sweep, he gathered up all Her Royal Highness Princess Luciana's hair and grasped it in one hand. With the other, he reached for a pair of scissors from his workstation and held them in the air. "Are you ready?"

"Yes," Luci answered for Luciana, who was speechless and terrified.

"I'll take off some of the length and then we'll truly begin."

"Do it," Luci eagerly agreed in anticipation. Luciana clenched both her teeth and her fists.

With just a couple of snips, Gabriel cut a good six inches from the length of hair and let it fall from his hands. He and Luci and Luciana all watched as it hit the black salon floor.

Luciana's mouth dropped open in shock.

"Can I offer you a coffee?" Gabriel asked.

"Absolutely," she answered without hesitation.

As Gabriel worked his ministrations on her locks, Luciana reflected on how this trip had turned into much more than what she bargained for. Not only was she cutting her hair and wearing pants and touring Florence at her leisure, something far more important had happened. A six-foot-three-inch something, to be exact.

Jeans fade and hairstyles grow out, but meeting Gio would linger with her for the rest of her days. Last night on the bridge was surely the most romantic interlude she could possibly conceive of. The way they watched each other's reflection in the water. How they turned to stare into each other's eyes. Then he'd kissed her. What's more, she'd kissed him back. A real kiss!

Which they'd immediately backed away from. Both understanding that nothing more could ever happen between them. Knowing that what already had happened was too much.

They'd stood in the courtyard of the villa when they'd returned from the river, neither of them wanting to go to bed. In that prolonged good-night, a piece of Luciana died. She'd realized the totality of what she would never have. This swirling dream she was dancing in could last for a few weeks, but that's all it would ever be, a milky vision to reflect back on like a photo in a memory album. That was all she'd be taking home with her.

Sleep had eluded her. It was too grand not to recall over and over again their walk along the banks of the river. The way they chatted and discoursed, even argued, about everything they could think of from politics to art history to the evolution of Grasstech. Gio's family was so progressive. They thought far and wide. They took bold chances and weren't afraid to fail.

Princess Luciana wished she'd grown up with people like that around her. Her mother had been, effectively, silenced long before she gave birth to a daughter. While in her heart she had the utmost respect for her father's decisions to preserve Izerote's natural beauty and its idyllic way of life, that wasn't what Luciana would have chosen for herself.

"Finito," Gabriel chirped with a flourish as he lifted a hand mirror to show Luciana the finished job. Luci smiled from ear to ear because it looked exactly as the wig did, but now it was hers. It belonged to her. She could float up on angel wings for her hair felt as light as a feather without the weight of its former length down her back. The color was dramatic and sophisticated. Luci complimented Luciana on looking like a self-assured young woman, no longer a little girl.

Thankfully, Gio had insisted on giving her some money to keep in her pocket, so she was able to pay for the salon services.

Gio said he'd take a lunchtime break to show her one of Florence's most visited sights, the original statue of *David* at the Galleria dell'Accademia. Viggo would pick her up in front of the villa soon. She decided to wander in what was essentially *her* neighborhood now. A bench at a small park beckoned, where she took in the noonday sun, let the rays shine through her new hair and replayed the electrifying kissing from last night.

A child's ball hit her on the leg and snapped her out of her meditations.

"Mi dispiace," a tiny voice apologized as a little boy

came to fetch the ball. Probably about four years old, he had dark corkscrew curls and huge black velvet eyes.

"That's okay. Here you go." Luciana rolled the orange ball back to the boy, who wasn't able to stop it. It passed behind him. The child stood only a few feet from the bench Luciana was sitting on and she had rolled it very slowly on the ground, so it was odd that he had missed it.

"Matteo!" A woman about Luciana's age retrieved the ball and brought it back to the boy. "Try again, bambino." The boy took the ball from her and ran toward the other six or so children in the park.

"Hi, I'm Luci. Do you care for all of them?" Luciana asked the woman.

"I'm Chiara and I suppose you could say that. I'm their teacher." She pointed to a small building attached to a church. "We've come out from the nursery school to play before the children take a nap."

Luciana watched the children, who were now chasing pigeons. She smiled at their lovely faces.

"Do you enjoy being a teacher?" she asked the young woman, whose hair was piled into a loose bun and who wore an airy blouse with a lot of stains on it. Probably everything from paint to clay to jam.

Her Royal Highness often made appearances at schools and children's charities in Izerote. Of course, when she toured a facility she was dressed as a princess and rarely given anything to do but meet the children, who stared at her as if she worked for Disney. Or she might be permitted to do a nonmessy craft with them for five minutes. Nonetheless, she treasured the visits.

While there, she might observe a particular quirk about a child. How one interacted socially, perhaps having trouble when another child was around, or crying at the slightest provocation. How much she wished she could formally study the behavior of children, to play a part in helping them grow up to be fully functioning adults.

"Of course, Luci." Chiara brushed some dirt from her own hands while her eyes never left the children. "To encourage the evolving young minds, to listen to their ideas. What could be better? What do *you* do?"

Obviously, she couldn't reply that she was a princess. "I'm finding my way," she answered wistfully. "I'd love to work with children."

The two women conversed a bit more, both keeping a vigilant eye on the needs of the children. As Chiara had just expressed, to watch each child interact during play held endless fascination for Luciana. While at university, she'd taken classes in child development, but how she longed to earn an advanced degree. To study different styles of learning, gender analysis, social conduct. To make a difference in the lives of precious, unrestrained children.

For a fleeting minute, Luciana felt like Luci, a denizen of this great city. A woman who had a direction and was at ease with herself, and who was in a secure relationship with a wonderful man.

What? Luciana caught her own thought. Even if she were free to love, Gio had made very clear that a serious relationship was most definitely not on his agenda. Last night's spontaneous kisses had probably meant nothing to him. Not only did he need to concentrate on the responsibilities of running an enormous corporation that was on top of its competitors, Gio was a man who lived out of a suitcase without entanglements. Just because he was spending time in Florence didn't mean that was immediately going to change.

Nonetheless, for just an iota longer, Luciana pictured her life as a Florentine schoolteacher in love. Imagining what she was going to cook for her man tonight and the warm embraces she'd have with him in their bed.

The boy with the big doe eyes threw the ball to Luciana again. She tossed it gently back and, again, he missed it.

"Chiara." Luciana leaned in toward her so the boy wouldn't hear. "I don't think he's seeing the ball clearly. Has he had his vision checked? I think he might need eyeglasses."

"That's a good observation, Luci. I will mention it to his parents when they come to pick him up."

After Chiara and the children left, Luci walked home to get ready to sightsee with Gio. Feeling very Luci indeed.

Although Luciana kept insisting that she wanted to see Florence as a typical tourist would, Gio was sure she'd just as soon not queue up for hours to see Michelangelo's *David* at the Accademia. Nor did he have the time to do so. Therefore, he was glad he had asked an assistant to book tickets in advance for a reserved entrance time. As it was he'd had to rearrange several meetings in order to free his schedule for a few hours. It was actually rather ridiculous that he was sightseeing in the middle of the day.

Gio himself hadn't seen what was one of the most visited locations in Europe in many years. He'd forgotten just how imposing and magnificent *David* really was until they approached the statue, ringed by tourists studying the work from all perspectives. The marble champion, who as the story went, was a young shepherd when he slew his powerful opponent, Goliath, with cleverness rather than might, stood raised on a pedestal for all to see.

"Michelangelo was only in his twenties when he carved this," Luciana commented to Gio while they both studied the details. "What an amazing achievement for such a young person."

"In addition to all of the other works he did in his career."

"One of the greatest artists the world has ever known. I've been waiting for so long to see this. Thank you for bringing me here."

"Look at how defined the eye sockets are. That gives him such a look of watchfulness."

"That's what they say about the biblical character it's based on. David has his slingshot there—" she pointed to the detail over his left shoulder "—that he used to defeat Goliath with only five stones."

They moved incrementally around the statue, carved from a single block of marble, observing every minute feature. The prominent veins in David's hands, the rigidity of his muscles, yet his bent left leg suggested the innocence of youth. The work was so well preserved and compelling that it felt as current now as it had been when Michelangelo created it in the early 1500s.

Gio felt himself relaxing. There had been a couple of stressful moments already today when he'd had to make decisions related to the employee structure of the company. People's jobs were on the line and it was up to him, and ultimately only him, to decree what was in the corporation's best interest. Which could be a ruthless job. He'd called his father at the vineyard. They'd discussed it over the phone and come to a decision.

He was especially interested in deciding on a new location for a manufacturing plant to produce his new slate of biometric products. With the dozens and dozens of offices and manufacturing sites Grasstech had amassed, Gio enjoyed bringing new and good-paying jobs to towns or villages whose citizens needed the employment.

"Do we have time to see some of the other works of art here?" Luciana asked after they'd circled David three times.

"I'm all yours."

Luciana looked at him with big eyes as a small smile fought to come across her mouth even though she resisted it with a bite to her lower lip.

Gio fought a grin, too, at the words that had come out wrong. He was hardly all hers, for heaven's sake!

Last night as they'd stood on the bridge, he didn't know what had driven him to kiss her, a move he hadn't been planning and knew he mustn't repeat. But there hadn't been a glimmer of censorship as his head bent down for that split second of contact with lips as pillow-soft as could be. Most unexpectedly, she'd lifted them to kiss him again and hadn't settled for the brief brush he had. No, she'd kissed him like a lover, bold and self-assured. With that, she'd rocked him to his very core.

After they'd lingered in the villa courtyard and finally said good-night, he'd lain awake in bed, high on Luciana. Like she was a drug that sent him levitating above his body. She was like no one he'd ever met, exhilarating and tragic all at once. Thoughts of seeing her again had popped into his head all night long in spite of his telling himself to get to sleep.

Gio had spent so much time alone. Even before the fiasco with Francesca, he'd been only casually dating, never able to see how a woman would fit into his life. A life dedicated to his mind and to creativity would be it for him.

Like many people who entered the world of computer science, he was not especially social by nature. More comfortable inside technology, absorbed in work. Like Michelangelo, who was said to sometimes lie down on the ground in his clothes and boots to sleep in small increments because he worked almost continually and barely ate. Gio understood how it was to get lost in a project, in the painstaking process of solving one problem after the next until he developed a solution.

Even with his parents' nearly sublime marriage as an example, Gio never imagined himself as someone who would settle down with a wife and children. He feared because of the attention he paid to his work that he would never be able to give a family the focus they deserved. Yet spending time with Luciana, it dawned on him that, with the right person, anything was possible.

"I want to see the slaves." Luciana brought him from his musings.

Taking her by the hand, and registering its smallness in his, he snaked through the crowd and led her to another hall in the gallery that held the works usually referred to as the *Prisoners*.

Four of them were on display here and others in museums elsewhere in the world. These Michelangelo works were considered *nonfinito*, or incomplete, although it wasn't known for sure as to whether he had left them unfinished on purpose as a way of explaining his own artistry.

"Michelangelo was quoted as saying something to the effect that he was merely a tool and that the sculptures were already there in the marble. His job was only to carve away what would allow the art to be seen," Luciana said.

"Ah, so we both studied art history at university. It was a good counterbalance for me to the world of science and mathematics."

"I've always been especially drawn to the Italian masters."

The four works were devastating. Each depicted a man who had not yet broken through and was still trapped within the marble. With a leg or a torso or a face not yet visible, they appeared to be half man and half stone.

"Some scholars speculate they represent man's struggle to be free," Luciana added pensively. Her face changed from admiration at the work to something personal and melancholy. Gio guessed it was the idea of being trapped in marble, bound, incomplete, unable to actualize one's full self, that had gotten to her on a profound level.

Out of the corner of his eye, Gio spotted two men wearing black suits who appeared to be looking their way. They didn't hold professional cameras or else he might have suspected that they were paparazzi that recognized Princess Luciana, although she'd told him that she was not a high-profile royal like some. Anyway, with that blond wig she was so enamored of and her new wardrobe of comfortable clothes, he doubted that the press would make the connection.

He dearly hoped that they weren't palace security from Izerote, a possibility that Luciana feared. That her father had been keeping tabs on her all along. That perhaps an arrangement had been made to allow Luciana a couple of days under the delusion that she was on her own when, really, she'd been surveilled by her father's missives all along. Who might pounce on her any minute, thereby ending this expedition that meant so much to her.

Although he was sure he would have detected it previously if they were being followed. Subtly glancing over to the men again, he saw they were now turned away from Gio and Luciana. Perhaps they were just undercover overseers for the gallery.

Strangely, he wanted to protect the princess. Fury bubbled in him as he watched her study the captives in marble, knowing she was in her own prison. Fury at her father and at a faraway land he didn't know, for forcing her to conform to outmoded conventions and gender rules that made no sense to Gio. If only he knew of a way to help Luciana's island of Izerote so that she didn't have to marry the neighboring king.

Why he'd come to care so much about Luciana in such a short time, he didn't know. Maybe it was his general disdain for injustice.

After Luciana had her fill of seeing a few of the other halls of art in the Accademia, they exited. "I can afford a little more time. Let me show you another tourist sight. Did you change something about your wig? It looks nice."

"This is the Ponte Vecchio." Gio swept his arm across the vista of the bridge filled with people.

"It's much different from the ones we saw last night." Luciana studied the bridge that was lined on both sides by shops and structures with windows.

"Centuries ago, it was butchers and fishmongers who sold their wares along this bridge. Now, as you can see, there are galleries and souvenir shops but mainly jewelers."

Indeed, Luciana and Gio walked past one small jewelry shop after the next. Gold, silver and other precious metals beckoned from the outward-facing glass cases the vendors used to attract buyers. Gemstones sparkled. Tourists pointed at items.

"It's an old saying that many a man lost his fortune by taking his wife walking along the Ponte Vecchio," Gio declared.

They observed as a man and a shopkeeper excitedly argued, their arm gestures and shaking heads indicating they had not yet reached a deal. A group of young women pointed at diamond rings from another vendor. Every few storefronts, instead of fine jewels, tables of figurines depicting the statue of *David* were for sale. Little *Davids* meant to sit on a desk as a memento of time spent in Florence. Naked *Davids* on cell phone cases. Luciana smiled wryly. Had she been princess of a larger monarchy, she might have ended up with her own likeness on a coffee mug.

From the bridge, they stopped to watch a sightseeing boat as it made its way underneath.

Gio bent his arm for Luciana to take, and they continued on.

A necklace caught Luciana's eye. Simple silver, its several strands of different lengths created a statement.

"Do you like that?" Gio inquired why she had fixated on that one piece.

"It's only that I have one very much like it."

"Did you sell it in Barcelona?"

"Not that one."

Suddenly, guilt thundered through Luciana's body. Had she completely lost her mind, selling palace jewels? Which technically didn't really belong to her. They were only hers to wear during her reign and would then be gracing her children and their children and so on. What right had she had to sell what wasn't even hers?

Her heartbeat sped to a rapid thump. In coming here, she'd rebelled against her father, who only wished for her protection. He was probably worried sick. If only he would have been more lenient with her, had let her travel, and had encouraged her to study and explore her curiosities. Or if she'd been more defiant, rather than always placating him. Then maybe she wouldn't have gone behind his back to take this drastic action most unfitting to her position. He must be in shock after his obedient daughter, who always thought first of pleasing him, had fled the island just weeks before her wedding! Yet she'd never meant to hurt him.

Absentmindedly, she touched her hair, still surprised by how silky and lightweight it was. Even Gio had complimented her on it today, without knowing why. She'd chosen not to tell Gio about the haircut. Not wanting him to think she'd taken on yet another form of disguise. It occurred to her that with his wealth and status, women left and right must present themselves in ways they think would attract him, whether it was their true selves or not.

Now she thought of her new hair as just another disappointment for her father. It would grow out. Just like the haircut, this crazy adventure would be a blip on her radar. Once she returned home, she'd take her rightful place. This city, the statue of *David*, Gio, would become pale remembrances that were completely incongruous with the life she was to lead.

Perhaps someday she'd return to Florence, to show her children the superlative art or to appear at an official occasion. She'd arrive on a private plane to be met by a limousine, and with bodyguards and palace personnel surrounding her like a butterfly net, she'd be escorted from one building into another. Never breathing fresh air, never strolling the backstreets, never watching children play ball in a park.

And she'd most certainly never, ever keep company with this fascinating and accomplished man who made her see herself as anything but a sequestered dusty relic on an island that no one cared about.

"You're regretting your decision to have sold some of your jewelry?" Gio leaned his head down close to hers as she fixed her gaze on the silver necklace.

"I don't know if I should have come here. I think I've made a terrible mistake."

"You won't regret this. It will help you along your path."

She looked him in the eye. "Why are you such a wise old sage for a techie?"

Gio laughed, a resounding guffaw that bounced through her, making her visualize yet again what it would be like to be married to a man with whom she could talk about big concepts and laugh with a dark sense of humor.

"You've learned about me already, *bellissima.* I have a mind for profound thoughts and no common sense in other matters. Which reminds me, I wanted to ask your opinion about the press statement for our new facility in Dallas."

Along the Ponte Vecchio, they chatted about catchphrases and wording. Luciana was grateful she had knowledge about *something* that was useful to him. Dealing with the media was a valuable thing her father had taught her, to be careful what she said and did because someone was always watching.

Her arm in Gio's, they sauntered on. She willed the yearning that rose when her body brushed against him to subside. There was no reason to think Gio had those same stirrings in return. He was not looking for love, and would not accept finding it, either. She sensed he'd been hurt by love, although he never went into any detail about it. That kiss between them had been spontaneous, and it was she who prolonged it. Nothing was going to change between them as a result of it.

Which was perfectly okay. In fact, it was essential. He could be relied on to keep her growing emotions in check. Because hers were moving into dangerous waters.

"I really do have to return to the office," he said, "but I'd like to share with you one other important thing that both locals and tourists do after they've been exploring our city's streets."

"What is that?"

"Let me show you."

They reached the opposite end of the Ponte Vecchio. The bridge emptied out to the Oltrarno, the other side of the river, the part of the city that had many historic places to see but was much less touristy.

Her arm in his, Luciana had a feeling she would follow him anywhere. He took her down one quiet street and then made a right into another and another until she thought they were secret agents outwitting evil foes.

With this little dash into the Oltrarno, he had brought them far from the crowds, from the doggy dishes with pictures of *David* on them, and the salt and pepper shakers shaped like the Duomo.

Finally, they reached their destination. Gelateria dei Frediano.

"Gelato, Princess. All the problems of the world could be solved with the right gelato."

He held the door open for her to enter the shop. The smell of fresh cream immediately took her by storm. Patrons sat on ice cream parlor chairs around small marble tables, giving the place a historic vibe. In fact, there was a sign above the old-fashioned cash register that read Established 1929.

Luciana eagerly inspected the cold cases that held silver trays of many flavors of gelato in small batches. From the caramel color to the pale green to the chocolate-studded white, each one promised to be more delicious than the next.

"How could one ever select?" Luciana exclaimed, glancing up to Gio, who had been watching her as she deliberated at the glass cases.

"Pick several. We'll have a tasting menu."

"They all look delectable. You choose."

"Why don't you have a seat over there?" He pointed to an empty table in the far back of the shop.

After a few minutes, Gio joined her with a tray of three small silver dishes, all containing scoops of the creamy treat.

"What did you get?"

"I'll let you guess," Gio said as he sat down and placed the tray on the marble table. "Close your eyes."

"What?"

"Close your eyes so that you can focus only on the taste of the gelato."

She was both entranced and horrified at the suggestions that she should close her eyes here in a public place. But she knew that Luci would think it was fun to shut out the distraction of sight so that she could become intoxicated by the flavors. For her sake, Luciana obliged.

With her eyes closed, she was hyperaware of Gio's presence next to her. Warmth and strength emanated from his direction.

Was he going to kiss her?

After a moment of almost unbearable anticipation, the first thing she sensed was the cold metal of a spoon as it touched her lips. Gio maneuvered the spoon a little bit so that it coaxed her lips to part. "That's right," he murmured softly, his voice crawling over her and making her twitch in her seat.

She felt the first bit of the gelato move from the spoon into her mouth. The pure creaminess coupled with the sweet flavoring made her tongue circle. "Oh," she moaned after the first of it slid down her throat, "that was so good."

"What flavor do you think it was?" he asked but then didn't give her a chance to respond as he slipped another spoonful of the same flavor between her lips.

"It tastes like nuts," she answered in a voice that didn't even sound like her own. Did Gio know how much he was arousing her with his little game? That as he fed her the ice cream, a secret pulsing was starting from down inside her body, in her most intimate center? And that the sound of his voice was only making the throb pound stronger and louder?

"Nuts. Good guess. But what kind?"

To get any last bits that could help her formulate her answer, she rolled her tongue all the way around her lips to catch every drop. At that action, a whisper-quiet groan escaped from Gio's lips, causing her to open her eyes.

"No fair, Luci. Close your eyes," he ordered and she obeyed.

"Is it hazelnut?"

"Very good." He dabbed at her lips with a napkin, and her spine sharply straightened. She knew that no one in the shop would be able to see them, as the table was in a dark corner and Gio's back was shielding them from view. But she did momentarily consider how wholly inappropriate this exercise was.

It was only a fleeting thought, though, before the metal touched her lips again, making her forget who she was, what she was, as she could only surrender to Gio's spoon and what it told her to do.

"This one is easy. It has to be strawberry. The pink one I saw in the display case."

"You're good at this, Luci." They both knew why he kept mentioning her Florence nickname.

He ran the tip of the spoon along her lower lip. Her tongue followed the motion to chase any specks of the fruity goodness that might have lingered. Then he abruptly took the spoon away, and the tip of her tongue darted out to try to catch it, though it was gone. Gio's easy laugh shot straight into the base of her belly.

"Are you ready?" He brought the spoon back to tease her lips apart again. Her eyes involuntarily popped open. His smiling face and the nod he gave her was an unspoken direction to close them again. Which she did, with a slow inhale that filled her lungs with the fragrance of the shop.

To the next creamy offering, she rolled the gelato around her mouth again. "Chocolate. A dark chocolate at that."

"Taste more," he said as he fed her another bite.

"Delicious."

"Exquisite."

"Did you have some?"

"No. I was talking about…" He stopped himself.

Luci raised her eyelids. Gio wasn't smiling anymore. His brows creased and his nostrils flared. There was a flush in his cheeks.

"Is something wrong?"

"No," he bit out. "I need to get back to work."

In a split second, his mood had gone from playful to upset. She didn't understand what had happened, and truth be told, she was intoxicated from the ice cream feeding. His displeasure was making her dizzy.

He shot up and pulled her so she was standing, too. Then he steered her out of the shop so fast her feet didn't touch the ground. With a quick wave, he hailed a taxi and secured her inside. "I'll walk to my office from here and see you later at the villa."

CHAPTER SIX

"Tell him we'll ship the first hundred thousand to him by November." Gio gave Samuele his verdict during their daily briefing in his office. It was late afternoon and the sun had moved away from the windows, letting a thick whiteness blanket the sky.

"That's a reasonable commitment. But what is bothering you?" The older man leaned forward in his chair facing Gio at his desk. "You are snappy and distracted."

Why did Samuele have to read him so well? Maybe because he was like an uncle? Because he'd been with the company since the beginning? Had watched Gio and Dante grow from young children into men?

Gio gave him a snarl, though it was quickly diffused by Samuele's loving smile.

The truth was, Gio still hadn't recovered from that gelato-eating-turned-erotic encounter he'd had with Princess Luciana a few hours earlier. Not to mention the explosive kiss the night before. He reprimanded himself for his impulsive behavior. There was no way that spoon-feeding sweet ice cream into her luscious little mouth was going to have been a good idea. What he hadn't realized was just how bad a move it was. Because while he may have satiated Luciana's appetite for the Italian treat, it had left him ravenous. For her. Which was not in the plan at all.

Indeed, as he played the guessing game with her and her eyes had closed, a craving came over Gio so powerful it almost pushed him to madness. Watching her pink tongue dart out to chase the ice cream was a sight he couldn't imagine would ever get old. A voracious surge had forced itself through him as he told her to keep her eyes closed, leaving her defenseless and in his charge.

There was more he wanted from her as he visualized at least a dozen places on her body where he'd like to sample gelato from. By the time that list was made, the hunger was visible on his body, and he'd had to shift sideways in his chair to keep the princess from noticing. It was at the most inopportune moment that she opened her eyes and was able to perceive his discomfort with the arousal.

Gio studied Samuele's face, wrinkled with age but still very much alive and present.

"Samuele, do you trust Ginevra?" Samuele's second wife. His first had died young.

"Of course. Without trust there is no love. And without love, life is not worth living."

"But do you really trust her? Do you keep secrets from her, about work or about your hopes or feelings? Because you're worried that one day she might use something against you?"

"*Mio amico*, what are you talking about? Of course I've trusted both of my wives with everything. Just as your father trusts your mother."

Gio's telephone rang. "Yes. Schedule that meeting for two weeks."

"I understand. This is still about that woman in Hong Kong."

Francesca. Samuele had guessed correctly. Gio had no idea how to reconcile the disloyalty she had dealt him with the love that the men around him had for the women in their lives.

With casual encounters his norm, it had been fairly simple for Gio to make his decision after Francesca showed her true colors. That betrayal had put his company in jeopardy, his family in jeopardy. She'd been the only woman he'd ever let get close, and so he was convinced that was that. He'd never let a woman in ever again. Nor did he have any inclination to.

Sure, he could date all the women he wanted. A new one every night if he so desired. Without intimacy, without even good faith.

Ever.

Easy.

Over and done.

So why was he questioning that proclamation?

"When you meet the right woman, you'll know," Samuele continued. "It fits perfectly with your coming back to sit at this desk, doesn't it? Firenze is your home again, and she will find you here."

"I think you're wrong."

"Love has a way of showing up whether you think you're searching for it or not."

When Samuele left his office, Gio replayed his words over and over. Maybe love was meant to be for Samuele, who had the good fortune to find it again after loss. However, it wasn't going to happen for Gio.

One thing he was crystal clear about was that the mischief at the *gelateria* with the princess hadn't been a good turn of events. For either of them. Whatever force had come over him while feeding the sweet ice cream into her scrumptious mouth needed to be locked back up, and quick.

It was probably another unwise plan that he told her they'd cook dinner together at the villa tonight, as they had been going to restaurants since the day she arrived. Being at home with her would be much too friendly. After he'd thought he might lift delicate Princess Luciana de la Isla de Izerote up onto the marble table at the *gelateria* and ravish her with a passion he didn't even know he had, spending the evening alone with her might be dangerous business he shouldn't dabble in.

But she was so excited when he'd told her he would come for her in time to visit the food stalls at the Mercato Centrale, he didn't want to let her down. It certainly wasn't her fault that his gentlemanly self-control was being tested to its limits. Technically, it was her fault for having such a swanlike neck and porcelain skin and caramel eyes as fine as the gelato she'd tasted. However, the internal struggle to keep himself from again pressing his mouth into those bowed lips was his, not hers.

If nothing else was able to hold him back, there was one truth of such importance that it would supersede any other impulses he might need to fight.

He didn't know it as fact, but he'd make an assumption.

Her Royal Highness was almost certainly a virgin.

A virgin bride, soon to be married. No matter how much Luciana protested that she would never love the widower king she was to wed, Gio could never live with himself if she gave her maidenhood to a man she met on a prewedding runaway holiday. And, man-to-man, however unpleasantly she described her fiancé, Gio wouldn't carry on his shoulders any part of her deception to him.

A gruesome thought came over him. No one still utilized medieval methods of examination to ensure a princess bride's virginity, did they? He didn't know if indignities like that were even historically factual or just folklore he'd heard of, but that was another thing he surely didn't want to spend his life worrying about. Because, much as he hated to admit, he had a premonition that he'd wonder about Princess Luciana long after she left Florence. He'd best be careful to leave his fantasies at just that. Not realities he'd mull over for eternity, knowing he'd done the wrong thing.

It was simple, then. Under no circumstances would he let anything else romantic happen between him and Princess Luciana. Not tonight and not ever.

"Florence's central market," Gio announced to Luciana when they exited the car.

An enthusiastic smile crossed her lips.

"So many people." She flipped her head from left to her right.

"Yes, this is one of the busiest parts of the city."

The streets that surrounded the old market building were filled with outdoor traders selling their wares under tarped canopies to shelter from any weather. Buyers thronged three deep to peruse the offerings.

"Can we look at these stalls before we go into the market?"

"Of course."

"I've never been to a place like this before."

Gio didn't doubt it. While he had wandered through the souks of Morocco, the bazaars in Istanbul and the Far East Asian night markets, Luciana had no such experiences. Being in crowds such as this would be considered too dangerous for a princess to walk through. Even with an entourage, he supposed the princess had probably never been in a crush of shoppers.

They maneuvered into the thick of the marketplace. Unlike the food and food-related products that dominated the *mercato*, the outdoor vendors sold leather, pottery, souvenirs, scarves and sunglasses. Each stall was attended to by a merchant or two, some yelling about their wares or special pricing.

Luciana was so aware of people all around her, her eyes darting this way or that when someone touched her.

"I'm not used to being so physically close to so many people."

"You're going to be bumped into, rubbed up against and even shoved. If you're uncomfortable, let's leave."

"Certainly not," she said, giving his hand a playful tug that brought a hitch to one corner of his mouth. "I'm not made of glass, you know. I won't break!"

Gio had a moment's caution when he thought of himself as responsible for her safety. Even though no one had put her under his supervision, he considered himself nonetheless to be her guardian. After all, she was a princess in a strange land.

Judging from the happiness on her face, though, she was having too much fun to be daunted with any further warnings. Besides, while there were surely pickpockets and thieves in the area, the San Lorenzo markets of Firenze were hardly dangerous places. He'd watch over her to make sure she used common sense.

"Look at those colors." She pointed to one stall that held a selection of silk scarves hanging from hooks. Bright pinks and purples and yellows, every color in the rainbow was utilized in the dying of fabric to create them.

An emerald green scarf captured Luciana's attention. She looked around to see how other shoppers inspected the merchandise, unsure how close a scrutiny was customary.

"You can touch it," Gio prodded.

Luciana reached out to a corner of the scarf, rolling it between her fingers, then holding it up to check the transparency.

"One for fifteen, two for twenty-five." The hawk-like merchant quickly seized on her interest. He added a sales pitch, "The color is beautiful with your eyes."

Luciana let go of the scarf and they started to move to the next stall.

"Wait," the scarf vendor called out, "try it on. I'll give you a deal."

Gio and Luciana smiled at each other. She glanced back at the scarf that she really seemed to like.

"Haggle with him," Gio said to her. "That's the way of these markets."

"I can't do that."

"Of course you can, Luci."

The green hue of the scarf was apparently enough to lure her back. The merchant detached the item from the dozens he exhibited on hooks. Luciana stepped closer and the man wrapped the long scarf twice around her neck, creating a very chic style. He handed her a mirror to see for herself. "I'll give you two for twenty, a special price, only for you."

"Do you see a second one you like?" Gio whispered in her earshot only.

She shook her head no.

"Then make him an offer."

"I only want one," Luciana stated to the merchant, but in a tentative voice.

"Usually I charge fifteen for one. I'm offering you two for twenty."

"No," she said with a firmer volume that made Gio proud. "If you'll give me two for twenty, then how about one for ten?"

"You'll have the other one for a gift," the vendor persisted.

When she returned to her home at the palace, Gio knew that Luciana was not going to be giving presents she'd bought at street markets. No, instead she would be spending weeks, if not months, trying to quell the anger of her father and her fiancé after she'd run away on this trip. Souvenirs were not going to be appropriate.

"Take the scarf off and hand it back to him," Gio counseled. "Then we start to walk away again."

The merchant grunted as she tried to hand him the scarf. "You drive a hard bargain, *bambolina*." He wouldn't take it from her, insisting that she hold on to it. "Okay. Thirteen-fifty for one."

Luciana shook her head. "Twelve."

"Twelve? You want to put me in the poorhouse?" he balked with a grin.

"Twelve," she said with resolve.

"Okay, okay."

Inside the old market building, as it had been for centuries, fresh food was for sale. As he and Luciana browsed the first aisle, several stands held the ripest- and juiciest-looking produce, from dark greens to crisp bell peppers to oranges with skin so bright you could almost smell them from a distance. Another stall had dried pastas in every imaginable shape, some tinged black from the ink of squids, others flecked with a beautiful green from spinach. A big wooden sign leading to a kitchen area read Pasta-Making Classes Here.

Another merchant sold a wide array of olive oils from regions all over the country, the amber of their color distinguishing the varieties. Yet another stand was lined with a case of fine cheeses, from the creamy and runny to the crumbly hard of the finest Parmesan.

“What would you like to cook tonight?” Gio asked Luciana as he enjoyed seeing the green scarf around her neck and recalled the negotiation for it with amusement.

“Perhaps pasta and vegetables? And cut fruit afterward.”

“Pasta with a sauce?”

“Last night at that restaurant by the river we had simple pasta tossed in olive oil and fresh tomatoes with basil. Let’s make that.”

Luciana chose a seller she thought had the most enticing offerings.

“I’ve never picked tomatoes before,” she confided to Gio. “I’m assuming they should be dark and firm.”

Together, they chose tomatoes from a big pile, showing each other potential candidates for the other to approve. The stall was supervised by an old woman in a knit hat who probably assumed that he and Luciana were a couple. Although they could be merely coworkers, or even siblings, or just friends.

Friends? Was that what they were? Gio barely knew how to understand these last few days let alone put a label on them. Friends had to start from some point but soon knew each other well, often seeing one another through the trials and tribulations of their days. He and Luciana weren’t that. They were friendly acquaintances, he’d grant only that much.

As he watched Luciana sort through the bunches of basil on offer, he contemplated whether she had hoped that romance would be part of her exploration here in Italy. Maybe she had longed to know attraction and lust before the arranged marriage she was to enter when she returned home. Maybe she'd imagined being swept off her feet by a swarthy and confident Italian Casanova, a stereotype perpetuated in movies and TV shows. He believed her to be virtuous, but he did wonder if she wanted to play at courtship in this most romantic of cities.

That was something he couldn't help her with. Too risky, for one thing, if his own body's reaction during the gelato tasting was any indication. And thank goodness she'd pulled away after that passionate kiss on the bridge. Gio wouldn't have the slightest notion how to pretend to woo a woman yet be expected to know exactly when to back off and put the charade down so that he kept it safe for her.

He wouldn't step foot in that territory. If he wanted something he took it, and nothing stopped him. Maybe he was that cliché of an Italian lover, after all. Because want Her Royal Highness he did, so he had to jerk back his own reins.

Luciana brought the tomatoes and basil to the old woman so that she could weigh them and charge her.

"Three-fifty," the woman said. Gio reached in his pocket for his cash and began to count it out.

"Three," Luciana challenged. The princess was apparently using her newly learned bargaining skills, not knowing that produce wasn't usually brought to auction.

"No, Luci," he said with a chuckle, "these are set prices."

After all the groceries were purchased, Gio and Luciana made their way out of the market and onto the street where Viggo was waiting to take them home.

In the car, Luciana scrunched her nose with concern. “I should have mentioned that I don’t know how to cook.”

“I’ve been living in hotels for years. I have no idea how to cook, either. But it’s just pasta, right? How hard can it be?”

At the villa, Gio used his key fob to open the doors to the main residence of the villa. Since Luciana had been staying at the compound, she’d never been inside the *big house*, as he called it.

“So this is where you grew up?”

“Here, and summers at the vineyard.” Gio had described the vineyard and winery in Chianti where his retired parents now lived.

As they stepped inside, Luciana admired the furnishings in the huge sitting room that faced the courtyard. Glass doors running the entire length allowed light, and fresh air if desired, to permeate the room. The space was divided into different sections. One sitting area was close to the doors, with two sofas facing each other and some armchairs. It was done with white and pink fabrics, giving it a cheerful mood.

A dining area with a long rustic wood table able to seat twenty or so took up another portion of the room. Comfortable-looking upholstered tan chairs surrounded it. A grouping of dark green chairs was arranged in a corner by a fireplace where tall bookcases lined the walls.

Everything was done in a casual sophistication befitting this most successful of Florentine families. It made her want to meet Gio’s mother, whom he credited for the interior design. Large mirrors everywhere gave the room an ambience that was stately without being at all stuffy. Art objects of historical significance sat on side tables, and Italian landscape paintings adorned the walls.

This was distinguished yet unceremonious. Stylish without taking itself too seriously. Comfortable in its own skin yet at the ready to summon strong passions.

Oh, wait. Luciana was reviewing the furniture, not Gio.

She couldn't resist a long gander at his visage as she caught it in profile in one of the mirrors. There was no doubt he was a breathtaking man. Although because he was, at heart, a scientist with his nose in a laptop much of the time, he was hardly the entitled playboy billionaire one might expect based on his family's success.

He'd mentioned that there had been women in his life he viewed as predators. Luciana didn't doubt that there might be many who saw only money and position when they looked at him. Women who were motivated by what they could get from him, be it a luxury lifestyle or a career gain. That must be tied into his reasons for staying single, not letting anyone get too close. He'd probably experienced personal betrayal, been used.

For her, being with Gio made her actually believe in trust.

And hope. And enthusiasm.

And a womanliness she had never known anything of before. Never to be nurtured in her, but it was nice to know that it existed.

Or was it torture?

She'd been having the most daring thoughts, ones that the kiss on the bridge and the gelato tasting only served to heighten. Gio made her want to explore something that wouldn't be found in a travel book. Luci, too, had begun to wonder about…

Lovemaking.

With Gio.

Could that be part of her awakening here in Florence? To know the pleasures of the flesh? That kiss had prompted a flood of desire, as if it had been shored up inside her and only Gio could set it flowing.

"This way to the kitchen." Gio jogged her out of those visions as he carried in the grocery bags they had bought at the central market. Luciana touched the green scarf still wrapped loosely around her neck. She knew that slip of fabric was going to be ultimately tucked into a back corner of a drawer in her bureau at the palace. Years from now and decades after that, she'd pull out the testament to the prewedding journey that changed her view of life, and herself, forever.

Perhaps it would have been better not to have taken this trip. Then she'd never have to live with the memories of bargaining at the San Lorenzo market or of taking in the sheer brilliance of Michelangelo's *David*. Of watching joyous children play in a piazza. And especially of Gio awakening her sexuality and forcing her to understand want. In the end, she might even hate him for showing her something she could never have.

What if she didn't go home? What if she could just stay here with him, in this beautiful villa, for the rest of her life? Would that smash her relationship with her father beyond repair?

She'd always put her father first, thought long and hard against taking any action that might displease him. Perhaps she should have better understood her own yearnings all along, and learned to negotiate with him rather than simply obey. Maybe then her need to catch her breath away from the demands of the palace wouldn't have become so desperate. Might her father in time have come to accept that she could not live her entire life denying her hopes and aspirations?

"Oh, how nice," Luciana commented when they entered the kitchen, brightening to appreciate the moment at hand. A black-and-white-tiled floor surrounded a large island workstation. Hanging light fixtures contributed to the slightly 1950s retro look, everything painted white with some red accents. Several ovens, refrigerators and an industrial-style dishwasher let her know that this was a kitchen created for entertaining. Built-in cupboards and pantries attested to the smart design of the space. A large rack that hung from the ceiling held copper pots and pans and baskets of other cooking tools.

"My grandmother used to cook up a storm in here. When all the family was here for a Sunday supper or a holiday, we were a formidable crowd. She'd have every implement in use."

"On her own?"

"My grandmother cooked everything. Mom and my aunts would pitch in to get everything on platters and served. They always left the cleaning to the kids. They said they didn't want us to get spoiled rotten. That cleaning the kitchen, which would look like a tidal wave had hit it by the end of the meal, would be good for us."

"Was it?"

"Of course. It built teamwork among the cousins. Plus, it was a big job so it forced us to develop a plan, delegate work, problem solve. Fabulous training for anything in life, really."

"I'm never allowed in the palace kitchen. It is attended to around the clock by staff. It's too risky for me to be in there. After all, a fork might fall to the floor." Luciana spit out sarcasm that surprised even her. "If I ever want a tea or something other than at mealtimes I, of course, merely press a button and it magically appears on a silver platter."

"Okay." Gio inventoried the ingredients he laid on the counter. "Spaghetti with diced tomatoes, basil, grated cheese and olive oil."

"Sounds wonderful."

"Why don't you wash the tomatoes?" he directed Luciana, who was only too delighted to have a task in the kitchen. She took note of the shiny skin and rich red color of the tomatoes they had picked. Turning on the tap at one of the small sinks, she rinsed their lovely selections and dried them on a nearby towel.

This was already great fun. She thought up a pretend scenario for her and Gio, preparing a simple weeknight supper just for the two of them. Perhaps they'd put the pasta into large bowls that they'd hold on their laps while they watched television. Both of them having changed from their workday clothes into loungewear, she'd wear striped fuzzy socks while Gio sat barefoot as they laughed at an American comedy show.

Never to be.

She watched as Gio filled a large pot with water. He carried it over to the stove and lit one of the burners under it.

"Right now, we can cut up the tomatoes and basil." He read the instructions on the spaghetti package. "When the water boils, we put the pasta in for eight minutes or until al dente."

"Why do you think it says *or* until al dente? Why wouldn't it be eight minutes every time?"

"Because the instructions don't indicate exactly how much water to use. It reads *'Fill a large pot with water.'*

If you had two pots of boiling water but of differing volumes, that could affect the time it takes to cook the pasta."

"Okay. That makes sense."

"Also, it reads *'Boil over a high heat.'* That's not very specific, as burners would vary from kitchen to kitchen. As a matter of fact, some are gas and some are electric, which would, theoretically, produce a different result."

About a half hour later, Gio and Luciana stared openmouthed at the sloppy mess on the stove. Splatters of tomato seeds and skins, and once-green basil leaves that had now turned black, dirtied the white marble countertop.

They peered into the colander that held their inedible meal.

"I wish my grandmother had taught me how to actually cook something." Gio shook his head in disbelief. "After all, it's chemistry. I should be good at it."

"What do you think went wrong?" Luciana lifted a slimy strand of spaghetti from the floor and then let it fall into the pile with the others.

"Maybe we shouldn't have put the tomatoes, basil and olive oil directly into the boiling pasta."

"I thought we would top it with the cheese."

"I have a hunch everything was intended to go over the cooked spaghetti. Nothing but the pasta was supposed to go in the boiling water."

"Ah, that's why the tomatoes exploded."

"Why didn't I look this up online?" Gio mashed his lips together.

"We thought it was going to be simple."

He brought over a small trash can, and used his hand to swipe some of the mess from the countertop into it. Luciana assisted by dumping the entire colander's worth of food into the trash, as well.

Next, Gio retrieved a couple of soapy sponges and together they cleaned up the disaster. Luciana had to admit to herself that even cleaning held a special satisfaction for her, as it was such an ordinary part of life for most people. Maybe King Agustin would allow her to take a cooking class if she expressed interest in it purely as a hobby. If he'd permit it, she'd be sure to pass anything she learned down to her children. Surely propriety of the throne wouldn't be compromised by young people learning how to cook an egg or a bowl of pasta!

Once they were done, the kitchen took on a hush.

"Now we need to figure out what to eat."

"I'm not that hungry after this afternoon's gelat…o." Luciana could barely get the word out as she was overwhelmed again by the recollection of Gio's sexiness with his game about the flavors.

Their eyes caught each other's for an extended moment. Longing bubbled out of her like an overly filled pot of boiling water would on the stove.

He picked up the one tomato they hadn't used for their fiasco. "Why don't we slice this tomato onto toast with a dot of olive oil?"

"Do you think we can handle that much food preparation?"

"Despite evidence to the contrary."

"Let's take it out to the courtyard."

There they sat close to each other, enjoying their beautiful tomato from one plate until all the stars came up in the sky.

"Your wig catches the moon's glow." Gio fixed on her blond locks. What he didn't know is that the hair he was admiring was real.

"Does it?"

"Let me show you," he said as he picked up a section to hold in front of her face. He realized that the texture felt different. "Wait a minute."

With his wide hand, he squeezed a cluster of her hair against her scalp. Expecting some movement from the wig atop her head. Nothing shifted. Another chunk, same result.

"I knew it didn't look the same as it did yesterday."

"I had my own hair cut and colored this morning to match the wig because I like it so much."

"I thought you said your father wouldn't approve."

"I don't care anymore."

"The tigress has been let out of captivity."

"You know," she said, licking her top lip, "it's you who are to blame. First you talk me into buying jeans, then you tell me I should wear my hair how I'd like to..."

Luci—it was definitely Luci—was unable to finish her sentence because without thinking about it first, she leaned over and kissed Gio's lips.

A groan exhaled through him and ricocheted to her, emboldening her to kiss him a second time.

He took hold of the back of her head and brought her closer toward him. Their mouths touched yet again, and with that, she was sure he set her on fire. They kissed more, his scorching lips pressing urgently into hers.

Flames licked at her legs under the table and quickly worked their way up her body. She had never been so fiery.

The contact of their tongues sent the blaze upward to totally engulf her. As their kisses went longer, the moon stood still and Luciana willed daylight never to come.

Please let this moment last forever!

Both of Gio's hands traced her hair until they slid

down to her shoulders. Which he took hold of and pulled her tight to him. When his lips traveled behind her ear and down her neck, she shuddered with uncontrollable pleasure. A moan she couldn't negate or retract came forth from deep within her.

A chill swept over her when he took an instant's break from the embrace. Yet it wasn't a bitter wind that put out the fire. Quite the opposite, the pause from his kisses only fanned the flames to make her want more.

Gio stood. Why? Where was he going? Her normal brain functions scrambled, not even processing her own questions.

"You are so difficult to resist." Gio raked both of his hands through his curls and took in a slow breath.

"Don't resist, Gio."

"There will be no turning back."

"Please."

With that, he reached down and picked her completely up off the chair and into his arms. Relief overtook her at the return of his touch. Her arms wrapped around his neck as if it was the most natural motion in the world.

She couldn't have anticipated what was happening, nor deny the fact that it was what she wanted. Needed. Luciana tried feebly to protest, but Luci handily silenced her.

He brought her from the courtyard table to the front of his guest cottage. With an elbow, he bumped open the door and lifted her through the threshold. Once inside, the layout identical to her cottage next door, Gio carried her up the stairs and into his bed.

CHAPTER SEVEN

ALL GIO COULD concentrate on was the two kinds of comfort invading his senses. One was the calm presence of the morning sun through the bedroom windows, letting him know that he'd slept later than usual.

The other lay next to him in his king-size bed. Her Royal Highness Princess Luciana de la Isla de Izerote slept facing him, her exquisite features in repose without flaw. The blond hair she favored bathed her face in gold. If only he was an artist so he could capture her beauty this morning and preserve it for all eternity. Or if Michelangelo was still alive, Gio would commission him to carve Luciana's likeness into marble.

Actually, he might not need anything to help him remember this morning, as the recesses of his mind had already snapped pictures he'd treasure forever.

Gently, Gio brushed away a strand of hair that fell from Luciana's forehead across her eye. She stirred the tiniest bit from his touch. The ever-so-small curl of her lips affected every inch of Gio's body, forcing his loins into an involuntary stretch.

With the mild temperature, he didn't perceive the need to pull the blanket over Luciana's alabaster shoulders. Instead, his eyes traced slowly downward to appreciate the curve of her breasts. He'd luxuriated for as long as he'd wanted to last night with the perfection of them in his hands, in his mouth. With his lips, his tongue, his teeth, he'd taken her entire body…

He'd done what?

Gio scratched his beard stubble as reality blew in the window. Late last night, after the disastrous attempt at cooking pasta and after they'd settled for tomato on toast and a humble table wine, the evening ended here. In his bedroom.

Where he took the virginity of a princess.

One who was engaged to be married.

Who was leaving Florence in a few weeks.

And whom he'd never see again.

It was hard to decide which of those truths was more disturbing.

Last night. With their laughter over their culinary foibles and her bargaining during their shopping expedition. Her cute yawn and outstretched arms as the evening got later. Finally her, no doubt, impulsive move to lean in and kiss him. He was unable to deny her. The faint voices in the back of his mind that had told him to be careful, to keep his distance, to remember that Luciana was to be a fleeting memory, had no strength last night. They went down without a fight.

All Gio had been able to hear was his own heart hammering in his chest and his gut stoking a fervor that couldn't be contained. It was the savage need that had been unshackled at the *gelateria* and never restrained, waiting, waiting, growing more powerful every hour. With every indication that it was what she wanted, too, taboos were cast aside as he carried her up the steps to his bedroom.

Her Royal Highness arched her back in her sleep and Gio's body firmed in response. Gazing at her, forgetting was easy. That she wouldn't be his. And how that was what he wanted. No love. No trust. Not to be depended on.

Why was the bravado of his credo fading further and further into the background?

"Good morning." Luciana opened her eyes and murmured a singsong.

"Good, indeed." Gio tickled a feather kiss onto her cheek and another to her bare shoulder.

Yes, ladies and gentlemen, Gio Grassi of world-renowned Grasstech had made love to a princess.

Those two starter kisses were not enough and he trailed another dozen down the length of her arm.

Their fusion last night had been a combination that shouldn't have worked, yet did. Primitive instincts had driven him while the purity in her eyes relied on him to go slowly, to measure her for pain or fear.

"Are you sure about this?" he'd asked once more.

"Yes, Gio, yes," she'd assured.

Relief swept across her face when he fitted on a condom. After that, soulful kisses and the sweetest of smiles informed the rest of the night. His satisfaction had been incomplete until he'd made certain that she'd experienced every pleasure a woman should know.

Eager to teach her more, he bent over to cover her face with a million kisses until the blankets were flung off the bed and the sun moved later into the day.

A lazy few hours later, Gio held Luciana in his arms. "I've got to get to work. You, lovely miss, are bad for business."

Of course he was joking. Because, in reality, after

making love with her he surged with energy and creativity. Ideas popped into his head about how to finalize the design for the new motherboard chipsets Grasstech was developing.

Funny how spending these days with Luciana hadn't been reducing his attention to his work but had been enhancing it.

As agonizing as it was, he separated himself from their embrace and got out of bed.

"*Bellissima*, do you want to help me with a magazine interview? That was part of our deal, wasn't it?"

She slid her fingers through her hair, visibly surprising herself with the feel of her new do, which she had apparently forgotten, causing Gio to laugh.

"Only if you'll take me to see more sights later."

"You're coming to the office with me."

"I am?"

"Up and out." He pointed toward her guest cottage. "Go get dressed."

After he heard her pad down the stairs and out the door, he stepped into a hot shower. For a minute he regretted not inviting her to join him, as the travertine shower was easily an ample size for two. But he really did need to get to work, and Luciana plus a steamy shower plus a bar of fragrant soap was not going to add up to getting him out of the house anytime soon.

They reunited in the courtyard. Viggo was outside and quickly ferried them to Grasstech headquarters.

"We'll go in through the back, shall we? I have a private entrance to my office. Better that the staff doesn't have something to gossip about."

"Absolutely, thank you. I appreciate that."

Her eyes were a bit glazed and something about her

didn't look as princess-proper as she usually did. Gio bit back the craving that threatened when he realized that the change was due to the girl who had now blossomed into a woman.

In his office, he slid one of his small desks to face opposite his large one. That way, he could easily work with her on the interview while he mapped out the design for the chipset.

Several hours passed in a most pleasant fashion. Gio not only liked glancing up from his computer to find Luciana opposite him, but she was really quite helpful assisting him in how to phrase his answers to the interview questions.

Despite the unalterable fact that she was going to be returning to Izerote, Gio's mind wandered in a direction it shouldn't have. He speculated on what it might be like to see Luciana every day.

In her perfect world, she'd be a teacher so she wouldn't be sharing an office with him. But perhaps in the mornings, after they made love and learned how to prepare breakfast, Viggo would drop her off at school on the way to Gio's office. On days when he didn't have meetings, he could meet her for her lunch break. And after the long day had passed, they'd rush home to each other's arms, where they'd stay entwined until the morning light arose once again.

There was nothing about that fantasy that had anything to do with reality. He was just daydreaming because he hadn't wanted to be with a woman this much in…well…he couldn't think of a time.

"Do you want to say something about the origin of the hacking incident?" she asked.

He was finally ready to share with Luciana the detail

he'd withheld. "I'm not going public with this information, but the hacker was a woman I dated." If that's how it could be categorized. Dated. More like worked and slept with. There were no candlelight dinners or tickets for the theater.

"Oh." Luciana looked up from the laptop with raised eyebrows. "I don't know why I assumed it was a man."

"In grungy black clothes surrounded by computers in a dark basement, right?"

"Something like that."

"I was fooled, too."

There wasn't much more to say on the topic. It was a humiliation he'd have to live with. But it was something he'd wanted to tell Luciana. Then he busied himself with other matters.

When the sun set over the city, Luciana asked him, "So, tour guide. Where are you taking me?"

He'd already thought that through. And he'd also come to the conclusion that he had every right to enjoy himself with this delightful woman. Circumstances were such that it was never meant to be more than a fleeting affair. A coming-of-age for Luciana. Why shouldn't he bask in her company while she was here and leave it at that? He'd had short-term flings with women before. He knew how to do that. When the goodbyes came, he and Luciana would part knowing that for that short time one autumn in Florence, two people were good to each other.

So why was it his heart had a hard time believing it would be easy to let her go?

"We're going back to the *mercato*?" Luciana inquired when Viggo dropped off her and Gio at the now familiar sight. Recognizing the old market building and the outdoor stalls where she had bargained for that green scarf, she knew exactly where they were.

"Follow me." Gio took her by the hand and maneuvered through the people heading this way and that. Entering the food market, they reached the stand where they had bought the pasta that they'd managed to render inedible. Gio walked her past the sign she remembered from last time: Pasta-Making Classes Here.

Through a doorway was a small commercial kitchen. Work counters were wedged in wherever they would fit. A pink-cheeked woman in a chef's coat welcomed them. "I am Chef Katia. You are here for the class?"

Gio provided her with his name, which she checked off from a clipboard she held in her hand.

"We're taking a cooking class?" Giddiness wiggled through Luciana. With her father considering the domestic arts irrelevant to royalty, and her and Gio's culinary debacle last night, if there was ever a person who needed a cooking class it was her. How thoughtful of Gio to plan this activity.

Speaking of activities, she was still in shock about the one she'd participated in last night. She blamed Luci for talking Her Royal Highness Princess Luciana into it, but nonetheless, it was clear to her from the first kiss that she was going to make love with Gio. She'd had to experience the hunger and intensity and ecstasy that two people could share. Need insisted she act with abandon, wildness even, and to learn the profound strength of her femaleness and her sexuality.

For all she might have hoped the intimacy would bring, it was infinitely more divine than anything she could have ever have imagined.

It was hard to picture leaving Gio now. She felt so

close to him in a way she'd never have thought possible. He'd even confided in her that the company hack that caused him so much anguish was of his own doing in trusting a woman who'd systematically figured out how to work through him to get what she wanted.

The pieces fit together. How suspicious he'd been of Luciana when she'd first run into him on the street after those boys harassed her. And how he'd said that some women he'd known were predators. This one, Francesca, had really got the best of him. It was utterly horrible that she'd pretended to genuinely care for him when, really, she was out for personal gain. His work and his designs meant so much to him, there could be almost no worse betrayal than to steal that. No wonder he'd resigned to stay single.

How would it play out if she didn't go back to Izerote? Would Gio come to trust again? She envisioned a life filled with freedom and peace where they could go anywhere, do everything, be anything. As long as they had each other, nothing could harm them. Would he take that leap of faith if it was offered?

"If everyone will take a place, we will begin." Chef Katia called the class to attention and pointed to the stations she had set up on the worktables. Each area had a wooden board, bowls of flour and eggs, rolling pins, towels and other accessories.

Gio and Luciana took spaces next to each other as the chef began her instruction.

"We'll make a mound of flour and then dig a well into the center of it." Glee filled Luciana as she burrowed her hands into the flour. She loved the cool, powdery texture of it through her fingers. "Into the center, we'll crack the eggs."

Neither she nor Gio knew how to properly crack an egg and both struggled, with giggles, to remove the shells that weren't part of the recipe. Chef Katia came over and demonstrated her technique. On the second egg, both Gio and Luciana shocked themselves by performing perfectly.

After forking through the eggs as instructed, the chef taught them how to gradually incorporate the dry flour into the wet well.

"You were right," Luciana said. "This is chemistry. Cooking is the magic combination of science meets art."

"Perhaps, then, I'll have an aptitude for it, after all."

"I think children should be taught basic cooking. Not only for practical survival purposes, but it's an excellent way to learn mathematics, don't you think?"

"Teaching children is something you've given a lot of thought to."

Luciana's forehead creased. Yes, of course, she'd contemplated how she'd like to teach if she ever had the chance. To make learning engaging and fun, and a discovery.

"Can I ask you something?" Gio reached over with the side of his wrist to brush some flour that had landed on Luciana's nose. "When you marry King Agustin and you develop these resorts on the island that are to bring jobs to your people, won't those employees need child care?"

"Yes, why?"

"Shouldn't that be provided for them, organized to make it a workable lifestyle for families?"

"Yes, of course."

"Why couldn't *you* play a part in that? You've told me that issues regarding children have always been on your official agenda, so it wouldn't be coming out of nowhere."

Luciana kneaded her pasta, unable to look Gio in the

eye as she answered, "Neither my father nor my future husband would be in favor of that."

"Doesn't what *you* want matter?"

What she didn't want was to lament about the realities that awaited her when she returned to Izerote. All she wanted was to be here right now, completely in the moment, with this mind-blowing man at her side who encouraged her to spread her wings. To see how high she could fly.

"It's unbearable to me, Luci, to accept the idea of you returning to a life where you are limited."

"I must. And it's as much my fault as anyone else's. I allowed my father to lock me up in the palace tower."

"What do you mean?"

"My mother died when I was eleven. A mentally unstable man crashed his car directly into the one she was riding in, killing her instantly."

"How terrible."

"By the time I was a teenager I could tell that my father was a broken man. So I dedicated myself to him. I decided to never cause him any pain. We're all each other has."

"He wasn't able to get over her death."

"My mother was not a happy woman and kept herself distant. I never really knew her. She and my father didn't have romantic love. But the sense of duty that was instilled in him meant he should have somehow protected her from harm, and he couldn't forgive himself for not being able to."

"So now he goes to every length to shield you?"

"He tries to protect all of Izerote from *everything*, which is why time has stood still for our people. And he keeps me as some sort of symbol of that. And I let him."

"I give you credit. I think if it was me, I would run away never to return."

"It's not all bad. I don't take for granted that I live a life of privilege."

"Do you?"

Those two words dangled in the air.

After crumbly messes of flour mixed with egg had been miraculously converted to smooth balls of shiny dough, they were set aside to rest. The cooking students were invited to have a glass of wine and sample olive oils during the break.

Across the market floor, past the produce vendors with their stacks of ripe fruits and vegetables of every hue, Luciana eyed two men in black suits who seemed to be watching her and Gio. They both wore earpieces. She'd seen a couple of similar-looking men when they were shopping for jeans. Was it paranoia, or was she being followed? It wouldn't surprise her if her father knew her whereabouts. Perhaps he didn't trust her note that promised she'd return to the island in time for her wedding. And who could blame him?

"Gio, inconspicuously turn around. Do you see a couple of men over there looking at us?" She gestured with her head in their direction.

But when they both subtly turned to check, the men were gone.

Chef Katia called them back into the kitchen. She showed them how to roll out the dough with a rolling pin and then feed it through a pasta machine. The process looked easier than it was. Luciana and Gio hand cranked their creations through the rollers. Eventually, they ended up with even sheets of pasta that they proudly showed each other. "You should be able to see the outline of your fingers underneath," Chef Katia instructed.

Luciana tested hers by lifting it up in her hand. Gio leaned over and laced his fingers through hers so that they could see their hands holding each other's through the veil of the thin pasta. They pivoted their hands this way and that, grooving on the sight of their fingers under the dough. At the sight of their hands beautifully intertwined, Luciana bit her lip.

Chef Katia demonstrated how to cut their sheets into thin strips that were ready to be tossed into boiling water. She had pots of water ready for those who wanted to cook and eat their pasta then and there. Some students, like Gio and Luciana, instead put theirs into plastic bags to take with them.

"Let's go home and try again," he said, making Luciana think about something different from dinner.

On the ride back to the villa, Gio put his long arm around her shoulders. She adored the smell of him, always clean and fresh. Her head rested so nicely against his solid and wide chest. When they were together, she was truly *with* him. Maybe that was what it was like to be in love, in harmony both physically and mentally.

Could she stay like this? Or could he come home with her where they'd demand the life they were entitled to? Why couldn't he be by her side at the palace, sharing dreams and passions?

Way down inside, she knew that was more make-believe. What had passed between them last night was only another souvenir for her memory box. The ex-virgin princess had simply got a taste of forbidden fruit, a secret she would carry to her grave. But that was it. It most definitely shouldn't happen again. It couldn't. It was too dangerous. She knew it and sensed that Gio did, too.

So why was it that after they'd successfully cooked and eaten a delicious pasta dinner, Luciana found herself sitting on Gio's lap in the courtyard? Why was she kissing and being kissed with an urgency that nothing in her life had ever demanded before? And why did it feel unquestionably right rather than wrong when, once again, he laid her down on his bed, his potent body hovering over hers as he showed her rhapsodies she had no knowledge existed?

CHAPTER EIGHT

GIO WALKED WITH a spring in his step like a schoolboy as he rushed to meet Luciana after work. He had told her to meet him in front of the Basilica Santa Maria Novella, the Gothic landmark church near the train station. It was hard to believe how much had happened since that fateful day when she'd arrived by train and he interceded to protect her from those thugs who were attempting to steal her jewels. He'd lived a lifetime since then and was astonished as he acknowledged how big a part of his life Luciana had become in such a short time. That wasn't like him. Yet all he wanted to do was both talk to and listen to her, and he'd had more conversation with her in the past few days than he'd probably had in a year.

Which was why he couldn't get to her fast enough. He hadn't told her where he was taking her, wanting to keep it a surprise. As had become their pattern, they'd meet at dusk while visitor attractions were still open for an hour or two longer. Where he was taking her today wasn't a typical tourist stop, but it was somewhere he thought she'd like.

Can't get to her fast enough. What crazy thoughts he was having. This wasn't supposed to be happening to him, caring whether or not he was with any woman, let alone a special one. Emotions were escaping his control. Sucked into an unexplainable whirlpool, his hours and days were delineated by time spent with Luciana and time waiting to return to her side again.

None of this was in character for him. He dealt in logic and probabilities, in calculus and abstracts that allowed him to understand a technological plane that would mystify the majority of people in the world. Feelings knew no logic, no mathematical equation that could be proved without doubt. He was in an uncharted operating system, and did not know his way around.

Which must have been why his heart skipped when he saw Luciana in the church square. She was wearing the *comfy* jeans, as she had come to call them, making him think of a carefree young woman on a metro bus. She looked like a proper Luci, a girl who dressed in whatever whim dictated, whose day was her own. Not one who lived by the regimented precision she had described on Izerote.

Was Luciana talking to someone? Yes, she was conversing with a woman who had a mop of hair pulled up in a bun. A few young children were running around them in a circle. Had she struck up a conversation with a stranger, or had the woman approached her?

One of the children pulled on Luciana's leg and she bent down to talk to the little girl. The expression on Luciana's face was one of pure dedication as she appeared to be answering the child's question. Gio noticed her easy manner with the girl, just as a boy grabbed her hand from the other side. Instead of being flustered Luciana divided her time between the two children, until she and the other woman were laughing by the time Gio approached.

"This is my friend Chiara. I think I told you we had met a few days ago."

"Oh, yes, the teacher. Nice to meet you."

"And you." Chiara called out, "Antonio, stop torturing that pigeon."

The boy ran closer and Luciana said to him, "Sweetheart, when you touch the pigeons you scare them. They don't like to be petted like dogs and cats do."

"Okay." The boy shrugged his shoulders.

"Chiara was taking the kids out for a walk and we ran into each other."

"Luci is actually wonderful with the children. She's been helping me."

"I don't doubt it." Gio glanced to Luciana, who looked like the ultimate Madonna with cherubic children circling her.

"I have to go. Their parents will be picking them up soon. Nice to meet you, Gio."

"You, too."

After watching Chiara and the children scurry away from the square, Gio pecked Luciana's cheek. "How was your time at the Uffizi Gallery?"

"Magnificent, of course. Where are we going tonight?"

Gio led her down a street off the church's piazza. They reached the front of a very unassuming building with big brass doorknobs.

"What is this?"

He turned the knobs and opened the doors. "The Firenze Profumo Farmaceutica. It's one of the oldest pharmacies and cosmetic shops in the world."

They entered the formal salon.

"Oh, my gosh." Her eyes lit up as she took it all in.

They had stepped back in time. Heavy burgundy drapery with gold pull cords lined the walls. Elaborate chandeliers hung from high frescoed ceilings, casting a yellowish light. A few red velvet benches were placed here and there atop the tapestried rug. Behind one long glass counter, three attendants assisted customers.

"The smell is incredible." Luciana inhaled the floral and spicy aromas that permeated the entire space as they walked farther in.

"The Dominican friars established this in the thirteenth century," Gio explained.

Luciana was drawn to the rows of glass cases. They held a dazzling array of perfumes, colognes, creams, lotions, shampoos and soaps. Some were in re-creations of bottles that matched the era when the particular product was created, such as the Acqua di Caterina from the 1500s, commissioned exclusively for Caterina de' Medici of the famous Florentine family. Other products were in simple bottles, pots and jars bearing the label of the *farmaceutica*.

"Come this way."

They passed into an interior parlor.

"What's this?"

The room had a large glass table in the center on which sat dozens of small amber bottles with droppers. One wall was filled with books. "Those were written by the friars, the original recipes for their preparations," Gio explained. Glass doors opened to an herb garden. "They make balms and ointments and tonic remedies here."

"How do you know about this place?"

"The de' Medici family, the leaders of the Florentine Renaissance, were proponents of medicine. In fact, their name is where the word *medicine* is derived from. Florence has always been a place to celebrate the healing powers and versatility of botanicals. My grandmother and hers before her and probably relatives even before that shopped here."

"How lovely of you to bring me."

"This is the room where they develop perfumes. I thought you might like to create a fragrance that's uniquely yours. When you smell it, you can remember your visit to Florence." *And me*, Gio thought but didn't say aloud. He hoped she would always remember him, as heaven knew he'd always remember her. More than he thought he should if his prediction proved correct.

Walking the streets of Florence with her had become natural now. When he wasn't with her, he felt off. Not quite right. Incomplete. Together, they seemed to grab something out of thin air and form it into something real and weighty.

A lone tear escaped from Luciana's eyes.

"Why are you crying?"

"I'm not. I'm just so touched that you thought of this. About making a perfume."

A middle-aged woman with her hair pulled tightly back and wearing a white lab coat entered the salon. "*Buona giornata*, I am Imilia and I will be assisting you today." She pointed to one set of the glass dropper bottles on the table. "These are some of our essential oils. Perhaps you'd like to start with one of those for our top note and then we'll add on to customize a fragrance."

Imilia laid several strips of testing paper on the table. From each bottle she squeezed a drop for them to smell.

After a few, Luciana was clear that she liked orange blossom.

"Now we'll choose a central note and a base note or two."

Gio loved seeing how seriously Luciana took the task, smelling the test strips several times before she eliminated any of them.

Selections were eventually made.

"Perfume is best aged. The scents will meld over time."

Gio whispered into Luciana's ear, "Think of me six months from today when the perfume has mellowed but my memories of you won't have."

As soon as those words fell out of his mouth, Gio regretted saying them. Soon enough Her Royal Highness Princess Luciana de la Isla de Izerote would not only leave Florence, but would leave him. Forever.

There was a king to wed. Heirs to produce. Her fates were decided. It was cruel to encourage her to remember him. Quite the opposite would be kinder. If he really cared about her, he'd hope she'd forget him the minute she left Italian soil.

How could he have allowed them to make love? Two nights in a row, no less. Even though he knew she wanted to as much as he did, he should have resisted. So what that their lips fit so seamlessly to each other's? So what that Luciana's lissome body went boneless against his, meeting his angles with her pliable curves? And so what that now they anticipated each other's movements, each of them in constant undulation around each other as if they were no longer independent beings?

She was never to be his.

No matter what, they couldn't make love again. What happened couldn't be undone, but Gio could keep from making matters worse. It was the least he could do.

Monarchy aside, Luciana was an inexperienced young woman. He should have been the stronger one. Defended her. The last thing he'd want to do was hurt her.

Nothing everlasting could ever be between them.

Could it?

Imilia asked if Luciana would like to name her fragrance and have a personalized label for the bottle.

"Let's call it Luci," she answered without hesitation. Of course. Luci being a different person from Luciana. The bottle of Luci that she'd no doubt keep hidden would bear witness to secrets the princess might never tell another living soul.

From the bottle that would bear her name, she rubbed a few drops of her fragrance onto the inside of her wrist, which she brought to her nose. Then she presented it to Gio to reconfirm that the scent was appealing. He lifted her delicate wrist, his fingertips memorizing every one of the tiny bones under her porcelain skin. The blend of the orange blossom, cloves, cinnamon and bergamot was a heady and pleasing combination.

Before he could stop himself, he topped off the examination of the inside of her wrist with a kiss. Just what he'd meant *not* to do. And without realizing ahead of time that the barest amount of physical contact would reverberate through his body and make him want to do things to Princess Luciana right then and there that would have the Dominican friars rolling in their graves.

"Chiara!" Luciana waved when, out for another walk in the Santa Maria Novella piazza, she spotted her new friend and the kids.

"Luci. Come sit. The children are playing." Chiara

pointed to a bench that allowed her to keep a close watch on her charges.

"So is that handsome Gio your lover?"

"No. He's just a friend." Luciana didn't know how to answer. Yes, she had made love with him. No, he was not her lover in any true sense of the word. Yes, she wished more than anything in the world that he was.

The princess would return to Izerote changed in more ways than would be visible to the eye. Hair cut and dyed, she'd have to face her father's scrutiny over something as petty as her appearance. He'd never know that she'd been forever altered internally, as well. That she'd known the earthquake of a man and a woman in the throes of passion, the planet moving beneath them, modifying the universe so that it could never go back to exactly how it was before. More important, not her father nor her future husband nor any other living soul would know that she herself had shifted like the tectonic plates under the earth, and would never be the same again.

"I saw how your eyes shined when he met you here yesterday," Chiara continued. "And he had the face of a man who thought he was the luckiest one alive when he found you in the crowd. Smells like lovers to me," she said in a cute lilt that made Luciana laugh.

"It's complicated."

"Isn't it always?"

Two of the boys were having a duel with the plastic spoons that they had been using to eat a snack. Jamming their implements at each other in a way that was going to lead to someone getting hurt. Chiara called out, "Boys, it is a gentleman's duel. Take two steps backward and bow to each other."

Which they did, eking a smile out of the two women.

"Do you have a boyfriend?"

"I go out with a nice enough guy, but he's not *the one.* My eyes don't flicker when I'm with him like yours did with Gio. I'm leaving Firenze soon, so it's best not to get serious."

The words banged between Luciana's ears. Of course when someone was planning to leave the place where they were, it was best not to allow any meaningful relationships to develop. That was so obvious Luciana would bet that even these children having spoon duels would understand. Any idiot would.

Except her, apparently. She did know that her feelings toward Gio had passed serious days ago and now had moved into critical. Which was not good.

"When are you going?" Luciana tried to distract herself by asking about Chiara's impending move.

"I'm half there now and half here on the days I work. I commute by train." Chiara had told her that her family, her mother and two sisters who were also teachers, were opening up a school in Salerno. A town in the south near Naples, it was a four-hour train ride from Florence. "To open a school is not a way to make a lot of money, but it's what we love. So I go down as often as I can to paint walls and buy furniture and network with the people who live there."

"Do you have commitments from families that are going to send their children to the school?"

"Oh, yes. We already have forty students enrolled."

"That's amazing!"

Luciana admired Chiara. Not only had she pursued her goal of becoming a teacher, but now she was opening her own business at it.

"What about you?"

To the outside world, they must look like two friends sharing a chat during lunch while the children in their care play. Perhaps that outside world might see Luciana as a teacher, too. Passersby would think them two young gals who were dishing about boyfriends and aspirations. "If Gio isn't your lover, what are you doing with him?"

Waltzing through the cloudy haze of a beautiful dream she never wanted to wake up from?

"I'm only in Florence for a short time," Luciana uttered softly. "I'm leaving, too."

"Ah, Gio was your passionate Italian fling?"

Princess Luciana winced at that characterization, thinking it cheapened the situation. Although perhaps that's exactly how she would recollect it decades from now.

"You're sad to leave him."

Chiara had no idea how right she was. But Her Royal Highness would have so much to distract her when she returned to the palace. There would be dull diplomatic lunches to attend, boring dedications to make appearances at and a man she barely knew to marry. How would she find the time in her schedule to pine for the magical man in Florence?

"I am."

"Have you rubbed the snout of Il Porcellino?"

"Not yet." Luciana knew about the legend of the bronze figure near the Mercato Nuovo. Lore had it that if you rubbed the nose of the boar, it meant you would return to Florence.

Luciana would do that before her trip was over, although her wish would be bittersweet.

Because even if she was to return, it would be too late for her and Gio.

"You don't want to go home, Luci?"

"I don't, and yet I can't stay here."

"Do you want to come work for me in Salerno?"

"Do I what?" Luciana could hardly believe the words she was hearing.

"Work for me. I can't hire you as a teacher until you earn a degree in early childhood education. But you can assist us. The children clearly love you."

Laugh or cry. Both options were equally viable. Princess Luciana de la Isla de Izerote had been offered her first job. In her chosen profession. In some families, that would be cause for celebration. In hers, it was a disgrace. *Laugh or cry.*

Even though she was supposed to have another two weeks in Florence, her departure was imminent.

The proverbial clock ticked.

Walls closed in.

There'd be no escape.

"A job."

With every blink of her eyes, she saw flashes of red.

Warning lights.

Danger signals.

Because Princess Luciana could not ignore that, once again, across the piazza, she noticed two men in black suits staring directly at her as they spoke into earpieces. Her stomach sank to her knees as the reality became impossible to dispute.

Chiara handed her a business card, which Luciana numbly slid into her jeans pocket alongside the pocket money Gio had insisted she carry.

"You can think about it. Let me know in the next few days."

* * *

Was she really thinking what she was thinking? The events of this past week made Luciana doubt every stronghold she'd ever embraced. Heady concepts like responsibility and sacrifice, honor and privilege, obligation and liberty were now all under question. Anything and everything was up for grabs.

Would she really be able to pull off the idea that was fighting for a place in her rational mind? It made sense and it made no sense at the same time. When Viggo dropped her off at her requested location, Luciana had been so lost in her dilemma that she'd hardly noticed the drive. She asked him to wait and stepped out of the car.

The Piazzale Michelangelo was a public square on a hill that afforded a breathtaking view of the city. From the river and its bridges to the bell tower of the Badia Fiorentina to the Duomo to the Tuscan mountains beyond, its breadth was spectacular. Overwhelming to take in all at once, the panorama had been known to make people weep. No different for the princess. Tears rolled down her face in a steady stream, chilled by the hilltop breeze.

The first tears were for Gio, whom in any scenario, she'd be torn from like a bandage that rips away the skin underneath it when it is removed. Other tears represented trepidation about what she was planning. If she failed, she'd have made even a bigger mess than what she'd already created. If she succeeded, there would be no turning back.

There were tears for the mother she barely knew. Who was unable to rise to her own duty. Although she didn't cause her own death, her spirit was laid to rest before her marriage at age eighteen. Part of Luciana's decision would be in her mother's honor.

Still different tears were for her father, whom in spite of all of this, she loved dearly and risked wounding. A young man himself when her mother died, he was ill-equipped to parent an eleven-year-old girl and turned to fear of loss as his only guidance.

And, because it had transformed her so drastically that no matter what road she took it could never be one she'd already traveled, she cried for Florence, which she'd miss every day of her life.

Luciana got back in the car and had Viggo drop her off at her next destination.

Chiara had been right. Il Porcellino was quite the tourist attraction. The open-air Mercato Nuovo was in full swing near the bronze boar, and the whole area was alive with Florentine bustle. As she'd seen elsewhere in the city, budding artists used colored chalk to draw replicas of famous paintings onto the pavement of city streets, putting out tip cups for passersby to show their appreciation. Many of the chalk renderings were excellent. Luciana took note of the young artists and wondered what their lives must be like, living and practicing their craft in this inspiring place.

Visitors queued up to touch the famous boar, and the princess took her place behind a tour group, all of whom wore matching plastic nameplates around their necks. English, German and Japanese were just three of the languages she heard around her. The bronze *porcellino*, or piglet, was covered in a green-brown patina except for its snout, which had been polished to a sheen by all the attention bestowed on it.

While she waited, she pivoted her head as far as she could to the left and then all the way to the right to take in the scene at the Mercato Nuovo until she found what she knew she would. Past a vendor specializing in wallets and belts, two men in black suits watched her. She couldn't tell if they were the same men from the piazza with Chiara earlier today, but it didn't matter.

She'd seen men in black suits outside the clothing store when she and Gio were shopping for jeans. There were two at the Mercato Centrale when she and Gio took the pasta-making class. Then today at the piazza. Part of her had been trying to deny the reality of what they represented. Now as her breath tightened and a blush burned her cheeks, she could pretend no longer.

King Mario de la Isla de Izerote had found her. Maybe he'd had her followed all along. She no longer believed that she was going to get the full three weeks of escape she had planned before returning to Izerote and her wedding. Today was her seventh day. A hunch in her gut told her it was her last.

This schedule was probably designed by her father. He, no doubt, instructed his security detail to have her located and surveilled but if she seemed safe, to let her have her silly little fun. Rage inched up her throat as she fully comprehended what must have happened. That she hadn't even had the small measure of freedom she'd hoped to cherish for the rest of her life. All she'd been granted was a longer chain than usual.

When it was her turn to touch the bronze boar's nose, she stroked it as lovingly as she would have had it been Gio's face. She threw her arms around its neck and held herself close. Because she was in love. With Luci, the young teacher who had the most marvelous boyfriend in the world.

If rubbing Il Porcellino's snout meant she would return, she'd rub it a hundred times before she let go.

Thank you, Florence.

Thank you, Gio.

Finally, she backed away to let the people who were waiting have their turn.

As she did, poison blackened her insides when she heard an unfamiliar male voice behind her say, "Princess Luciana, may we speak with you for a moment?"

Luciana didn't turn around to acknowledge him.

"And we'd like to speak with the gentleman you've been keeping company with."

Those words sliced like a lash across her back. The most unbearable consequence of her actions would be if Gio was brought into the chaos she'd made. He had plenty of his own issues to deal with. He'd been nothing but kind to her and deserved better.

Blood vessels throbbed through Luciana's skull. What she was scheming was her only hope. A far-fetched Hail Mary. Worth a try because, at this point, she had nothing to lose.

She suddenly bulleted forward and dashed into the outdoor marketplace.

If she could just get away from these security men right now, she'd carry out her plan immediately. Making an abrupt right turn, she tore through an aisle of merchants who were all selling tablecloths and bed linens displayed on hooks so that the fabrics danced in the afternoon wind. As the bedsheets swayed, Luciana was able to maneuver quickly between one and around another until she got to the other end of the market.

A quick glance backward confirmed that she'd done it. The men weren't trailing her!

With no time to wait for Viggo, whom she'd asked to return in an hour, she hailed a taxi to return her to the villa. Which she slipped into, seemingly unnoticed. As she bounded up the stairs of her guest cottage, her heart thundered. The ticking bomb was about to explode. Time to hurry.

She picked up the phone on the night table beside her bed. It had been seven days since she'd held a phone, the hard plastic harsh and now unfamiliar in her hand as she punched in a number. "Chiara, it's Luci."

After the call, she yanked her suitcase out of the closet and tossed it on the bed, unzipping it to unpack the items she had left buried inside. The ones she had hoped never to need. The ones that were now her last chance.

"Luciana?" Gio's voice called up to her bedroom from the courtyard a half hour later. "Luciana?"

What was he doing home? It was hours before he was to finish work and join her for their usual early-evening sightseeing. They were to finally tour the Duomo, which she had been greatly looking forward to.

"I'm up here," she yelled through the open doors to the Juliet balcony, hoping not to have to see him.

"I was so worried," he continued shouting up. "Viggo said he went to pick you up but you weren't there."

"I'm fine, Gio. Go back to the office."

Luciana had already written him a note to leave on the table in the courtyard. An in-person goodbye was more than she could handle.

"Come to the balcony, Luciana."

"No, Gio. Please go back to work." It was agony to tell him to go, but if he knew what she was planning, he'd try to stop her.

"Luciana! Luciana!"

The low timbre of his bellow was too much for her to fight. She'd allow herself one last time the sight of his exquisite face and the tall muscular body that had educated her in ecstasies she'd never expected to learn.

With a last check in the mirror before she'd have to tell Gio the truth, Princess Luciana confirmed that her look was complete. When she'd arrived in Barcelona after stowing away on that supply ship leaving Izerote, she'd bought not one but two disguises. Her *just in case* would be put to the test right now.

The boy's brown suit fit her about right, appropriately shapeless to skim over any womanly curves. The white shirt and brown shoes matched it. And the dark wig cut above the ears gave her the appearance of a teenaged boy, perhaps on his way to a school interview or reluctantly forced to get dressed up for an occasion. No, the delicate skin and regal bones of her face were not very masculine, but she knew that some boys had fine features. Walking down the street, no one would give her a second glance.

She stepped out onto the Juliet balcony to face Gio.

"The men who have been following you?" Gio asked upon seeing her in the ensemble.

"How did you know?"

"I saw them, too. I didn't say anything because I hoped you hadn't noticed. I didn't want to ruin your precious time here with the news."

"I can't go back to Izerote, Gio. Not after everything that happened here. Not after you."

She inhaled the full view the balcony afforded. The old buildings, the chirps of birds sharing a song with the horns of taxicabs. The splendid mixture of the ancient and the modern that was this city. And the high-tech billionaire here who'd keep her heart.

Luciana moved away from the balcony and back into her bedroom. Closing her suitcase, with the bag of jewels that were her only currency inside, she made her way down the stairs and out to the courtyard where Gio stood waiting.

"Where are you going?"

"Chiara offered me a job at her new school in the south, near Naples. If I can get away without being caught, maybe I have a chance. I'll disappear there. I'll find a way to contact my father and tell him that I'm not coming home."

Desperation had driven her to the unconceivable.

"Don't leave," Gio implored. "We'll figure it out. There has to be a way."

"There is none. Not when they're closing in on me. On us. As it is, I've dragged you into this further than I ever meant to."

His hands circled her wrists, handcuffing her in his grasp. "No. You're not leaving."

"Maybe someday I'll be able to return. I rubbed the nose of the boar. Maybe a Florence miracle will be ours."

"I'll help you. I'll drive you there. At least then I'll know exactly where you are. When it's safe we'll be together again."

"No. They'll follow you. Go back to the office. When they question you, say I disappeared without a trace. Say you don't know anything."

"You've never been on your own. I'll worry about you every day of my life. I can't let you go."

"Let me go, Gio. For both of our sake. You have your company to protect. And I can't have you take the place of my father. I have to try something of my own or else I'll never know what freedom is."

She lifted up on her tiptoes and craned her neck so

that her lips would reach his. For one goodbye kiss that contained the sun, the moon and all the stars in the sky.

Then she broke away from him, grabbed her suitcase and fled out through the entrance tunnel that led to the street.

Chiara was to meet her at the train station, so Luciana rushed in that direction, disguise in place. But within seconds, a black car screeched to a stop beside her on the street. The two men who had been following her at the bronze boar got out of the car.

"Princess Luciana, at your father's request we are here to take you home."

Speechless and unsure what to do, she covered her mouth with her hand. In her heart of hearts, she knew she'd never be able to outrun these men, and even if she did they—or others like them—would be back again the next day. It was a foolish attempt. Her father had decided that it was time for her journey to come to an end. Just as she always figured he would.

She looked back toward the villa. Gio had chased after her and stood a few paces behind. The two men glared at him, and then one of them took hold of Princess Luciana's arm. The other opened the passenger door of the black car. He stated flatly, "Time to go."

Using no small amount of force, the man began to marshal Princess Luciana into the car. In doing so, her wig came off in his hand. The blond lob that had now become her real hairstyle spilled around her face as tears pooled in her eyes. She turned back one last time and called out, "I love you, Gio! I love you."

With that, she surrendered into the back seat and the door was closed after her. The two men got into the front seat, and from the clicks and beeps she heard, she knew she had been securely locked into her motorized jail.

Her Royal Highness Princess Luciana de la Isla de Izerote jerked around to look out the back window as the car pulled away. Gio ran toward her, sprinting after the car, picking up his own speed as the vehicle did, too. But when the car took a big lead over him, the last thing she saw was his mouth saying something to her. She'd spend the rest of her life wondering what it was.

CHAPTER NINE

"I LOVE YOU, too, Luciana! I love you, too."

Gio stared blankly out of his office window replaying the words he had screamed at the top of lungs yesterday as the black car drove his heart away from his body.

Yesterday. When the world was a different place. Because Luci was in it. Luci, the whip-smart, fun-loving, sensual breath of fresh air that had shaken Gio to his core, was gone forever. Oh, certainly Princess Luciana de la Isla de Izerote still lived and breathed. To marry and bear children, and hopefully remain healthy and strong for decades to come. But the part of her that had spent this enchanting week with Gio had disappeared into thin air as quickly as she had arrived.

What was she doing right now? Begging her father's and her fiancé's forgiveness? For stealing seven days? Who could blame her for wanting that? How could that be considered an offense? Gio's fists clenched at the injustice.

For her.

For him.

She was supposed to have three weeks. He'd been planning to take her to his family's vineyard in Chianti. To show her the charming coastal towns of the Cinque

Terra. The lush terrain of the Emilio Romagna region. Perhaps a few days in Venice.

Cruelly, their time together was cut short. But the week they'd had changed the course of his life. Because once you loved, you could no longer pretend that it wasn't important. That it was something you could live without. That it wasn't worth the risk.

That it wouldn't destroy a person once it was gone.

Destruction wasn't an option for Gio. Family loyalty demanded that he run this empire. The responsibility was on him.

He turned his concentration to work. As he drafted a public statement to announce the next generation of DDR SDRAM that would render everything currently on the market obsolete, Princess Luciana's suggestions to him came to mind. She'd remind him that it wasn't technical mumbo jumbo that the public would respond to. It was people being their genuine selves that made an impression.

How right she was. His fingers flew over the keys as he typed. Grasstech might be a leader in the computer industry, but it was a company started by one man and now under the care of his sons. With thousands of employees throughout the world, each of whose diligent work contributed to the company's success. For the new RAM, Park Baek Yeol in Seoul had worked for years on its development. Adil Pannu's group in Mumbai tested hundreds of designs until they found one that could be produced at much less expense than its predecessor.

Once Gio had crafted a statement he was pleased with, he was ready to share it with his marketing team. After hitting the send button, he shut down his computer for the night.

As he was leaving the office, Samuele locked in step with him in the corridor. "*Mio amico*, we must decide where we are going to manufacture the biometric products. This is an enormous undertaking for us. Have you given it any thought?"

"I will, Samuele. Thank you. I want you to know how much I appreciate you."

"Why are you so wistful?"

Gio couldn't bring himself to explain about Luciana. Not yet, anyway.

At home, he pushed open the door to the villa. There was no doubt that the envelope on the table in the courtyard was for him. Luciana had left it, hoping to make a clean exit without having to say goodbye. Luck, or serendipity, spoiled her plot. As bad as it was to watch her being driven away by her keepers, it would have been far worse not to have bid her farewell. After she'd been transported long out of sight, he'd shuffled back to the villa but couldn't bear to read her note.

Recognizing the Grasstech logo embossed on the top left corner of the envelope, Gio nodded to himself. Of course, even in order to leave him a message, she'd had to borrow an envelope and probably the piece of paper it was written on. Which of his pens had she used? Anything he had was hers for the asking, yet it brought a crinkle to his face that she hadn't brought royal stationery with her from Izerote. No, she was too busy bringing wigs and palace jewels in her attempt to clinch time without her tiara for just one holiday.

Gio slid his finger under the flap to open the envelope. Having never seen her handwriting, he was awed by its feminine and stately precision. Every line symmetrical, every word incorporating as many swirly flourishes as it could hold.

Ache pushed through him as he appreciated the beauty in the way Luciana had written his name.

Gio.

You have no idea how much you have given me in addition to your generosity. You have shown me a modern world full of excitement and potential, where ambition and innovation are celebrated.

I vow to you now that I will find a way to teach that to my children, and to tell them about the brilliant man in Florence who taught it to me.

You are the only man I will ever love, and I will love you until my dying day.

Yours forever, Luci.

Uncharacteristic mist filled Gio's eyes as he peered up to the Juliet balcony of Luciana's guest cottage, knowing only too painfully that she wouldn't be appearing. Because darn if the words he yelled as he tried in vain to catch up to that car weren't true. He loved her. And now that he knew what love was, he was sure it was something he'd never known before.

With Francesca, until she betrayed him, there was lust. And the commonality of working in the same industry. A similar lifestyle. Work came first, and there was never any worry about dividing his energies.

But his heart never lurched out of his chest at the mere thought of Francesca. He'd surely never had sunny visions of a home built together and children to share it with. A foundation that sparked his creativity. Celebrating successes and enduring challenges as one, an entity stronger than the sum of its parts.

Luciana made those possibilities dance through his head. In fact, he couldn't stop obsessing over them. So much so that those visions had bent to include royal life. It would take adjustment, but he could see himself accepting the obligations and rules that would come with being at the princess's side. They'd find a way to protect some amount of a private life for themselves. Love gave everything potential.

After sitting down at the courtyard table to pick at the pasta left over from their cooking class, Gio let his mind travel to faraway places. To the island of Izerote. To imagine what his heart was doing at this very moment. To miss her.

When he had wallowed for as long as he could stand, he forced his mind to turn a corner. The next issue on his agenda was where the biometric products were to be produced. He could give them to one of the India plants, although the crews there already had plenty to do. In fact, he'd like to shift some of the ongoing manufacturing he had operating out of Mumbai to somewhere else. The Tokyo plants were overworked, too. A new location might be what was in order. The components were all small parts that didn't require massive production equipment, so that opened up a lot of options.

The strangest germ of an idea popped into his mind. With some research and phone calls, he began to envision a prospect. The next morning, he summoned Samuele to his office and included his father at the winery in the discussion via FaceTime. Gio announced where he was taking new manufacturing.

If he had his way.

Which he was about to find out.

"Samuele, I have no idea how to reach my destination. Book a trip for me."

"Your Royal Highness, may I ask you to lift up your arms?" Three dress fitters swarmed around Luciana. She obliged, although the tight lace sleeves of the wedding gown didn't allow much flexibility of movement. "Just a bit higher, Princess, please. Most appreciated."

With the three-paneled mirror set up in front of a dais that provided easy access for alterations to the gown, Luciana was on display like a pirouetting ballerina in a child's wind-up jewelry box. One tailor slowly circled the bottom of the gown, pinning it for a perfect hemline. The other two attended to the rest of the fit.

"Would you prefer us to add a large lace flower at the waistline?" one of them asked. The question caught Luciana by surprised as it was the first one anyone had asked her since she was returned to the palace yesterday. Every last detail of her upcoming wedding had been decided on by the royal wedding planners and her father. She supposed that having disappeared for seven days she had further forfeited her right to any say in the matter. Although she was the bride, she felt like a mannequin that was only one element in the whole of the affair, of equal importance to the cake or the table settings. The fitter held a lace rose to the waistband of the gown. Then withdrew it for comparison.

The dress was so undeniably hideous the princess didn't think it much mattered whether yet one more adornment was added. At her father's request, the design had been modeled on the one worn by her great-great-grandmother at her own wedding. While a style that was hopelessly out of date could have a kind of retro charm, this one did not. She was reminded that the unbearable confines of this gown were what propelled her to finally stow away on that supply boat, and to take her fateful trip to Italy.

A stiff collar led to a fitted lace bodice and sleeves. The silk layer under the lace extended upward almost to the neckline, eliminating any hint of sexiness or even femininity to the décolleté area. Past the waistband, the skirt portion was full-on poof, round with gigantic petticoats that made her think she might be wearing a hot air balloon. Perhaps she could float up toward the clouds and be carried away.

A veil was affixed to her head. It was long enough to hoist beachcombers from Barcelona onto Izerote. The ensemble was finished off with uncomfortable matching pumps with decorative buckles—yes, buckles—encrusted with crystals.

"Princess?" The fitter was still waiting on her opinion about the lace rose at the waistband.

Luciana lazily shrugged her shoulders. She was defeated. Gio was right. She'd never been independent and she never would be. Why should she decide if the gown should have a flower on it? Let the dresser choose.

The royal planners had buzzed themselves into a tizzy as soon as the princess had been delivered back to the palace, with everyone told that she had been temporarily called off the island to lend her support to an urgent humanitarian crisis. A palace public relations spin, in action. But which, in essence, was accurate as far as she was concerned. Although, even if they knew the truth, she wouldn't have expected any sympathy from anyone at the palace about her own human need to soul search before she dedicated the rest of her life to the service of the crown.

Returning wasn't so easy, as she'd been changed by her journey. So her new goal would be to become more like her mother. To shut down, check out, not have an opinion about anything. She'd keep the life she wished she led alive in her mind, but walk through her real one.

"Kindly allow me a few minutes of privacy with my daughter." King Mario de la Isla de Izerote's stomp, then voice, reverberated off the walls as he shooed away the wedding staff. They assisted the princess down from the alterations dais before taking their leave.

Surely Luciana's father was the person least able to understand why she had to go to Florence. In fact, he hadn't even welcomed her back last night, merely sending a representative to convey his relief at her safe return. His wrath was to be one of the prices she'd pay for her defiance.

It was worth it, though, she confirmed to herself with a bite of her lower lip. "Father," she exhaled bravely.

"What have you done to your hair?"

"I had it cut and colored."

"That much is obvious."

As was expected of her, Luciana had always shown her father the utmost respect and deference. She loved him. If only he'd been a perceptive enough parent to see that spending her life isolated on this island where time stood still was a fate his daughter couldn't bear.

"I didn't mean to cause you worry," she stated with her head slightly bowed so she wouldn't have to make eye contact. "That's why I left you a note promising my return."

"It would have been proper protocol to ask my permission, not to stow away on a supply boat."

As she suspected, she'd been surveilled from the very beginning of her voyage.

"If you were following my every move, Father, why didn't you allow me the three weeks my note to you promised?"

"I received information that you were keeping company with a man. There was an incident involving *gelato*," he spat, as if it were a bitter taste in his mouth, "that my operatives interpreted as highly improper. I decided it best to sever that liaison as soon as possible, in your own best interest."

The princess brought her hand over her mouth in absolute mortification.

After a painful silence she said, "My best interest. I've tried to be a perfect daughter and a perfect princess."

"Is your idea of a perfect princess who is soon to be married one who cavorts around Florence with a man who isn't her fiancé?"

"That wasn't something I had planned." Nor was falling in love.

"Perhaps. But it was most undignified. We all have rules we must abide by, girl."

"I'm not a girl."

"You have acted like one."

No, he was wrong. For the first time in her life, Luciana had been a steel-eyed, rock-solid adult. Gio had taught her that. In seven short days, she'd learned more about being an adult from him than she had in her entire life.

Amazing Gio. Who thought for himself. From big-picture revelations to infinitesimal technological solutions. How often during her too-brief time with him had he asked her what she wanted and, if she didn't know, challenged her to find her answer? He shaped her into the woman she would now be. Which ruined her at the same time. As it was the man before her now to whom she was truly bound.

"It doesn't matter anymore. We live like museum pieces. We're fossils. I'll just turn to stone like mother did."

"Don't you think I know what you're feeling? I'm not so old that I don't remember what it was to be young. To crave drama and abandon. But I came to accept, as my forefathers did and as you will, too, that the honor and onus of the crown is far more important than any selfish goals that might try to lure us away."

Deep down, Luciana knew that her father was not the enemy. She could blame her fates if she wanted to. What good would that do her in the end?

"You will marry. And bear children. Your days will be full. These longings you have will pass. In time, you'll forget them."

"I don't love King Agustin." She loved Giovanni Grassi. And although she would never see him again, she would hold her love for him like a precious jewel in her hand until her last breath.

"And your mother did not love me." King Mario spoke a truth they both already knew. "Duty, Luciana. You'll truly be an adult when you stop battling your destiny."

Luciana shifted her eyes to the three panels of the dressing mirrors. There she stood in the ugly wedding gown she was to wear when her father would escort her down the aisle. Her father, who'd endured a loveless marriage that produced only one, ungrateful heir. A man who had to receive the middle-of-the-night phone call that his wife had been crushed to death in a car accident. Who did what he thought was his best with his only child.

"King Agustin will bring the jobs to our island we so desperately need," he reminded.

"Eroding our natural resources with tourist resorts? Is that really what's good for our subjects in the long run?"

"Without industry, we have no means to employ our people. It might not be the most inventive idea. However, it's what we're being offered."

Luciana studied her father's reflection in the three mirrors. His hair was still more pepper than salt. Shoulders that had always stood straight outlined a king with many decades left on the throne.

"Father, we have to think bigger."

"There is no other way."

There simply had to be. Despite her outward resignation, a whisper inside her heart told her she would not walk down that aisle to marry the widower king.

That evening after she'd changed into her nightgown and slippers, Luciana unpacked the suitcase she'd brought to Florence, refusing to let an assistant do it for her. As if they were as fragile as eggshells, she placed the two pairs of boyfriend jeans, the emerald green scarf from the San Lorenzo market and the bottle of Luci perfume in the back of the bottom drawer of her bureau. On top of them, she stacked a pillow and a blanket in the hope that her treasures wouldn't be discovered.

Slipping on her dressing gown, she stepped out onto the terrace of her sitting room. From this vantage point she could survey the north side of the island, facing toward the Spanish mainland.

It was a quiet night on the island, as always, with the

crash of the waves against the rock bluffs the only sound to be heard. The sea was rough, water bursting over and over again upon itself with turbulence similar to what she felt in her own center.

No matter how hard she tried, Luciana could not get her mind off Gio. It would eternally haunt her to ponder what it was that he had mouthed to her as the security detail forced her into that black car and squired her away from him. She knew what she hoped he had said. The same words she had screamed out to him, the last words she would ever speak to him.

What was he doing at this very moment? She allowed herself to imagine that it wasn't a palace terrace she looked out from tonight but, instead, the wrought iron Juliet balcony overlooking the courtyard of his villa. With its fragrant lavender and colorful flowers. That he was standing in the midst of it, gazing up at her, his sparkling eyes bright in the dark of night. Beckoning her to come down to him. To his embrace, to his kiss.

The moon tonight was high above the sea. Its distance made her think of a movie plot she'd heard of in which a woman had to be separated from her child. To ease her young son's mind, she promised him that every evening they would each look up to see the same moon. That no matter their distance, because they could both see the moon that would mean they were together.

Oh, Gio, please be looking at the moon. Please be with me tonight.

After staring at the sky with Gio in her heart for as long as she could take it, her eyes drifted to the hills and valleys of the island. To the west sat two abandoned factories, side by side. The eyesores were a constant reminder of the failures of Izerote, one of the reasons why the island's leadership could not provide enough employment for its citizens.

Those two factories had been built by a manufacturing company with the utmost in environmental protections as to not disturb the pristine ecosystems of the island. Engineering and construction were costly in such a remote location. Materials were brought by boat and with the use of the small airstrip that allowed private planes to fly in.

What the business investors had failed to take into consideration was that the machine tools they were manufacturing were heavy in weight and that shipping the finished product back to Barcelona for distribution was so costly all of the profits were eaten up. Within two years, the factories closed and the employees were again out of work. It was not only a catastrophe for the local economy, it was an embarrassment to the king and his advisory team.

If only those factories could be repurposed. If only a small, lightweight product could be manufactured or assembled there, an enterprise that would learn from the mistakes made in the past.

An idea stirred within Luciana.

It might not work. She might not get the necessary parties to agree. Without much knowledge on what the operation would involve, it might be an impossibility.

But what if the impossible was possible? What if?

Her mind swirled with a million thoughts and as many questions. She'd get them all answered. Tomorrow.

By the time dawn broke, she'd spent all night typing everything she'd thought of into her laptop. Ready to take action. She stepped again out onto the terrace to greet the day, assuming that if Gio had seen the same moon, her love would share the sun with her, as well.

Good morning, my exquisite Gio. Can you help me again?

Wasn't it rather early in the morning for a small airplane to be landing onto the island's airstrip?

As the private plane he'd hired descended for landing, Gio got his first glimpse of the island of Izerote. Luciana had not exaggerated when she'd explained to him just how remote her home was. After the flight to Barcelona, Gio transferred to the small aircraft that shuttled him the rest of the way. Finishing the glass of blood orange juice the lone flight attendant had presented to him earlier, he surveyed the island from the window beside his seat.

Untouched mountain ranges covered much of the terrain. From his vantage point, he spotted three small coastal towns and two more inland. They appeared to be like most towns in Europe. Gio could make out a center area in each, the commercial core dense with buildings erected closely together. Surrounding those in something of a ring were the residential areas with the structures a bit farther apart, homes with small yards. And farther out still from the town center were the more rural properties, some with plots of farmland.

He even saw livestock dotting the green fields. Although not much, according to Luciana, who had explained that most of the food for the island's inhabitants was shipped or flown in. Which explained why goods and services were very expensive, thereby contributing to the reasons many of the citizens were moving off the island. A complex set of issues faced this tiny land. He hoped to be part of the solution.

In a valley, he saw two large buildings that looked like factories. From what Gio could see, they appeared to be empty. If that was the case, his purpose here could be even more easily accomplished. He vaguely remembered Luciana telling him about some ill-thought-out industry that had gone into business here only to fail. That disaster pushed her father even further toward deciding on the arranged marriage between Luciana and the widower king from the neighboring island.

Which was about to be called off, if he had any say about it.

When the palace finally came into view, Gio's pulse quickened. Somewhere within those walls was his love. Picturing Luciana still asleep in a royal bed, no doubt blanketed in the finest of fabrics with her lovely head upon the fluffiest of pillows, filled him with happiness. He could hardly wait to bring his lips to hers. To taste her sweetness. To hold her softness against him.

There were many obstacles to cross before he'd have her in his arms again. But he'd get there.

After touchdown onto the island, Gio located the hired car that had been reserved to take him to the palace. Thank heavens for Samuele at the office in Florence, whom Gio could always count on to get the job done. Samuele had also spoken with palace staff to make an appointment for Gio to speak with King Mario, as a formal meeting with the monarch seemed the most appropriate method of introduction.

Once at the palace entrance, the driver opened the car door for Gio to step out. He took in what he could see of the palace grounds. The whole of it was rather small, befitting the size of the island. Nonetheless it had the foreboding of a fortress with its surrounding barricades of stone.

Upon giving his name at the security gate, Gio was

directed to the offices of the king. He passed through entrance doors into a reception foyer. A large oak desk stood in the center. A telephone bank and computer suggested that the desk was useful to operations, although its chair was empty at the moment. Gio took stock of the computer equipment setup and deduced that Wi-Fi was available. Which answered one of the questions he had regarding the idea he'd come to speak to the king about.

A wooden door to Gio's right opened, and a young man in a jacket bearing the palace insignia on the breast pocket emerged but was called back before he exited. He didn't see Gio, and spoke loudly enough to whoever was behind the door that Gio was able to hear them.

"I'll take care of it, King Mario," the attendant continued while Gio eavesdropped. "Also Your Highness, Mr. Giovanni Grassi should be arriving shortly for your appointment. Palace Intelligence has just informed me that Mr. Grassi is the gentleman Princess Luciana had kept company with during her sojourn in Italy."

Uh-oh. Gio had hoped that the king wasn't going to find out the connection between him and Luciana prior to their meeting. He was sure that, as an overprotective father, he would disapprove of Gio after finding out he had been touring Florence with his daughter. Gio wanted to first discuss his plan with the king before he got on to personal business. And, indeed, there were urgent personal matters to discuss. But if the king knew who Gio was at the outset, his anger might bias his ability to hear him out.

"Very well, Your Highness, when Mr. Grassi arrives I'll let him know that you were unexpectedly called away and that your schedule is full for the foreseeable future."

Gio needed to think fast.

If this attendant saw him in the foyer and Gio introduced himself, he'd be escorted out of the palace grounds immediately. Now that the king had gotten word of Gio's association with Luciana, the original course of action was ruled out. He had to find a safe place to reevaluate.

"Thank you, King Mario." The attendant uttered his last words before he closed the door on the king's office.

Not knowing what else to do but disappear before he got caught, Gio hurried down a corridor that led away from the foyer. In his dark blue suit and carrying his Italian leather attaché case, he looked like a legitimate palace visitor. If he encountered anyone along his way, he could feign being lost on his way to an official conference.

Mentally taking note that the corridor was leading him west and then north, he decided that what he needed to do was find Luciana. She'd shelter him and then they'd speak with the king together. Not to mention the fact that every second he'd been apart from her since she left Florence two days ago had been torture. By her side was where he wanted to be as soon as possible, for now and for always.

When he observed a housekeeper wheeling a cart of bed linens up ahead, he assumed he had reached the residential section of the palace. He was on the right track. Trying first one then another, he finally found an unlocked door and ducked into a room before the housekeeper saw him. From behind the closed door he listened until the cart was rolled past.

Tapestries depicting nature scenes adorned the walls of the room he found himself in. Antique or antique-style furniture sat in the center of the room, which appeared to be a parlor. The decor was as oppressive as Luciana had described, mismatched pieces that wouldn't have even been stylish in their day. Even the telephone on the claw-footed table was of an old style, connecting to the wall through a cable. Plenty of lighting suggested that the electrical systems were fully functional, though. He wondered about the wiring on the rest of the island.

Glass doors opened from the parlor onto a stone terrace. Gio stepped through and out into the fresh air, quickly taking note of where security cameras were placed so that he could avoid them. The sea breezes were bracing. As he made a careful assessment, he could see that one terrace led to the next and the next all in a row, each separated by a wall.

Leaning forward and around to the adjacent terrace he saw that it was empty, and was able to get a footing and swing himself over to it. Keeping from view, he peeked into the windows of the room there. Another parlor area with no one inside. He made his way to the next terrace, then peered into that sitting room.

Luciana! He'd know his love anywhere even though he saw her only in profile as she sat at a small desk typing into a laptop. Blood surged through his veins at the sight of her, and he could hardly wait to reunite with the kindheartedness and intelligence that lay beneath her staggering beauty.

The blond hairdo she was so proud of was pulled into a ponytail. She wore one of her conservative dresses, this one in brown, and looked ready to shake hands and have her photo taken at an official function. Maybe this was how princesses dressed every day, whether or not they had an engagement to attend. He'd have much to learn about palace life in the future.

Not wanting to scare her, he rapped lightly on one of the panes of the glass door. When she glanced up and recognition slowly took hold, tears leaked out of her eyes.

He'd kiss away each one.

She sprang out of her chair and rushed to open the door. Throwing her arms around his neck, she fluttered a hundred kisses all over his face and pulled him into the room, shutting the door behind her.

He swallowed his breath with a mixture of relief, yearning and joy beyond any jumble of emotions he had ever imagined possible. One disastrous scenario that had run through his mind before coming was that once he arrived, she'd not want any more contact with him. That she was ready to move forward with her fates and would not be open to his plan. Her response assured him otherwise.

"Gio," she cried, kissing him passionately on the lips and then holding him tight. "My Gio."

CHAPTER TEN

AFTER THEY COULD momentarily tear themselves away from celebrating their reunion with hugs and kisses, Gio explained how he had wanted to meet with her father but that the king had refused. "I want to manufacture my biometric products here. I'll establish a production plant and a development center on Izerote."

Luciana could hardly believe Gio was really here, flesh and blood, in her sitting room at the palace. Florence seemed a world away. Her mind ping-ponged in a hundred directions. "I had the same idea! I was reminded of these factories we have on the island, and then one thought led to another. That maybe it would be good for both your business and for my people. I was going to contact you."

"With a different solution to create jobs on the island, surely your father won't force you to marry King Agustin."

Tears trickled down Luciana's cheeks again. Because Gio had thought of a way to save her from marrying a man she didn't love. How fundamentally considerate he was, even though she didn't doubt that this arrangement would benefit him, as well.

But after the shock of his arrival subsided, she reminded herself that Gio wasn't here to give her the rest of her life with the man she loved. He was on Izerote to do business. He'd made it clear that he wouldn't devote himself to a woman and was not interested in building a family. There was no cause to think he'd changed his mind simply because they had been physically intimate.

She thought of her last minute in Florence. How, as she was being escorted into the car that would take her away, she yelled out to Gio to tell him that she loved him. She'd never expected to see him again after that, but she'd wanted him to know. And she'd needed to hear herself say it out loud, if only once in her life. Gio had mouthed something back to her that she hadn't heard. What was it? She couldn't bring herself to just come right out and ask.

"I spotted the factories from the plane," Gio said. "Can we go see them?"

He needed all of the information he could gather in order to prepare a presentation for her father. She had to think of a way to let him see those factories and decide if they were usable for his enterprise.

She dared not disappear again. And she couldn't very well call for a palace driver and exit her sitting room with Gio in tow. Hmm…

Recalling that fateful night when she'd climbed off her terrace to hike down to the shore where she'd stowed away on the supply boat, she remembered that her path took her straight past the factories. Gio could go that same way, and she'd go by car and meet him there.

"Good thinking, Princess." Gio planted a passionate kiss onto her lips before he hopped over the terrace wall like a swashbuckler in an old movie.

When Luciana told the driver where she wanted to go,

he balked. "Your Highness, I don't believe there is anyone on the premises there anymore."

"Thank you, Nico. If you'll just proceed, I'll take it from there." It turned out Gio must have brought a little of Luci with him from Florence. Because the princess was finished with acquiescing to what everyone, including a palace driver, thought she should be doing.

Regardless of the outcome of her plan with Gio, there was no turning back. If she refused to marry King Agustin, what could he and her father do? Throw her in jail? That didn't scare her. She was already in one.

Telling Nico to return for her in an hour, she found Gio on the property inspecting the buildings. Windows on all sides allowed them to get a good look into the inside of the factories. Gio was pleased that they were in good condition, and he could tell from the solar panels and lighting design that the structures were built with energy efficiency. He made guesstimates about the size of the work floors and how many assembly stations he could set up.

"This is really quite perfect," he said as he took her hand, his palm bathing her in instant warmth. Even if they were to be tied together only in business, Luciana thanked the universe that she'd at least have Gio in some way if they could bring this to fruition. Her world was a better place with him in it, even if he wasn't going to be at her side like she wished he would.

"Yes," she echoed. "Perfect." *Well, almost.*

They walked together to a grassy embankment behind the factories that overlooked the coast. She studied his profile while he looked out to the waves.

It was incongruous, his handsome face on *her* island. The magnificent curls blowing in *her* sea breeze.

"Luci," he said, using the distinction in her name. "I didn't come to this idea only because it would be good for my corporation. Or even to help you get out of your forced engagement to King Agustin."

"You didn't?"

"No, *bellissima*." He turned to her and took hold of both of her shoulders. His strong hands traced their way inward to her throat and then rode upward to caress her jaw, until he held her face in his hands. "My actions are not merely intended to keep you from another man. I'm here because I want you. I won't say I want you to belong to me. Because you belong to yourself. You're more than capable of standing on your own two feet. And I want to walk beside you. I want to catch you if you fall. I want you to catch me, too."

He placed a light kiss on her lips. Luciana shivered with cold abandon when he let his hands drop from her face. Then her spirit soared again when he went down on one knee and looked up to her with a sparkle in his eyes that she'd swear was more beautiful than all the gemstones in the world.

"I thought I would never partner with someone. That I wouldn't make time, that I wouldn't trust. Until I met you. You fill me up rather than deplete me. I don't know if you heard me declare my love to you in Firenze as the car was taking you away from me. I love you. I have never loved before. And I never will again. My love is only for you."

She covered her mouth as the shock settled in. "But I am bound to live here in Izerote. Someday I will be queen."

"I've lived all over the world. I'll make my life here in order to be with you. I can adapt. Home is where you are. Our wills are strong. We can make this work. Your Royal Highness Princess Luciana de la Isla de Izerote, will you marry me?"

Luciana fell to her knees to meet him eye to eye. Mouth to mouth. "Yes, Gio, we *will* find a way. You are my one true love, too. Of course I'll marry you."

The clack of King Mario's boots against the wooden floor was thunderous even from behind his closed office door as Luciana and Gio approached.

"Princess." The attendant in the blazer with the palace insignia whom Gio had avoided earlier now marched toward them. "Please allow me to notify the king that you wish an audience with him."

"Thank you, Joaquin, but I refuse to make an appointment to speak to my own father," Luciana rebuffed him as she opened the office door.

Gio slipped in behind her and closed the heavy door until he heard it click shut.

"Luciana." The king looked up from his audible pacing across his office floor.

"Giovanni Grassi," Gio introduced himself and hurried to meet the king face-to-face, thrusting out his hand for a proper handshake.

King Mario merely looked at his hand and continued on his walking course.

"Bow," Luciana mouthed to Gio.

Bow? Gio couldn't believe such an antiquated custom was still used on this remote little island that, frankly, had no relevance on the world stage. He knew that bowing to royalty was protocol in formal settings, but he somehow expected a man-to-man shake would be more appropriate to this private meeting.

The king returned to his paces.

It was with a grinding of his teeth that Gio bowed his head. "It's a great honor to meet you, sir."

He wasn't sure if *sir* was an acceptable address, but Gio was doing the best he could.

King Mario sized him up, his approval or disapproval impossible to read.

Gio decided to forge ahead with a preemptive, "Your Highness, I do apologize that our acquaintance begins so unusually. After I received the intelligence that you were unwilling to meet with me, I took a bold action in conferencing with the princess."

The king finally stopped his pacing and stood facing Gio, crossing his arms over his chest. "Indeed."

"I hope that when I, when we—" Gio gestured to Luciana, who stood beside him "—fully explain our proposal, you'll agree that the plan benefits all concerned."

"So, you and my daughter have already mapped out the future of Izerote? Mr. Grassi, you've known of the existence of this island for exactly how long?"

"A week, Your Highness. Please allow me to explain."

King Mario said nothing, merely nodding his head once. Princess Luciana straightened her spine and made herself taller, which Gio took as a positive sign of her willingness to stand up to her father.

Fortunately, from the minute Gio had had this idea, he'd been compiling scores of information. As he talked of his plan to bring the manufacturing of his biometrics to Izerote, he was able to emphasize Grasstech's eco-friendly practices that Luciana had told him were very important to her father. They were the sticking point that had caused him to reject other propositions in the past for enterprise on the island.

The strategy appeared to be working because King Mario listened attentively. "And depending on your preferences, if you so choose we could operate the factories on a twenty-four-hour cycle, with three sets of staff working eight-hour shifts, allowing us to employ thousands of your citizens."

"Not to mention that Gio will be able to bring the highest level of technology into our homes and throughout all the other businesses on the island," Luciana chimed in.

"At my expense, sir. We'd seek to modernize Izerote on a full scale."

Luciana surprised Gio by taking his hand. Which felt so right, Gio's chest swelled.

King Mario took note of the hand-holding.

The act was a declaration of independence that was difficult for her father. Just the same, Gio was proud of his beloved for doing it.

"I suppose you two have got all of *that* figured out, as well," the king stated flatly as he gestured to their hands in each other's.

"We do."

"I love Gio, Father. I knew it from the moment I met him."

"Your Highness, I will admit that I'm an informal man. My employees address me by my first name. Most of the time I'm wearing a pair of jeans and sipping a cappuccino as I hover over a computer." Although he had donned his finest dark blue Savile Row suit to meet the king today.

Luciana smiled at the comment about the jeans. Gio's mind paraded back to their time in Florence when Luci had first bought the pairs of baggy jeans that she was so thrilled to wear while they took in the sights.

He and his love locked eyes, making the world disappear. With her gazing at him like that, the affection and closeness they'd come to share, Gio could conquer the world.

"I'm well aware that as a commoner, sir, I have a lot to learn about palace etiquette. Therefore, again I beg your forgiveness if I'm not following royal decorum when I ask you for your daughter's hand in marriage."

"You are already engaged." King Mario's glare could shatter glass.

"To a man that I don't love."

"Perhaps you will in time, child."

"I'm not a child and I could never love King Agustin. Because I love Gio and there would never be any room in my heart to love another. Father, I know that you and Mother didn't have the kind of romantic love that only the lucky few are destined for. But I've been chosen. Don't you think that brings its own duty? Even though you didn't have it, don't you want that for me? I believe my mother would have."

The king's face transformed dramatically, morphing into one of a much softer man, changing into a loving father.

"I know this is a lot to take in all at once, Father. May we please sit down together?" She pointed to the dark wood conference table and chairs in front of the bay windows. "We want to tell you so much more about our plan for Grasstech on Izerote."

An hour later, Gio didn't know whether King Mario had admitted defeat or had been simply won over by his and Luciana's enthusiasm. There had been enough of the occasional half smiles and several nods indicating his comprehension of the plan that Gio was satisfied.

He wanted to conclude the meeting while things were still going well.

Just one more part of the endeavor needed to be outlined. "King, there's a final matter we need to discuss."

"How do I look?" Gio buttoned his jacket and modeled for Luciana as they prepared for the public address.

She lifted up on tiptoe to give her handsome fiancé a kiss on his mouth before she applied her lipstick. "My love, you look as fine in your bespoke suits as you would in a tuxedo or in swim trunks." And added with a wink, "Or in nothing at all."

"I can't believe how nervous I am. I've spoken in public many times before."

"It's the palace balcony bit. Intimidates the best of us."

Allowing a royal dresser to approve them as they passed through the corridor, the princess and her soon-to-be husband were escorted to the inner chamber that led to the official balcony. Luciana could hear the murmur of the citizens on the grounds below. It was a din she'd heard often enough to be able to estimate that it was a packed crowd with most of Izerote in attendance.

She had to admit to some jitters herself, as she generally appeared beside her father as a porcelain doll who merely waved and rarely spoke. Today, she had a lot to tell her subjects.

King Mario joined them and they were announced as His Royal Highness King Mario de la Isla de Izerote, Her Royal Highness Princess Luciana and honored guest Mr. Giovanni Grassi of Florence.

Gio looked to Luciana for instruction, and she pointed for him to step out onto the balcony. The crowd below stretched as far as the eyes could see. With the palace grounds not able to hold the mass, people stood all the way back to the entrance lawn in order to get a glimpse of the royal family when they took to the balcony. Their appearance was met with loyal applause and cheers.

Luciana peered down to the people and worked to spot individual faces in the crowds. A young father held his toddler up on his shoulders, the boy's arms wrapped around his neck. Teenaged girls looked up to Luciana with palpable admiration. An older couple linked arms.

Truly, Luciana loved Izerote. The untamed natural beauty. The cordiality and goodness of its people. She slanted her eyes sideways to steal a glance at Gio. With this man by her side, she could do her duty to these citizens. As a pair they would not only change the island for the benefit of these deserving people, they'd leave a future of stewardship and prosperity for generations to come. Luciana again focused on the little boy atop his father's shoulders in the crowd.

"Princess." King Mario leaned in to speak only to his daughter. "You've forced me to see how much my own fear has suffocated you. I love you, daughter. You've become a wise woman. You'll make a fine queen someday."

"I love you, too. Dad." The corners of both of their mouths tipped up in a private almost smile that they alone shared.

King Mario then thrust his shoulders back and faced his subjects.

"Thank you, citizens of Izerote, for joining us today," he spoke through the standing microphone placed on the balcony. The crowd cheered. The king explained the arrangement he'd made with Grasstech to create jobs and futures for the island's population. He invited Gio to speak.

"My father began Grasstech forty years ago," he began, "at a time when computer technology was ancient compared with what it is today. He founded the company with the command to his employees to think deep, to think wide, to think far outside of the box. King Mario has told you a bit about what we plan to do here in Izerote. But, in reality, that is only the beginning. We don't yet know how high we can fly, how fast we can soar. I can hardly wait for us, together, to find out."

The throng roared with approval. Luciana filled with pride at Gio's inspiring words.

Now it was her turn to stand in front of the microphone. She peeked over to Gio, then took her place in the center of the balcony, righteous and strong.

"I am pleased to see so many children here." She pointed to six or so in her sight. "Because any actions we take today affect them tomorrow. Gio has outlined our plans to bring living wages and enduring jobs to our people. As parents, and as future parents, we understand that in order for us to be successful in our work, we need to know that our children are being meaningfully looked after. That's why I'm pleased to announce the formation of the Luci Foundation, a new initiative that will create free, quality child care for our youngest citizens until they are old enough to go to school."

Many in the audience applauded, especially the women.

Luciana bowed her head to her father, who, after she and Gio laid out their intentions for this element of the plan, had consented.

"In addition to devoting myself to you as a monarch," she continued, "it has always been my own personal dream to work with young children. To help parents raise confident, happy, creative and secure children who will grow into the big-thinking adults Gio just spoke of. I ask you today to support me in my quest. I would like to continue my education to earn an advanced degree in early childhood education so that I can lead the Luci Foundation with experience and expertise, and work together with you to bring Izerote the progress and prosperity I know we can achieve."

Her speech was met with ovations of endorsement.

In reality, Luciana had always known that her father was wrong when he insisted that the citizens of the island did not want advancement and modernization. It was only he who feared it. The protective king didn't want to put his people, or his daughter, in danger and thought that by keeping them sheltered and separate he could better safeguard them.

She and Gio would teach him. Slowly, in a way that was comfortable to him.

Her lovely Gio had already broken the ice when after the meeting in the king's office yesterday, the conversation turned friendly and Gio taught his future father-in-law how to check the weather and the world's stock markets on his smartphone.

King Mario handed something to Gio, who nodded knowingly. She'd spied them having a private tête-à-tête this morning but didn't know what the topic was.

His Royal Highness moved to the microphone. "Our family has another announcement to make. Princess Luciana has made a change in her personal plans. She will not be marrying King Agustin de la Isla de Menocita. I spoke with the king this morning and he wishes everyone on our island peace and prosperity in the future."

A hush of shock swept across the gathering. Luciana swallowed hard, knowing that she was perhaps disappointing people with this news. She was compelled to take over the microphone from her father and speak candidly.

"Are any of you in love?" she asked her subjects. Bellows and yelps came from different areas of the grounds. Couples kissed. Others smiled. "I hope you'll agree that there's no predicting love. Quite unexpectedly, I have fallen in love. To a man I wish to marry. Although he is a commoner, I hope that you will accept him and learn to love him as much as I do. Together, we will earn your trust. Ladies and gentlemen, Mr. Giovanni Grassi is not only the genius mind who will help us take our island into the next generation and beyond, he is also the man I will marry and bear children with."

Gio stepped forward and opened his hand. It held Luciana's great-grandmother's wedding ring. She remembered the family stories about Esmerelda being the only one in her lineage who fell in love with her husband after an arranged marriage.

Luciana mouthed *Thank you* to her father.

Her fiancé placed the ring on her finger.

The princess took his hand in her left and her father's in her right. The three faced the crowd, who went wild with well-wishes.

Gio and Luciana had their first official kiss as an engaged couple, which was welcomed with resounding cheers that echoed all the way to the blue skies above.

* * * * *

RESCUING THE ROYAL RUNAWAY BRIDE

ALLY BLAKE

For my husband, Mark, who loves nothing more than looking to the stars.

CHAPTER ONE

THE DAY COULD not be more perfect for a royal wedding, thought Will as his open-topped hire car chewed up miles of undulating Vallemontian roads.

The sky was a cerulean-blue dome. Clusters of puffy white cumuli hovered over snow-dusted mountains and dotted shadows over rolling green hills filling the valley that gave the small European principality its name.

By Will's calculations, snow should fall on the valley any day. Instead, the delicate bite of a warm sun cut through the washed-clean feeling that came after lashings of rain. It was as if the influential Vallemontian royal family had wished for it to be so, and so it was.

But Will Darcy did not believe in wishes. He believed in the human eye's ability to find millions of colours in a drop of light; the resultant heat of distantly burning stars; that weather forecasting was an inexact science.

This coming from an astronomer; his field truly a game of extrapolation, using ancient evidence to build current theory, relying on calculations that pushed against the edges of the range of known values. One had to be part cowboy, part explorer, part decoder, idealist and seer to do well in the field—something he'd addressed as the keynote speaker at the Space and Time Forum in London the night before.

It had been a late night too. Hence the fact he'd flown

into Vallemont only that morning, and would arrive at the palace just as the ceremony was about to start.

The delayed flight had also given him plenty of opportunity to back out if need be. There was the lecture on worm holes he was due to give at the University of Amsterdam a few days from now, after all. The podcast with newyorker.com. The notes from his editor on the second edition of his graduate-level astronomy textbook due any day. And then there was the virtual-reality game set in the Orion Nebula for which he was both investor and technical advisor.

Reasons enough to forgo the trip.

But only one reason to get on that plane.

To see his old friend tie the knot.

A day for knots, Will thought, choosing to ignore the one that had formed overnight in his belly at the thought of what this day might bring.

He pressed down on the accelerator on the neat little convertible his assistant had hired for him in the hope he might "realise how damn lucky he was and take a moment to enjoy himself". The chill wind ruffled his hair as he zoomed through the bucolic countryside until the road narrowed, heralding yet another idyllic Arcadian village.

Around a tight bend and he was in the thick of it—tightly winding cobblestone streets dotted with gaslight-style street lamps, stone houses with thatched roofs tucked tightly together and wedged into the side of a steep hill, their windowsills abundant with brightly coloured flowers; history in crumbling stone walls, mossy pavements and the occasional brass sign telling of times past.

The engine on the low-slung sports model growled as Will changed down a gear. The suspension knocked his teeth together as it struggled against the ancient stone beneath, but it was all he could do to avoid the crowd spilling from the thin footpaths onto the road.

Festive they were. All smiles as they headed to pubs and parks and lounge rooms all over the country to watch the wedding on television. Pink and gold ribbons had been strung across the road. Handmade banners flapped from weathervanes. Pink flower petals covered the footpaths and floated in tiny puddles.

All because Will's oldest friend, Hugo, was getting married to some woman named Mercedes Gray Leonine, no less. Though those who had strung the ribbons and scattered the petals knew the guy as Prince Alessandro Hugo Giordano.

Then the roadway cleared and Will aimed for a stone bridge crossing the rocky river that trapped the village against the hillside and hit open space again.

It was all so very green, rain having brought a lush overabundance, shine and glisten as far as the eye could see.

And on he drove. Until he reached a tunnel of trees running parallel to the river.

Glimpses of fields pushing into the distance sneaked through the dark foliage. The ever-present mountains cast cool shadows through the sunshine. And, if his GPS wasn't glitching, any moment to the east…

There. Sunlight bounced off arched windows and turned pale sandstone turrets into rose-gold. Pink and gold banners flapped high in the breeze while the Palace of Vallemont sat high and grand on its pretty bluff, like something out of a fairy tale.

And the knot in Will's stomach grew so that it pressed hard against his lungs.

The first time he'd been invited to the palace had been well over a decade before. Circumstances—by way of a skiing accident—had seen to it that he'd been forced to stay at his grandparents' mausoleum of a townhouse in London that summer, leaving his sister, Clair, to visit the royal family as Hugo's special guest on her own.

Only a few weeks later, Will's life had been irrevocably, tragically altered. The boy who'd already lost so much became a young man who'd lost everything. And Vallemont, this postcard-pretty part of the world, had been a throbbing bruise on his subconscious ever since.

Memories lifted and flurried. He'd handled things less than admirably at the time. This was his chance to put things right. He held the steering wheel tighter and kept moving forward.

The thicket filled out, the view narrowing to the curving tunnel of green and rutting muddy road that hadn't had the benefit of recent sunshine. A herd of sheep suddenly tripped and tumbled their way across the road.

Will slowed again, this time to a stop. He rested his elbow on the windowsill, his chin in his hand, his finger tapping against his bottom lip. If life wasn't so cruel, random and insensate, he might one day have attended a very different wedding in this storybook place. Not as a ghost from the groom's past, but as best man and brother, all in one.

He shook his head.

What ifs were not relevant. The world simply kept on turning. Day would dissolve into night. And tomorrow it would start all over again.

The last of the sheep skittered past, followed by a wizened old man in overalls holding a crook. He tipped his hat. Will returned with a salute. And then he and the knot in his belly were off again.

He kept his speed down as rain had dug deep grooves into the ancient mud and stone. The trees hung dangerously low over the road, dappling sunlight over the windscreen, shadow and light dancing across his hands, hindering his vision for a second, then—

Will slammed on the brakes. He gripped the wheel as

the car fishtailed, mud spattering every which way, the engine squalling, the small tyres struggling to find purchase.

Then the car skidded to a jarring halt, momentum throwing him forward hard against the seatbelt, knocking his breath from his lungs. At which point the engine sputtered and died.

His chest burned from the impact of the belt. His fingers stung on the wheel. Blood rushed like an ocean behind his ears. Adrenaline poured hotly through his veins. And beneath it all his heart clanged in terror.

He'd heard a noise. He was sure of it. The growl and splutter had been punctuated with a thud.

Expecting carnage, axle damage from a fallen log, or, worse, a lone sheep thrown clear by the impact, Will opened his eyes.

Sunlight streaked through the thicket. Steam rose from the road. Wet leaves fell like confetti from a tree above. But there was no sheep in sight.

Instead, dead centre of his windscreen, stood a woman.

He blinked to make sure he wasn't imagining her. So pale, sylph-like in the shadows of the dark, dank vegetation, she practically glowed.

As if in slow motion, a leaf fluttered from above to snag in a dark auburn curl dangling over her face. Another landed on a fair bare shoulder. Yet another snagged on the wide skirt of a voluminous pink dress three times bigger than she was.

Those were details that stampeded through Will's mind during the half-second it took him to leap from the car. The mud sluicing over the tops of his dress shoes and seeping into his socks mattered only so far as the fact it slowed him down.

"Where are you hurt?" he barked, running his hands through his hair to dampen the urge to run them over her.

Not that she seemed to notice. Her eyes remained

closed, mouth downturned, black-streaked tears ran unstopped down her cheeks. And she trembled as if a strong gust of wind might whip her away.

Best case scenario was shock. Worst case… The thud still echoed against the back of his skull.

"Ma'am, I need you to look at me," he said, his voice louder now. It was the kind of voice that could silence a room full of jaded policy-makers. "Right now."

The woman flinched, her throat working. And then she opened her eyes.

They were enormous. Far too big for her face. Blue. Maybe green. Not easy to tell considering they were rimmed red and swollen with dark tears.

And every part of her vibrated a little more, from her clumpy eyelashes to the skirt of her elaborate dress. Standing there in the loaded silence, the hiss and tic of his cooling engine the only sound, he knew he'd never felt such energy pouring off a single person before. Like the sun's corona, it extended well beyond her physical body, impinging on anyone in its path.

He took what felt like a necessary step back as he said, "I cannot help you until you tell me whether you are hurt."

She let out one last head-to-toe quiver, then dragged in a breath. It seemed to do the trick as she blinked. Looked at his car. Lifted her hands into the air as if to balance. Pink diamonds dangling from her ears glinted softly as she shook her head. *No.*

Will breathed out, the sound not altogether together. Then, as relief broke the tension, anger tumbled through the rare breach in his faculties.

"Then what the holy hell were you doing jumping out in front of my car?"

The woman blinked at his outburst, her eyes becoming bigger still. Then her chin lifted, she seemed to grow an inch in height, and finally she found her voice. "I beg your pardon, but I did *not* jump out in front of your car."

Will baulked. The lilting, sing-song quality of the Vallemontian accent that he had not heard in person in years was resonant in every syllable. It took him back in time, making the ground beneath his feet unsteady.

He refocused. "Jump. Leap. Swan dive. It's all the same. You had to have heard me coming. My car engine isn't exactly subtle."

That earned him a surprisingly unladylike snort. "Subtle? It's a mid-life crisis incarnate. *You* should have been driving your overcompensation more slowly! Especially with the roads being as they are after the rain we've had."

"It's a rental," he shot back, then gave himself a swift mental kick for having risen to the bait. "Speed was not the issue here. The pertinent fact is that you chose to cross at a bend in the road shaded by thick foliage. You could have been killed. Or was that your intention? If so it was an obtuse plan. Nearly every person in the country is already at the palace or sitting by a TV to watch the royal wedding."

At that she winced, her pale face turning so much paler he could practically see the veins working beneath her skin. Then she broke eye contact, her chin dipping as she muttered, "My being right here, right now, was never part of any plan, I can assure you of that."

Okay. All right. Things had gone astray. Time to bring everything back to fundamentals. "So, just to be clear, I did not hit you."

She shook her head, dark red curls wobbling. "No, you did not."

"I could have sworn I heard a thud."

Her mouth twisted. Then she looked up at him from beneath long, clumping eyelashes. "When I saw you coming I did the only thing I could think to do. I threw a shoe at you."

"A shoe?"

"I'd have thrown both if I'd thought it would help. But alas, the other one is stuck."

"Stuck?" Will was aware he was beginning to sound like a parrot, but the late night, early morning, the knotty reality of being in Vallemont after all these years were beginning to take their toll.

He watched in mute interest as the woman gathered her dress and lifted it to show off skinny legs covered in pale pink stockings. One foot was bare. The other foot was nowhere to be seen—or, more precisely, was ankle-deep in mud.

Will glanced back at his car. Then up along the road ahead.

Time was ticking. Hugo's wedding was looming. Will wasn't sure of the protocol but he doubted a soon-to-be princess bride would be fashionably late.

The woman in pink was calmer now, the static having dulled to a mild buzz. Best of all she was unhurt, meaning she was not his problem.

Will did not do "people problems". His assistant, Natalie—a jolly, hardworking woman who performed miracles from a desk at home somewhere in the Midwest of the United States—was the only person in the world to whom he felt beholden and only because she told him every time they spoke that he should. Even then her efforts on his behalf were well-compensated.

He preferred maths problems, fact problems, evidentiary problems. His manager would attest that time management was Will's biggest problem as he never said no to work if he could find a way to fit it all in.

And yet… He found that he could not seem to roust himself to wish the woman well and get back on his way.

There was nothing to be done except to help.

Decision made, he held out both hands as if dealing

with a wounded animal. "Any way you can jiggle your foot free?"

"Wow. That's a thought." It seemed she'd hit the next stage of shock—sarcasm.

"Says the woman who threw a shoe at an oncoming car in the hope of saving herself from getting squished."

Her eyes narrowed. Her fists curled tighter around her skirt. Beneath the head-to-toe finery she was pure street urchin itching for a fight.

Shock, he reminded himself. *Stuck*. And she must have been cold. There wasn't much to the top part of her dress but a few layers of lace draped over her shoulders, leaving her arms bare. The way the skirt moved as it fell to her feet made it look like layers of woven air.

Air he'd have to get a grip on if he had any hope of pulling her free.

Will slid the jacket of his morning suit from his shoulders and tossed it over the windscreen into the car. Rolling his sleeves to his elbows, he took a turn about her, eyeing the angles, finding comfort in the application of basic geometry and calculus.

She looked about five-feet-eight, give or take the foot stuck in the mud.

"What do you weigh?"

"Excuse me?"

"Never mind." It would come down to the force of the suction of the mud anyway. "If you don't mind, I'm going to take you from behind."

A slim auburn eyebrow rose dramatically. "I thank you for asking first, but I do mind."

Will's gaze lifted from the behind in question to find the woman looking over her shoulder at him. Those big eyes were unblinking, a glint of warmth, laughter even, flickering in the blue. Or was it green?

Right. He'd heard it too. He felt his own cheek curving

into an unexpected smile. "My intentions are pure. I only wish to get you out of your…sticky situation."

Her right fist unclenched from her skirt, her fingers sliding past one another. Then her eyes dipped as she gave *him* a thorough once-over to match the one he'd given her.

Will crossed his arms and waited. He was the preeminent living name in modern astronomy. Eyes Only at NASA. An open invitation to the UN. On first-name terms with presidents and prime ministers alike.

Yet none of that mattered on this muddy country road as, with a deep sigh of unwitting capitulation, the woman waved an idle hand his way and said, "Fine. Let's get this over and done with."

First time for everything, Will thought as he moved into position. Adrenaline having been sapped away, he was now very much aware of the damage incurred by his footwear. He attempted to find purchase on the boggy ground. "Ready?"

She muttered something that sounded like, "Not even close." But then she lifted her arms.

Will wrapped his arms around her waist. There really was nothing of her. More dress than woman. He grounded his feet, and heaved.

Nothing happened. She was well-bogged.

"Grip my arms," he said. "Lean back a little. Into me."

In for a penny, she wrapped her arms over his, her fingers shockingly cold as they curved over his wrists. But right behind the chill came that energy, like electricity humming just beneath her skin.

Will said, "On three I need you to press down strongly with your free foot, then jump. Okay?"

She nodded and another curl fell down, tumbling into his face. He blinked to dislodge a strand from his eyelashes. And a sweet, familiar scent tickled his nose till he could taste it on the back of his tongue. *Honeysuckle.*

"Here we go," he grumbled. "One. Two. And…three!"

He felt her sink into the ground and as she pushed he pulled. With a thick, wet *schlock* her foot popped free.

She spun, tottered, her feet near slipping out from under her. And finally came to a halt with her face lodged into his neck.

There she breathed. Warm bursts of air wafted over his skin and turned his hair follicles into goose flesh.

Then he felt the moment she realised she had one hand gripping his sleeve, the other clamped to his backside for all she was worth.

The breathing stopped. A heartbeat slunk by. Two. Then she slowly released her hold.

Only, the second she let go, she slipped again.

With a whoop she grabbed him—the sound shaking a pair of bluebirds loose. They swooped and twittered before chasing one another down the tunnel and away.

And suddenly she was trembling in earnest. Violent shakes racked her body, as if she were about to self-destruct.

Dammit. Computing how best to separate her from her trap was one thing, but this was beyond his pay grade.

She made a noise then. Something between a squeak and a whimper. The next time she shook she broke free with a cracking laugh. Then more laughter tumbled on top of the first. Braying, cackling, riotous laughter—the kind that took hold of a person until they could barely breathe.

Will looked to the sky. He wasn't built for this kind of roller coaster of emotion. It was so taxing and there was no logical pathway out.

Ready to take his leave before things turned again, Will took her firmly by the arms.

Another curl fell to dangle in front of her face. She crossed her eyes and blew it away with a quick stream of air shot from the side of her mouth. When she uncrossed her eyes she looked directly into his.

Spots of pretty pink sat high on her pale cheeks, clear even beneath the tracks of old tears. As her laughter faded, her wide mouth still smiled softly. Light sparked in the bluish green of her huge eyes, glints of folly and fun. And she sank into his grip as if she could stay there all day.

Instead of the words that had been balanced on the tip of his tongue, Will found himself saying, "If you're laughing because your other foot is now stuck I will leave you here."

A grin flashed across her face, fast and furious, resonant of a pulse fusion blast. "Not stuck," she said. "Muddy, mortified, falling apart at the seams, but the last thing I am any more is stuck."

Will nodded. Even though he was the one who suddenly felt stuck. For words. For a decision on what to do next. For a reason to let her go.

Which was *why* he let her go. He unclamped his fingers one at a time, giving her no reason to fall into his arms again.

The woman reminded him of a newly collapsed star, unaware as yet that her unstable gravitational field syphoned energy from everything she touched.

But Will wasn't about to give any away. He gave every bit of energy to his work. It was important, it was groundbreaking, it was necessary. He had none to spare.

"Look," he said, stopping to clear his throat. "I'm heading towards court so I can give you a lift if you're heading in that direction. Or drop you…wherever it is you are going." On foot. Through muddy countryside. In what had probably been some pretty fancy shoes, considering the party dress that went with them. From what Will had seen there was nothing for miles bar the village behind him, and the palace some distance ahead. "Were you heading to the wedding, then?"

It was a simple enough question, but the girl looked as if she'd been slapped. Laughter gone, colour gone, dark tears suddenly wobbled precariously in the corners of her eyes.

She recovered quickly, dashing a finger under each eye, sniffing and taking a careful step back. "No. No, thanks. I'm… I'll be fine. You go ahead. Thank you, though."

With that she lifted her dress, turned her back on him and picked her way across the road, slipping a little, tripping on her skirt more.

If the woman wanted to make her own way, dressed and shod as she was, then who was he to argue? He almost convinced himself too. Then he caught the moment she glanced towards the palace, hidden somewhere on the other side of the trees, and decidedly changed tack so that she was heading in the absolute opposite direction.

And, like the snick of a well-oiled combination lock, everything suddenly clicked into place.

The dress with its layers of pink lace, voluminous skirt and hints of rose-gold thread throughout.

The pink train—was that what they called it?—trailing in the mud behind her.

Will's gaze dropped to her left hand clenched around a handful of skirt. A humungous pink rock the size of a thumbnail in a thin rose-gold band glinted thereupon.

He'd ribbed Hugo enough through school when the guy had been forced to wear the sash of his country at formal events: pink and rose-gold—the colours of the Vallemontian banner.

Only one woman in the country would be wearing a gown in those colours today.

If Will wasn't mistaken, he'd nearly run down one Mercedes Gray Leonine.

Who—instead of spending her last moments as a single woman laughing with her bridesmaids and hugging her family before heading off to marry the estimable Prince Alessandro Hugo Giordano and become a princess of Vallemont—was making a desperate, muddy, shoeless run for the hills.

Perfect.

CHAPTER TWO

"YOU CAN'T BE SERIOUS."

Sadie swallowed as the man's voice echoed through the thicket. Or she tried at the very least. After crying non-stop for the last hour, her throat felt like sandpaper.

In fact, her entire body felt raw. Sensitive. Prickly. As if her senses were turned up to eleven.

Adding a near-death experience hadn't helped a jot.

Well, pure and utter panic had got her this far and she planned to ride it out until she reached the border. Or a cave. Or a sinkhole that could swallow her up. Where was a batch of quicksand when you needed it?

She gathered as much of her dress as she was able and kept on walking, hoping her sardonic liberator would simply give up and drive away.

Unfortunately, his deep voice cut through the clearing like a foghorn. "You've made your point. You can stop walking now."

Sadie's bare foot squelched into a slippery patch of mud. She closed her eyes. Took a breath. Turned. And faced down the stranger in her midst.

When she'd heard the car coming around the corner her life had flashed before her eyes. Literally. Moments, big and small, fluttering through her mind like pages in a picture book.

Not yet school age, screaming, pigtails flying behind

her as she was being chased through the palace halls by a grinning Hugo. Her mother waggling a finger at her and telling her to act like a lady.

At five, maybe six, Princess Marguerite gently reminding her not to hold her hand up to block the bright lights from the TV crew. Hugo standing behind a camera making faces as she sat on a couch in the palace library, answering questions about growing up as a "regular girl" in the palace.

The blur of high school without Hugo at her side—the first sense of feeling adrift without her safety net.

Her attempt to overcome that feeling—wide-eyed and terrified, landing in New York when she was twenty. Then grabbing that safety net with both hands as, teary and weary, she fled New York and moved back into the palace at twenty-five.

Her memory had not yet hit the anxious, fractured, out-of-control mess of the past few weeks when she'd spied the driver on the muddy road.

For time had slowed—imprinting on her mind wind-ruffled dark hair, a square jaw, a face as handsome as sin. A surge of drama at the end. *At least the last thing I'll ever see is a thing of beauty*, she'd thought.

Of course, that was before he'd proceeded to storm at her for a good five minutes straight.

Quite the voice he had. Good projection. With those darkly scowling eyes and that muscle ticking in his impossibly firm jaw she'd first thought him a Hamlet shoo-in. From a distance, though, with those serious curls and proud square shoulders he'd make a fine Laërtes. Then again, she'd had a good grip on that which was hidden beneath the suit. A dashing Mercutio, perhaps?

Though not in one of her high-school productions, alas. One look at him and her twelfth-grade drama students would be too busy swooning to get anything done.

That, and she'd been "encouraged" to take a sabbatical from her job the moment she'd become engaged. The palace had suggested six months for her to settle into her new role before "deciding" if she wished to return.

"Ms," he said again, and she landed back in the moment with a thud.

Focus, her subconscious demanded, lucidity fluctuating like a flickering oil lamp during a storm. Her brain seemed to have kicked into self-protect mode, preferring distraction over reality. But, as much as she might wish she was living a high-school play, this was as real as it got.

"Ms—"

"Miss," she shot back, levelling the stranger with a *leave me be* glance. Oh, yes, she was very much a "miss". Her recent actions made sure of that. She remembered the rock weighing down her left hand and carefully tucked it into a swathe of pink tulle.

"As I said I'll be fine from here. I promise. You can go." She took a decided step back, landing right on the cusp of a jagged rock. She winced. Cried out. Hopped around. Swore just a bit. Then pinched the bridge of her nose when tears threatened to spill again.

"Miss," said the stranger, his rumbling voice quieter now, yet somehow carrying all the more. "You have lost both your shoes. You're covered in mud. You're clearly not…well. It's a mile or more to the nearest village. And the afternoon is settling in. Unless you have another mode of transport under that skirt, you're either coming with me or you're sleeping under the stars. Trust me."

Trust him? Did he think she was born under a mushroom? *Quite possibly*, she thought, considering the amount of mud covering the bottom half of her dress.

Not witness to the conversations going on inside Sadie's head, the stranger went on, "How could I look myself in the mirror if I heard on the news tomorrow that a woman was eaten by a bear, the only evidence the remains of a pink dress?"

Sadie coughed. Not a laugh. Not a whimper. More like the verbal rendering of her crumbling resolve. "Bears are rare in Vallemont. And they have plenty of fish."

"Mmm. The headline was always more likely to be *Death by Tulle*." He swished a headline across the sky. *"'Woman trips over log hidden entirely from view by copious skirts, lands face-first in puddle. Drowns.'"*

Sadie's eye twitched. She wasn't going to smile. Not again. That earlier burst of laughter was merely the most recent mental snap on a day punctuated with mental snaps.

She breathed out hard. She'd walked miles through rain-drenched countryside in high heels and a dress that weighed as much as she did. She hadn't eaten since... when? Last night? There was a good chance she was on the verge of dehydration considering the amount of water she'd lost through her tear ducts alone. She was physically and emotionally spent.

And she needed whatever reserve of energy, chutzpah and pure guts she had left, considering what she'd be facing over the next few days, weeks, decades, when she was finally forced to face the mess she had left behind.

She gave the stranger a proper once-over. Bespoke suit. Clean fingernails. Posh accent. That certain *je ne sais quoi* that came of being born into a life of relative ease.

The fact that he had clearly not taken to her was a concern. She was likable. Extremely likable. Well known, in fact, for being universally liked. True, he'd not caught her in a banner moment, but still. Worth noting.

"You could be an axe murderer for all I know," she said. "Heck, *I* could be an axe murderer. Maybe this is my *modus operandi*."

He must have seen something in her face. Heard the subtle hitch in her voice. Either way, his head tipped sideways. Just a fraction. Enough to say, *Come on, honey. Who are you trying to kid?*

The frustrating thing was, he was right.

It was pure dumb luck that he had happened upon her right in the moment she'd become stuck. And it was dumber luck that he was a stranger who clearly had no clue who she was. For her face had been everywhere the last few weeks. Well, not *her* face. The plucked, besmeared, stylised face of a future princess. For what she had imagined would be a quiet, intimate ceremony, the legal joining of two friends in a mutually beneficial arrangement, had somehow spiralled way out of control.

She'd had more dumb luck that not a single soul had seen her climb out the window of the small antechamber at the base of the six-hundred-year-old palace chapel and run, the church bells chiming loud enough to be heard for twenty miles in every direction.

Meaning karma would be lying in wait to even out the balance.

She looked up the road. That way led to the palace. To people who'd no doubt discovered she was missing by now and would search to the ends of the earth to find her. A scattered pulse leapt in her throat.

Then she looked at the stranger's car, all rolling fenders and mag wheels, speed drawn in its every line. Honestly, if he drove a jalopy it would still get her further from trouble faster than her own feet.

Decision made, she held out a hand. "Give me your phone."

"Not an axe murderer, then, but a thief?"

"I'm going to let my mother know who to send the police after if I go missing."

"Where's your phone?"

"In my other dress."

A glint sparked deep in her accomplice's shadowed

eyes. It was quite the sight, triggering a matching spark in her belly. She cleared her throat as the man bent over the car and pulled a slick black phone from a space between the bucket seats.

He waved his thumb over the screen, and when it flashed on he handed it to her.

The wallpaper on his phone was something from outer space. A shot from *Star Wars*? Maybe underneath the suave, urban hunk mystique he was a Trekkie.

The wallpaper on the phone she'd unfortunately left at the palace in her rush to get the heck out of there was a unicorn sitting at a bar drinking a "human milkshake". Best not to judge.

She found the text app, typed in her mother's number.

But what to say? *I'm sorry? I'm safe? I screwed up? I would give my right leg to make sure they do not take this out on you?*

Her mother had been a maid at the palace since before Sadie was born. It had been her home too for nearly thirty years. If they fired her mother because of what Sadie had done…

Lava-hot fear swarmed through Sadie's insides until she imagined Hugo's response to such a suggestion. No. No matter how hard he might find it to forgive her for what she'd done to him today, he'd never take it out on her mother. He was that good a man. The best man she'd ever known.

Maman

Good start.

By now you know that I'm not at the chapel.

Another deep breath.

I couldn't go through with it. It wasn't right. Not for me and certainly not for Hugo. If you see Hugo…

She paused, deleted the last line. Whatever needed to be said to Hugo, she would say herself.

I'm so terribly, desperately sorry for all the confusion and complications that will come of this and I promise I will make everything right. But today, right now, I have to lick my wounds, clear my head and prepare. Know that until then that I'm whole and I'm safe. xXx

Before she could change her mind, she pressed "send". Only remembering belatedly that her mother wouldn't recognise the strange phone number.

In fact…

She found the camera app, held up the phone and said, "Smile!" Her benefactor turned and she took a photo.

She quickly started a new message. Added the picture.

I've borrowed this phone from the gentleman in this picture, so do not message back. I'll call when I can. Love you.

The picture slid up the screen as the message was sent. The top of his head was missing, and an ear, but it was still him in all his grumpy glory. His hand was at his tie, giving it a tormented tug. His dark eyes bored into the lens. He wasn't smiling but there was something about the shape of his mouth, a curving at the corners, the barest hint of what might—under just the right circumstances—become a dimple.

Her thumb hovered over the screen as she thought about sending a text to Hugo too. What if the poor lady-in-waiting she'd sent off into the palace with the note to Hugo clutched in her white-knuckled grip hadn't managed to get through to him? Even if she had, Sadie still needed to tell him…to explain…

What? That she was nothing but a scaredy-cat?

She slid her thumbs away from the screen.

"Done?" the phone owner asked.

Sadie deleted the conversation. She hoped her mother would heed her warning or her cover as a possible axe murderess would be blown.

She solemnly gave him back his phone. "And now I'll go in your car with you."

"You're a brave woman."

"You have no idea."

His mouthed twitched and…there. Dimple. Heaven help the women of the world who got to see that thing in full flight.

Not *her* though.

If her mother had taught her anything it was to beware instant appeal; it had everything to do with genetic luck and nothing to do with character. A handsome smile could be fleeting, and could be used to hide all manner of sins.

With that in mind, it had taken her twenty-nine years to agree to marry Hugo and he'd been her best friend since birth. And still, when it had come to the crunch, she'd run. Something she'd learned from her father.

Sadie felt the backs of her eyes begin to burn as the home truths settled in. But she was done crying. She mentally forced the tears away.

She'd made a choice today. One that had sent her down this road alone. And alone she had to remain if she was to get her head on straight and figure out what the heck she was going to do with the rest of her life. But Grouchy Dimples wasn't going to leave her alone unless she let him do his knight-in-shining-armour bit and get her safely out of sight.

So Sadie picked her way back through the rivulets of rock and dirt and mud.

The stranger moved around to the passenger side of the car, opened the door, bowed slightly and said, “My lady.”

Sadie’s entire body froze. Only her eyes moved to collide with his.

She looked for a gleam of knowledge, a sign that he knew exactly who she was. But the only sign she got was the return of the tic in his jaw. He couldn’t wait to get rid of her either.

“Sadie,” she said before she even felt the word forming. “My name, it’s…just Sadie.”

“Pleasure to meet you, Just Sadie. I’m Will.”

He held out a hand. She took it. He felt warm where she was cool. Strong where she was soft. His big hand enveloped hers completely, and for the first time in as long as she could remember she found herself hit with the profound sense that everything was going to be okay.

The sensation was so strong, so unexpected, so unsought, she whipped her hand away.

Will held the door for her once more. “Let’s get this show on the road.”

Taking a deep breath, Sadie gathered up as much of her skirt as she could, tucking and folding and looping the fabric under her arms. Then she squeezed backside-first into the bucket seat.

After Will closed the door with a soft snick, Sadie let the fabric go. It sprung away, filling the space right up to her chin. Relief at not being on her feet, on the run, in the open, rolling over her like a wave of bliss.

Will slid into the driver’s seat and curled long fingers over the leather steering wheel. He surreptitiously checked his watch again. He still thought he had a wedding to attend, Sadie realised, and for a fraught second she thought he might simply drive that way.

"You mentioned a village," Sadie said, pointing over her shoulder in the opposite direction to the palace.

"The village it is." Will gunned the engine, carefully backed out of the muddy trench, executed a neat three-point turn and drove back the way he had come.

A minute later, Sadie glimpsed the palace through the trees. The afternoon sunlight had begun to cast the famous pink and gold highlights across the sandstone walls which had lent the small principality the beautiful, romantic, quixotic colours of its banners.

Home.

But after what she had done, could she ever go back there? Would they even let her through the door? And what would happen to her mother, a maid who had lived and worked under the palace roof for the last twenty-nine years?

Sadie put the flurry of unpleasant questions to one side and closed her eyes, letting the dappled sunlight wash across the backs of her eyelids. There was nothing she could do about all that right now.

Later. She'd figure it all out later.

Will leant his elbow against the window of the car, feigning a relaxedness he did not feel as he drove over the bridge he'd navigated not long before. Back in the village, banners still flew. Music poured out into the streets. The roads were now bare, since everyone had moved inside to be in front of their TVs in order to see the bride make her first appearance. Little did they know they were looking the wrong way.

If Hugo hadn't yet discovered his bride was missing, he soon would. Search plans would be afoot. Containment plans.

Will was forced to admit that his immediate plans would need to become fluid for the moment as well. But first…

As the engine's throaty growl gave him away, Sadie sat upright. "What are you doing? Why are you slowing?"

"We need petrol," he said as he pulled off the road and up to a tank wrapped in rose-gold tinsel that flapped in the light breeze.

He used the collective noun very much on purpose. He'd read enough books to know that, in hostage negotiations, making the hostage-taker feel they were on the same side was paramount. Though which one of them was the hostage here was debatable.

He pulled over and jumped from the car. But not before surreptitiously sliding his phone into his pocket.

Meanwhile, Sadie had slunk down so far in the seat she was practically in the footwell. All he could see was acres of crinkled pink and a few auburn curls.

"Can you breathe down there?"

A muffled voice professed, "Most of the dress is organically grown Australian cotton. Very breathable."

"And yet I'm not sure it was intended to be worn over the face."

Two hands curled around the fabric and a small face poked out. "Point made."

She blinked at him through huge red-rimmed eyes above a pink-tipped nose. Her full lower lip was shiny from nibbling. When she wasn't acting so bolshie and stubborn she was rather pretty.

Will pushed the thought away. He turned his back and splashed a nominal amount of petrol into the tank before heading for the shop. Inside, he gave the guy behind the counter a wave. Then, finding a private corner, he made the call, using a phone number he could only hope still worked.

It answered on the second ring.

"Yes?" came the voice from Will's past. The voice of the Prince.

Will leaned against a shelf. "Hey, mate, how's things?"

A beat. “Darcy? Look, I can’t—”

“You can’t talk because you’re meant to be getting married but your bride seems to have gone missing.”

The silence was deafening. Then footsteps echoed through the phone as Hugo obviously set to finding himself a private corner of his own.

“How the hell can you possibly—?”

“She’s with me.”

Will gave a very quick rundown of the events. Leading to his decision to keep her close.

Hugo’s voice was uncommonly hoarse, even a little cracked, as he said, “I was given a note just before you rang by a maid refusing to leave my doorway. Written in lipstick, on the torn-out page of a hymnal no less, telling me she couldn’t go through with it. I didn’t believe it until just now. Yet at the same time it felt like I’d been waiting for that note all my life. I— *Dammit.* Excuse me a moment.”

Hugo’s voice was muffled. Will imagined him covering the mouthpiece of the phone. His tension was palpable in his short, sharp responses to whomever had disrupted their conversation.

It had been years since he’d seen Hugo in person. Even as a teenager there’d been gravitas about the Prince, the weight of the world sitting easily on his shoulders. Until his own father had died in a car crash and that world had collapsed.

Will had born Hugo through that horrendous time. Hugo had tried to return the favour after Clair’s death only a few months later, putting aside his own grief, but Will had rejected Hugo’s counsel out of hand.

Will had been mistaken then. He would not turn his back on the Prince now.

Will waited, glancing around the petrol station. Pink and gold streamers hung limply from the ceiling to the cash register. The guy behind the counter hunched over a small TV while sipping pink milk through a straw. The vision showed a variety of invited guests smiling and waving as they walked up the gravel path to the palace gates.

A frisson of tension pulled tight across Will's shoulders. Everything had happened so fast—the near crash, the rescue, the discovery, the uncommon decision to get involved—the repercussions that went far beyond his inconvenience didn't hit him until that moment.

An entire country held its breath in anticipation, clueless as to the axe that had already begun to swing, while Hugo sat somewhere in the palace, looking into the face of an emotional ruination that he did not deserve. Again.

"Apologies," said Hugo as he came back on the line.

"Mate," said Will, his own voice a little rough. "What the hell happened?"

The silence was thick. Distant. Elongating the miles and years between them.

Hugo's voice was cool as he asked, "Is she injured? Is she distressed?"

"She's shaky but unhurt."

"I'd very much like to talk to her."

Will thought *he'd* very much like to kick her out of his rental car, and dump her on the side of the road; force her to face the bedlam she had unleashed. But it was clear Hugo was not of the same mind.

If Will's intention in coming to Vallemont had truly been to put things to rights with his oldest friend, then it seemed he'd been gifted the opportunity to do just that. The fact it would not be easy was ironically just.

"In full disclosure, she doesn't know I'm talking to you. In fact, she doesn't know that I'm aware of who she is at all. I believe that's the only reason she agreed to let me give her a lift."

He let that sit. When Hugo made no demur, Will went on.

"I can give her the phone or I can keep her with me until you send someone to collect her. Unless, of course, you want me to bring her back right now so you can work your magic and marry the girl."

He half hoped Hugo would say *Bring back my girl*—then Will could deliver her and tell himself he'd achieved what he'd come to Vallemont to do.

"If you could stay with her I would very much appreciate it," was Hugo's eventual response. "I'll send for her when I can. Till then, keep her safe."

Will nodded before saying, "Of course. And you? Where do you go from here?"

"That, my friend, would be the question of the hour."

"As opposed to, *Do you take this woman?*" Will imagined a wry smile filling the silence. And suddenly the miles and years contracted to nothing.

"Yes," was Hugo's dry response. "As opposed to that."

The Prince rang off first. No doubt plenty on his to-do list.

It left Will to stare at the picture he'd linked to Hugo's private line; the two of them at seventeen in climbing gear, grins wide, arms slung around one another's shoulders, mountains at their backs. Clair had taken that picture the day before Will had broken his leg.

By the end of that summer Clair had been taken ill. A week later she'd been diagnosed with an incurable brain disease. Mere months after she'd taken that photo she'd left them for ever.

Will slid his phone into his pocket. He tucked the memories away too before they started to feed on him rather than the other way around.

Hugo wasn't the only one with things to do.

Only, while Hugo would no doubt be fending off a buffet of advisors as he determined the best way forward, Will had to go it alone.

It was a concept that didn't come easily to a twin, a concept that had haunted him for a long time after his sister was gone. Until one day, while hiding from his economics professor at Cambridge, he'd slipped into a random lecture hall. Taken a seat at the back. Discovered it was *Stars and the Cosmic Cycle*. And found himself skewered to the seat.

For Clair's last gift to him, one she'd planned to give to him on what would have been their eighteenth birthday, one he'd only found in her bedroom after she'd died, was a telescope.

As a man who'd never believed in signs, he'd gone with it. As the lecturer had talked of the universe as unmapped, unchartered and mostly incalculable, many in the lecture hall had twittered and shifted on their seats, finding the concept overwhelming.

For Will it had changed the concept of being "alone" for him completely. And it was that ability to dissociate from the everyday, to enjoy a high level of dedicated solitude, that had paved the way for his being the pre-eminent voice in modern astronomy.

Will paid for the petrol, steadfastly refusing to look at the pre-wedding coverage on the monitor. He was halfway to the car when he remembered.

He wasn't alone.

He had Sadie.

She peered up at him from the mound of wriggling pink as he slid back into the car, her curls flopping onto her pale shoulders, her big eyes filled with pandemonium. This woman was chaos incarnate, and she was leaving a widening swathe of trouble in her wake.

"Everything okay?" she asked. "You were gone for a while."

"Was I?" Will started the car with more gusto than required.

He'd come to this country, pained at the thought of having to watch Hugo marry someone who wasn't Clair, quietly wondering if the invitation was his penance for having laid the blame for what had happened at Hugo's guiltless feet for all these years.

Now he realised he'd miscalculated. *She* was his penance. Mercedes "Sadie" Gray Leonine. Looking after her on Hugo's behalf, keeping her out of sight until he could send word to Hugo where he could find her would go some way to ameliorating past wrongs.

And when it was done, he might even be able to get an earlier flight out. It was meant to be an unusually clear night, a rare opportunity to spend some time with London's night sky.

Feeling better about the world, Will shot Sadie a smile, which faded a tad at the way her eyes widened as he did so.

"The tank is full, the sky is blue." Will tapped the car's GPS. "North? South? East? West? Coast? Mountains? Moon? Where are we going?"

CHAPTER THREE

SADIE NIBBLED SO hard on the tip of a pale pink acrylic nail, the thing snapped right off, so she carefully hid it in the door pocket and racked her brain for an answer.

Where are we going? Will had asked. As if she were following some kind of plan.

Her only goal had been to get as far from the palace as possible without being seen. Her luck would not hold out for much longer. Her best bet now was to hole up, get in touch with Hugo somehow. Apologise, grovel, make him see that while her timing had been terrible it had been the right decision, for both of them.

"A room," she said. "To stay for a night. That's what I'd like."

"Excellent. Do you have a place in mind?"

"Not exactly. Some place…quiet would be fine." Discreet. Not one of Hugo's palatial resorts, for example. "Where are those dodgy motels you see in American cop shows when you need them?"

"I'm sorry?"

Sadie glanced at her companion, thankful to find he was back to looking at her as if he was barely containing his impatience. That momentary flash of perfect white teeth as he'd smiled had been disconcerting to say the least.

She usually went out of her way to make people feel comfortable. Hugo joked that her need to be liked by everyone was pathological. Sadie simply wanted to make sure everyone around her was happy. But in these circumstances a little distance felt safer. It was easier to think of the man as a means to an end rather than a collection of dimples, warm hands and crinkles at the edges of his eyes as he smiled. Especially now, when she was feeling so untethered. In the past her decision-making skills had not been at their peak at such times.

She turned on the seat; her skirt bunching under her hip. "You know, the kind where the anti-hero in the vintage brown Cadillac hooks around the back of some dreary, anonymous, flat-roofed roadside joint where the ancient woman with a cigarette dangling from her cracked lips doesn't even bother to look up from her crossword as she signs the guy in?"

He glanced at her and said, "Flat-roofed?"

How odd that he focused on that. It was the kind of detail that usually tickled only her. When she found herself looking into those dark eyes of his a beat too long, she glanced at her fake fingernails instead. One down, nine to go. "You know—squat. Like it's been flattened by the weight of the world. Why doesn't Vallemont have places like that?"

"Because it's Vallemont," he said, and he was right.

The sentiment wouldn't have made as much sense to her as a kid.

Watching Hugo go away to school had made Sadie itch to see the world, to see life outside the borders of the peaceable country in which she'd been born. And eventually she'd managed to talk her way into a four-year acting course in New York.

At first it had been a dream. Auditioning, waitressing, living in near-squalor with three strangers in a studio in Brooklyn. Walking streets where nobody knew her story, with its urban canyons, subway smells, its cracked sidewalks and manic energy, as different a place from Vallemont as it was possible to find.

Halfway through she'd begun to feel lonely, the brilliant, fraught, nerve-racking, ugly, beautiful and eye-opening experience taking its toll.

By the end of that year she'd realised that it wasn't the noise and hustle and energy of a big city she had craved, but control over her life. Taking control over her narrative. That's what she loved about theatre. Not acting, but the chance to shape a play from beginning to end.

She'd lasted another year before she'd come home. Giving up a dream many would kill for.

And oh, that land of rolling hills and green pastures. Of crystalline streams fed by snow-capped mountains. And towns of cobbled streets and dappled sunshine and quiet, happy lives. The relief had been immeasurable.

And here she was again—gifted a rare opportunity and she'd thrown it all away.

Sadie groaned and let her head drop back against the seat.

"If it's accommodation you're after, what about this place?" said Will, the car engine growling as he slowed.

Sadie cracked open an eye to find herself looking at a place as far from a dreary, anonymous, flat-roofed roadside joint as possible.

A sign reading "La Tulipe" swung from the eaves of a ramshackle dwelling, three storeys high, with a pitched roof and balconies all round. Bright purple bougainvillaea was starkly stunning as it crept over the muddy brick. Oddly shaped, it dissected two roads, one heading up the hill to the left, the other dipping down the hill sharply to the right, creating an optical illusion that made it look as if it had a slight lean down the hill. Or maybe it *was* falling down the hill. It had an ancient, ramshackle appeal either way.

A skinny black cat skittered across the way as Will pulled into a spot on the low side of the building. He turned off the engine, got out of the car and reached into the back seat for a soft black leather bag.

Sadie sat up straight. "Ah, what are you doing with those?"

"I plan on seeing you inside. And I'm not leaving my bags in the car while I do so."

Sadie peeked over her shoulder. A gentle breeze skipped autumn leaves over the cobbled road. A small brown bird danced from one semi-bare tree to another. Other than that, there was no one as far as the eye could see. "We're not exactly a crime capital here."

Will followed her gaze, paused a moment, then, ignoring her, heaved his other bag—a big square silver case—out of the car and set it on the footpath. "Coming?"

Sadie heard voices—a couple laughing as they crossed the street at the bottom of the hill. Time to get inside. Except…

"I can't go in there dressed like this. I look—" Like the girl who'd left the country's most eligible bachelor standing at the altar. She'd be less likely to be recognised naked than in that dress. She'd heard knock-offs were already available. "A total mess. What do you have in your bag? Or your case?"

Will's hand went to the battered silver case. It was big enough that she might even fit inside. For a brief moment she considered asking.

"Anything I might be able to borrow? I'll take it off the minute I get inside a room."

That muscle ticked in his jaw. Another flickered below his right eye. He appeared to be making a great effort at keeping eye contact. And Sadie realised what she'd said.

Feeling a wave of pink heat rising up her neck, she backtracked. "I mean I'll find something else to wear, even if it's a bed sheet, then you can be on your way."

Her reluctant knight breathed for a beat or two, his dark eyes pinning her to her seat. Then, muttering under his breath, he lifted the leather bag and plonked it onto the driver's seat.

Then he moved down the footpath and away from the car, his back to her, giving her some privacy. Not ideal, but needs must.

Inside his bag she found an expensive-looking knit sweater. Black. Soft as a baby's bottom. It smelled delicious too. Like sandalwood, and fresh air and man. Like the scent she'd caught in that strangely intimate half a second where Will had put his arms around her, pulling her back into the nook of his strong, warm body, before yanking her out of the mud.

She cleared her throat and shoved the sweater aside, rifling until she found a utilitarian tracksuit top. Black again. And some black tracksuit pants. The guy sure liked black. Maybe he was a spy. Or a magician. Or clinically depressed.

She glanced over her shoulder to find he still had his back to her as he stood on the footpath, hands in pockets, face tilted to the sun.

Even in a suit it was clear he was built like a champion diver—all broad shoulders and thick, roping muscle. His profile as he squinted down the street was strong, sure, forbearing. He might not be the most easy-going man she'd ever met, but there was no doubting he was very comfortable in his own skin.

Not depressed, then. Perhaps he simply liked black.

She pulled out the tracksuit pants, shuffled up onto her knees, twisted her hands over her shoulder to attempt to rid herself of layers of lace embedded with tiny pink crystals…no luck. She twisted around the back of her waist. Still no luck. As panic tickled up her spine she thought about ripping the thing over her head, but it was so dense she'd probably find herself caught in a straight-jacket of her own making.

Sadie bit her lip and looked up at the sky. Cloudless. The brightest blue. Such a happy sight. She muttered a few choice words under her breath.

Then, "Ah, excuse me. Will? I need some help here."

He spun on his heel so the sun was behind him, his face in shadow. Resistance was evident in the hard lines of his body as he said, "Help?"

She flapped her hand towards the trillion pearl buttons strapping her in.

It was his turn to mutter a flurry of choice words before he took a few slow steps her way. "What do you need me to do?"

"Start at the top? Truth be told, I wasn't paying much attention as I was strapped in." Trying not to panic had been higher on her list of priorities.

Will took in a long, deep breath before his hands moved to her neck, surprisingly gentle as they pushed her hair aside. So many curls had dropped during her run from the palace. She helped, taking them in hand as she tipped her head forward.

A beat later, Will's fingers worked the top button, which was positioned right against a vertebra. That was what it felt like anyway, as if he'd hit a nerve cluster. Goosebumps sprung up all over her body.

With a sweet glide, it unhooked, Will's warm thumb sliding against her skin as he pressed the fabric aside.

"Sadie?" he asked, his voice deep and low and close enough to cause a rumble.

"Yes, Will?"

"There are about a hundred-odd buttons on this thing."

"One hundred and eight." One for every year the Giordanos had been the governing family of Vallemont. Seriously. When the small wedding she and Hugo had planned had twisted into the kind of circus where the number of pearl buttons on her dress had a backstory, that was when she ought to have put her foot down and called the whole thing off.

Will said, "Take this as a serious question, but are there…layers underneath the dress?"

"Layers?"

"Ah, under…garments?"

She'd not been able to pin down his accent until that moment. It was crisp and clear, but worldly. As if he'd travelled a great deal. In that moment it was pure, upper-crust, Queen's English.

He sounded so adorably repressed, she was unable to stop herself from saying, "Are you asking if I've gone commando?"

A beat, a breath. Then, "Sure. Why not?"

"No, Will. I am not naked beneath my dress. There are undergarments to spare."

"Glad to hear it. And are you planning on wearing your dress again?"

"Once this thing is off I never want to see it again, much less wear it!" A tad effusive perhaps?

"Excellent. Here goes." Solid nails scraped lightly against her shoulder muscles as his fingers dived beneath the fabric. Then with a rip that split the silence he tore the dress apart. Buttons scattered with a pop-pop-pop as they hit the dashboard, the steering wheel, the metal skin of the car.

As the fabric loosened and fell forward across her chest, Sadie heaved in a big, gasping breath. The first proper lungful of air she'd managed in hours. Days even. Weeks maybe. It might well have been the first true breath she'd taken since she and Hugo had shaken hands on an agreement to wed.

She felt the moment Will let the fabric go, the weight of his warm hands lifting away. More goosebumps popped up to fill the gaps between the others.

"Thank you," she said, her voice a little rough, as she wriggled free of the thing until she was in her bra, chemise and stockings.

Out of the corner of her eye she saw Will turn away again, this time to lean his back against the car.

As the chill autumn air nipped at her skin she hastened Will's clothes over the top. There was that scent again. This time she also caught layers of leather and skin and cologne. Subtle, expensive and drinkable. The sooner she was out of his clothes the better.

Kicking her dress into the footwell with more force than was probably necessary, Sadie got out of the car.

The stony ground was freezing against her bare toes. Bracing.

When Will's tracksuit pants—which were far too big for her—began to fall, she twisted the waistband and shoved it into the top of her knickers. The jacket falling halfway down her thighs covered the lump.

At last, she bent to check herself in the side mirror. And literally reared back in shock at the sight. Her hair was an absolute disaster. Her cheeks were blotchy and windchafed. She could barely recognise herself beneath the rivers of dried mascara bleeding down her cheeks.

Licking her thumbs, she wiped her face clean as best she could. Then she set to pulling out the thousand pins from her hair. Dislodging the hairpiece was a blessed relief.

Once her hair was all her own again she tipped over her head, ran fingers through the knots, and massaged life back into her skull. With practised fingers, she tied the lot into a basic ponytail. No longer a clown bride. Now she was rocking more of an athletic goth look.

An athletic Goth with a mighty big engagement ring on her finger.

She glanced Will's way. He was checking something on his silver case.

She looked back to the ring. It was insanely ostentatious, with its gleaming pink diamond baguette in the rose-gold band. But was it her? Not even close.

Hugo's face slid into her mind then, with his oh-so-familiar laugh.

"My grandmother left it to me, which was a matter of contention in the family, as you can imagine. Her intention was that I give it to my bride. I'm sorry."

"Sorry for what?"

"It looks ridiculous on you."

"Thanks a lot!"

"Seriously. Your fingers are so scrawny, it looks like you're trying to balance a brick on the back of your hand. Take it off."

"No. Never. Do you remember the first time you said you'd marry me? I do. I was four and you were seven. Kind woman that I am, I never planned to hold you to it back then. But I'm not letting you off the hook now. This ring is what it is: a symbol. If a brick is what will help keep roofs over both of our families' heads, then it seems like a pretty fine symbol to me."

Another promise broken, Sadie slid the brick from her finger. The fact that it came right off, without even the slightest pressure, seemed like a pretty big sign in and of itself.

She quickly tugged down the track pants, found a ribbon hanging from her garter and tied the ring to it with a nice tight knot. Then she gave the jacket one last tug. "Okay, I'm ready."

Will pressed away from the car and turned. His dark gaze danced over her clothes—*his* clothes—her bare feet, then up to her hair. It paused there a moment before dropping to the hand clutching the bouffant of fake curls. At which point his mouth kicked into a smile. Dimple and all.

As it had been the first time, it was as unexpected and magnificent as a ray of sun slicing through a rain cloud and Sadie's heart thumped against her chest.

"What?" she shot back.

Will held a hand towards the doorway of La Tulipe. "I didn't say a thing."

Sadie grabbed the hood of his jacket and pulled it over her head. Then, scooting past him, her chin imperiously high, she said, "You didn't have to."

As soon as they entered the lobby of the old hotel, Sadie's adrenaline kicked up a notch. For all her efforts to escape, everything could fall apart right here, right now.

She tucked herself in behind Will, breathing through her mouth so as not to drink too deeply of the deliciousness of his cologne. Skin. Washing detergent. Whatever.

"Sadie," he said, turning so she was face to face with his strong profile. The heavy brow, nose so perfect it could have been carved from marble, the hint of that dimple.

"Mmm?"

"Have you heard of a little something called personal space?"

"Sorry," she said, searching desperately for a sane reason why she might be snuggled into him as she was. "I'm… cold."

If Will didn't believe her, he didn't say so. No doubt he already thought her a lunatic, considering her behaviour thus far.

As they approached the desk, over Will's shoulder Sadie

saw a girl in her late teens wearing jeans and a plain pink T-shirt, her long brown hair in a side ponytail.

Will came to a stop, tipping his big silver case back onto its wheels and readjusting his leather bag on his shoulder.

The girl smiled as they approached. "Hello!" she sing-songed. Then she seemed to notice Will anew, as along with a little sigh came a breathy, "Oh, my. Oh… Ah. Didn't think we'd see a soul today. The entire country has its nose up against its collective TVs. Waiting for the wedding to begin!"

She motioned to her computer monitor and Sadie was bombarded with a montage of images—crowds lining the path leading to the palace waving Vallemontian flags and throwing pink peony petals into the street. The front doors of the St Barnabas Chapel were open, inviting, a mouth waiting to swallow a bride whole.

"Prince Alessandro is so dreamy," said the girl, "don't you think? Those eyes. That voice. He's like the hero from some novel. To think, there is a woman out there who gets to be his heroine."

Sadie let her head fall, gently landing on one of Will's shoulder blades. "A room," she stage-whispered. "Ask about a room."

Will cleared his throat. "We were hoping for a room."

The girl blinked, seemed to suddenly notice Sadie hiding behind Will's shoulder.

Having been seen, Sadie fixed the hood tighter over her head, then gave the girl a little wave. She held her breath, waiting for the moment of recognition. But the girl merely gave her a nod before her gaze slid right back to Will.

"Right. Well, lucky for you the Tower Room has just come free. The couple using it had a wicked fight. She stormed out. He followed, looking most chagrined. It was all very exciting. Like Beatrice and Benedick in person."

Sadie perked up. The girl was into *Much Ado About*

Nothing? It was Sadie's absolute favourite play. She taught it to her senior students every year. Perhaps this place was a good choice after all.

"Anyway," said the girl, "it's our finest room. Canopy bed. Kitchenette. Balcony with views that extend all the way to the palace."

Sadie's perk was short-lived. Views of the palace? No! *No, no, no...*

She must have said it out loud, as Will leaned back an inch. "No?"

Sadie bit her lip.

"Oh. Well, I'm afraid that's the only room we have. And you're not likely to find another this close to the palace. We've been booked out for weeks. Ever since the date of the royal wedding was announced. Prince Alessandro is a favourite. Many a heart broke the moment the news came through that he was to settle down for good."

"Did they, now?" Will asked, with something akin to humour edging his voice. A catch. An aside. Like an inside joke. Or was she imagining it? "The Tower Room sounds just perfect? Thank you."

A beat slunk by, followed by another, after which Sadie realised Will was waiting for her. As this was the point at which she was meant to give her details. And her money.

She lifted herself a little higher, high enough she could mutter near Will's ear, "I don't exactly have my wallet on me right now."

"In your other dress?" he muttered back.

"Uh-huh."

His hand slid between them, grazing her belly through his tracksuit top. She gasped, her breath shooting past his ear.

He turned to stone. "Sadie," he said, his voice seeming even lower than normal.

"Mmm-hmm?"

"Wallet's in my back pocket," he said.

"Right. Sorry."

Sadie rocked back onto her heels, giving Will room. When he slid a shiny black card from inside, Sadie wasn't exactly trying to catch his name…not really. But catch it she did.

Dr William Darcy.

Dr Darcy, eh? Doctor of what? William suited him more than Will. Will was a friendly name. Will Darcy—

It was Sadie's turn to turn to stone.

Surely Mr Tall Dark and Grouchy wasn't *the* Will Darcy—schoolfriend of Hugo's from his murky boarding-school days and the only person Hugo had insisted they invite to their wedding back when the plan had been to keep it small?

Her gaze danced over the back of the man's head and neck, as if hoping for clues. But alas his collar gave nothing away.

All the while, Will's finger pressed down hard on the card and stopped its counter-slide. "Dare I ask what might the room rate be at this late date?"

The girl looked at Will, looked at his shiny card, then with a bright smile quoted an exorbitant nightly price more suited to a famous Fifth Avenue penthouse than a crumbling old village building. "Blame the wedding."

"Oh, I do," Will grumbled as he slowly lifted his finger from the card.

And Sadie felt the ground tip out from under her.

It *was* him. It had to be.

It was him and he knew. He knew who she was, he knew what she'd done. It all made sense! His coolness towards her, his insistence she go with him, the fact he was being so obliging, despite the fact he ought to have been fretting about getting to the wedding late.

The cad had been lying to her about who he was the entire time!

Okay, fine. She was lying too. But her reasons were *life and death*. Or near enough. In the olden days she would have been stoned for the move she'd pulled.

His motivation could not possibly be so clean.

"Lovely," said the girl after swiping and checking Will's card. "All set. Here are your keys."

What was that? Keys? Plural? Hang on a second. Sadie opened her mouth to let the girl know she only needed one, but Will had already picked them up.

"I'm Janine," said the girl as she came around the desk. "If you need anything, anything at all, I'm your girl. Until then, head up both sets of stairs; your door is the last on the right. I trust you'll find it wonderfully comfortable. The Tower Room also has its own fireplace. Fur rugs throughout. Super-comfortable sofas. And the most gorgeous bed you will ever see. There's no TV, of course, because it's our honeymoon suite."

Of course it is, thought Sadie, right at the moment Will said the exact same words.

A bubble of crazed laughter escaped her throat, though it sounded more like a whimper.

"Have a lovely stay, Dr Darcy and…friend."

"Thank you, Janine," he said, tapping his forehead in a two-finger salute and earning himself another sigh.

Then he turned to face Sadie. "Ready?"

Sadie gave him the same salute.

When his mouth twitched, that dimple showed for one brief second. Sadie ducked her chin and took off for the stairs.

The Tower Room was as advertised.

Exposed brick walls covered in romantic prints by Waterhouse and Rossetti. Polished wood floors gleamed in the fading light of day. Soft couches looked as if you'd fall in and never want to get out. A fireplace big enough to sleep in.

It was charming, inviting and terribly romantic.

Only then did she see the bed.

For there it was, perched on a slightly raised platform at the end of the room. Soft, cream-coloured blankets covered the mattress. Pretty gold gauze trailed from a canopy, falling into pools on the floor at each corner while fake ivy twisted around its beams and posts.

It looked like something a fairy-tale princess would sleep in.

Panic welling within her once more, Sadie looked for an out. Stumbling to one side of the room, which from the outside mirrored a classic castle keep, she pushed open the French windows and stepped onto the tiny, round balcony.

Gripping the cold metal, she gulped in great lungs full of crisp, late autumn air, hoping not to be sick all over Will's clothes.

When she finally got her stomach under control she opened her eyes.

Janine was right. The view was breathtaking.

The village lay before her, all warm, tumbling brick and thatched roofs. Early lamplight laced together rambling cobbled paths. Flower pots, green corners and naked-branched trees were scattered prettily about.

And then she looked up.

The glorious jagged mountains that surrounded their landlocked little corner of the world thrust up into the sky. And right smack dab in the middle of the view, like a gem in the centre of a ring, sat the Palace of Vallemont.

Pink ceremonial flags flapped in the breeze, all across the rooftops, heralding the big occasion. And then, as if someone had simply been waiting for her to watch, the flag atop the highest tower slid slowly down the flagpole.

If the raising of the flag signified glory, honour, rejoicing, the lowering was a sign of a death in the family, a tragedy in the country, a moment of great national sorrow.

The news was out.

Soon everybody would know she had run.

Talk about breathtaking.

CHAPTER FOUR

SADIE BACKED SLOWLY into the room, feeling as if her insides had been scooped out.

When she'd come home from New York she'd felt like such a disappointment. She'd let down everyone who'd rooted for her. Having to tell the story of her withered dream over and over again had been an out-of-body experience.

This was way worse. Millions of people she'd never met would be reeling with dismay.

Sadie was not used to being disliked. In fact, her likeability was the cornerstone of her identity.

Her story was well-known all across Vallemont, she having been born literally on the road to the palace.

Her father—a less than exemplary model of manhood who had been dragging his pregnant girlfriend across the country to avoid debt collectors—had taken one look at newborn Sadie and fled. Luckily, the wife of the reigning Sovereign Prince—Hugo's Aunt Marguerite—had been driving past when she found them, huddled on a patch of grass. The Princess had famously taken them in and given Sadie's mother a job as a palace maid, allowing Sadie to grow up as a palace child. Sadie had been a firm favourite ever since.

The very thought of all that hatred coming her way

drained the blood from her extremities until she could no longer feel her toes.

Someone cleared their throat.

Sadie's focus shifted until she saw her reluctant rescuer, the living embodiment of unfavourable judgment, standing in the centre of the room holding his bags.

The only person she could possibly turn to, the only person she could lean on, ask for advice, was looking at her with all the warmth of a shadow. His dark energy added layers to her discomfort, making her feel edgy. Awkward. Hyper-aware.

Okay, she thought. This situation seems overwhelming, impossible even. But all you can expect yourself to do is handle one thing at a time. Starting with the thing right in front of you.

Dr Will Darcy.

He was the right age to have gone to school with Hugo. That elevated level of self-confidence was certainly comparable. Though where Hugo oozed sophistication and class as if he'd been dipped in them at birth, Will had the personality of a wounded bear: gruff, unpredictable. Dangerous.

She nibbled on one of her remaining fake nails.

In the end it didn't matter. What mattered was thanking him and sending him on his way.

She moved to the small table behind the couch and grabbed some La Tulipe stationery and a pen. "Will. Thank you. So much. Truly. You've gone above and beyond. If you leave your contact details I'll know where to send the money to pay you back. Petrol, car cleaning, laundry, the hotel bill. Whatever expenses you've incurred."

He slowly shook his head. "Not necessary."

Sadie flapped the stationery his way. "But it is. Necessary. I don't like being beholden to anybody."

"Really."

Wow. Passive-aggressive, much? Sadie's shoulders snapped together, annoyance rising in her belly. He *really* didn't like her and wasn't even trying to hide it. Well, he was no prince either. Sadie held back the desire to tell him so. Barely. Years of practice at being nice coming to the fore.

"Okay, then. I officially relieve you of your knight-in-shining-armour duties." Sadie waved her fingers as if she were sprinkling fairy dust in his general direction.

Will's expression changed. It was a miniscule shift. Barely akin to an intake of breath. But she felt it. Like a ripple of energy beneath the gruff exterior. *Game on.*

He hefted the smaller bag onto the couch. Then he nudged his muddy shoes off his feet in the way men did—using the toes to shove them past the heels. He picked them up, dropped them at the door, then padded into the small kitchenette.

"I'm thirsty. You?" he asked.

With an exaggerated yawn, she said, "I am exhausted though. I think the first thing I'll do after you have your drink and go is take a nice long nap."

Will took his time filling a glass with water from the tap. Then he turned, leaning against the bench. His voice a rumble across the room. "I'm not going anywhere just yet."

A strange little flicker of heat leapt in her belly before she smacked it down. *That* wasn't what he meant. Even if it was, now was not the time, or place…

The corner of his mouth lifted, as if he knew exactly what she was thinking. It was unnerving. *He* was unnerving. She'd been so sure he didn't like her. But maybe she had it all backwards and—

Then he said, "My tracksuit. I'd like it back."

Right. Of course! He was waiting to get his clothes back. What was wrong with her?

She was a mess, that was what was wrong. Scared,

disoriented and emotionally wrecked. Not at all herself. She felt a small amount of relief at the realisation that that was why every little thing Will did—his every look, every word, every dig—was getting under her skin.

She managed a laugh. “Right. Sorry! What a goof. I’ll just…find an alternative. Get you your clothes and then you can be on your way.”

He took another sip of water and gave her nothing in response.

She spun around. Near the bed was a pair of doors. Behind one was a bathroom. Ooh, how lovely! A bath the size of a small car. That would go a long way to getting her back on track. But first… *Voilà!* A closet! With a pair of fluffy pink robes with rose-gold stitching and matching slippers, no less. *Viva Vallemont!*

She turned around. Will had moved to the lounge room and was sitting on the couch, looking right at home.

Sadie thought of the bath. Her head felt like mush. Her muscles ached. Even her bones were tired. Happy-go-lucky reserves fading like an empty battery, she said, “Give me ten minutes.”

With that she headed into the bathroom.

There she stripped off Will’s clothes and took off her chemise.

Something rubbed against her thigh. The garter. Thankfully the ring was still attached. Hugo’s grandmother’s ring. Not only was it part of the royal collection, and worth more than the building she was standing in, but also it didn’t belong to her any more.

Not that it ever really had.

She carefully slid the garter down her leg and over her foot, placing it on the bathroom sink.

Last came her stockings, mud-covered and torn. Without a shred of remorse she threw them in the bin.

Then she turned the taps on the gorgeous big bath to as

hot as was manageable. She found complimentary bubbles and squeezed until the bottle was empty and watched as the room became misty with steam and the bubbles threatened to topple over the sides.

And, as water tended to do, it began to unlock and unwind the knotty thoughts, opening the way to the simplest plan for dealing with the problem in front of her—moving Dr Will Darcy on.

Will leant back into the big, soft couch, checked his watch and adjusted the map of his day yet again.

He hadn't given up on making the late flight home, even as the afternoon faded, but then evening began to creep in, painting golden tracts of sunlight across the wooden floor.

It flipped a memory to the front of the pack. A crumbling cottage made of stone; cosy and warm, with a fireplace and rugs on the wooden floor. His parents' house—his and Clair's—before his mother and father had died.

His grandmother had insisted he'd dreamt it. No Darcy would dare live in such a place.

But something about this place made the memory feel solid. Perhaps it was the surrealism of events. Or the fact he was thinking so much about Clair.

He rubbed his hands over his face, then reached for his phone, dashing off a quick message to Hugo giving him their location.

Within seconds a message came back:

Well done.

As if he'd known Sadie-wrangling wouldn't be easy.

Needing a distraction, Hugo made another call.

The phone was answered. "Boss man!"

"Natalie. How are you?"

"Frantic. Busy. Overworked."

"Happy to hear it."

Will's assistant laughed, the jolly sound coming to him from somewhere in the Midwest of the United States.

Natalie had worked for him going on seven years now, after having been attached to his case by a publicity firm the week his textbook was first published. Finding her tough, keen and pedantic, he'd offered her a permanent position as his assistant and she'd snapped it up. They'd never actually met, working purely online and over the phone which suited him. Less time wasted on personal chit chat that way. She ran his bookings, planned his travel and was the gatekeeper between him and his business manager, clients, institutions, conglomerates and governments the world over.

"Now," said Natalie, "Garry is breathing down my neck like a dragon with a blocked nose, wanting to set up a meeting."

Will's business manager. Probably wanting to talk career strategy, aka Slow Down Before You Break Down. He'd heard it before, mostly from whoever he was dating at the time. Perhaps it was time for a new business manager too.

"When are you coming home?"

Will knew that by "home" Natalie didn't mean London. He had an apartment there, as he did in New Mexico, Sweden, Chile and many of the best star-gazing spots in the world, but he was rarely in one place longer than any other. By "When are you coming home?" Natalie meant, when was he getting back to work?

"What's coming up?"

Natalie listed a string of upcoming engagements. Full to bursting. Just as he liked it.

Without the onus of family, his work was the sun around which his life revolved. Whether he was looking through a telescope, hooking a crowd of eager-faced college students, putting the hard word on funding to a room filled with industry leaders, chipping away at the whys and wherefores of the universe, he was as engrossed now as he ever had been.

The rare times he loosened his grip, took a short break, said no to opportunity, he felt his life touching on the ordinary—and with it a creeping sense of futility. Of being indolent and inadequate. Just as his grandmother assured him his parents had been.

"You've also had meeting and speaking requests from a talk show in LA, a finishing school in the south of France, and…this is my favourite." She rattled off the name of a big-time rapper, who was keen on investing in new digital mirroring technology that Will had funded from day dot. NASA were liking the looks of it and the musician wanted in.

"Fit them in."

Not surprised with his answer, Natalie barrelled on. "And the prime minister would like five minutes next week."

Will perked up. "The agenda?"

He could all but see Natalie's grin as she said, "The Templeton Grant."

Will smacked his hand on his thigh. "Finally! Make the time. Day or night. I'm there."

Professor Templeton was the man who had conducted the first lecture Will had ever attended. He had become a mentor over the years until he had passed away a few months before. The long-running grant the professor had directed for the university was in danger of being phased out. Will was determined not to let that happen. He'd petitioned parliament to ask they continue in perpetuity, and to rename it in Templeton's honour. So far unsuccessfully.

The prime minister—a smart man, a good man, a man of science—was his last hope.

"You bet," said Natalie. And Will was certain she'd make it work.

Until then, so long as he was on the first plane out in the morning, he could roll from one commitment to the next like the human tumbleweed that he was.

"Anything else I can do for you, Boss Man?" Natalie asked.

"Tell Garry we'll make time soon. And send through the changes to the calendar when you have them."

"Shall do." A beat then. "So is it true?"

"What's that?"

"That the royal wedding didn't go off as planned?" Her sing-song voice dropped, as if they were sitting across from one another at a café. "It's all over the news. Apparently, the bride-to-be had a change of heart."

"You don't say."

Will glanced towards the wooden door when the sound of running water stopped. He listened a moment before he heard a splash. He imagined Sadie stepping a muddy foot into the bath. Then a long, pale calf, then…

Natalie sighed, bringing his vision to a halt. "She looked so nice too. Fun. Smiley. Someone you could be friends with. What did you think? I mean, before she did a runner? Did she seem as lovely as she looked in the magazines?"

Will knew better than to engage. He rubbed his temple instead.

"Aw, come on, Boss Man! My cousin Brianna works for a reality TV producer. I don't get many chances to one-up her in ways she understands."

"Alas."

"Fine. I'm guessing by the stoic silence she's not all she's cracked up to be. I mean, did you get a load of the

Prince? Oh, me…oh, my. I guess a real-life, normal girl marrying a prince is simply too much to hope for."

"Hang in there, Natalie."

"I'm all right. You're the only man I need."

"Lucky me."

And then she was gone.

It seemed word was out. If Natalie was busy making negative assumptions, tucked away in her cottage in Wisconsin, it wasn't looking good. Things had gone up a notch. This was no longer simply a case of keeping Sadie in sight until Hugo came to get her, but actually keeping her safe.

Something he'd not been able to do for Clair.

Throat feeling unnaturally tight, Will lifted a hand to his neck, tugged his tie loose, then pulled it free and tossed it on top of his bag.

He wasn't built for this. All this…emotional disarray. It wore down a man's sharp edges. He liked his edges. On a day like today—with the whole world looking to others with a need to "share"—those edges were a requirement.

Ironic that he'd thought Clair's memory would be the biggest battle he'd fight today, instead it was the reality of Sadie. Yet somehow it was all intertwined. Choices, decisions, reactions, repercussions.

The door to the bathroom opened. He pulled himself to standing. Turned. And whatever ethical dilemma he'd been mulling over disintegrated into so many dust motes as his eyes found Sadie.

Gone was his oversized tracksuit, the piles of messy curls, the tear-soaked make-up.

Her hair was wet, and long, and straight. Her cheeks were pink from the heat of the bathroom. Freckles stood out on the bridge of her straight nose. Without the black make-up her eyes were even bigger. *Blue*, he thought, catching glints of sky. Wrapped in a big, fluffy, shapeless robe, she seemed taller. Upright. More graceful somehow. Long, lean and empirically lovely.

Something tightened in his gut at the sight of her. Something raw and unsettling and new. Like the deep ache of a fresh bruise.

Her brow knotted and she ran a self-conscious hand over her hair.

Will came to; realised he'd been staring.

"Better?" he asked.

"Much. I did wonder if you'd still be here when I got out."

Will held out his hands. "Not going anywhere without my favourite running gear."

Sadie seemed to remember she was holding his clothes. She padded over towards him and handed them over. She was careful not to touch him.

He threw them atop his bag and her eyes followed, glaring at the clothes as if by sheer force of will alone she could unzip his bag, pack the clothes away and make him leave.

"Now that you have them…"

Will put his hands into his pockets. Right. How to convince her to let him stay without coming across as a Neanderthal. Or a Lothario. Without giving her actual cause to run.

"Will," she said.

"Yes, Sadie."

She lifted her gaze, bright eyes snagging on his. Then she laughed, a sound both sweet and husky. But there was no humour in it. "I was going to eke it out. To keep you hanging. Make you suffer. But you look like you're about to pull a muscle with the effort at keeping this up. I saw your credit card downstairs. You're Will Darcy. You were heading to the wedding at the palace today because you were invited by Prince Alessandro himself."

Will should have been prepared for this eventuality.

He was a man of angles after all. And control was an illusion. The universe chaotic. Any number of factors altered the possible futures of any given body, making accurate projections near impossible. Still, he found himself unprepared.

"Are you going to deny it?" she asked; gaze steady, that humming energy of hers now turned up to eleven.

He shook his head, *No.*

As if she'd been hoping for a different answer, Sadie deflated, crumpling to sit on the arm of the couch. "Okay. Next question. I know the answer but I want to hear it from you. Do you know who I am?"

Will crossed his arms over his chest as he decided how to play this; fast and loose as he had so far, or absolute truth. As a man of science, the decision was elementary, and a relief.

"You were Hugo's intended. Now you are his runaway bride."

Her eyes were wide, luminous in the fading light. "How?"

"The dress. The tears. The determination to be as far from the palace as you could be. But it was the ring that clinched it. I'd seen it before. We were at school when his grandmother sent it to him. After..."

"After Prince Karl—Hugo's father—died in a crash," she finished, her gaze not shifting a jot. She was far tougher than she looked.

Then she shifted, her robe falling open. The slit separated at her ankles, then her knees, revealing one long, creamy pale leg. She had freckles on her knees. A small bruise just below. Her hands delved up inside the robe and, before Will could even look away, with a wriggle she pulled a frilly pink garter down her leg.

The fact that this rather intimate move had been meant

for Hugo later that evening was not lost on him. Neither was the heat that travelled through him like a rogue wave.

Will pressed his feet harder into the floor and thought of England.

Holding the garter scrunched in her hand, she took a deep breath and opened her palm. And there, tied to the thing with a length of pink ribbon, was the Ring of Vallemont.

Then, tucking the ring back into her palm, she held out her other hand. "Mercedes Gray Leonine. Pleased to meet you."

He took it. Her hand wrapped around his—soft and cool and impossibly fine. He could all but feel the blood pulsing beneath her skin, the steady vibration of the perpetual electric impulses that made her tick.

His voice was a little rough as he said, "Will Darcy. Pleasure's all mine."

She let go and used both hands to slide the garter back into place. "But it's not your pleasure, not really, is it?"

Will said nothing, holding his breath so long it grew stale in his lungs.

"I'm a drama teacher, you know. Or I was...before. Body language—understanding it and duplicating it—is my job. You've hardly hidden the fact that you would rather be anywhere but here." She blinked at him. "If it helps any, I'd rather be pretty much anywhere but here too."

It didn't. It only made his task more complicated than it already was. He didn't want to see her side of things. He certainly didn't want to empathise. He wanted to keep her from running away again and gift her back to Hugo in one piece. Then leave.

He saw the moment she realised it too. She sat taller, and narrowed her eyes his way. Something hardened in her gaze, like steel tempered by fire. And Will couldn't press his feet into the floor hard enough.

Her eyes drilled into his as she said, "He'd never mentioned you before, you know."

A deliberate barb, it scored a direct hit. Will crossed his arms tighter.

She noticed. A small smile tugged at one corner of her mouth. "And suddenly, with the wedding, you loomed large. This friend from school he hadn't seen in years. A falling-out he never explained, no matter how maddeningly I prodded. With all that, I imagined you hunched and brooding. More Holden Caulfield, less..."

"Less?"

"Mr Rochester." She waved a hand his way as if it was obvious, her eyes dashing from his chest to his hair and back to his face. Her cheeks came over such a sudden pink he knew he'd have to track down this Rochester fellow the moment he had the chance.

She looked down at her toes, where he could see the nails painted in some kind of animal print, making him wonder if this palace rebellion of hers had been coming on for some time. Then she asked, "How did you imagine me?"

"I didn't." It was true. He'd done everything in his power not to know anything about her. He was no masochist. Though the longer he chose to stick around this woman, the more he'd question that fact.

Sadie crossed her arms, mirroring his defensive position. "Seriously? Then you have a better hold over your curiosity than I do. Well, how about now? Am I the kind of girl you imagined Hugo would one day marry?"

Will ran a hand through his hair. Hell. This was worse than masochism. He'd found himself on the pathway to hell.

"Forget it. It doesn't matter," she said, shaking her head. "Okay. So, cards-on-the-table time. What are we doing here, Will? What's your end game? I know something happened between you and Hugo, something regrettable. If your intentions aren't above reproach, if you're out to humiliate him in any way…I'll…I'll cut off your whatsit."

Even though he knew she was all bluff, Will's whatsit twitched in response. "I think he's had quite enough humiliating for one day, don't you?"

Her gaze dropped to his…whatsit.

Will's voice was dry as he said, "I was talking about Hugo."

Another hit. This one flashed in her eyes like a bonfire. "Leave him out of this."

He shook his head.

"Why? Wait. Have you spoken to him? Is he okay? Does he know we're here?"

Will pulled the phone from his pocket. "Call him. Ask him yourself."

Sadie's arms loosened, her hands dropping to grip the arms of the couch on which she sat. She pulled herself to standing. Then reached out and took Will's phone.

Their fingers brushed, static electricity crackling through his hand.

Her eyes shot to his. She'd felt it too. Breathing out hard, she asked, "Are you sure? I mean, will he even take my call?"

"Call him."

She nodded and took a few steps away, before turning back.

"Today—not going through with the wedding… It wasn't a decision I made lightly. I usually make a much better first impression. I'm very likeable, you know."

"I'm sure."

She looked at him then, all ocean-blue eyes and electric energy. With her brow twitching a moment, she said, "No, you're not."

And then she stepped out onto the balcony and was once more gone from his sight.

With leaden feet, Will sat back on the couch. Feeling like he'd gone ten rounds.

She was right. After what she'd done today, to his oldest friend, he wasn't convinced that he would ever come to like her. But there was no denying she'd made an impression he'd not soon forget.

CHAPTER FIVE

SADIE'S HEART STAMMERED against her ribs.

In front of her, the palace was glowing gold in the final throes of the dying light.

Through the gauzy curtains behind her, a man was all but keeping her hostage. A man who'd made no bones about the fact he wasn't a fan. A man who made her feel unsettled and antsy and contrite.

And in her hands was a link to her Prince. Her friend. The man she'd wronged.

With the fall of night came a brisk wintry breeze cascading off the snow-topped mountains in the distance, skipping and swirling through the narrow valley and tossing Sadie's damp hair about her shoulders.

She pulled her gown tighter, sat on a small wrought-iron chair and tucked her feet up beneath her. And typed in Hugo's private number.

As unexpected as it was sudden, Hugo's picture flashed onto Will's screen as the phone rang. Will was in it too. They had their arms around one another as they stood atop a mountain somewhere. Young men. Grinning. Happier times.

The phone stopped ringing.

"Darcy?" said Hugo, in his deep bass voice. "What's happened?"

Sadie pictured him sitting behind the grand old desk

in his study, foot hooked up on the other knee, hand gripping his chin.

Sadie closed her eyes and swallowed. “Hugo—” Her voice cracked. She cleared her throat. “Hugo, it’s me.”

Sadie couldn’t remember a time when she’d been so scared of a response. Not since calling her mother to let her know New York hadn’t worked out as hoped and that she was coming home.

She’d felt like a failure then. As though she’d let everyone down. Right now, she *knew* she was a failure. She *knew* she’d let everyone down.

Finally he spoke. “Leo.”

Sadie nearly sobbed with relief. Hugo was the only person in the entire world who called her that and the fact he used her nickname now meant so much. It meant everything.

“Hey, big guy. How’s it hanging?”

“Tight and away.”

Her laughter was croaky. “Yeah. Figured as much. I’m assuming you got my note?”

“The one about deciding not to marry me after all?”

“That’s the one.”

The moment she’d realised there was no way she could go through with the wedding, she’d also known she couldn’t go without letting him know.

Finding him would have been impossible without making a huge scene. At the time not embarrassing Hugo in public had seemed the most important thing. Now she realised she’d simply postponed the inevitable.

So she’d torn a page from a hymnal, grabbed a stick of lipstick left behind by the make-up artist and scribbled down the best short explanation she could. She’d given it to the sweet maid who’d been left to “keep her company” and, using every ounce of charisma she had in her arsenal, had convinced the young girl to deliver it to the Prince.

Then she'd climbed out of the old stone window and run.

"The poor girl who gave it to me was so terrified she left fingerprints in the thing."

Sadie laughed, even as a rogue tear slithered down her cheek. She dashed it away with the sleeve of her gown. "She needs a raise. A big one." Then, "Is it crazy over there?"

"That's one way of putting it. It was agreed that Aunt Marguerite would make the announcement to the guests. One line—the wedding would not go ahead but the after-party would. Then everyone was promptly herded into the ballroom. The champagne is flowing. The music is loud. The doors are bolted shut."

"She's hoping they'll not remember any of it in the morning?"

"Very much."

Sadie heard a squeak. He was definitely in the leather chair behind his desk. She wished she was in there now, lying on the big, soft rug, using a throw cushion as a head-rest, annoying him as he tried to work; chatting about her latest class play or Netflix addiction; niggling him about some movie star who'd claimed to have a crush on him; listening as he took calls from foreign leaders, or those interested in his divine resorts.

"So," he said, his voice nothing but a rumble. "You've met Darcy."

"Mmm-hmm." Suddenly uncomfortable, Sadie adjusted her gown. Then her sitting posture. Then the garter which had begun to feel scratchy now her tights were gone.

"What do you think?"

"About?"

Hugo waited. No surprise that he saw right through her. Born two years apart to the day, they'd grown up in one another's pockets. The Prince and the daughter of a palace maid. As the story went, she'd told anyone who would listen that she'd one day marry Hugo before she could even pronounce his real name properly.

"Oh," said Sadie, "you mean Will? He's..." *dogged, grouchy, brooding, infuriating, enigmatic* "...a very good driver."

Hugo's chuckle was pained. "You playing nice?"

"Of course I am! I'm the epitome of nice. Ask anyone." A beat. "Well, maybe give it a few days." *Weeks. Months. Millennia.* "I'm not sure there's a person in the world who'd have a good thing to say about me right now. Hugo—"

"Leo. It's okay."

"But—"

"Truly."

"No. I need to say it. I wronged you. Terribly. I screwed up more than even I ever imagined I could and that's saying something. And I plan to do everything in my power to fix it. I'll write an official apology to the palace. I'll take out a full-page ad in the *Vallemont Chronicle*. I'll go door to door telling every man, woman and child that my running away had nothing to do with you. That you are the Prince they know you to be, while I am a complete flake. Anything."

"Anything except marry me."

She opened her mouth to...what? Tell him to give her another chance? That this time she could go through with it, if it was what he really wanted. What he needed. But for some reason Will's face popped into her head right at that moment. Those intensely dark eyes of his boring into her as if he'd accept nothing but the truth. Her truth. However unpopular it might be.

The tears flowed fast and furious now. "God, no. Anything except that."

Hugo laughed, as she'd known he would. Never in the

history of history had there been a better man, meaning that he deserved a better woman.

Sadie shifted on the seat. "He doesn't like me, you know."

"Who?"

Right. They hadn't been talking about him, she'd just been thinking about him. "Your old friend, Will Darcy."

"Not possible."

"Something to do with my actions today, perhaps?" But even as she said it, Sadie knew it wasn't that. Not entirely. It was something deeper. Something about her made him uneasy. Not what she'd done but who she was. And to think she'd thought she couldn't feel worse!

"I know you. Making people feel comfortable is your special skill. You'll work him until he adores you. You always do."

"Alas, once I give him his phone back he's outta here." No response from Hugo. Which gave her pause. "Unless I'm missing something."

"I'd like him to stay."

Sadie sat up so fast she nearly fell off the chair. The thought of being *stuck* in the hotel room with Will—"working him until he adored her", no less—made her feel itchy all over.

"Hugo—"

"I'd feel better knowing that you had company. At least until I can send for you."

"A babysitter, you mean. So that I don't get up to more mischief than I already have."

"If you like."

The ease of his about-turn gave him away. "You don't think I need a babysitter. You think I need a bodyguard."

How bad was it out there? For the first time since she'd run she wanted access to a TV. She remembered Janine from downstairs saying "the honeymoon suite" didn't have one. Maybe she could ask Will if she could check out the news pages on his phone.

"Send Prospero," she tried, imagining Hugo's big, neckless, mountain-sized, actual bodyguard.

"Prospero wouldn't leave me if ordered him to by royal decree. It has to be Will."

She dropped her forehead into her hand.

"Humour me," Hugo said.

He didn't say, *You owe me this much at least*, but Sadie read between the lines. He'd been born into a royal bloodline, a flourishing principality run by very smart, savvy, forward-thinking people. Hugo could be a master manipulator when he wanted to.

If making things right meant having to put up with Will Darcy's disquieting presence, then Sadie would just have to handle it.

"And what would you like me to tell your friend about this arrangement? Not my biggest fan, remember."

"Just tell him I asked."

"Really? He doesn't come across as the kind of man who blindly follows."

"Just tell him."

"Fine. And when things die down? What then?"

"Then I'll send someone to bring you home."

Home.

Sadie stifled a whimper.

That Hugo could sit there, in the middle of the scandal of his life, and truly believe she could ever move back into his venerable ancestral home after what she'd done… He was the best man she'd ever known times ten.

"Anything you need until then?" he asked.

Clothes. A phone. Money. Her mum. A hug. A new place to live. For her students not to be out there thinking badly of her. For the people who knew her best to believe she'd had no choice. For the world to forget her name.

"I'm fine."

"As for Will?"

"Mmm?"

"Take it easy on the guy. If he's the same man I knew back then, he comes across as a big, gruff loner, but deep down he's a good guy."

"It'd have to be *waaaay* deep down."

"Leo."

"Fine! I'll be sweetness and light."

"I know you will. Now… Sorry. Hang on a moment." Hugo put her on hold.

The village below was quiet in the looming gloom of late autumnal dusk. Through the curled iron of the balcony she watched a small, battered Fiat bump slowly along the street below. When a group of revellers pushed their way out the front door of a pub down the road, she ducked down so they wouldn't see her.

And she suddenly felt terribly alone.

But while he had people clamouring to do his bidding, Hugo was far more alone than she was. He always had been. It came with the position, with the expectations thrust upon him from birth, with not knowing if people liked you for who you were or what you had to offer. And now, without her at his side, she feared he always would be.

Was that why she'd planned to marry him? Maybe. Partly. If so, at one time it had seemed like reason enough.

After a most inauspicious entry into the world, Sadie's life had been blessed.

Educated by royal tutors. Given music lessons, dance lessons, drama lessons. During the latter, she'd discovered the direct link between putting on a show and having people look to her with smiles on their faces. Thus her love of theatre had been born.

But who deserved that kind of luck? Truly? People who earned it, who were grateful for every ounce; who were nice and kind and likeable; who made sure not to let down all those who'd been instrumental in giving her the chances she'd had.

The Muzak stopped as Hugo came back on the line. "Apologies. It was Aunt Marguerite."

"Ruing the day she rescued my mother and me?"

"Asking if you are all right."

Of course. "What did you tell her?"

"That if you're not yet, you soon will be."

Sadie let her feet drop to the ground, the freezing cold tiles keeping her in the here and now.

"I should go," Hugo said.

"Me too. Busy, busy! You don't have to send someone for me, you know. I'm a big girl."

"I don't have to, but I want to."

Her eyes fell closed. Giving him that was the least she could do. "Do it soon."

"As soon as I'm able. Stay safe."

With that, Hugo rang off.

Sadie uncurled herself from the chair, shivering as she stood. The temperature had dropped fast as night closed in quickly. The sky was now a soft dusty blue, the mountains guarding the borders of her tiny country glowing white.

Just before she turned to head back inside, the first star popped into sight. She thought about making a wish, but had no idea what to wish for.

Will was on the couch, one foot hooked over the other knee, fingers running back and forth over his chin.

He looked up at the sound of the French door sliding closed, a slice of moonlight cutting his strong face in half. "All's well in the state of Denmark?"

Sadie's mouth twitched. She could count on one finger the number of men who'd quoted Shakespeare at her without knowing what a geek-fan she was.

She walked over to Will and gave him back his phone,

then took a seat on the other couch. "Princess Marguerite is hosting the party to end all parties in the hope of either giving everyone the night of their lives so they leave with only good to say, or they are too hungover to speak of it."

"Seems a pity to be missing it."

Sadie coughed out a bitter laugh. "For some strange reason, I'm struggling to imagine you partying. You seem a little straight for all that. More of a cognac and non-fiction tome kind of guy."

Will breathed out hard, his hands coming together, fingers running over fingers in a hypnotic pattern. "Is that what you came in here to say?"

Well, no. But it had felt good to have a dig at the guy anyway. Hugo clearly thought more highly of her "working it" skills than she did.

Enough dilly-dallying. Time to get this over with. Hugo seemed to think Will would stay simply because he'd asked him to. Hugo believed Will was a good guy. And that had to count for something.

So, while the words felt like stones in her mouth, she managed to say, "While I feel like I'm taking the feminist movement back decades by asking this, is there any chance you could stick around until Hugo sends someone to whisk me out of here?"

Will sat forward. His hand went to his watch—big, fancy, classy—twisting it about his wrist as he made his decision.

It hadn't occurred to her until that moment that he might say no—claim work, or play; claim a jealous wife or a sick child or a job that needed him more. That he might leave her here, in this honeymoon suite with its princess bed and its view of the palace.

"And how long might that be?"

"I…don't know. As soon as humanly possible."

"Is this a request from you, or Hugo?"

"Does it matter?"

The slight tilt of his head told her it did.

Well, buddy, you rub me up the wrong way too. The funny thing was, though, sitting there beside him, her hairs standing on end, a tornado in her tummy, prickling under the burn of his hot, hard gaze, being on his bad side felt like the safer option.

Sadie shuffled forward on the chair, held her hands out in supplication and said, "Look, I get that I'm not your favourite person."

There, now it was out there. Maybe that would alleviate the tension sapping the air from the room.

"But neither am I some damsel in distress, if that's what you think."

To that he said nothing.

"The truth is, you don't know me. You just happened upon me at just about the crappiest moment of my entire life. And now I'm exhausted. And hungry. And stuck in a hotel room with a stranger. Which isn't going to bring out my best. I promised Hugo I'd be sweetness and light, but I'm not sure how long I can keep that up. So, stay, don't stay; right now I'm done caring."

Will looked cool as a cucumber as he said, "Is self-sabotage a habit of yours?"

"*Excuse* me?"

"I'm simply going by the evidence. I've known you a couple of hours and in that time you've rejected a prince and done your all to convince me to throw my hands in the air and give up on you."

"I'm not! I—"

"Then my staying won't bother you."

Oh.

"Not a jot," she said.

She lied. *He* bothered her. But that was just the price she had to pay.

"Then that's that," said Will.

Sadie breathed out hard and flopped back into the couch, feeling better about having a plan, even if it wasn't hers.

Will opened up his battered silver bag to pull out a laptop. He flipped it open, long fingers tapping in a password. "Now, if you don't mind, I'm going to get some work done."

Sadie flapped a hand his way, barely wasting a thought wondering what that work might be. He was a doctor of some sort. Did they give doctorates in such pedantic things as forensic accounting, or comment moderating?

She closed her eyes for a second. When she peeled her eyes open—five seconds later, or five minutes, she couldn't be sure—it was to find Will looking at her strangely.

Sadie followed the path of his gaze to find her gown had fallen open. Not much—enough to show her collarbone and a little shoulder. Maybe a swell of something more, but nothing to get excited about.

When she found his eyes again his jaw clenched, as hard as stone. His nostrils flared with the fervour of a racehorse, then with patent effort tore his gaze away.

Sadie was surprised to find her hands shaking as she surreptitiously tugged her dressing gown back together. And her heart beat like gangbusters.

He didn't like her. But it turned out he was very much aware of her.

The horrible truth was that she was aware of him too. The sure strength of his arms, the scent of his neck, the intensity of his gaze had been playing like a brutal loop in the back of her mind whenever she felt herself begin to relax.

And now they were stuck here, in this romantic hotel room.

It was going to be a long night.

* * *

Sadie had fallen asleep on the couch almost instantly.

A few hours later she lay there still, breathing softly through open lips, her lashes creating dark smudges beneath her eyes. Her gown…

Will looked away from her dressing gown and ran a hand over his face. A move he'd made so much in the past day he was in danger of rearranging his features permanently.

Will refocused on his laptop—not that it looked any different from the way it had ten minutes before. The internet was prohibitively slow, meaning he couldn't check Natalie's updates to his calendar. Or access Hubble's latest infrared take on Orion that was due to land, eyes only, that morning. Or open the latest incarnation of the Orion's Sword game sitting temptingly in his inbox.

And he'd had no word from Hugo.

Edgy and frustrated, Will rolled his shoulders, got up, started a fire and checked out the kitchen, to find only a few mini-bar items. He could have done with some real food, but, since he wasn't lucky enough to be at the non-wedding reception—aka the party to end all parties—he had to make do with instant coffee and a bar of chocolate-covered ginger.

The fire made short work of the cold room, so, needing some fresh air, Will headed to the balcony. The village was spread beneath him like something on the front of a Marks and Spencer biscuit tin.

Sipping on the bitter brew, he looked up. And promptly forgot to swallow.

For the perfect day had given way to an even more perfect night.

The combination of minimal light pollution from the old-fashioned gas lamps below, the elevated position of the hillside hotel and a first-quarter moon had made the galaxy come out to play.

* * *

From his cramped position tucked into the corner of the small balcony, Will found a nice angle on his target and racked up the focus.

His serious telescope—with long exposure CCD camera attachment—which lived in the permanent glass box atop his London town house, had collected more detailed images of the nebula's famous irregular, translucent fan-shaped cloud, and ultraviolet glow. But this telescope—smaller, older, less sophisticated—was the one he took with him all over the world.

It was the last gift he'd received from Clair.

He'd added to it over the years. Modified it to keep it relevant. And right now, as always, it did right by him, giving him a really nice shot of vivid grey-green mist enshrouding a distant star.

But what he was really hoping for was—any moment now— *There!* A shooting star. And another. The annual Orionid Meteor Shower in all its glory.

Will sat back in the freezing wrought-iron chair and did something he rarely took the time to do nowadays: he watched the sky with his own two eyes. The moment seemed to require it.

It was late. A ways after midnight. And the entire world felt quiet. Still. Slumberous and safe within the cradle of jagged mountains all around. It was as though this spot had a direct link to the heavens.

"Will?" Sadie's voice cut through his thoughts.

His chair scraped sharply against the tiled floor of the small balcony as Will arose.

Sadie stood in the French windows, nibbling on a bag of peanuts. "What are you doing out here? It's freezing. You should… Oh." Her eyes widened comically as she spotted the apparatus taking up most of the balcony. She stepped out onto the tiles, wincing at the cold beneath her bare feet. "Was this here the whole time?"

Will laughed, the rough sound drifting away into the darkness. "I brought her with me."

"Her?"

Will put a hand on the body of the telescope. "Sadie, this is Maia. Maia—Sadie."

"Pretty name. An old flame?"

"A young star. Found on the shoulder of Taurus." Will pointed unerringly towards the bull constellation without even having to look.

"So *that's* what you had hiding in your silver case! By the measly contents of your other bag I'd have bet you were planning on skedaddling tomorrow at the very latest. And yet you lugged this thing all the way here? Why?"

"Did Hugo not mention what I do for a living?"

She grimaced. "No. Maybe. He mostly told stories about your time at school. How you led him to the dark side, teaching him how best to ditch class. Or the time he dared you to petition the school to reinstate Domestic Science and you won. So many *Boys' Own* adventure stories I may have drifted off now and then." Her eyes darted to the telescope and back again. "So…this. This is what you do? What are you? Some kind of…*astronomer*?"

Will nodded.

And Sadie's eyes near bugged out of her head. "Really? But that's so cool! I imagined you in a career that was more…phlegmatic. No offence."

None taken. In fact, he took it as a compliment. A high level of impassivity was necessary to doing his best work. Besides, Will was too busy noticing she seemed to imagine him a fair bit. But he kept that noticing to himself.

"Hugo's friends are all in their family business—money, politics, ruling." She scrunched up her nose. "But not you. Unless astronomy *is* your family business…?"

"My family business was holding on tight to old money. And my grandmother's version of ruling was browbeating the butlers until they quit. This seemed a better choice."

Her hair rippled in the light breeze. "I would have thought that kind of thing was done by computers nowadays. Super-robots."

"Computers can certainly extrapolate data, make comparisons, find patterns in big, random, violent actualities that rise and fall over billions of years before we've even seen their first spark of light in our sky. But—as my old university mentor, Professor Templeton, used to remind us—the first step, the human element in all that, is to wonder."

"I like the sound of your professor."

"He was one of the good ones."

"You've surprised me just now, Will Darcy. Quite a bit. So what are you looking for?"

"That's a big question."

Sadie laughed. And waggled her fingers at the telescope.

"Ah," said Will. "You mean in there."

She laughed again, her eyes gleaming. The quiet, the dark, the late hour…they all promoted a sense of playfulness. Or maybe that was simply her: mischievous, bright, irreverent, with an agile open mind.

Will rubbed a hand over his chin to find it rough. Somehow he'd forgotten his nightly shave. Reminding himself to fix that tomorrow, he said, "This telescope isn't big enough for any serious research. I bring it with me more out of sentimentality than anything else."

"You? Sentimental?"

"Apparently so. It was a gift." *Swallow.* "From my sister." He braced himself against the jagged knot tightening in his belly. Then he moved on. "What would you like to see?"

"Me? Wow. I suddenly feel really ignorant. I don't know all that much about what's out there apart from, you know, moon, stars. The earth is the centre of the universe."

Will's mouth twitched. Then he leaned down, adjusted direction and focus and found the general direction of his telescope's namesake. Then he pushed back the chair, and motioned for Sadie to have a look.

Adjusting her robe, Sadie shuffled in closer to the telescope. Will had to press himself hard against the railing so as not to be right behind her as, fingers lightly gripping the eyepiece, she bent to have a look.

Sadie's mouth stretched into a slow smile. "Oh. Oh, Will. That is…spectacular."

"Pleiades," he said. "Otherwise known as the Seven Sisters. Maia is the fourth brightest."

She stood and blinked up into the cosmos. "Show me more. Show me your very favourite thing out there. Show me something that makes a man like you gasp with delight."

Will cocked an eyebrow. "I'm not sure I've ever gasped, in delight or otherwise."

Her grin was bright, even in the low moonlight. "Maybe you're just not doing it right." She flicked a glance to the sky. "Maybe you could lighten up a little. Put that frown of yours away for a bit and find the delight. Maybe you just have to look harder."

He looked, but not at the sky. At her profile, open and bright. At the dishevelled way she'd tied her gown. At her leopard-print toenails as her toes curled into the cold floor.

For the first time since Natalie had rung him about the invitation, Will purposely wondered about the girl Hugo had planned to marry, opening the part of himself he preferred to keep under lock and key—that place that bred *what ifs* and *if onlys.*

It was his turn to imagine as he attempted to picture the

Hugo he knew with this restive, indefatigable, unkempt creature.

And couldn't.

Deep down in a place both unfamiliar and disquieting, Will wondered how Hugo could have chosen a woman who was so clearly not meant for him.

Will cleared his throat and did a mental about-turn.

Nothing was *meant* in this world. Nothing was for ever. Planets collided, suns faded, worlds were destroyed by their own cores, imploding in on themselves in utter self-destruction. The universe was random and chaotic and it was foolish to think otherwise.

"Move aside." He gave her a nudge with his hip so that he might shift the telescope a smidgeon.

"Should I prepare myself to be amazed?" she asked as they swapped places again, this time the front of her dressing gown brushing against his arm. His hairs stood on end, chasing the sensation.

His voice was gruff as he said, "I would think the purpose of preparation was to avoid surprise."

"We shall see," she said. This time Sadie held her breath. Her voice revenant, she whispered, "What am I looking at now?"

"That would be Orion. A diffuse nebula in the Milky Way. Around one thousand five hundred light-years from here and containing thousands of stars, it is the nearest star-forming region to Earth."

Will had heard Orion, so optically beautiful, described as "angel's breath against a frosted sky". He believed its true beauty was that it was their best glimpse into how the universe had begun.

Sadie pulled back. She looked up at the sky for a good while. Then, her voice rusty, she said, "I can't even find the words, Will. It's beautiful, to be sure. But also...somehow hollow. Like if you look at it too long, all that darkness would see your darkness until it becomes one. 'Stars, hide your fires; Let not light see my black and deep desires.'"

Her last words had been so soft he wasn't even sure she'd meant to say them out loud. The order tickled at the corner of Will's brain. He sorted through the databanks of information he'd stored over the years and found a match. *Macbeth.*

Catalogued under cosmic quotes he'd kept note of over the years, he found, "'When beggars die there are no comets seen; The heavens themselves blaze forth the death of princes.'"

She blinked as if coming out of a trance, then turned to him, incredulous. "Seriously?"

"Seriously what?"

"You're quoting Shakespeare. Again."

"I'm very well-read."

"I'm beginning to see that." She shook her head. "Because that's my thing, you know. My mission in life is to show attention-deficient young adults how to concentrate long enough to get through an entire Shakespearean play. Huh. I just realised. Will. Will Shakespeare. You have the same name."

As her gaze held his and didn't let go, Will felt the air shift between them. A wind of change. A disturbance in the force. Electric currents zapped and collided until he was all but sure he'd see sparks.

But deeper, beneath it all, a sense of recognition; of shared experience; of lives lived parallel; of truth. Will felt its pull like a physical thing.

People spoke of chemistry being the reason people were drawn to one another. But it was gravity that caused one body to revolve around another. That said the denser gravity of a planet could draw on the lesser gravity of a meteor, leading to destruction, sometimes on a grand scale.

Sadie's gaze snapped to something over his shoulder.

"Did you see that?" Sadie gasped. "Keep watching. Keep watching… There!"

Will looked up. He watched as another shooting star flashed, flew and disappeared, disintegrating into a mass of scattered space dust.

If he'd believed in such things he might have taken it as a sign.

CHAPTER SIX

SADIE WOKE UP with a start.

It was deep in the heart of the witching hour; that time of night when every sound, every thought felt heightened. Her skin prickled with sweat. Unfamiliar sheets twisted around her legs. Her chemise had ridden high enough to nearly strangle her.

She wriggled and rolled, kicking off blankets, and scrambled up towards a mound of pillows. Holding her legs to her chest, she stared into the semi-darkness. Embers crackled in the fireplace below, the eerie golden glow casting light and shadow over the room. And over the man sleeping on the couch.

She couldn't make out much detail bar one bare arm dangling off the edge, fingertips nearly grazing the floor. A large naked foot hooked over the arm rest.

It was more than enough.

She looked away, towards the French door, towards the palace; towards her bed, her pillow, her home. She wondered if Hugo had managed to fall asleep or if he was still awake, lamenting what might have been, or relieved she'd let him off the hook.

She slid back down into the big, soft bed, pulling her sheets up to her neck and trying to recapture her dream. But all she remembered were insubstantial threads, like ribbons in a storm.

A few moments later she lifted her head, checking to make sure Will was actually asleep. His arm lifted and fell, as if in time with long, slow breaths.

Whatever. Sleep or no sleep, as soon as Hugo sent someone to get her, chances were she'd never see Will again.

There hadn't exactly been time or opportunity to uncover why Will and Hugo had been estranged since school, despite the fact there was clearly great mutual respect. But it must have been significant. A great fight? A deep betrayal? Or had she simply read *Macbeth* so many times she saw potential drama everywhere she looked?

No. Something must have happened. In her experience, men didn't lash out like wounded animals unless they felt cornered.

Her father had been the first. Taking umbrage to the fact Sadie's mother had dared love his child as much as she loved him. For that he had left and not looked back.

Then there had been her acting coach in New York. An older man, a faded Paul Newman wannabe, he'd been her teacher, then her mentor, dangling the string of success for a couple of years. Once she'd bitten he'd become her agent. Not a good one, but the fact he'd seen something in her had felt like enough. Until the day he offered her a part—not the lead—in the "adult" film he was producing. When she'd refused, point blank, he'd kicked her to the kerb, leaving her homeless, the entire experience telling her it was time to head home.

She'd even seen how implacable Hugo could be, if those in his care were under attack. It was the very reason he'd wanted to marry her, after all.

Will's "self-sabotage" accusation hovered on the edge of her subconscious, but she brushed it away.

She'd heard them called "the rational sex", but in her experience men made decisions based on emotion over common sense far more than women.

From what she'd seen of Will Darcy so far, he'd not proven to be any different.

More awake than asleep now, Sadie laid herself out as flat as she could, becoming one with the mattress, and closed her eyes. She breathed slowly through her nose and wondered… Did Will dream? If so, of what? Supernovas and little green men? Or was he a classicist—dreaming of memory, hope, wishes, flying, falling, desire…

Just like that, her own dream came back to her in a rush. Hurtling through a sky filled with planets, a great, hot sun and bright, thrusting comets. Only she wasn't falling, she was being held. Protected. By a pair of strong, warm arms. While also being shown the moon and stars.

She grabbed a spare pillow and shoved it over her head.

Will woke feeling as if he'd been hit by a truck.

Every muscle, joint and bone ached from trying to curl six feet two inches onto an over-soft two-seater.

He pressed himself to sitting, then rubbed both hands hard over his face in an effort to put all the bits back into the right place.

Will checked his phone. It was a little after seven. He had had eleven missed messages overnight. Not unusual. The stars were always out somewhere in the world. He listened to them all, took mental notes and sent word to Natalie how to deal with each.

She hadn't yet sent word about a meeting time with the prime minister regarding the Templeton Grant. He nudged her to make it the number-one priority.

The moment he'd heard the grant was in jeopardy he'd felt a strange compulsion, a knowledge deep in his bones, that he had to use the power of his reputation for more than simply work.

For Professor Templeton's gentle patience had been Will's deliverance at a time when things had gone either way, and it seemed only right that he make sure the next generation of students would have the chance to find their path as he did that long-ago day.

Following that one random astronomy class, Will had doubled up on his degree, joined as many research projects as would have him. He'd worked nights, checking the university's telescope minute by minute for whichever project needed data at the time. And eventually he'd earned the Templeton Grant himself for his independent study on the Orion Nebula. It had paid his way through university, in one fell swoop giving him complete independence from his grandparents and showing them he was neither indolent nor inadequate. He was bloody hardworking and exceedingly bright. Despite them.

Clair would have been the same, if she'd been given the chance. So what choice did Will have but to take every opportunity she'd never had?

Keeping watch over Sadie had nudged him off course, which was not a comfortable place for him to be. Nevertheless, after a prolonged beat, he sent another message to Natalie asking her to cancel or postpone—with apologies—everything he had on for the next twenty-four hours. To keep the day after that on standby. And please not to injure herself when she fell over in shock.

Then he threw his phone into his leather bag and stood.

He rolled his shoulders. Cricked his neck.

Glancing towards the raised platform, he could make out the lump of Sadie's form. Fast sleep.

Weak, dreary sunlight attempted to breach the curtains before seeming to give up.

Hunger gnawed at his belly. If Hugo wasn't here soon he'd have to head out and source some real food.

But first…needs must.

He grabbed his leather bag and headed to the bathroom. Since he couldn't get there without passing Sadie's bed, he found her splayed on her stomach like a human starfish, one hand hanging off one side, a toe hanging off the other. The sheets were twisted around her and tugged from their moorings. Her hair was splayed out across the white sheets like a red wine spill.

An empty chocolate packet lay open on the bedside table. And below it, in a pile on the floor, was her dressing gown. Meaning beneath the twisted sheets she wore…

Will kept his eyes straight ahead as he moved into the bathroom and shut the door. Two minutes later he was stripped and standing beneath a hot shower. And he did what he always did near water: he closed his eyes and let his mind go.

It wasn't an unusual phenomenon that his most complete theories had come to him while in the shower. Having nothing else to worry about, the mind travelled in disparate directions and made random connections it would otherwise miss.

He waited for his mind to mull over tricky calculations he'd been asked to weigh in on. Or the three-dimensional graphics of the Orion Nebula the gaming team in Oxford were working on.

But instead his head filled with silken, wine-red hair, soft, cool skin, eyes so deep they seemed to go on for ever.

Jaw clenching, he dragged his tired eyes open.

So, no stream of consciousness, then. Purposeful analysis was the order of the day. He began, as he always did, with known data.

Fact: he'd been on edge for days. Weeks even. Knowing he was set to face Hugo, to face his part in the derailment of their friendship, knowing that watching someone else take his sister's place at Hugo's side would be…difficult. No, it would be insufferable.

Fact: stress led to surges of adrenaline, a natural human response to an extraordinary amount of stimuli. Biological readiness for a fight or flight led to heightened senses. Which then led to a natural physical response to the attractive woman he was sharing a hotel room with.

Fact: he clearly wasn't the only one suffering this… natural human response.

He was suddenly back on the balcony the night before, Sadie's energy tangling with his, the stars shining in her eyes. Gravity, attraction, the heady pull of mutual intrigue, of the thrill of discovery drawing them together.

He was not unduly attracted to his old friend's runaway bride. It was simple science.

And yet he turned off the hot water and stuck his head under the cold until it began to burn.

When he'd punished himself enough, Will turned off the water, shaking off the chilly droplets. And stilled. Listening.

He'd heard something. A knock at the front door?

Hugo.

He reached for a towel to find the nearest towel rail empty. A quick glance found Sadie's towel flopped over the side of the bath.

Upon a thorough search he couldn't find another. So, grabbing her towel, he rubbed himself down, straining to hear voices. But the room seemed quiet.

"Sadie?" he called, his voice echoing in the small, steamy room. No response.

There. The front door opening. And closing.

"Dammit. Sadie!"

He couldn't seem to get himself dry. Because the towel was damp. Redolent with the scent of honeysuckle.

"Saaadiiie!"

The bathroom door swung open and with the rush of clear air came Sadie. "What's wrong? Are you okay?"

Will swept the towel around his waist, clamping it together with one fierce hand at his hip. "Hell, Sadie!"

"What?" she said, swallowing a yawn. "You were the one bellowing my name."

Her hair was crushed against one side of her head where it had dried while she was sleeping. A crease from her pillow lined her cheek. Thankfully she was now wearing her dressing gown, though it sat twisted, half falling off one shoulder. When she absently tugged the sash tight it made no difference.

"I thought maybe you'd slipped, or…something." Her words faded as she seemed to realise his state of undress.

Under her unchecked gaze, Will felt the water dripping off his hair and rolling over his shoulders. His skin felt tight, and sensitive. Even with the heat of the shower still filling the room, goosebumps sprang up over his arms. When he felt other parts of himself beginning to stir he gathered the towel more tightly and growled, "Sadie."

She blinked. Slowly. Then she swallowed. Her next breath in was long and slow. Then her eyes rose to his. "Hmm? What? No? Wait… What on earth…?"

She took a full step towards him. Close enough that he saw the genuine worry in her eyes, the constellation of slightly darker freckles on her left cheek. Close enough that her hand hovered an inch from his chest.

She reached a hand towards his chest. Will clenched all over. Now what was she playing at?

Then she asked, "Is that a bruise?"

Will looked down to find a dark variegated stripe angling across his chest. He lifted a hand and ran it over the contusion. Thinking back, he came to a likely conclusion.

"I slammed on my brakes," he said, his voice rusty. "My seatbelt did its job."

Her eyes whipped to his. Energy crackled through the fog, the level fit to reach the back of a large theatre. "That's happened when you stopped for *me*? Does it hurt?"

She lifted her hand again, and this time he knew she was set to touch him.

Will caught her an inch from ground zero, holding her hand at bay. Her skin was cool against his. His thumb rested on her wrist, picking up the scattered throb of her pulse. Or perhaps it was his own.

Her pupils were huge and dark. Her cheeks high with colour and her breath no longer at ease.

Gravity. Attraction. Intrigue. Discovery.

"I'm fine." Will pressed his hand towards her before letting go. Then he turned and dug about inside his bag. Needing a break from those eyes. "Who was at the door?"

"The door?"

"The reason I called your name. I heard a knock."

"Right. Yes. I thought it might be Hugo… Alas. When I checked no one was there. But there was a gift basket left outside. Decorated in little love hearts for the honeymoon suite, no less."

Will gripped the edges of his bag. He was not a praying man, but in that moment he understood the impulse.

"Thank goodness, right? Because I'm starving."

Starving. Will's belly felt empty and his head a little light. A man his size couldn't live on adrenaline and chocolate-covered ginger alone. Food would help. It would alleviate the pangs. And he could recalibrate from there.

Oblivious to his internal bargaining, Sadie went on, "There's champagne, strawberries, chocolate, almonds, Vallemontian ginger. Some crackers and crisps. Even a tub of honey. I call the ginger."

"All yours," he managed, contemplating the veritable cornucopia of aphrodisiacs. "I don't have much of a sweet tooth."

"What a shock."

He looked up then. To find her gaze was on his chest once more. Not the scar—the rest. He could have told himself the aspiration in her gaze was all due to the food talk, but what would be the point?

Clearly a cold shower and rationalisation weren't going to do the trick.

He'd been on the back foot since this entire escapade began—a feeling he was neither used to nor welcomed.

Enough was enough. It was time to take charge.

He turned, reached into his bag, grabbed the tracksuit she'd worn the day before and threw it at her.

She caught it. "What's this for?"

"Put it on. It'll be warmer than what you're wearing. And it's a grey old day out there."

"Thanks. That's really nice of you."

It was completely self-serving. "Was there something else?"

"No, but…I was just thinking about what the gift basket fairies might leave next? A collection of sonnets? Some massage oils? There's no TV so I guess that rules out—"

"Sadie."

"Yes, Will?"

"Get out."

"Yes, Will." She spun on her heel, all but scurrying from the room, closing the door with a loud snick.

That left Will to dress in the only clean clothes he had remaining—jeans and a black cashmere sweater.

He wiped his face, hung up his towel and tidied away his toiletries. He left no trace of himself behind.

And prayed when he checked his phone again Hugo would have sent word.

Will was back at the couch, repacking his bag for the tenth time that day, clearly wanting to be ready to go the moment she was off his hands. While Sadie—after living off strawberries, chocolate and champagne all day—felt super-twitchy and a little claustrophobic.

"Bored, bored, *bored*," she chanted under her breath.

Will turned, jaw tight, brow furrowed as if she'd interrupted him doing something terribly important. "Did you say something?"

"Nope. Maybe. I'm bored."

Will gave her a look. "Why don't you tidy up a little?"

"Nah."

"You are clearly used to having a maid."

"Are you kidding? My mother *is* the maid. At the palace. So was I, at times." She shuddered. "When Hugo was away ditching school with you, I begged Marguerite to put me to work. I helped look after the smaller royals—teaching them to clean up after themselves, to make their beds, to cook easy meals. Have you ever had to clean up the same Lego day after day after day?"

His blank look gave him away.

"That's right, you had a butler. Well, if you spend enough time cleaning up that stuff, one day you wake up and think, what's the point?"

"I never cleaned up my own Lego, Ms Gray, because my grandmother was rather old-fashioned when it came to the raising of children and did not believe in frivolous toys. That said, if the zombie apocalypse ever comes I'll be able to fence myself to freedom."

He went back to packing and she poked her tongue out at his back. Then she spun, held out fake pistols and muttered, "This room ain't big enough for the both of us."

"You definitely said something that time."

She blew invisible smoke from the top of a finger before sticking it back in her imaginary holster.

Things couldn't go on like this. This constant tension was messing with her equilibrium.

Like out on the balcony the night before—there'd been a moment when the wintry air had turned thick and steamy, when she'd looked into Will's dark eyes and seen something. Seen *him*. It had felt intimate, and thrilling, and terrifying. It was the kind of moment where something might have happened. The kind of something you couldn't take back.

And then in the bathroom this morning…she'd woken with a fright to the sound of his voice, the grit as he'd called her name. It hadn't occurred to her she might walk in on him half-dressed. Make that quarter-dressed. It had been too early in the morning to react sensibly to so much man. And how close had she come to feeling the guy up? He'd had to physically stop her from running her hand down his hard, muscular, naked—

Sadie sucked in a breath and shook her head.

Hugo had been right. Making friends with Will had to be better than…whatever was going on between them now.

She lifted her chin, manufactured a blinding smile and said, "So, Will, do you have a girlfriend waiting for you back in…wherever it is you're from?"

Wow. Excellent sentence-making skills, Sadie. Had she left her renowned charm in her "other" dress too? Apparently so, because Will wasn't charmed.

He kept on folding, waiting until everything was precise and in its place before deigning to reply. "No," he said. "And I was born in London."

No surprise. Grey, damp, so much snarling traffic they all but outlawed it, London was the polar opposite to the wide open, verdant green that was Vallemont. Though Hugo had taken her there for her eighteenth birthday, to see *The Tempest* in the West End, and that had been phenomenal.

Huh. Funny that Hugo hadn't made the effort to get in touch with Will, then, either. So whatever had happened between them was already in play. She'd get to that. But first:

"Really? No saucy smart girl with a lab coat, glasses and big brain to go home to?"

He gave her a sideways glance, still not giving an inch. And she knew there was no point even trying. He was just too…Will. He seemed to respond best to cool, clinical honesty.

Oh, well, here goes. "Come on, Will. Give me something. I'm drowning here."

"And what exactly do you mean by *something*?"

His deep, gravelly voice did things to her spine. Zappy, tingly things. She decided that was a little too much honesty and kept it to herself. "A little light small talk to while away the hours might be nice."

"Small talk?"

"Sure, why not?"

"Because it's asinine."

"Asinine? There you go. Something juicy for me to chew on." She took a deep breath and once again put on her best cowboy voice. *"Now, who do you think you are, calling me asinine?"*

He blinked. "I didn't. I said *small talk* was—"

She flapped a hand at him before plopping down on his couch, one foot under her backside, the other knee hooked up on the seat. Then she smacked the cushion, requesting he join her. "Sit. Let's get to know one another better. We might be here for days, after all. We might be here for ever."

Will lost a little colour at that last prediction.

"Sit. I dare you."

The colour returned.

He sat. The couch seemed to shrink, leaving her bent knee mere inches from his. But she held her ground. *All good here! My physical nearness to you is not a problem at my end!*

"So, where were we? No girlfriend. Great. I mean… fine. Okay. Glad we have that sorted." Then, because champagne and chocolate and boredom and…some new level of sadomasochism seemed to have taken her over, "But you do like girls, right?"

A slightly raised eyebrow and a flicker of his dimple was his only response.

"So, you *like* girls but you don't *have* a girl. Got it. I'm assuming it's that you're simply between girls and not because you're as much of a relationship screw-upper as I am."

His only response to her eventual silence was a look; dark and broody and gorgeous. Did she just say gorgeous? Only inside her head this time, which was okay. Except it wasn't even slightly okay!

Maybe it was some kind of Stockholm Syndrome. He'd practically kidnapped her, after all, and dragged her off to an actual tower, where he was keeping her hostage… Who knew what he had in mind for her?

Sadie wriggled on the seat, trying to shake off the tingle in her spine that didn't seem to want to go away. While also trying desperately not to let her knee touch his, because every time they touched, every time she bumped into him in the kitchen, or shuffled past him on the balcony, or passed him a cup of tea there was this spark, and warmth, and fast-spreading heat, and…

Will was still looking at her. His gaze locked on to her, not letting go. She could feel her heart rate speeding up and was getting that fuzzy feeling at the back of her skull. Like when a man was about to…

"My work is very important to me," said Will, thankfully cutting off her train of thought before it got away from her completely. "More than important. It's critical. It's also not conducive to long-term relationships."

She swallowed, hard, before managing, "How's that?"

"I work a great deal. I travel often. My plans change daily. I have a place in the Americas and Scandinavia as well as London, but my mail forwards to my assistant in

Wisconsin. My publisher is in New York. The stars are always out somewhere in the world and so can I be too."

"Doctors work a lot. Firefighters too. Soccer players travel constantly. Many manage to settle down, have families." She could have just said, *That's nice*. Why was she pushing this?

"Ask those families if they'd prefer to have their partners and parents home more. I believe you'll get an unequivocal yes."

"So your singlehood is benevolent."

"Entirely." The way he said it, with a hint of humour in that whisky-rough voice of his, hit a spot deep down inside. Echoing. Reverberating. Before making itself at home.

"Well, good for you."

He nodded. The best she could manage was a toothless smile. Then, before she even felt the words coming, she said, "You must have questions."

Will's eyebrow twitched. "Many. Though they usually bend towards the esoteric—why are we here, how did we get here, what might happen next?"

"I meant about me…and Hugo."

Will went straight into his statue impersonation. Not moving, not breathing, not giving anything away. He was very good at it.

"No? Then let's start smaller. How about what's my favourite colour? Do I prefer ice cream or sorbet? What did I want to be when I—?"

"How long were you together?"

"Together? You mean Hugo and me? Hugo and I were never *together*."

The guy could win a statue competition, hands down.

"We were the closest of friends since we were tiny tots. He'd pull me around in his little red wagon when he was three and drive me around in his big red Maserati when he was eighteen. And, because it never failed to bring a smile to someone's face, I'd declare to anyone who would listen that one day I was going to marry him."

"But you didn't mean it."

Sadie's breath caught. He'd known her a day and he got her. Those who'd known her a lifetime didn't have a clue.

She dragged her gaze away, the break of eye-contact a blessed relief. "Sure, we kissed a couple of times over the years—spin the bottle, three minutes in heaven, that kind of thing—in case it actually worked. But it never did. Not the way it should. It was to be a marriage of convenience. Separate quarters. Separate beds—"

Now Will moved, holding up a hand. "I know what a marriage of convenience means."

"Okay."

"But what I don't understand is why. Why get married at all?"

It was entirely her fault, but now they were moving into territories she wasn't comfortable talking about. It wasn't just her story to tell after all.

With a smile she said, "You've met the guy, right?"

"Several times. Wouldn't marry him, though."

"If you remember, neither would I."

Will shot her a look. Intense, intrigued. A life lived in the public eye, and she'd never felt quite so much as if she was under a microscope as she did now. Then, "Wait. Are you in some kind of trouble? Is that why he agreed to marry you?"

"Wow. You make him sound so gallant, deigning to stoop to—"

"Sadie."

"No," she allowed. "Not in the way you mean."

"Then in what way?"

She wondered if Will had a clue that he'd suddenly sat up taller—shoulders back, fists braced on his thighs as if preparing to take on the as yet unknown trouble that had her in its thrall.

While she was trying so hard to appear cool and unaffected, it unglued her. He unglued her. Every time he went all gruff and protective on her behalf.

In the short time they'd been thrown together, he'd managed to see through her plucky façade to the truth. Her truth. In a way no one else had ever managed. She wondered now if anyone else had even bothered to try.

"Stop it," she said, her voice raspy. Her hands gripping one another in her lap, hanging on for dear life.

"Stop what? I didn't say a word."

She licked her lips. "But you were thinking it. I can see it. All those big, heroic, take-over thoughts whipping around inside that ginormous brain of yours. Synapses firing at supersonic speed, sparking lights in your baby blues."

"Baby *what*?"

She waggled a hand towards his face. "Your eyes. Why, do you have something else blue on your person that I don't know about? Inner nostrils? Belly-button lint? No, I would have seen it when you called me into the bathroom this morning. And what was that really all about? You couldn't have pulled on some clothes beforehand?"

Sadie's gaze dropped to Will's chest, saliva actually pooling in her mouth as she remembered.

"Wasn't it Shakespeare who had something to say about a lady protesting too much?"

She coughed out a laugh as her eyes swung back to his. So intense, so clever, so unrelenting. "Seriously? This is the conversation you want to be having?"

When he didn't demur, she knew she had to get out of there. But where? The steamy bathroom and her memories of Will half-naked? The balcony, where anyone could see her? With its palace view and memories of looking at the stars with Will? Maybe it was time to run again. At least she was wearing a tracksuit this time…

She made to stand, but as soon as her foot hit the floor she realised it had gone numb. Unable to take her weight, it collapsed and with a *whoop* she toppled.

Will reached out and caught her with all her gangly limbs and flailing panic. He braced, taking the worst of the impact as they landed in a heap on the couch. A telling *oomph* shot from his lungs as her knee jabbed him in the thigh, her elbow slamming him right in the solar plexus.

As she waited for her own aches and pains to show themselves, she couldn't feel anything bar the fact her body was all up against Will's. She felt as if she had a hundred senses, not the normal five. Each one focused on hard muscle, strong arms, warm, masculine scent.

"Sadie," he said. "Sadie, are you hurt?"

She squeezed her eyes shut and shook her head.

"Are you sure? Because you're shaking."

Trembling. She was trembling. Emotion, adrenaline, lust, fear, exhaustion, confusion—all were rolling through her in satiny, liquid waves.

Will reached up to brush her hair from her face, tucking it behind her ear.

Her eyes flickered open in surprise and landed on his.

He should have let his hand drop then. They both knew it. Instead his thumb lingered, just a moment, brushing over the high sweep of her cheek. Following the sweet, warm rush of heat rising in her face.

The move was so unexpected, so gentle, so *tender*, she couldn't handle it.

She shifted, and he grimaced. Not with agony. She knew the way a woman knew. He was bracing himself against the slide of her body against his.

Even before Will's hand moved around her back, sliding up her ribs, into her hair, he said, "Stop. Moving."

"Okay." She licked her lips. "But I have to move eventually."

"Just not yet."

When he breathed she felt it against her mouth, her neck, everywhere. It was a rush. A terrible, wonderful, overwhelming rush, asking too much, not asking for enough.

She could not want this man. Not the way her body was trying to tell her she did. He was Hugo's friend. A man Hugo had trusted to be on her side, meaning that Hugo thought Will was on his side.

If this whole debacle had taught her anything, surely it was to stop thinking she could make it work with men she couldn't have.

Her acting coach in New York had adored the way she had looked up to him. The estimable Prince of Vallemont adored her as a friend. And insular, unreachable, closed-off Dr Will Darcy…

There was no adoration here. Only attraction. Compulsion. And a sweet, raw, formidable urge to pack away her need to be liked and simply get real.

"Will," she said, her voice soft, her heart aching with regret.

"Mmm?"

"I'm sorry you got caught up in all this. But I'm also not sorry at all."

The look in his eyes was tragic. Tortured.

Then he opened his mouth to speak—

But Sadie never got to find out what he'd been about to say next because just then someone knocked on the door.

CHAPTER SEVEN

FEELING AS IF he'd swallowed a lead balloon, Will said, "Expecting anyone?"

Sadie shook her head, her hair sliding over his collarbone like silk. Her next breath in she was shifting her body over his, her next breath out she seemed to melt over him like chocolate on a summer's day.

Then she blinked, her oceanic eyes widening. "Well, apart from whoever Hugo plans on sending in to whisk me away." She swallowed. "Has he sent word?"

"Nothing since yesterday."

The knock came again. Not the dainty taps that had heralded the gift basket but harder, more insistent, like a secret code.

Then, even though he was not in the right frame of mind, or body for that matter, to talk to anyone, Will found some reserve of inner strength in order to lift her bodily away, place her back in the chair and heave himself to standing.

He took a few moments to bring himself back under some semblance of control before he moved to the door and looked through the peephole.

What he saw made him take a literal step back. As time contracted, and his gut squeezed tight, he considered ignoring the knock. The moment passed, as moments tended to do. And good sense returned. *This* was what he wanted. This was what he'd been waiting for.

"This'll be cosy," he muttered, widening the door.

And there stood Hugo.

Taller than Will, just. Lines fanning out from the edges of his eyes where there'd been none before. A short dark beard now covered his jaw, but the chronic wealth and the resplendent royal Vallemontian bloodline was evident in every cell. With the antiquated newspaper rolled up under one arm, the way the collar of his button-down shirt was turned up at the neck it was simply so particularly Hugo, Will burst into laughter.

And reached out a hand.

Hugo's face split into a matching grin as he shook it. "Good to see you too, my friend."

Hugo glanced back towards the neckless, black-clad man-mountain with the bald head and the frown standing guard at the end of the hall. "I'll message when we're done."

The man-mountain nodded and hulked down the hall.

Only then did Hugo step into the breach to wrap Will in a manly hug. Double back-slap and all. And just like that the years between them faded to nothing.

"Hugo?"

Sadie's voice cut through and both men turned to face the room.

"Oh, my God! Oh, my God!" Like the Doppler effect, Sadie's voice lifted and grew as she vaulted over the back of the couch and ran towards them, her hair flying behind her.

Hugo had about half a second to drop his newspaper and the overnight bag he'd had slung over his shoulder before she leapt into his arms. Like a teddy bear with Velcro hands, she buried her face in his neck. Hugo's eyes squeezed closed, his voice rough even though muffled by her hair.

"Leo."

"What the heck are you doing here, you great fool? I assumed you'd send a lackey. Or maybe just a car. You didn't have to come."

"Of course I did."

Imagining them together was one thing. Theorising why it made little sense was another. Watching them, like this, their affection a real, live, pulsing thing, Will gripped the door handle so hard the thing creaked in protest. "Perhaps we ought to move this reunion inside."

Hugo's eyes found Will; filled with a level of understanding Will knew the man couldn't possibly have. Then he nodded his agreement and walked inside with Sadie still attached like a limpet.

Will shut the door, perhaps a tad harder than necessary.

At the sound, Sadie lifted her head. She tapped Hugo on the back and when he placed her on the ground she peeled herself away. "I can't believe you're actually here."

"Yet here I am."

"Excellent. This is just excellent." She glanced at Will, her cheeks now pinking like crazy.

And what Will thought was, *She's about to give us away entirely*. Except there was nothing tangible to give away. Only a little gravitational theory. And a whole lot of misplaced heat energy.

It didn't matter now. Hugo was here. Will's job was done. It was time for him to bow out. To get on a plane. To get back to work.

"Come in!" said Sadie. "Tell me everything. No, not everything. I might need a little Dutch courage before we get to that."

Hugo smiled as Sadie took him by the arm, but the look in his eyes showed he was pensive.

And from one breath to the next Will knew he wasn't going anywhere. Not just yet.

Not that he didn't trust Hugo, but the Prince's interests were divided. Naturally so. He had his own legacy, his own future to consider. He also had an entire royal house breathing down his neck. Will had been charged with keeping Sadie safe, so he'd stick around a little longer and finish the job properly.

He moved the overnight bag—Sadie's by the looks of it—to the door and picked up the newspaper Hugo had dropped, giving the front page a quick glance. The non-wedding was the headliner. No surprise there.

When he looked up, Will noticed Sadie had bypassed the nearest couch to sit Hugo on the other. The one Will *hadn't* slept on. The one on which they had not just been wrapped up in one another…

Will cleared his throat. When Hugo looked over he pointed to the newspaper, asking, "Any concern with this lot on your way here?"

"We were careful."

"Be grateful you're not British," said Will. "Or they'd be camped out on the roof, climbing the trellis, crawling out of the toilet bowl by now."

"I'm grateful of that each and every day."

Old jokes. Old friendship. All new tension in the air as Sadie sat on the edge of the couch, leg jiggling, nibbling at her bottom lip, energy levels spiking.

"How long have you and the man in black been special friends?" Will asked.

Hugo's cheek twitched. "Since an attempt was made on my uncle's life a year ago. While he was picnicking with Princess Marguerite and the twins."

That was half the Vallemontian succession plan right there. Another tragic event would have brought Hugo within sight of the throne. "I hadn't heard."

"It was kept quiet."

"Were they all right?"

"Shaken up. But unharmed." Hugo sent Sadie a comforting wink. "Against my express wishes, Prospero turned up the next day. I have offered him gainful employment in any number of positions since, and yet I can't shake the guy."

"It must be a constant struggle, being so beloved."

"And yet I never let the hardship get to me."

Sadie laughed. Quieted. Laughed again. "Who the hell are you two and what have you done with Hugo and Will?"

Hugo gave her a pat on the knee. Chummy. Friendly. "Don't tell anyone but all men are teenaged boys in the bodies of grown-ups. Now, I'd kill for a glass of water."

Sadie sprang out of the seat. "I can do better than that. Will, you start the fire. Hugo, you tidy the coffee table. I'm sure I saw designer beers in the bottom of the fridge."

Will watched her bounce into the kitchen. "Where's the, *Please, Your Majesty*?"

"Ask her," said Hugo. "I dare you."

"Hey, Sadie?" Will called.

Sadie pulled her head out of the fridge. "Mmm?"

"I hid some cheese and crackers in the pantry so we wouldn't starve."

"Perfect!"

Hugo laughed under his breath. "Coward."

Will crouched to pick out kindling and a good-sized log. "At least she gave me the manly job. She has you on tidying duty."

"Fair point. Leo?" Hugo called.

"Mm hmm."

"Do I have to tidy?"

"It builds character."

"Fine," Hugo mumbled, before making space on the coffee table.

Leo? Will thought. Oh my god. *Leo.*

Will had quietly wondered why he couldn't remember Hugo mentioning Sadie while at school, if they'd known one another as long as she'd intimated. But flashes came back to him now. Hugo talking about *Leo's* terrible taste in music. Rock climbing with *Leo.* Plans to hit Oktoberfest with *Leo.*

Hugo had spoken as if talking about a great mate. Not even the slightest hint of romance. While the stories had been about Mercedes Gray *Leo*nine, naturally Will had thought "Leo" was a boy.

Giving in to a sudden urge to whistle a happy tune, Will set to starting a fire. Out of the corner of his eye he saw Sadie with a packet of crackers hanging from her teeth, cheese hooked into her elbow and a knife between two knuckles, three beers in one hand. Barefoot, hair cascading over her shoulder, her small frame swamped by his tracksuit.

Either Hugo had become less observant over the years or he was holding off from passing comment on the story behind the outfit. Odds were the latter; the question was *why.*

When Will stood it was to find Hugo leaning back in the chair, hands behind his head, looking content.

"Here you go, big guy," said Sadie.

Hugo held out a hand and Sadie dutifully handed him a beer. "Much appreciated."

Then Sadie placed a hand on Hugo's knee as she leant over his legs to hand a beer to Will. "And one for you."

He took it with a nod.

She smiled quickly and pink heat flushed her cheeks again. He felt it too. The echo of a pulsing red haze that had come over him on the couch; her soft body flush against his, her hair sweeping against his neck.

Will tipped his drink towards her. She took a big swig of hers, then dumped the rest of the picnic on the coffee table.

"S'cuse," she said, nudging her way past Hugo's legs, taking a quick survey of the space and choosing a piece of floor in between them. "Tell me, in gory detail, how is it out there?"

"I'd say it's pretty mild for this late in the year."

"Jeans and jumper weather?" Will asked.

Hugo nodded. "I'd take a coat, just in case."

"Boys," Sadie chastised, shooting each of them a glare. "This is a war meeting. Not a party. Now, what do I need to do from here? How can I help mitigate the damage? For you. Your family. My mother—"

"Your mother is fine," said Hugo. "In fact…"

"In fact what?"

"She handed in her resignation."

"She *what*?"

"Apparently she told Marguerite she has been wanting to retire for years. She has quite the nest egg, an eye on a small cottage in the village near your school and a penchant to travel."

"Why didn't she say anything to me?"

"She didn't want to disappoint you."

"Disappoint *me*? But the entire reason I agreed to marry you was so that she could stay on after she stops working. I mean, *part* of the reason, because, well, I'd been told there'd be a tiara in it for me. A really big one. And you are, of course, you."

Hugo waved an understanding hand her way.

But Will realised he'd stopped with his beer halfway to his mouth. "Can we rewind just a second?"

Hugo and Sadie glanced his way—expressions of barely restrained patience exactly the same.

"Did I just hear that you were marrying this lug so your mother could live in the palace after she retires?"

Sadie answered, "That was a deciding factor. Yes."

Will sat forward, and turned on Hugo. "And why the hell were you marrying her?"

"Whoa," said Sadie. "A tad too effusive in your level of disbelief there, cowboy."

Hugo laughed. "He makes a fair point. I am ridiculously eligible."

Sadie batted her lashes at Hugo. "And rich."

"And devilishly handsome."

Sadie ran a hand through her hair; most of it settled back into place but some hooked on the hood of Will's track top. Light from the fire inside sparked off the russet tones like flares from the sun. It would take nothing to unhook it for her, to let it run through his fingers.

Nothing but his dignity.

Will's voice was a growl. "Get a room already."

Hugo looked around. "I could say we already have one, but this has a little too much chintz for my taste."

Will let his half-drunk beer drop to the coffee table and rubbed a hand over his chin as he attempted to sort the actual evidence from the white noise, only to find he'd forgotten to shave yet again. Unlike him.

He ran his hands through his hair instead, as if that might massage his brain into gear, and said, "The attempt on Sovereign Prince Reynaldo and his family—it was more of a near thing than you made out. If it had been a success, you would have been damn near the front of the succession line. Reynaldo is a serious ruler. A serious man. That realisation had him rethink the leeway you've enjoyed since your father passed. He made you an offer. Or a threat."

"Wow," said Sadie. "You're good."

Hugo's smile was flat. "Since my mother is not of royal blood, and Australian-born, her position here is precarious. Especially now that she has remarried—a Frenchman, and a commoner no less. The law is clear: without my father she lives at the palace at the grace of the family until I come of age."

"At…?"

"Three and thirty."

"Next year. And then?"

"If I marry she may stay. If not…"

"I see."

"Do you?"

"She must leave the palace."

"Without citizenship, without naturalisation, without a partner from Vallemont to sponsor her, my mother would be forced to leave the country."

Will coughed out a laugh. It was laughable. Archaic. Nonsensical. And by the twin expressions looking back at him, true. And then he was laughing no more. "So he was marrying you for real estate and you were marrying for the sake of…" He looked to Sadie. "What? Security?"

"Don't knock it. Security is pretty sought after. Especially for those who don't have it."

Hugo offered up a hand for a high five.

"So you were both being altruistic to the point of sadomasochism?" Will was right to stay a little longer. He ran a hand through his hair, tugging at the ends. "You're cracked. The both of you."

"And you're so very British," said Hugo.

"Isn't he?" Sadie agreed. Then, to Will, "Our sensibilities are not as draconian as yours. It is normal for Vallemontians to openly marry for any number of reasons: business, property, partnership, companionship. Even—shock, horror—for true love."

Hugo stopped her there. "Don't bother, Leo. They say no man is an island, but even before he discovered the stars Will was always a planet."

"Hugo," Sadie chastised.

But Will stayed her with a smile. "I was trying to remember why we hadn't seen one another in an age, but now it's all come back to me."

Only it hadn't. Not until that moment. Somehow he'd been so caught up in protecting Sadie—from herself, it turned out—he'd not seen Hugo and thought *Clair.*

From the flash of pain in the Prince's eyes Clair's ghost was now on his mind as well.

"What?" said Sadie. "What just happened there? What am I missing?"

But words were not possible. Will's throat had closed up. The edges of his vision blurring. Clair was not something he spoke of. In fact, he hadn't spoken to anyone who'd actually known her in years. It was too brittle. Too terrible. The loss of her was as much a part of him as his ribs.

But Hugo, it turned out, was not so bound. "Do you remember my friend Clair?"

Sadie looked at Hugo and back to Will. "Clair. You mean from the high school near yours? Of course. She came to stay that summer."

"Clair was Will's twin sister."

Will had seen Sadie shaken, seen her scared and he'd seen her cry. He'd seen her eyes warm and melt. But he had not, until that moment, seen her focus, the cessation of energy coming from her position like a sudden black hole.

Then she said, "You're *Clair's* brother. The one who was meant to come to Vallemont that summer, but couldn't because you..."

"I broke my leg."

She clicked her fingers at him. "Yes! From what I remember Hugo had quite the crush on young Clair. Followed her around like a puppy. I might have even been a mite jealous—because I hadn't had him to myself for months—if not for the fact I had a bit of a girl crush on her too. She taught herself to play the guitar, remember, Hugo? From nothing. And she was obsessed with Marguerite's accent. She had the impression down pat. She was rather too taken with Ibsen to truly be trusted. But she was fun. And you say you're her twin? Will wonders never cease?"

On her saunter down memory lane Sadie was clearly missing the undercurrents. For Hugo had gone deadly quiet, while Will was eating up her every word. He was swimming in visions of Clair laughing, creating, keeping the palace in thrall. Filling in gaps of the time he'd missed. He'd spent so long blaming Hugo for stealing those last days, when the truth was Will's old friend had given her a wonderfully rich final summer.

It wasn't Clair's death that had ripped their friendship apart. It was Will's anger. His grief. The fact that he'd been eviscerated. The next couple of years were a wretched blur. Until he woke up again in that astronomy lecture, and never looked back.

Never truly faced his grief. Never truly let go.

"Whatever did happen to Clair?" Sadie asked. "Why isn't she here? Too heartbroken over the one that got away?"

Will's gaze shot to Hugo to find the Prince looking deep into his beer. *Come on, Hugo, give me a hand here.* Hugo took a long, slow swig, but refused to look Will's way.

It seemed Will would have to find the words after all. "She fell ill."

"Oh, poor thing."

"No… I mean, years ago. Clair died not long after that summer."

Sadie's hand went to her mouth as she rose to her knees, her gaze zapping between the men. "No. I can't believe it."

Will nodded.

"I'm so sorry, Will, I had no idea. And there I was, fluffing on about ridiculous impressions and how gaga we were over her."

"It's okay," Will said, surprised to find he meant it. "It

was actually good to hear. To think of her having a good time."

Sadie looked into his eyes, deep, searching, demanding honesty. "How did she die?"

"Sadie," said Hugo, speaking up for the first time.

"If Will doesn't want to talk about it he'll tell me. You on the other hand don't get to weigh in here because this is all news to me and that is your fault. What happened?"

Will twisted his knuckles, easing out the tension, and soon found himself saying, "It started with memory loss. Personality changes. Depression. You met her, she was… sunny. When we'd all gone back to school I started receiving letters in which she sounded anxious, aggrieved. I figured she must have fought with Hugo even though he denied it. I asked my school to allow me to check in. As a known truant they refused me, so I begged my grandmother to intervene. My grandmother was not moved. It wasn't until the first seizure that anyone else thought anything was wrong. By the time they had Clair in hospital her speech was impaired, her balance dysfunctional. Pneumonia hit three weeks later. And then she was gone." Will's voice didn't feel like his own. It felt a hundred years old. "I had not seen her in person since I broke my leg."

"Since Vallemont?"

"That's right." Out of the corner of his eye Will saw Hugo shift in his seat.

"Is it hereditary?" Sadie asked.

A note of concern in her voice had Will lifting his eyes. "No. It was the spontaneous misfolding of a protein. Nothing anyone could have done."

"So, you're okay?"

"I'm okay."

"Okay, then." Her eyes caught the reflection of the fire as she turned on Hugo. "Alessandro Hugo Giordano, what were you thinking in not telling me?"

Hugo refused to answer and Sadie rocked back onto her feet and stood. "I'm sorry to hear about your sister, Will. But I can't look at him right now. I need a moment."

And with a withering look sent Hugo's way, she went. The creak of the French windows opening was followed by a stream of chilly air.

"That went well," said the Prince.

"Oh, hello," said Will, grabbing his beer once more. "You've been so quiet I'd forgotten you were here."

"Nowhere else in the world I'd rather be."

"I vote for the Bahamas."

Hugo raised his beer. Will gave it a clink. And together they drank. Unlike the beers they'd secreted during not-so-secret parties their American dorm-mate used to host in his room after hours, this felt more like a wake. A toast. To Clair.

The girl they'd both loved. The girl they both missed. And just like that Will felt as if a weight that had rested on his shoulders for years lifted.

Hugo shifted. Cleared his throat. And changed the subject. "So, Will, how's life been treating you these last million years?"

"Can't complain."

"My mother showed me an article about you in a magazine a month or so back. Which one was it?"

"Time? New Yorker? American Scientist?" He could have named dozens.

Hugo clicked his fingers. "*Top Twenty: sexiest living scientists* issue. I particularly liked the 'living' addendum. Clearly if they'd opened up the field to intellectuals of eras past you wouldn't have stood a chance."

Will's laughter now came without restraint. No one in his life today had known him before he was someone. Before the university awards, the publishing deal, the infamy in his field. No one in his life had known him as a troubled kid with an incorrigible twin sister he'd loved more than anything.

But he was that kid. He'd had that sister. Pressing it deep down inside, never to be talked about, had not made it go away. Did not make it hurt any less. It only made it fester.

Time to let in a little sunshine. Time to heal.

"So how do you like my Leo?" Hugo asked.

And as if he couldn't stop himself now, Will laughed again. "I like her just fine."

"Really? Because every time you look at her you roll your shoulders as if trying to shake her off. She's under your skin, my friend."

Will's gaze slid to the open French window. Like a moth to the flame. "Stick anyone in a room with her for twenty-four hours and she'd get under their skin."

"And that's the truth. She had a hard beginning to things, you know. Father left her and her mother on the side of the road the day she was born."

Will ran a hand up the back of his neck. "Hell."

"Could have been. Marguerite found them and took them in. The entire country adopted her as their own. It would be difficult to find one's feet under so many watchful eyes. I've handled it by creating a life, a purpose, separate from the renown. She handled it by being the sweet, funny, happy, grateful kid she thought everyone expected her to be."

Hugo rested a finger over his mouth.

"She's the one person in my life I can trust to call me on my bullshit. And I care for her more than I care for anyone. But I also clearly misread her. What she must have suffered—to go through with my plan for this long and then run. I know she is determined to take the blame, but this is entirely my fault. She'll forgive me when she finally realises it—she's all heart. But I'm not sure I'll ever forgive myself."

Will knew Hugo wasn't looking for a response, merely a listening ear. So he listened. He heard. And he tried with all his might not to let it colour his feelings for Sadie. They were convoluted enough as it was without adding pathos to her tale. She had a sweet, determined kind of dauntlessness. But it was best to remember her as an unexpected variance in his life's path. And nothing more.

"Anyway." Hugo pulled himself to standing and Will did the same. "I'll just make a quick stop and then it's time for us to leave."

Hugo reached out a hand. Will took it.

The Prince tipped his head. "Thank you for stepping up in my stead, old friend. She couldn't have landed in better hands."

Will's gut clenched, looking for signs Hugo meant the words in a way other than how they appeared. But he seemed only grateful.

Will nodded. "I'm glad I could be of help."

Hugo let go, patted Will on the shoulder, then jogged towards the bathroom. The moment his friend was out of sight, Will turned his gaze east. Towards sunset. Towards night. Towards the stars.

Towards the open French window and goodbye.

Sadie looked up into the sky. The first stars had begun to twinkle high above her, the deep red sunset over the mountains masked the rest. The small village below was even quieter than the evening before. As if everyone had simply gone on with their lives.

She breathed in long and hard as her mind flipped through memories of Clair, her breath shaky as she let it go. It was silly really, feeling so bereft about a girl she'd known for a few weeks so long ago. She could barely even remember what she looked like apart from dark wavy hair. A quick smile. Bright, mischievous eyes.

When Hugo had come back from school at the end of that next year, and not mentioned her again, she'd assumed they had drifted apart. And, knowing Hugo as she did, she'd let it go. All the while he must have been in such pain.

And to think that warm, funny girl was cool, clever Will's sister. His twin sister, no less. How must losing her have affected him? He'd been, what? Sixteen? Seventeen?

Sadie felt swamped. Off kilter. As if everything she thought she knew about Will had shifted just a fraction to the right. Where there was a two-dimensional thorn in her side, now there was warmth, sorrow, angles, depth, adding rabid curiosity to what had been, up until that point, rabid physical attraction.

None of which mattered a jot.

Hugo was here.

She was leaving with him.

Will would…do whatever it was Will did with his time wherever in the world he did it. The fact that she couldn't quite imagine what that might look like made her feel even worse.

She gripped the railing hard. The air had turned so bitterly cold it felt as though it might even snow.

Her breath hitched before she even knew why. And she turned to find Will stepping over the threshold and onto the balcony.

She gave him a small smile. He gave her one back. Then he moved to stand beside her, his hands gripping the freezing cold railing mere inches from hers. But not touching. Things unsaid swirling about them like a storm.

"Time to go?" she asked.

Will nodded.

"But where?" she said. "That is the question."

"Home?"

"I'm not sure where that is any more."

"Not a bad thing in my experience. Where would you like to go now you have the chance?"

"I have no idea. I truly hadn't let myself think past yesterday. Not to the honeymoon, or to my new living quarters, or to how I was going to get my job back. I think, deep down, I was sure someone would call us out, that it would never actually happen." She shook her head. Old news. The future was now. "Anyway, I should… I was going to say pack, but I have nothing. No home, no prince, no job. Just me."

"Sounds like you have plenty."

At the note in Will's voice—husky and raw—Sadie's eyes swept to the man beside her. The dark curls, the strong face, those profoundly deep eyes—he looked like some Byronic hero. He looked…so beautifully tragic, her entire body began to unfurl. To reach for him. To ease his aches and pains. And, yes, her own.

How had she come to be so used to having him in her life? It had been a day and a half, for Pete's sake. How had she become so attuned to the subtlety of his movements, his expressions, his breaths? So responsive to the quiet questions in his eyes?

She closed herself back in, crossing both arms over her chest. "Thank you, Will. For the tracksuit, for the bed, for putting up with me."

"I won't say it's been my pleasure—"

She smiled, as she was meant to do.

"But it has been educational."

Sadie reached out, laid her hand on Will's arm. "From a smart guy like you I'll take that as a compliment."

"From a generous spirit like yours, I wouldn't expect anything different."

Sadie should have let go. Instead she stepped forward, tipped up onto her toes and pressed her lips to Will's cheek.

Even as it happened she knew she would never forget

the scent of him—soap and heat and man. Or the warmth of his body, enveloping hers. The scrape of his stubble against her lips. Or the telling shiver that rocketed down his arm and into her hand. Like a perfect circuit.

When she pulled away, her heart was clanging in her chest. Breaths were difficult to come by. The intensity in his eyes was nothing like she'd felt in her entire life.

And once again the spell was broken by a knock at the door.

Shaking her head, literally, she landed back on her heels. Then she took a step towards the room. "Did Hugo go out?"

But Will put a hand over the door, protecting her. "No. Wait here."

She didn't wait, she followed. He might harbour a protective streak a mile wide, but she could look after herself. To find Hugo was already at the door, eye at the peephole.

He opened the door with a flourish to reveal Prospero filling the doorway.

"Prospero," said Hugo. "Excellent timing. We're ready to—"

The big man held out his phone. "Your Highness."

Hugo winced. "For the hundredth time, it's Hugo, please."

The big man's expression didn't falter. "Your Highness, you need to see this."

"Fine." Hugo took the phone, his expression blank. Until it wasn't. His brow furrowed, his mouth thinned. He seemed to grow out of his shoes until he looked for all the world a king. His voice was sharp as he demanded, "Where did you find this?"

"Internet alerts," said Prospero. "Any hint of a news article about you comes into my phone. I need to be prepared." The big man's throat worked ever so slightly, the only sign he was in any way concerned. "I blame myself.

They must have followed us from the palace. I have failed you at the first sign of trouble. I will resign the moment I get you to safety."

Hugo gave him a look. "You're not quitting. I've only just got used to having you around. And it looks like I'm going to need you tonight."

When Will stepped forward, Sadie realised she'd been tucked in behind him, taking his protection for granted. She moved past him and tugged on Hugo's sleeve. "What is it? What's going on?"

Hugo glanced over her shoulder at Will.

Sadie took Hugo by his royal chin and forced him to look at her. Out of the corner of her eye she saw Prospero move in. To the big bald man she said, "Back away." To Hugo, "And you. Tell me what's going on. Right now."

Hugo gave over his phone.

Sadie recognised the website. It was the kind that traded in online gossip, most of it made up. All salacious. Whatever their opinion on the wedding upset, no one would take it seriously, surely.

And then she saw the art.

There was Hugo walking into a building. Crumbling brick. Bougainvillaea. A swing sign with a tulip carved into the wood.

She looked up at Hugo. "That's you. Walking in here. This afternoon."

"Keep going."

Finger shaking now, she scanned down. Her hand moved to cover her mouth as she saw the worst of it.

More pictures. This time it was later, darker. The shots angled up at the Tower Room balcony. Some images weren't even in focus but every one of them was all too clear.

Picture after picture of Sadie and Will. Hands an inch

apart as they held the railing. Looking into one another's eyes.

Sadie's throat tightened as she madly scanned through the lot. Thankfully the pictures stopped before she had taken Will by the arm. Leaned in. Kissed him.

Small mercy. For under each picture the banner read, "Prince Alessandro busts Lady Sadie with new lover in secret village pad."

She'd known the balcony wasn't secure. The entire village was spread out below with its houses and shops and bars. Will's self-sabotage theory grew roots and shoots and twisted around her like a creeping vine.

"Hugo, we were just talking." That was Will, looking over Sadie's shoulder as she slowly scrolled back.

"I know," said Hugo.

"I mean, it was right now. Just happened. Look at the clothes. The angle of the shadows—"

"Will, I know. I trust you weren't just romancing Leo on the balcony like something from one of her plays. It's okay."

Head swimming, tummy tumbling, Sadie shoved the phone at Hugo before it burned her hand, clueless as to whether to apologise or smack him.

She turned to Prospero, ready to flay him for bringing the press here, but the big guy looked so desperately disgraced that in another place, another era, he might have popped an arsenic tablet and been done with it.

She looked around the room for answers. It really was a sweet room. If one had to get stuck somewhere for any length of time it was a wonderful choice. She'd miss it. Or maybe it was the simplicity. The time to do nothing but reflect on the life choices she'd made. The company…

It didn't matter. For now it was time to go.

Hugo broke into her reverie. "Will, what's your plan?"

"London."

"Take her with you."

In the gap left by Will's revealing silence, Sadie said, "Am I the *her* in this situation?"

Her eyes flickered between theirs. Hugo had gone full prince—looking down his nose imperiously, as if he was about to bestow a knighthood. While Will was pulling his statue move. These men…

"Will can't just take me with him. He works. He has a life." Sadie realised she wasn't sure what that entailed. Despite the intensity of the past couple of days, she didn't really know the man at all. "Tell him, Will."

But Will was watching Hugo, the two men having some kind of psychic Man Conversation of which she was no part.

Sadie looked to Prospero for help. "Prospero, tell them they're overreacting."

Anguish passed over Prospero's face. "Sorry, m'lady. But His Highness is right. The sooner you are gone, the easier it is for me to protect the Prince. It's best."

Sadie threw her hands in the air. "'It's best'? *It's best* is how we got into this mess in the first place!"

Knowing the barb was meant for him, Hugo finally looked at her. She took her chance. "If Will and I are seen together, leaving the country no less, those pictures will take on loaded meaning where right now there is nothing but two separate, uninvolved people on a balcony. Chatting. About…stuff."

Only she couldn't stop the strangely guilty warmth rising in her cheeks, because for her it had meant more than simply chatting. If Hugo noticed he didn't say, but something passed over his face, nevertheless. Ruefulness? Or maybe it was release.

Sadie turned on Will, getting desperate now. "Will. You say the word and we can put an end to this idea."

Will's gaze turned to Sadie. All deep soulful eyes and tight, ticking jaw. And he said, "It's fine."

"Wow, how to make a girl feel wanted."

A flash of fire lit the depths of his eyes, of *want.* It lit a twin fire in her belly, lower. Higher. All over. This was going to be a disaster.

"Don't you see you're off the hook? You're not my baby-sitter any more. You're not my bodyguard."

"Then what is he?" Hugo asked.

"He's… He's…" So many conflicting answers rushed to the front of Sadie's mind, none of which she could say out loud.

Hugo took her silence for acquiescence. "Exactly. It's done. Prospero?"

"I'm on it." And then the big man was off, striding down the hall.

Hugo shoved an overnight bag at her. "I had your mother pack for you, just in case you decided against coming home right away. Clothing, toothbrush, et cetera. A book. Your phone. Charger. And your passport."

Passport? She'd run out of excuses. Unless she wanted to be hunted in her own backyard, she had to go. It was best.

Will gathered his leather overnight bag and his battered silver case. *He'd* been packed, ready to go, from the moment they'd arrived. "Let's do this."

And then they were off. Hugo at the head, Sadie in the middle, Will at the rear.

"Breathe," Will murmured.

"Don't want to."

Then his hand slipped under her elbow and he walked beside her. "Do it anyway."

"Story of my life."

His rough laughter made her feel as if she'd stepped

into a warm bath. The tingling in her toes diminished and her anxiety eased.

Striding down the hall, down the stairs and into Reception, they saw that Prospero had taken up residence with his back to the front door.

Janine of the ponytail was at the desk once more, watching Prospero like a hawk. When she looked up to see Will bearing down on her, her whole face brightened. "Why, hello! If it isn't the lovebirds from the honeymoon suite!"

Sadie blanched. Not that Janine would have noticed. Her eyes were now comically jumping from Will to Prospero to Hugo.

"Heading out?" Janine called. "It's cold out there—" Her voice came to a halt as her mouth dropped open into comical shock. "You're…him. You're the… Oh, my."

Hugo stepped up to the plate, blinding smile in place. "Prince Alessandro. Pleased to meet you. Is there, by any chance, a back entrance to this place? We seem to have collected some unsavoury hangers-on."

Janine, good girl that she was, did not need to be asked twice. She was out from behind the counter in a flash. "This way," she stage-whispered, tiptoeing dramatically.

Will, Hugo and Sadie followed, edging through the old kitchen, and out into an alleyway filled with limp bougainvillaea petals, bins and a half-dozen stray cats. As luck would have it they could see the bumper of Will's hire car out the other end.

To Will Hugo said, "Take care of her as if she is your most precious possession. Take care of her as if she is family."

Will's nod was solemn.

"Thanks again, Will," said Hugo, shaking the other man's hand. "I owe you."

"You owe me nothing."

"Can you let Maman know?" asked Sadie.

"Of course." Hugo gave Sadie a quick bear hug. "Try not to cause too much trouble."

She laughed. "Way too late for that."

"Go. Now."

Will grabbed Sadie's bag from her shoulder and strode towards the car. Sadie followed, noting it had started to snow. Big, soft, romantic flakes that dissolved the second they hit skin.

Her feet ground to a halt as she neared the end of the alley, and moonlit hit her toes. "Just a second."

She ran back to Hugo, who was waiting in the darkness, delved deep into the zip pocket in the side of her track top and found the ring which was still attached to the garter. She gave it to Hugo.

He winced. "Maybe I ought to gift this thing to the twins and be done with it."

"Don't say that. You'll find someone one day. Someone wonderful. Someone who adores you. Someone who doesn't cringe at the thought of kissing you. Someone who doesn't answer back all the time and isn't such a bad sport at board games as I am. Someone, maybe, a little like Clair."

A moment of torment crossed her old friend's face like a cloud passing the moon, and she wondered that she'd never noticed before.

Then he pulled himself free of it and gave her a smile. "Take care, Leo."

"You too, Hugo."

And with that, Sadie ran and hopped into the car. Or she tried, but her wedding dress was still smooshed into the footwell, her hairpiece sitting pathetically on top.

She hopped out of the car, dragged out the wedding stuff, went to the bin in the alleyway and threw it all away.

Back in the car she looked at Will, his face a familiar expression of barely reigned-in patience.

"Are you ready?" he asked.

Her heart clunked against her ribs just at the look of him. "Not even close."

But as the engine growled to life, Sadie felt lighter. Like an untethered helium balloon. Even though, as they took off into the night, leaving Vallemont behind, she knew not when, or if, she might ever return.

CHAPTER EIGHT

DARKNESS HAD LANDED by the time their private plane—organised with stunning speed by Will's apparently unflappable assistant, Natalie—hit English soil. While the snow falling through the crisp Vallemontian air had felt dreamy and romantic, London's weather was damp and grey.

A driver was waiting for them at a designated point. "Where to, sir?"

Will gave an address in Borough Market and it wasn't long before they were pulling down a dark concrete alley to a warehouse conversion with rows of arched leadlight windows and striped metal security bars.

Sadie walked hesitantly inside.

Will dragged his battered silver case with Maia the telescope inside to a spot beside a long, black leather couch, then moved about, turning on lights, turning on the heat.

Industrial lamps splashed pools of cool light against walls of rustic exposed brick. Insanely high ceilings criss-crossed with massive steel and wooden beams. There was a fantastical Art Deco staircase that went up, up, up. Huge, gunmetal-grey barn doors shut off whatever rooms were behind them. Everything was dark, seriously arty and hyper-masculine. There was an old wooden plane propeller mounted to the wall above the TV, for Pete's sake!

It was an amazing place, to be sure. Only it didn't mesh

with what she thought she knew of Will. Not even close. She would have said Will's defining feature was how confident he was in his own skin—in his cleverness, his quirks, his self-containment. This place was pure mid-life crisis—all it was missing was wood chips on the floor, a Lamborghini in the lounge room and the scent of beer in the air.

Coming here had been a mistake. A huge, colossal mistake.

Will touched her on the shoulder and she near leapt out of her skin.

When she realised he was taking her overnight bag she let out a shaky laugh. "Sorry. I was half expecting the bogeyman to have followed us here."

"We weren't followed. I'm sure."

"Prospero was sure and he's a professional."

"Prospero's neck is so thick he can't turn his head to check his side mirrors."

Sadie laughed and a small measure of her nerves faded away.

Then she realised Will's fingers were still hooked into her bag, on her shoulder, the heat of them tingling through her arm. She let him slide the strap away.

Then she moved further into the space. So much space. "How long have you lived here?"

"I've owned it about eight years. Ten maybe. Quite a place, isn't it?"

"Quite."

"But?"

"Did you hear the but?"

"It's written all over your face."

His arms were crossed as he watched her move through his home, but his face was gentle. He didn't seem to mind her hesitance, he was more…curious than anything else. The Will she knew was curious. Painfully so. It made her nerves fade a little more.

"But…where's all your stuff?"

He looked around. "In its place."

What place? There was nothing there. No rugs to soften it, no cushions to add comfort. No bookshelves, even though Will was an educated man. No knick-knacks, no family photos. Not even a telescope pointing out the expanse of windows. No sense of Will at all.

"I wasn't expecting company."

She dragged her eyes away from the man cave to shoot Will a flat stare. "Big shock. But even if you were, all of this feels more like a concerted effort to scare people away."

He didn't react. Didn't even blink. But then a smile kicked at the corner of his mouth and his dimple came out to play. Sadie tried to settle the resultant shimmer in her belly, as she wondered if maybe she had him figured out after all.

The she turned on her toes and came to a halt, her mouth dropping open at the huge, twenty-foot-high wall covered in the most stunning wallpaper—a black background scattered with the names of constellations and such in chunky white font.

"That was the clincher," he said, his voice near as he moved in behind her. "My publisher had rented the place and a stylist had decked out that wall for a publicity shoot before my first book came out. I found I wasn't comfortable pretending the place was mine for the book jacket photographs, so I bought it. As is. *Stuff*—or lack thereof—and all."

Sadie wasn't au fait with London real estate but she knew enough. "Who knew gazing at the stars paid so well?"

"It's not all star-gazing, Sadie," he said, his voice going gruff in that way it did when she had him on the ropes. He was so easy that way.

"No?"

"Consultancy, publishing, speaking, teaching. I do okay. Not as well as a prince, mind you."

"Ha! Turns out, for me, that's not all that much of a selling point."

Will's brow clutched. And Sadie, belatedly, heard what she'd said.

"Not that you were *trying* to sell me anything, of course." *Stop. Stop talking right now. Nope, more words coming.* "But if you were… I'm out of a job, out of a home and on the shelf. You in the market for a wife?"

It had been a joke. *Absolutely.* She had meant to alleviate the tension that had been humming between them since they'd taken off in Will's car. Or maybe it had been since the first night on the balcony. Or the first time she'd seen Will's smile.

It didn't work. Tension rippled through the air like a living thing, smacking against the stark brick and overwhelming glass and rocketing back at them like flying knives.

Feeling the pink beginning to rise up her throat, Sadie flapped a lazy hand at Will. "I changed my mind. Now I've seen this place I realise the neat freak thing wasn't a one-off. And I'm a delightful slob. It would never work."

She feigned a nonchalant yawn which turned into the real thing.

"You look exhausted."

"Why, thank you," she said on yet another yawn.

"You hungry?"

"Not a bit," she lied. Knowing she had to head somewhere quiet, alone, to collect her thoughts before she said something even less appropriate than mock-proposing to the guy.

"Then I'll show you to your room."

Sliding the strap of her bag over his shoulder, Will headed for the stairs, leaving Sadie to follow. The heating system must have been state of the art as she was starting to feel all thawed and fuzzy already.

Up the big black stairs they went, past more barn doors—she spied a sliver of sterile-looking office behind one, fancy gym equipment behind another, which explained the man's physique—until Will stopped in front of a neat, light room with huge, curtainless windows and a view of a whole lot of rooftops of post-industrial London.

Will handed over her bag and waited on the threshold as she went inside. "There's a private bathroom through that door. The remote on the bedside table darkens the windows." A beat. Time enough for his cheeks to lift before he said, "Knowing how much you like borrowed clothes, there are spares in the cupboard."

She sat on the corner of the neat grey bed and patted her bag, holding it close to her chest to try to stop the *ba-da-boom* of her heart at the sight of that smile. "I'm all good."

"Excellent. If I'm not here in the morning there'll be food in the fridge. I'll leave my assistant's contact details on the kitchen bench. She knows where I am at all times."

"Okay."

"Okay. Goodnight, Sadie."

"Goodnight, Will."

Will went to slide the door closed, but Sadie stopped him with a breath. "They'll figure out who you are, you know."

"I know."

"They'll make assumptions without fact and write about it. They'll take those pictures and turn them into something ugly. Over and over again, the stories getting bigger, wilder, further and further from anything resembling truth." She knew. She'd seen it happen to other members of Hugo's family. Tall poppies ripe for cutting down.

"I'm aware."

"Are you? Because the thought of it impacting your career, of you having to explain me to your friends… I sense that, for all the speaking and publishing and teaching and consulting and international jet-setting, you're a private man, Will. Should you call your family?"

"No family to call."

"None?"

"Sadie, don't worry about it."

"But I will. I do. I worry all the time. The thought of someone out there not liking me, or being angry at me, or blaming me…" She ran a hand over her eyes. "You're right. I am exhausted."

Will's toe nudged over the line at her door before he stopped himself. "Whatever happens tomorrow, or next week, the sun will rise, the earth will turn, and it will be forgotten. We all will be forgotten. Nothing lasts for ever."

Sadie laughed. "Was that meant to make me feel better?"

"You're laughing."

"So I am."

"Sleep."

"Yes, sir."

With that Will slid the door closed, leaving Sadie in his big grey room, in the big, bold house, in a big, strange city, her thoughts a flurry, her heart confused, her oldest fears playing on the edges of her mind.

Alone.

"I'm back."

"The Boss Man's back!" Natalie paused as she mulled over Will's words. "Back to work or back in London? Or back in Vallemont? I've lost track."

Will lay back on his uncomfortable couch in the main room, staring up at the propeller jutting out from the floating wall, wondering if there might be a button somewhere to make it work, he'd simply never cared enough to find out. "London. Work."

"Fantastic! I'll set up newyorker.com for you for… tomorrow afternoon your time. No appointment set up with the prime minister as yet, but I've managed to become firm friends with his secretary, Jenny. She gave me an amazing recipe for mulberry jam. And I can let Garry know he no longer has to berate you for never taking a break, as you've just had two whole days in the gorgeous countryside of Vallemont! Was it amazing?"

"Amazing," Will said.

"You're not even listening."

Will sat up straight. Focused. He checked his watch to find it had been five minutes since the last time he'd looked. And twenty-five minutes since he'd left Sadie to sleep in his spare bedroom.

He rubbed a hand over his chin to find his beard now long enough to leave a rash, and said, "New Yorker. Jam. Sadie. I got it."

"Will."

"Yes, Natalie."

"Who's Sadie?"

Will held the phone away from his ear as if it had just grown legs. Dammit. How distracted was he.

"Will? Will!" Natalie's voice chirped through the phone.

Will slowly brought it back to his ear. In time to hear his assistant ask, "Is that what you were doing the past two days? A girl?"

Will pinched the bridge of his nose. For all her voracious work ethic and killer travel-arranging skills, Natalie was ridiculously focused on his private life. She had been since she saw a photo of him once in *GQ*, attending the Kennedy Centre honours for a previous president with a Victoria's Secret model on his arm.

The fact that his date was a space buff who'd been in

contact with Garry, his manager, asking for advice on which university was best for post-grad studies was beside the point as far as Natalie was concerned.

"Will," she shouted. "Don't you lie to me. It's the one non-negotiable of our contract together."

"No, it's not."

"Fine. But tell me anyway. I worry about you. From all the way over here. Garry does too. And Cynthia."

His publisher? Please don't say they'd all been talking about him.

"Knowing you had a nice girl in your life would go a long way to alleviating our concerns."

"Natalie, do I not pay you enough?"

"Oh, no, Boss Man. I cannot complain on that score. Not a single bit."

"Do I push my luck, ask too much of you, underappreciate you?"

"Often, sometimes and absolutely no."

Not the answer he'd expected. Into the moment's pause Natalie said, "Will, did you or did you not meet a girl in Vallemont?"

He stared up at the propeller once more and thought of the look of incredulity in Sadie's eyes as she'd spotted it. He'd had dates in his London pad before. They'd either not noticed the thing, or they'd thought it inspired. Sadie had known, in a second, that it wasn't something he'd ever have chosen.

"It's complicated."

Natalie whooped. And clapped. For so long he wondered if she was giving him a standing ovation.

"It's not what you think."

"You have no idea what I think."

"You think I'm skiving off work because I've found myself a woman who's made me realise human relationships are more important than work can ever be."

A long pause. "Well, have you?"

"No, Natalie. I have not. For which you ought to be thankful, as it is my work that keeps you in mulberry jam."

Natalie went quiet. Then, "Will Darcy, it is my skill that keeps me in mulberry jam. It's your work that keeps you from rocking in a corner. Check your calendar; it's updated. And packed to the rafters, just as you like it. Goodnight."

Will threw his phone to the end of the couch, where it bounced and settled. Knowing he ought to check his calendar in order to be prepared for the next day's work, he instead headed upstairs, ignoring the lift of his pulse as he passed Sadie's closed door, and headed into his room.

He showered—and shaved, *hallelujah*—put on fresh pyjamas, and hopped into his own bed.

Then stared at the ceiling knowing he'd never been further from sleep in his entire life.

Natalie's words floated around and around his mind like so much space junk.

He had relationships. They were simply shorter, more condensed or more peripheral than others might be used to.

And, while his work was at the centre of his life, it wasn't the thing that held him together. If he had to give it up one day, he could. Yup, even he heard it—he sounded like a junkie. *Who's Sadie?* Natalie had asked.

Sadie was the reason he felt a gnawing self-reproach at having missed work for two days apart from a little gazing at the Orionid Shower.

Sadie was the reason he was holed up in his London house, when he should be in the outback, a desert, anywhere but the high-density cityscape that was London, where it was so grey out he'd see nothing but soup.

Sadie was the reason he was wide awake.

He rolled over, and closed his eyes. Sleep would come. This restlessness wouldn't last.

Nothing ever did.

Sadie was used to things going bump in the night. She'd grown up in a several-hundred-year-old palace after all.

But it didn't make a lick of difference. As tired as she was, knowing Will was out there was making her restless.

Restless in a way she hadn't been before the kiss on the cheek.

Before the photos of them looking so…so…

Before he'd gone above and beyond, whisking her away to his private residence.

She rolled over, rifled through her overnight bag. Hello! Her phone.

It was only slightly charged. And she had so many messages her mailbox was full. She paused a half-second before deleting it all. And she made the only call she needed to make.

"This is Genevieve."

Sadie rolled her eyes. "It's *me*, Maman. And I know you know because my number comes up when I call."

A beat slid by in which Sadie imagined her mother's imperious stare. Only then did her mother launch into a series of very important questions.

"Mercedes Gray Leonine, did I not teach you anything about getting into cars with strange men?"

"No. You did not."

"Really?"

"It never came up."

A beat, then, "Are his eyes as blue as they look in the photo?"

"Oh, yeah."

"Some might call that extenuating circumstances."

Some, but not Genevieve. It had been her life's mission

to make sure her daughter thought once, twice, three times before taking anyone at face value. Men in particular. The better looking, the more charming, the more she was encouraged to stay away. It was as if she'd had to defy her mother by falling for her acting coach in New York—an older man, beautiful but fallible—to finally see she had a point.

Leading her to Hugo. The one man in her life, and her mother's life, who had always been the exception to the rule.

Still Sadie had run. And where had she learned that, again?

"Now Hugo tells me you are *living with* this man?"

"Not living. Staying. In his spare room. He is a dear old friend of Hugo's. He's been amazingly…unruffled by the situation. A self-contained sort of man." Yikes, she was making him sound like a doddering uncle. She heard Will's voice accusing her of *protesting too much* and eased back. "It's easier this way."

"Hmmm. And how good-looking is he?" her mother asked. "Because if that photograph was even close you need to beware—"

"Maman. Any chance we can talk about something other than Will?"

"But why?"

"Because I ran away from marrying a prince yesterday and I thought you might have an opinion on that. And I hear that you have retired and moved out of the palace and I wondered if you would like to hear my opinion on that?"

"Not so much."

Sadie rolled onto her back and stuck her legs in the air, the huge, lacy white nightie she had never seen before that her mother had so kindly packed for her falling to her hips as she twirled her ankles one way and then the other. "I've been thinking."

"Yes?"

"About my father."

Never a fun topic.

Sadie's toes clenched as she waited for her mother's, "I see."

"About the similarities between us."

"You do have his eyes." Genevieve sighed. The love of melodramatics also an inherited trait.

"I mean, that he was a runner. And so, it seems, am I."

"Oh, darling. My sweet girl. What you are is discriminating. You will not be shaken. You will not be swayed. You know kindness and you know how to put people at ease."

"I know when I'm being hustled."

"That's my girl. No point being sweet unless it's wrapped around a core of steel."

"That's right, Maman." Sadie let her feet drop. She rolled to her side, watched moonlight play over the painted wood floor. "Have you really moved out already?"

"I really have. To a lovely little cottage on the edge of the grounds. Marguerite has been saving it for me for years. You have a room here too, my darling. If you want it."

Sadie rolled onto her front, to the foggy grey view out the window, to the light from the converted homes nearby, the city beyond. Growing up in the country, she'd dreamed of living in a big city one day—close to the best theatres, surrounded by crowds and people who had no clue who she was. Who didn't watch her every move. Where she could be anonymous.

New York hadn't worked out. Maybe this was a second chance.

"Thanks, Maman. I'll let you know as soon as I know what I decide to do."

Her phone started to buzz. Low battery. She promised to call soon and hung up.

She rolled to sitting. Her toes reached to the floor before curling away from the cold grey. Only… Her toes tapped against the floor to find it warm. Toasty, in fact. Underfloor heating. Naturally.

She was thirsty. Or hungry. Or something.

Whatever she was she couldn't sit here pretending to sleep. It was early—maybe that was it. She needed to stretch her legs. Or watch a little TV. Hugo had mentioned a book in her bag… No. A book wouldn't do it. Surely this place had a TV somewhere.

Grabbing the heavy comforter off the end of the bed, she wrapped it around her shoulders and heaved open the door and—

The comforter slid off her shoulders and landed in a puddle on the floor as she came face to face with Will.

He'd stopped in the hallway, a cup of coffee in his hand. A pristine white T-shirt—creased from where it had just come out of its packet—did magical things to his chest. Or was that the other way around? Dark grey pyjama bottoms hung low on his hips. His feet were bare.

Moonlight sliced across his strong face. He'd shaved, making him look younger somehow. Clean-cut. All crisp edges, and smooth lines. Much like the statue he seemed too fond of incarnating. Except for the banked heat in his eyes.

"I don't remember that being in my spare-clothes drawer."

"Hmm?" Sadie followed his gaze, glancing down at her matronly nightgown with its neck-to-ankle pin-tucks. "My mother packed it for me."

"Is there a chance she wants you living at home with her for ever?"

Sadie laughed out loud, recalling the phone call she'd literally just had. "Could be."

For a man who came across as so dry, he had a way at cutting to the heart of things. The humanity. Like this strange house of his—cool and intimidating on the outside, but warm to the touch.

"Did you need something?" he asked. His deep voice rumbled over her skin like a blast of heat.

Did she? Did she need something? Maybe. Maybe what she needed was right here in front of her.

No. Don't be stupid. You don't need Will. You've just gotten used to having him near. You like having him near. You want to have him nearer still.

Boy, was that a bad idea. He was Hugo's friend, for one. He was a self-confessed workaholic, existing in the rarefied air of the intelligentsia, whereas everything she did was navigated by her heart. And security was crucial to her; knowing she had a safe place to go home to if everything else in her life fell apart. His home clearly meant nothing more to him than a place to occasionally sleep.

If she stood a chance of doing this right one day, she'd need a stayer. Someone solid and settled and present. Someone to pin her feet to the floor. Someone she could trust not to bolt. Someone not like her father. *Someone not like her.*

She needed someone else.

But she wanted him.

He took a step closer and she gripped the comforter for all she was worth.

"Are you hungry? We could go out— No. Bad idea."

Will smiled. It did things to his face, encouraging things, that had Sadie feeling warm all over. It had to be some kind of glitch in the space-time continuum to find the only astronomer in the universe who could do more for a white T-shirt than Marlon Brando.

"I could order food in. I think Natalie had my cleaning agency pin some takeaway menus to a door somewhere."

She shook her head no.

"How about a book? I know there are plays in my library. Funny, I hadn't remembered until that moment that Clair used to read herself to sleep when it wouldn't come on its own."

Funny; she wondered if he realised that here, alone with her, he was able to say Clair's name and not look as if he was being stabbed in the heart as he said it.

Funny how well he knew her that he understood she was a lover of words.

Not so funny that all of that burned him a little place marker onto her heart.

"The building came with a fully stocked library when I bought it. I'm sure even Shakespeare is in there somewhere."

Maybe it was the moonlight, maybe it was the man—heck, maybe it was the fact that he kept quoting Shakespeare—but Sadie dropped the comforter on the floor, stepped over it, took Will by the front of the T-shirt, pulled herself up onto her toes and kissed him.

Time seemed to stand still as her lips met his. Her fingers curled harder into the cotton as every nerve ending zinged as if all the energy in all the world had coalesced into her body in that moment.

Which was why it took a moment to realise he wasn't kissing her back.

Her eyes fluttered open to find his dark. Impenetrable.

She pulled back. A fraction. A mile. It didn't matter. So long as she had those eyes on hers. For she knew she hadn't misread the signs—the way he looked at her, how he found excuses to touch her—had she?

The urge to let go, to step back, to apologise, make a joke, make light, to *run* was near overwhelming.

But this time the want was stronger.

She squeezed the cotton tighter in her grip, holding on for dear life. And…there. The thump of his heart against her knuckles gave him away. It was galloping, out of control.

"Will?" she said, her voice barely a breath.

With a growl that seemed to come from some primal place inside of him, Will's arms were around her, holding her so close not a sliver of light could get through, then kissed her like there was no tomorrow.

Colour exploded behind her eyes as heat and want and desire and relief swirled together in a heady mix of intense sensation. His kisses were like a dream, pulling her under until her thoughts were no longer her own.

Her hands ran over his hard shoulders, diving into his curls. Her knees lost all feeling and she felt an almost insatiable need to cry.

Then, just when she thought she might dissolve into a puddle of trembling lust, his arm slid under her knees and she whooped as her feet left the ground.

Laughter spilled from her as Will stepped over the comforter and carried her to the bed. He dropped her so she bounced. Her laughter grew patchy, breathless, as he hovered at the end of her bed.

He stood perfectly still in a patch of moonlight, every inch of him illuminated in its silvery spotlight.

She felt as though she could see past the impermeable Will wall and into the heart of him for the very first time. Substantial, stoic, strong and sure. But above all solitary. A lone wolf.

Her belly fluttered in warning. *Be careful. Be sure.*

This had all the markers of self-sabotage he'd observed in her. Only it didn't feel the same. It didn't have the same breathless desperation with which she made so many big decisions. She felt…calm. Present. As if she'd been waiting for this moment her entire life.

"What are we doing, Will?"

"If you need me to tell you that—"

"You know what I mean. This, us, it's just a normal reaction to the stress of the past few days, right?"

He said nothing. But she'd been stuck in close quarters with him long enough now to read his supremely subtle body language. The heat was no longer banked, the spark of attraction was aflame. But he was as conflicted as she was.

But then his gaze travelled down her body, roaming over her hair, her shoulders, down her voluminous nightdress to her feet, leopard-print toenails curling and uncurling in the soft grey sheets. It left a trail of warmth, of anticipation, of promise in its wake.

And he said, "I've never been comforted by the idea of normal. Not when there's the option to reach for more."

"All the way to the stars?"

He smiled then, a deeply sexy smile in which his dimple came out to play. Then he climbed onto the bed and thought became something other people did.

His hand started at her ankle, then moved slowly up her calf. She jerked as it hit the back of her knee. Then it was gone, over the top of her nightgown now, sliding over her hip, slowly moving over her ribs. Her muscles melted one by one. All except her toes. They curled so far back on themselves they hurt.

She grabbed him by the T-shirt and dragged him towards her. He caught himself so he didn't hurt her, muscles in his arms straining as he pressed her back, even as she pulled him down.

Then his fingers were at her neck, tracing the edge of her nightgown. She realised he was looking for a button. A release.

She reached down to her knees to grab the hem, before wriggling the acres of fabric over her head. Dangling it daintily over the edge of the bed, she said, "Unless you'd prefer I fold it and place it neatly in my bag..."

Will shoved it to the floor, and hauled her into his arms. The heat of him burnt through his clothes, searing her bare skin. It was as if now he had her he couldn't stand to let her go.

Dangerous thought.

This was a man for whom sentimentality was a four-letter word. He *would* let her go. And that was okay.

Funny; the fact that he would never expect anything from her made him all the more of a prize.

As she hovered on the edge of no turning back, her eyes once more found his, moonlight no longer giving her insight, forcing her to respond to the truth of his touch, his pulse, his presence.

"Nothing's going to be the same, is it?"

He smoothed her hair off her face. Kissed her nose. Her forehead. Her chin. And found her eyes again. "Nothing ever is."

Then he lowered himself to drag his lips across hers, slow, gentle, before settling perfectly into place and stealing her breath away, taking her to some other place where thought was lost, memory became a dream and nothing mattered but the moment.

And neither of them said a thing for a good long while.

CHAPTER NINE

WILL WOKE LATE. Not that he could remember what he might be late for. Or what day it was. Or what country he was in.

Then he heard Sadie shift, muttering and murmuring as she rolled onto her belly, the sheets twisting with her, her hair cascading down her back, like liquid fire in the morning light.

The urge to join her again hit fast and furious. To sweep her hair away and run his hand down her back. To trace her spine with kisses. To see her smile.

To feel her open to him. To silence her moans with a kiss. To see that look in her eyes, the raw emotion, something beyond attraction, beyond a mere spark, as she tumbled over the edge.

But, while the night before had felt inevitable, the burning away of the tension that had simmered between them from the moment he nearly ran her down, waking her with a kiss would be a very different thing.

For he was in London, it was Monday and he had work to do.

Will slid out of Sadie's bed, picked her nightgown up off the floor and shook it out, preparing to fold it. He stopped himself, tossing it on the edge of the bed instead.

Stretching out his limbs, he turned at the door and looked back. Took stock.

He would give her sanctuary so long as she required it, and he could get back to real life, driven by a brutal calendar, living on the rush of his work, banking his meticulously architected reputation to make sure he was in the rooms of power.

But now he had finally slayed the sentimental obstructions that had been dogging him for years, he did not intend to replace one kind with another.

Stepping over the comforter in her doorway, Will went back to work.

Sadie felt like herself for the first time in days. Weeks even.

It could be the jeans.

While packing her a nightgown fit for Queen Victoria, Sadie's all too clever mother had also packed her favourite jeans. Soft from wear, skin-tight and worn away at the knees. Add a warm top, an oversized cream jumper and a leopard-print scarf and she was happy as a clam.

It could also have been the coffee.

She'd managed to find an espresso machine in Will's concrete kitchen and actual ground coffee. Not instant, or pods, but fresh ground: manna from heaven.

Of course, it might well have been Will.

Last night had been…unexpected. Not the fact that it had happened. Something had had to give, what with the tension that had been building between them in incremental steps for days. But the way of him—intense as he was in the everyday, all dark, brooding eyes and devastating detail. But also tender. Cherishing her. Making her ache so sweetly, all over, so deeply, she'd lost all sense of place and time. She didn't remember falling asleep so much as drifting away as if on a cloud.

Then, as though she'd closed her eyes and opened them again, it had been morning. And she'd been fully awake.

Every fibre, every cell, every hair follicle switched on. As though the night before had acted like some kind of psychic system reset. As if things would be different from hereon in, she just had to figure out how.

But first…coffee.

Sipping, she stared across the great expanse of Will's plane-hangar-sized abode. The weak morning sunlight did nothing to make the living space appear homelier. While stunning in its über-masculine detail, it was sterile. The perfect pad for the man who'd leapt from his car and accused her of being obtuse.

But what about the man who'd held her in his arms, caressing a length of her hair, breathing softly into her neck as they'd floated into slumber together? There had to be proof of him here somewhere.

She began a room-by-room reconnoitre.

The kitchen cupboards were mostly bare. His office had not a pencil out of place. It was as if he'd deliberately not left his mark on the place. As if being packed, ready to leave a place, wasn't the mark of a well-seasoned traveller but a way of life.

Despite the underfloor heating and the coffee in her system, Sadie suddenly felt the cold.

What brought a man to the point where being alone was the only choice?

The few times Sadie had managed to solicit her mother to talk about her father, Genevieve had admitted she'd been smitten. That his passion, his joie de vivre, his dashing good looks had been hard to resist. That she'd been so blinded by it she'd never for a moment imagined he'd desert her the way he had.

Cradling the cooling coffee, she wandered aimlessly about the upper level, bypassing small doors probably leading to storage areas and a ladder that went up to who knew where.

And then she found the library.

She stepped inside the cool, shadowy room. The heavy dark shelves were covered in books organised by colour and shape rather than author or title. Visually stunning, but futile.

Nevertheless, she searched. For something she couldn't be sure was there but was certain all the same. Going over each row, each column until… There.

She pulled down the textbook, its pages soft and heavy in her hands. Then she turned it over to see the cover, her heart lodging in her throat at the words on the cover—*Waiting to Be Known* by Dr Will Darcy.

Swallowing hard, she looked inside. The title, it explained, was taken from a quote by Carl Sagan. Reviews included praise by famous scientists. The dedication read simply, *"For Clair."*

She flicked through the rest to find that from there it went into full scientific-textbook mode. Words upon words, diagrams, maths and the occasional colour picture to break it up. Clever man, this friend of Hugo's. This friend of hers.

But waiting to be known? Could it be?

She put the book down and looked a little further until she found a large, softcover book amongst the hardbacks. Its spine was creased with use. A book someone had actually read.

She pulled *The Collected Works of William Shakespeare* from the shelf. Opened it to find dog-ears. A handful of notes in the margins. The sign she'd been looking for. The sign *someone* had lived here. Someone had left something of themselves behind.

A piece of paper fell out. A receipt that had been used as a bookmark. By the date, it had been bought after Will had moved in, meaning Will had bought the book himself. Read it. Made notes.

She brought the heavy tome to her chest, pressing it against her rocketing heart. The brand he'd burned there the night before pulsed like a fresh wound as the tendrils of his life twisted a little tighter around hers.

Why was she doing this to herself? Looking for connections? Just because she felt as if she'd glimpsed the core of the man, it didn't mean she ought to keep digging. It didn't mean that knowing him, understanding him, would get her what she wanted.

And she wanted… No.

Will had said it himself—she had a predilection for self-sabotage. Or maybe, she was beginning to wonder, was it more of a compulsion? Do unto herself before someone else did unto her.

If so, not any more.

She'd woken up that morning and she was never going to fall asleep to her life again.

It was long dark by the time Will returned.

And it had been a hell of a day. Determined to get back on track, he'd made a dozen phone calls, finished research papers and begun others, fitting a trip out to the Royal Observatory with a meeting with the gaming crew. He felt as if he could only remember half of it. Probably for the best, as the game had major holes—meaning he had to front up more money, and agree to replace one of the designers, in order to get it back on track. A paper was rejected, as the core theory had already been covered by a fellow scientist from Tulsa. And Natalie was still stubbornly unhappy with him for not being more "sharing".

Music was playing as he headed to the front door and for a second he found himself checking he was outside the right warehouse. When he opened the door he was overcome with the scent of home cooking.

It was so foreign, so specifically outside the basic absolutes of his life, and yet so sorely welcome after such a long, difficult day, he nearly shut the door.

But then he heard the clang of pots and pans. His natural curiosity had him edging inside to find Sadie behind the kitchen bench wearing an apron he didn't know he had, using pots he'd never seen, dancing along with Otis Redding coming from a record player somewhere, cooking up a storm.

She looked up, lips puckered around the end of a wooden spoon, then slid the spoon away before calling, "Honey, you're home!"

It was so sexy Will found himself in the middle of an out-of-body experience—pleasure warring with good judgment. He gripped his briefcase hard enough to break.

Then she burst into laughter. "I'm kidding! Oh, my God, you should see your face. Come in. Put down your stuff. Sit. And wipe that look of abject terror off your face. All this is me going a very small way to making it up to you for being my babysitter, and my bodyguard, my newfound friend."

Will found himself holding his breath as he waited for another title. When none came it felt insufficient.

He dropped his briefcase by the couch, then moved towards the kitchen. Antennae on the blitz, he wasn't sure whether to kiss her on the cheek and ask after her day, or keep the bench safely between them.

In the end, he moved around to the working side of the bench. Plates and cutlery, napkins and wine glasses were lined up ready to be filled. He looked in the pot. Some kind of soup was bubbling away. It smelled amazing. Rich, decadent and wholesome.

"Where did you find all this?"

"In the cupboards. And a local grocery store delivered the ingredients."

"You cooked this?"

"Of course I cooked this. I'm fixing things in reverse, you see. Stitching up the mess I've made, starting with thanking you."

He looked up to find her nudged in beside him. Not touching, but close enough to see the light dusting of flour on her cheek. The sparks of gold in the ends of her hair sticking out of the messy topknot on her head. Her jeans fitted like a second skin and on her feet she wore a pair of socks he would have sworn were his.

Tendrils of attraction curled around him like a fast-motion creeper, twisting and tugging, shooting off in random directions until he couldn't tell where it all began. "I assumed..."

"That I lorded it up in the palace? I *learnt* in the palace. Thank goodness too. When I lived in New York I shared a tiny studio apartment with three other starving actors who waited on tables on the side. I worked in hotels, so I didn't get any of the leftover food they did. For me it was cook or starve."

"You lived in New York."

Her gaze swept to his. Snagged. Whatever she saw in his gaze had her pupils growing dark. A pulse beat in her neck.

Brow furrowing, she moved away from him to clean a bench that already looked pretty clean. "For a few years, in fact. In order to...expand my dramatic education. Why? Do I seem that parochial?"

"Yes."

She laughed, the sound tinkling up into the rafters. And Will found himself imagining coming home to this every day. Not the food, though his taste buds were watering like crazy. The woman. Her smile, her impudence, her interminable optimism.

"I get that," she said. "But, as I keep telling you, you didn't meet me at my best. I can be quite erudite when the situation calls for it. Charming too. And I know some of the best dirty jokes you will hear in your life."

Will breathed out hard, trying to find some kind of equilibrium. He was so out of sync, he felt like coming through his own front door and trying again.

It was his fault. Work or no work, he shouldn't have left as he had, not without discussing what had happened. Without putting their night together into some kind of sensible model—with margins, and objectives, and a deadline.

He'd just have to do it now.

First, he turned to pour himself a large glass of water, but he stopped when he saw the open book on the bench next to the fridge. His textbook. Open to a page about a third of the way through. A couple of bookmarks fashioned out of kitchen towel poked out of the top. And she'd scrawled question marks in the margin.

"You read my book?"

"You read Shakespeare. Seemed a fair exchange. Hungry?" she asked.

"Famished," he said, his voice a growl.

She ladled a hefty amount of soup into each bowl, tore some bread apart and lathered it in butter, then finished the look with a small pinch of herbs. *"Voilà!"*

Will breathed it in. And rubbed a hand up the back of his neck.

"You okay? You look like no one ever cooked you soup before."

"The kitchen at my grandmother's place was three floors down and locked away in the servants' quarters. The house smelled like demoralisation and thousand-year-old paintings. It never smelt like this."

"Well, then, you're welcome." A second slunk by before she said, "You were raised by your grandmother, weren't you? Were your parents not around?"

"They died when we were five."

"That's rough. I can't imagine not having my own mother around, baffling woman that she is. Is that why you always call it your grandmother's place and not home?"

"As you call the place you grew up 'the palace'."

"Huh. Do I really?"

He looked to Sadie, hip nudged against the bench, holding a glass of wine in her hand, watching him. She was the very picture of friendly nonchalance.

Except he knew better. For all the happy chatter, she was on edge. Her energy level was at altissimo, pitching and keening. His pitched with it. An echo. Her shadow. The dark to her light. North to her south.

He moved in closer.

She swallowed, her wine dropping a fraction.

"Nowhere I've lived has ever smelt like this."

"Because I live out of a suitcase, Sadie."

"Or a soft black bag and battered silver telescope case."

He smiled and it felt good. The best he'd felt all day since leaving her bed. "Or that. The truth is I can't stay in one place longer than about a month before it starts to feel too comfortable, my work suffers and I leave. Relationships follow the exact same pattern. I don't like it when my work suffers. When it suffers—"

"You suffer?"

He moved in closer again and she put the wine on the bench.

"The data I am able to collect, collate, decipher and impart is important."

"To whom?"

"To the entire world."

An eyebrow kicked north. "Wow. That's a lot of pressure."

"I like pressure," said Will, moving in close enough that the tips of his leather shoes prodded her socks. "I live for the pressure. Pressure is my bliss."

Sadie crossed her arms but her feet stayed put. "Will, is this some kind of warning?"

"Sadie, since you came into my life I have no bloody idea what I'm doing."

He slid a hand into Sadie's hair, tucking his hand over the back of her neck. He gave himself a moment to soak in those eyes, the freckles, energy enough to keep this place alight for a week.

"Wait," she said on a whisper, "what are we doing?"

"Again, if you need me to tell you that—"

"Will."

It was the perfect moment to explain to her the margins and objectives, and a deadline.

Instead he ran his thumb over her cheek and leaned towards her. Her mouth opened on a sigh just before he put his lips to hers.

A second later her hands crept up his chest, sliding under his collar and pulling his head closer. She opened to him, pressing her body against his. Making sweet little murmuring sounds as she melted into his arms.

He held her tighter still. So tightly she lifted off the ground. Swinging her around, he sat her on the bench.

Her eyes flashed open and her hands flew away as the cool of the concrete seeped into her jeans. And then she smiled against his lips.

This. This was what he'd been thinking about all day. Coming home to this. The intimacy he'd been avoiding his entire adult life. It was terrifying. It was irresistible.

She pulled back just enough to slide his jacket from his shoulders, letting it drop to the floor.

"You're a bad influence," he murmured as he tried to go in for another kiss.

But she pushed him away, moving to undo the buttons of his shirt, one by slow damn one. Once his shirt joined his jacket she ran a hand over his chest, following the line of the now purple and yellow bruise. "Does it hurt?"

"Not right now."

She laughed, the sound sexy as hell.

Then she kissed the bruise, right at the top, and Will sucked in a breath. He held it still as she pulled him into the cradle of her thighs and kissed him. On the jaw, the cheek, the tip of his nose.

Her kisses were so delicate, so exquisite, he felt as if he could barely hold himself together. As if he might crack right down the middle if he breathed too hard.

But then she touched her lips to his, ran her tongue over the seam and tugged his head to hers and he fell apart anyway.

He'd been overachieving by every quantifiable measure of success. But it had been a straight and narrow road. He hadn't been living until that moment.

Pathways opened up inside of him as he ran his hands over Sadie's hair, as he pressed into her warmth and swallowed her gasp in a kiss that changed his world.

He grabbed her by the backside and lifted her off the cold kitchen bench. She wrapped her arms about his neck and didn't break the kiss for even a breath as he carried her upstairs. But still Will held on tight.

She had a habit of running when the going got tough. Making her feel safe enough to stay would take finesse, timing and patience. The hours he'd spent behind the eyepiece of a telescope attempting to focus on precise celestial bodies light years away proved he had the staying power.

At the top of the stairs he turned left, heading into his room this time.

They never did get around to eating that soup.

"Do you have a warmer coat?"

Sadie looked up from her coffee to find Will had come

home early. Then down at the clothes she'd had on the day before. Her underwear was clean, so she figured that was winning. "I do not."

"Wait here."

"Okay."

Will ducked back upstairs, into his bedroom, and came out with a familiar black tracksuit top.

"Hello, old friend!" she said, putting it on under her jumper, letting the hood fall out of the top. "Now what?"

"Now we go out."

"We can't go out."

"Well, we can't stay here. Not for ever."

"If we go out there someone might see you."

"I've been seen before."

"But they'll see *me*, with you."

"Let them."

He gave her a look then, a look she'd never been given in her life before. Yet she understood it all the same. Deep down in the most primal, private, female part of her she knew.

Will Darcy was staking his claim. Not for ever. He didn't believe in for ever. But for now. Which, for him, was still a very big deal.

"Are you sure about this?"

Will took her by the hand and tugged her into his arms. "I called our friend the Prince this morning."

Whoa. "And said what?"

Will rubbed away the frown that popped up above her nose. "I gave him a brief, G-rated, rundown of your stay. He asked how the soup was. I changed the subject."

She coughed out a laugh.

"We had a long talk about many things and found ourselves in absolute agreement."

"You did?"

They had. "The first thing we agreed on was that the

mourning period was over. The photos of us are true and the world has to get over the fact that they are out there. Time to get on with getting on."

"The palace won't like it."

"The palace can bite me."

"Wow, Will Darcy, them's fighting words."

"I was always good in a fight, even as a kid. Scrappy. Not one for following the rules. I've also never been one to skulk in doorways, and I don't plan on making a habit of it now. So what do you say?"

But she couldn't say a single thing. She was too busy trying to find her feet. Not sure whether to laugh or cry or scream, or turn cartwheels. The only thing she didn't have the urge to do was run. She simply placed her hand in the crook of his arm and smiled.

Outside, the day was glorious. Freezing, as if the first tendrils of real winter were coming, but sunny.

Sadie took a great big, bracing breath. "Are we waiting for the car?"

"I thought we'd walk." And off they went.

Once they hit the end of his street, the crowds began to swell. Tourists and locals. Shoppers and workers. A bustling, noisy, energetic mob.

Being around people once more, for the first couple of minutes Sadie panicked any time someone looked their way, but as Will pointed out landmarks—places he drank coffee, a half-court where he played basketball, the Shard—she began to relax. Besides, no one looked at her twice. Not when she had Will at her side. He drew enough gazes, both admiring and envious, for the both of them.

"So, what do you think?" he asked.

Sadie smiled at Will before realising what he was looking at. A good-sized Tudor building—white with brown trim—lay just ahead.

The Globe Theatre—the modern-day "home" of William Shakespeare.

Sadie wasn't sure she could feel any happier than she did in that moment. Until Will pulled two tickets out of his pocket. "*Much Ado About Nothing*—what do you think?"

Speechless, she nodded. And followed as Will led her inside.

And as the play unfolded before her, a simple, brilliant telling of a complex, bittersweet tale, she knew she was done forcing Shakespeare down the throats of high-school kids who weren't even close to being ready to appreciate the language she loved so dearly.

It was a job she had revelled in for its battles and its victories. A job that had fallen her way. A job people expected her to love.

Just as New York had been something everyone had assumed would be a dream come true.

But defying expectations wasn't such a bad thing. And if it meant following her heart, doing what made her happy, and tapping into her bliss, then even if people didn't quite understand the choice, surely that had to be better than the alternative.

She glanced at Will to find him watching her.

And, not caring if anyone was watching, if anyone knew who they were, she gave him a smile that started at the little place marker he'd burned onto her heart. She slipped her hand through his arm, leant her head on his shoulder and let Beatrice and Benedick sweep her off her feet.

Will could not remember the last time he'd taken a morning off work on purpose. But it had been worth it.

He'd followed the play to a point, but had found Sadie far more entertaining: the spark in her eyes, the grin that near split her face in half and the tears when everything came good. She saw the world like someone who was on earth for the very first time.

She was practically skipping as they left the theatre. "That was amazing. Just…wonderful. It's been so long since I've seen a real, live, professional Shakespearean production not put on by sixteen-year-old kids. I feel like I've been banging my head against a wall for years! That, Will Darcy, was an epiphany. I cannot thank you enough." She threw herself at him then, wrapping him in a hug that took him only a second or two to return. "Now I have to check out the gift shop."

While she did so, Will checked his phone. A dozen calls had come in while his phone had been on silent.

Not wasting time to check the messages, he rang Natalie.

"Hello?"

Will checked his watch. Dammit. It was late over there. "Natalie, apologies. I didn't check the time—I'll call back later."

"No, wait! Give me a second to get to my desk." Much shuffling and banging of doors, a squeak of a desk chair and… "Right. So I've been on to his secretary and she seems to think we've lost our chance but—"

"Sorry. Whose secretary?"

"Ah, the prime minister's." A pause, then, "Did you not get my messages?"

"I've yet to listen—"

"Why on earth? You always check your messages. In fact, you're pedantic to the point of anally retentive. My cousin Brianna read somewhere that men with your looks, your brains and your sex appeal—"

"Natalie."

"Yes. Sorry." A breath, then, "He had space for you this afternoon. At two. Then he was flying out of the country for eight days."

Will checked his watch. It was a little after four.

"Send me the number, I'll call—"

"I've already checked. It's too late, Will. He's gone."

Eyelids lowering, Will swore. Swore some more. Then pressed his phone against his forehead.

"Will? Will, are you there?"

"Thanks for trying, Natalie."

"That's okay. I wish I could have done more."

"It's not your fault," he said, right as Sadie came out of the gift shop, her gaze scanning the area before landing on him. "It's mine."

Something was wrong.

After all the excitement of the play, the sweet thrill of freedom and the hot, burning delight of love that was pulsing through her like radio waves, all the extra layers in the world couldn't have saved her from Will's chill.

Once they were back inside the warehouse, thawing out, she got up the guts to ask, "Will, is everything okay?"

"No, actually."

"What happened?"

"It's nothing. A work matter."

As soon as he mentioned work, she felt him pulling away, heading into a bubble inside his head. Her instinct was to let him, but something bigger made her reach out and clamp a hand around his arm.

"Will, tell me. Maybe I can help."

He looked at her then, the creases at the edges of his eyes deeper, but not from smiling. Her heart slowed, her blood turning sluggish, as if preparing itself for a winter freeze.

"I may have mentioned my old professor at some point."

Her memory skipped and raced until it found the moment she was looking for. "The one who encouraged you to wonder."

"He passed away earlier in the year, not long before your wedding invitation arrived, in fact. Which is by the by. Anyway, he had been point-man for a research grant at our old university for decades. On his death it was marked to shut down. It's cumbersome and prohibitively expensive. But it's also imperative to the long-term success of astronomical research in this country."

"What an amazing legacy."

Will's eyes flashed and she thought she had him back, but he ran a hand up the back of his neck, dislodging her hold on his arm at the same time.

"I was guaranteed a chance to meet with the prime minister to urge him to continue the grant and have been waiting for news of the time. It came through this morning while we were walking. The meeting was set for the same time the play began."

Sadie swallowed, the burn of ignominy tingling all over her skin. "Can't you reschedule? Go bang on his door, right now?"

Will looked down at the floor, hands deep in the pockets of his jeans. What had Hugo said? Will wasn't an island unto himself, he was a planet.

"Will—"

"My work, my achievements, my reputation open doors for me where others wouldn't even get a look-in. But this was my chance. My last chance to truly honour a man who made all that possible. I forgot myself and screwed it up."

Sadie's stomach clutched at the disappointment in his voice. Worse than disappointment. Devastation.

Her throat was like a desert as she said, "It's my fault."

He looked at her then, really at her. And she realised in that moment that he held her heart in his hands.

"It's mine. For thinking I could do this."

Sadie didn't ask what "this" was. She didn't have to. She'd been right with him as this thing between them had played out, unravelling, exploding, taking them over. She'd held his hand on the street, she'd felt his eyes on her as they'd watched the play. They'd both been held in thrall of a moment in time where their worlds had aligned and all things had seemed possible.

He was determined to take the blame, but Sadie knew it was all her. This was what she did. She got intoxicated by possibility, by the chance that this time things would be different. She dragged others along for the ride, only to end up bathing them in her chaos.

She wrapped her arms around herself in an attempt to stop the trembles that were taking her over, years of practice helping her summon a smile from nowhere. "Don't be so hard on yourself. You've been amazing. Heroic even. I know how much you've sacrificed in rescuing this damsel in distress. And if there's anything I can do to make it up to you—"

"You are no damsel, Sadie, and right now I've never felt less heroic in my life."

He gave her a long look. Of ruination and despair. But beneath it all hummed that heat. The magnet that kept pulling them back together even when circumstance, fate and history had tried telling them it wasn't to be.

It felt as if the universe was holding its breath.

Then he took a step away. "You're right. I can't take no for an answer. I need to attempt to fix this. Look, do you mind if I…?"

"Go. Go! I can take care of myself."

"Good. Thank you, Sadie." Then he jogged up the stairs towards his office, pulling the door shut behind him.

And Sadie brought a shaking hand to cover her mouth.

She was in love with Will.

She knew it. She'd spent the morning bathed in it like a divine glow. But even that hadn't been enough to stop her from being his downfall.

Sadie couldn't feel her feet as she made her way to her room. And there she slowly, deliberately, packed her things.

She took off Will's jacket, folded it neatly and put it onto the chair in her room. She made the bed, tucking in the corners like an expert. She grabbed some tissue and wiped down every surface she'd touched.

All she'd ever wanted was to feel safe somewhere. Or with someone. Even while her life raged in chaos around her, she'd felt safer the past three days in Will's company than she could remember feeling ever before. His stoic strength, his quiet confidence, were like a balm to her frenetic soul.

Which was a big part of why loving Will, and leaving him, meant now she was scared. Terrified. Shaken from the top of her head to the tips of her toenails.

But she had to do this. For him.

With one last look around the room she made her way to Will's office.

He was on the phone, pacing, papers strewn across the surface of his desk.

He was an important man doing important work. Work that he believed made him the man he was. Sadie would have begged to differ, but she knew he wouldn't hear it right now even if she stripped naked, sat on him and forced him to listen.

He put his hand over the microphone. "Sadie, sorry, you're going to have to give me some time here."

"I'm going one better." She hitched her bag on her shoulder and he stopped pacing.

Grey clouds swarmed over his face. He opened his mouth, no doubt to tell her she was being dramatic, and maybe she was, but she stopped him with the international sign for stop. "I've called a car service. They'll be here in ten."

Running a hand down his face, he hung up the phone and strode around the desk until they were toe to toe. The creases around his eyes were so deep, so concerned. Frustration poured off him in waves. "Do you really have to do this now?"

"I really do. It's past time. And you know it too."

Hands on hips, he looked over her shoulder, into the middle distance, his big brain working overtime. "I'm not a selfless man, Sadie. I'm not going to make a song and dance out of this. I'm not Hugo."

"I'm very glad you're not Hugo." It ached not to tell him why. To tell him that she loved his particular brand of strength. His stoicism. She loved his stubbornness and his lonesomeness.

She loved him.

"You've been incredible, Will. A good friend to Hugo. A good friend to me. You gave me sanctuary when I needed it most. But you've given up enough to help us. Too much. Today proved that."

She tried to put it into words he'd understand. *Nothing lasts for ever.* But the words wouldn't come. It hurt too much.

Instead she leaned in, placed a hand on the bruise over his heart and kissed him on the cheek. Then, because she wasn't perfect, she took him by the chin, fresh stubble scraping the pads of her fingers, and turned his face so she could kiss his beautiful lips.

He resisted, caught in that vortex of disappointment and frustration. But only for a fraction of a second. Then he hauled her against him and kissed her with everything he had.

If it had been any other man kissing her so that her kneecaps melted, she might have put it down to the urge to get his own way. But Will was not a game player. He was a man of integrity and might.

If she was a betting girl she might have thought that kiss was his way of showing her he was beginning to fall for her too.

But all bets were off. It was time for her to go.

She pulled away, pressed herself back, held herself together by the barest thread. “Thanks, Will. For everything.”

He said nothing. No goodbyes. No understanding nods.

But neither did he look like a statue. He looked ravaged, like a man braced against a perfect storm.

Holding that image in her heart, she turned and walked away, down the stairs, out the front door and into the car waiting to take her to the airport. Where she’d take her chances with being recognised, holding her head high.

For she was running again, but this time it wasn’t out of fear. This time she was running away for love.

As the tears ran down her face she felt as if she’d done the absolute right thing for the first time in her life.

No one would throw her a parade, or pat her on the head and tell her *well done.* She’d make no new fans out of this. But she knew, and that was what mattered.

CHAPTER TEN

SADIE PARKED HER car under a tree, leapt over the ancient, crumbling brick wall edging the field and walked across the same expanse over which she'd fled not that long ago.

The bottoms of her jeans were soon damp, her boots beginning to chill. But she ploughed on until she found herself standing outside the antechamber, staring up at the façade of the palace.

It was strange to think she had grown up here, and now it only looked like a building. A beautiful building, to be sure, glorious and charming and strong. But it was no longer her home.

Not about to head up to the front door and knock, but also not keen on bumping into anyone in the private quarters, she went with a hunch, pushed her way through the garden brambles and tested the window. It opened easy as pie.

It was ironic to find herself climbing in through the very same window out of which she'd climbed just a few days ago. Or maybe it was necessary. A kind of bookend.

The antechamber was much as she'd left it bar the wedding paraphernalia, which was no doubt at the bottom of a rubbish bin somewhere.

She checked through the door to make sure the coast was clear, then headed off, through the palace.

Five minutes and a few close calls later, Sadie sat huddled beneath the fluffy, double-thick blanket she'd nicked from the back of a couch in the library, secure in her favourite spot in the palace. She was atop the turret of the tallest tower, feet dangling over the side, the country she loved at her feet.

Her gaze tripped over snow-capped mountains, verdant green fields dotted with fluffy black and white sheep. Over the lights of a dozen quaint villages tucked into valleys and sprawled over hillsides.

One of them had to be the village of Bellponte in which she and Will had stayed. If she'd seen the palace from La Tulipe, then surely she could see La Tulipe from here. But she'd never had much of a sense of direction, and couldn't be sure.

Shivering, Sadie tucked her feet up beneath her and wrapped the blanket tighter.

She hadn't realised it at the time, but her life had changed in that chintz-filled tower room. She'd grown up, faced her demons, faced herself. And she'd begun to fall in love.

"Hey."

Sadie sniffed, wiped her cheek against her shoulder and spun to find Hugo framed by the heavy brick doorway.

He said, "Only the Keeper of the Flags is meant to have a key to this spot."

Sadie lifted a finger from its warm cocoon to tap the side of her nose. "I have contacts."

Hugo ambled to Sadie's side. He sat, then swore at the freezing cold of the brick beneath his hands.

Sadie offered him some of her blanket. He refused with a manly shake of the head.

Together, in silence, they looked out over Vallemont as they had a zillion times before. He'd first brought her up here when she was six or seven. She'd also found him here a few weeks back, after Prince Reynaldo had made him the offer he couldn't refuse.

Sadie asked, "How did you know I was here?"

"At least half a dozen people told me they'd seen you sneaking through the palace, heading this way."

"Oh. I thought I'd made it without being seen."

"A running theme in your life of late."

Sadie groaned. "Tell me about it. A few hours ago I thought I'd made it all the way through Heathrow unseen before a pair of Americans asked me for a selfie."

Hugo shot her a smile. "And there I was thinking you were still in London. In fact, I had the funny feeling you were going to be there for some time."

"Nah. This is where I belong." Sadie rested her chin against her knees and glanced at her old friend. "If I hadn't run, would you have gone through with it?"

"Of course," said Hugo without missing a beat.

"Even though you don't love me, and never have."

"I do—"

"Hugo, come on. Does your tummy tighten every time you lay eyes on me? Do you come out in goosebumps if I simply brush your arm? Do you ache for me when we're apart?"

Hugo's silence was answer enough.

"Then consider yourself lucky one of us was smart enough to walk away."

Hugo nodded. "Done." And like that they put the Great Hiccup of their lifelong friendship behind them.

Then, with a bump to her shoulder with his, Hugo asked, "When did you develop such specific parameters for what it means to be in love?"

Sadie bit her lip.

"Because I've never heard you talk that way. You're always so blasé about such things. I'm assuming this is a new development. Very recent, in fact. Days old, at the very most."

"Drop it."

"No, I don't think I will. Why aren't you in London, Sadie?"

If she could have pulled the blanket over her head she would have. But that would have been the old Sadie—make a joke of things, do a little tap dance to distract everyone from anything unpleasant.

So why wasn't she in London? As difficult or ugly as they might be, the new Sadie was all about the truths.

The truth was she might not physically be there, but her heart was. And her head. And she wasn't going to sit there and do nothing about that any more.

She pulled herself to standing and threw Hugo the blanket.

"Come on, get up."

"Why?"

"You and I have some work to do."

A week later Will sat staring at his laptop.

Or *through* his laptop would have been a more fitting description, as the words of the position paper he was attempting to outline were swimming before his eyes.

He could be doing this on a plane to Geneva, where he was due to present his famous "Scenes from the Orion Nebula" lecture the next day. He did some of his best work on planes, alone, uninterrupted, the white noise creating a prefect creative cocoon.

Instead here he sat, in a village pub, with no Wi-Fi and limited phone reception, waiting to feel the satisfied glow that came from one of the best weeks of his career.

An offer had come through on the Orion Nebula game, and he'd sold, tripling his investment overnight.

An array of radio telescopes in Chile had picked up

space noise for a few seconds in the direction of Orion's Belt and he'd been there to hear it.

He'd been offered the European Space Agency's top spot on the Future Commission—focusing on how best to channel research and funding for telescopes to be launched into space.

Best of all, an unknown benefactor had gifted five years to the Templeton Grant. Natalie had connected the call from the prime minister, who'd bashfully agreed to join forces now that he didn't have to justify the initial expense, promising to announce it at the World Science Symposium later that year.

But no glow came.

His phone rang. In pure relief, he answered it without looking at the caller details. "Darcy."

"Where are you?"

Hugo. Will sat up so fast he knocked his beer, the froth sloshing over the rim and onto his laptop.

Mopping it up with a napkin, he said, "Is everything all right? Is she okay?"

Hugo laughed. "Sadie's fine. As far as I know."

"What do you mean, as far as you know? Isn't she with you?"

"Of course she's not with me, you damn fool. In fact—No. Yes. I'm going to say it. She should be with you."

Wincing, Will screwed the napkin into a ball. "You don't know what you're talking about."

"I'm a well-educated man. I have seen the world. And I am a prince. Therefore, I am never wrong."

It was so unlike Hugo to pull the prince card, Will actually coughed out a laugh.

"She left of her own free will," said Will.

"Did you ask her to stay?"

"You know as well as I do that there's no telling her anything. I've never met anyone as stubborn." *As quick to laughter, as emotional, bright, indefatigable, raw, sweet, thoughtful, warm.*

"Hmm. I feel as if I have."

Will tossed the damp napkin onto the table.

Hugo went on. "I have never seen you as relaxed as you were when you were with her. She was the best thing that ever happened to you, my friend. How the hell could you have let her go?"

Will knew Hugo was pushing for a reaction. He was good at it.

"Right back at you," Will gritted out, unsurprised when Hugo laughed down the phone.

"So, where are you?"

Will looked up from his laptop at the rustic walls, the craggy-mountain motif carved into the bar, the framed picture of the reigning Prince of Vallemont on the wall, the pink and rose-gold trim on the bar towels. All he said was, "In a pub."

"Alone?"

Alone. Funny how that word had been his touchstone for so many years. A motivator, a goal. He'd held on to the fact that his aloneness gave him an edge, time and motivation to work hard, to better focus, to give himself over to the study of the whys of the universe.

Now the word felt like an open wound.

"Yes, I'm alone. I just felt the need to stretch my legs."

Stretching them all the way to a small pub in Vallemont. With a view over the thatched rooftops of Bellponte to the top corner of a crumbling hotel with a lopsided Tower Room that looked as though it might fall off the side of the building at any moment.

Will asked, "I am an important man with much work to do. Did you call me for a reason?"

"Go online, stream Vallemontian station, Channel Four, at five o'clock our time."

"And why would I want to do that?"

"Because, old friend, for all the stars and moons and planets and galaxies you have unravelled in your search for the meaning of life, I'd bet the palace it won't compare to what Channel Four is about to teach you."

Will drummed his fingers against the table top and looked up at the TV playing silently above the bar. The logo at the bottom of the screen said Channel Four. If that wasn't a sign he had no idea what was. "Fine. I'll track it down."

"My work here is done," said Hugo, and then he was gone.

Will checked his watch. Fifteen minutes until five.

He closed his laptop and worked on his beer. A low hum of pub chatter and occasional laughter punctuated clinking glassware and the ting of the cash register as Will watched the clock tick down.

Just on five a "special presentation" graphic flashed onto the screen.

A young woman's smiling face mouthed words Will couldn't hear. Closed-caption text scrolled across the bottom of the screen, stating the journalist's name, stipulating that she was a former pupil of the Vallemont School of Drama and therefore a one-time student of Mercedes Gray Leonine, and was happy to be able to facilitate the evening's special event.

And then…there she was.

Will felt his stomach drop away at the sight of her. Her mussed red hair was slicked back and pinned off her face with a clip. Long, sparkly earrings swung against her shoulders and a pale floral top clung to her elegant frame.

She looked different—still, somehow, serene. She looked so beautiful it hurt to blink. And even with the sound turned down he could hear her voice. The bravado.

The humour. The strength. The vulnerability. As if she were sitting right beside him.

God, how he wished she were sitting beside him. How he wished he could touch her, hold her, kiss her, hear her voice for real; watch her animated face as she told a story; watch her quiet face as she listened to one of his.

For a man who didn't believe in wishes, they came so thick and fast he couldn't keep up.

The interviewer leaned forward and the camera pulled out to show Sadie sitting on a white couch in a large, old-fashioned-looking room that was no doubt in the palace. And there Hugo sat, right beside her.

Even without sound it was clear how fond they were of one another. Nothing more. No romantic tension. No sideways glances. Just friendship. And honest remorse at the way things had been handled.

"Turn it up!" someone called from across the room. "The TV—turn it up."

The barkeeper did as asked, and Sadie's voice blasted across the pub.

"Our reasons were private, but we hope you believe us when we say they were just and good. We were blinded by a need to do the right thing; we just…didn't think things through to their logical conclusions. And if a man like Prince Alessandro says he'll marry you it's pretty hard to say no. Just look at him!"

The interviewer laughed. Blushed. A woman at a table behind Will said, "Oh, I'm looking."

"If you take anything from this interview, know that your Prince is one of the very best men you could ever hope to meet. Second-best at worst. He's just not the man for me."

And then Sadie looked into the camera. She looked right into Will's eyes. It was a split second, a blink. But he felt that look as if she'd reached out and grabbed him by the heart and squeezed.

"And you, Prince Alessandro—is Mercedes not the woman for you?"

He smiled, and Sadie turned to him, which was when Will saw the clip in her hair. Silver, sparkly, a shooting star.

Will didn't realise he was on his feet until someone behind him politely asked him to sit down.

"Don't answer that," she said. "He'll just say something charming so as not to hurt my feelings. But I'd have driven the Prince crazy. And Vallemont does not need a crazy prince. Look at Prince Reynaldo—such a benevolent leader, so forward-thinking. So generous."

Will noted that Hugo looked down at that point, hiding a wry smile.

"Not only on a personal level—having always been so kind to me, the daughter of a palace maid. Did you know he's recently personally invested in a number of international grants towards the arts and sciences, making Vallemont not only the most beautiful country in the world, but also one of the most progressive?"

The interviewer looked dutifully amazed. "Well, that is news."

The interviewer then turned to Hugo, asking him a spate of questions that Will barely heard. While Sadie leant back in the chair and breathed out long and slow. Only then did Will see how tired she seemed, the slight smudges under her eyes that even television make-up couldn't quite hide.

Sitting through the rest of the interview was the hardest thing Will had ever done in his entire life, but he had to, in case she had any more hidden messages for him. For that was what the interview had been. That was why Hugo had made him watch.

By the end of the interview it was made very clear that this would be the only time they would talk of it; that they believed their explanation and apologies were done. A great big line had been drawn under the day Sadie left Hugo at the altar. This chapter of the country's history was well and truly closed.

Then it was over.

Will's glass sat in a puddle of condensation next to a very large tip as he dashed from the pub.

Outside, he had no idea which way to turn. He grabbed his phone, jabbed in Hugo's number.

Hugo answered on the first ring. "Hey, mate, how's things?"

"Where is she?" Will asked, walking just to feel as though he was going somewhere.

"Now he's in an all fire rush—"

"Hugo."

Hugo chuckled. "She moved out of the palace the day she came back."

"What's her mother's new address?"

"She's not there either. For now she's taken a room in that dilapidated old hovel you holed her up in for those first couple of days."

And suddenly Will was running, scooting around people blocking his way, leaping over a display of boxes holding masses of pink flowers. His shoes slapped against the uneven pavement, his jacket and scarf flying out behind him.

"Probably a good time to tell you I'm heading away for a while."

Will made a left, realised he'd taken a wrong turn. Spinning on his heel, he made a right instead. "Where are you going?"

"Not sure it matters right now. I just wanted you to know so if you don't hear from me you understand why."

Reading between the lines, Will knew: Hugo had taken the olive branch.

Will turned the corner to find himself facing La Tulipe. The window to the Tower Room was open, the gauzy curtain flapping in the wintry breeze.

His lungs burned from the icy air. His neck itched from the heat of the woollen scarf. And as he shook out his cold fingers he realised he'd left his laptop, his notes, his life's work behind in the pub.

The fact that he felt zero compunction to leave this spot to collect his all-important work was final proof of how fundamentally his world view had broadened. Made room for diversion, for insouciance, for the contents of the room above. And it would still be there when he got around to picking it up. This was Vallemont, after all.

Will breathed out fast and hard. The last of his breath leaving on a laugh.

"Everything all right, Darcy?" Hugo asked over the phone.

"It's been a big few days."

"Tell me about it."

"Promise me something. Next time you agree to marry a girl, you actually go through with it."

Hugo laughed. "I don't think that will be a problem I will ever have to face again."

After a loaded beat, Hugo hung up.

Will put the phone in his pocket and stared up at the open window.

She had left. And he had let her go. Because when you lose enough of the people you love, letting people go became a fallback position.

Only here he was. Because he'd been looking at it all wrong.

Gravity wasn't entirely destructive. It helped hold the entire universe together.

Looking around, he picked up a small stone. He threw

it towards the window, hearing it skitter across the balcony floor.

A few seconds later he picked up another and tried again. This time the stone hit the glass door.

His heart was thundering in his chest by that stage, as if it were trying to kick its way through his ribs.

Then the door moved, the curtains sucking inside the room.

And there she was. Beneath a fluffy pink beanie with a pompom on top, her hair bobbed on her shoulders. Her lips were painted a pretty pale pink. A dark floral dress flared at her wrists and landed just above her knees. Brown tights disappeared into knee-high boots.

"Sadie."

"Quite the aim you have."

"Had to do something when we skipped out on school. Skimming stones at a local lake was right up there."

Her hands gripped the railing. "Were you just passing through?"

"I was, in fact, enjoying a quiet beer in a pub down the way when I saw you on the television."

"You did?" She licked her lips. "Was it any good? I couldn't bring myself to watch."

He moved closer to the building, so that he could see her better. "I liked your hair clip."

Her hand moved to her beanie, her cheeks pinking.

"I do have one question for you though."

She leant her arms against the railing. "What's that?"

"It was Reynaldo behind the Templeton Grant. And you were the one behind Reynaldo."

"That's not a question."

"How on earth did you swing it?"

"Prince Reynaldo put the hard word on a friend of mine once. I figured it was time someone did the same back to him."

"What did you give up in return?"

A slow grin spread across her face. "A promise to never again agree to marry anyone in his family. It was a difficult decision but in the end I felt it was the right one for me."

"Not only for you," he said.

She breathed out hard and fast. Her smile was open and warm, and just like that he let it in. He let her in. Let her fill him up. Take him over. And it was as if he'd opened his eyes fully for the first time in his life.

Had the sky been that blue a moment before? The buildings that many shades of yellow? Did winter ever smell this good?

Will could no longer feel his feet. It was as if gravity had simply stopped working. Only one way to be sure—he moved closer to the building and took a better look at the bricks. He grabbed hold of a couple and gave them a wiggle.

"What do you think you're doing?" she called. "Do not climb up that wall!"

A beat, then, "Well, I can't go in the front door. Janine will see me. And then she'll start quoting *Much Ado About Nothing.* Or she'll want to know how I know the Prince, and I'll never get out of there—"

"Sod it," said Sadie, tossing a leg over the edge of the balcony.

What? No. "You have to be kidding."

"I'm no damsel in distress, remember."

Right. It didn't stop him from standing beneath her with his arms outstretched, ready to catch.

A few of the bricks had seen better days, sending sprays of crumbing shale to hit the ground and turn to dust. But she made it down, feet first, pulling bougainvillaea flowers from the front of her dress.

"You quite done?" he asked, his voice rough.

She looked at him then, her eyes full, her whole body

quaking with the kind of energy that could no doubt be seen from outer space.

Then she was in his arms before he even knew they were moving. The scent of honeysuckle filled his senses, and the grey blah that had held him in its grip the past few days melted away.

And then he took her face in his hands, her sweet, lovely face, and he kissed her. And kissed her. And kissed her. "I should never have let you go. No. Let me start again."

"I thought you started pretty well," she said, her voice a husky croak.

"I was right to let you go. For you can go wherever the hell you want, whenever the hell you want. What I mean is, I should never have let you go without telling you what you have come to mean to me."

"Okay."

"I'm used to being alone."

"Big shock."

He should have known she wouldn't make this easy. But that was what he loved about her.

What he *loved* about her. *He loved her.* Where first there was something that took up no space at all, suddenly he was inundated. Because he, a man who believed in things he could see, measure and explain, was in love.

"What I am trying to say, if you'll shut up and let me, is that I'm used to being alone, the way you are used to being surrounded. Your life is here. Mine is everywhere else. You are an untidy grub—"

"While you are so fastidious I don't know how you manage to leave the house in the morning." Sadie blinked up at him, all sleepy-eyed, as her fingers curled into his hair, tugging at the ends every few seconds, sending shards of electricity right through him.

Screw it.

"I love you, Sadie."

The twirling stopped.

"I am in love with you. I have all the evidence to back it up too. Physical, intellectual, anecdotal. But I don't care. The only important thing is that I feel it, right here."

He slapped a hand over his heart and wished with every ounce of his being that she might believe him. Then, with a rush of inspiration that could only have come from somewhere beyond the realm of his understanding, he brought out the big guns. *"'Doubt thou the stars are fire; Doubt that the sun doth move; Doubt truth to be a liar; But never doubt I love.'"*

A little *Hamlet* right when it counted. She grinned and laughed, tears now streaming down her face. "I don't doubt. I believe it," she said. "I believe you."

To think this alternative reality had been out there in the universe all this time and he'd closed himself off to it. He chided himself as a man of science and vowed to explore every angle of this new discovery.

Starting with Sadie's mouth. Her soft, pink, delicious mouth. The sweetest taste there was.

After an age, she pulled away, straining for breath as she rested her head against his chest. "I love you too, you know."

Will tipped her chin so he could look into her eyes. "I didn't actually. But that is good to know."

She grinned, the grin turning into laughter. Then she let him go, flinging her arms out sideways, tipping her head to the sun. "I'm totally, madly in love with you. Which is crazy, right? That this happened. Imagine if Hugo and I had never come up with our fool plan. Imagine if we'd come to our senses earlier. Imagine if I'd never run. The chances were high that we'd have never met. There's only one possible explanation for it. This was always in the stars."

"Sadie."

"Yes, Will," she said on a sigh as she brought her hands to his shoulders.

"As a man of science, I'm going to pretend I didn't hear a word you said past 'madly in love'. Okay?"

"You do what you need to do. Just know that I do love you. Physically." She lifted onto her toes to place a kiss at the corner of his mouth. "Intellectually." She dragged a kiss over the edge of his jaw. "Anecdotally." With that she bit down on his earlobe.

"Good afternoon."

Sadie slowly edged her teeth away from Will's ear before as one they turned to look over Sadie's shoulder.

A local baker was riding by on his bicycle, a bag of baguettes poking out of the basket at the back. He gave them a jaunty wave.

"Good afternoon," they said as one.

"Just saw your interview on the TV," said the baker, letting his foot drift to the pavement as he pulled to a stop. "Very nicely handled. If the rest of your generation is as savvy as our Prince, then our country is in for a grand future. Now you can hopefully get on with your lives."

Will's hand drifted to Sadie's lower back right as her hand curled around the back of his neck. She said, "Sounds like a plan to me."

With that the baker sat back onto his bike and rolled down the hill, whistling as he went.

Will pressed his lips against Sadie's ear. "Shall we? Get on with our lives?"

She plucked a purple flower from his shoulder, then smiled into his eyes. "Let's."

EPILOGUE

SADIE WOKE UP. Sensing it was still the middle of the night, she thought about rolling over and going back to sleep but instead she stretched, hands and feet reaching for the four corners of her glorious, big new bed.

It took up the entire platform in her bedroom in the Tower Room at La Tulipe. No canopy, no fake ivy, no net curtains. Nothing princessy about it at all.

She'd bought the bed for Will as a gift when they'd moved in. He'd bought her the building to put it in, so fair was fair.

She let her hands and feet relax, her breaths slowing, a smile spreading over her face as she thought about her plans for the coming day.

There was a meeting with the architect and project manager first thing, as refurbishment was beginning in the old foyer next week—the administration offices of the brand-new Vallemont Royal Youth Theatre Company.

As patron, Hugo had requested something dry, esoteric, modern for their first play. As chief financial officer, Natalie had told Hugo to keep his intellectual nose out of things he didn't understand. As front office manager, Janine hadn't stopped smiling long enough to have a decided opinion. As director, Sadie had smiled and nodded and told everyone she'd certainly take his thoughts into consideration.

Rehearsals for *Romeo and Juliet* began that afternoon.

As for the rest of La Tulipe—it would eventually become home. So far, they were living out of the Tower Room and would do for some time. The place was crumbling, with so many add-ons and temporary walls built over the years it would be like a puzzle to undo it all and bring it back to its former glory. But they had time. Years. Their whole lives.

She breathed in deeply and rolled over, ready for sleep to come again.

But something stopped her.

Her eyes sprang open. She sat bolt upright. Weak moonlight poured into the room and she struggled to make out shapes in the semi-darkness. There! By the couch. The overnight bag on the floor.

Will was home.

Sadie leapt out of bed and wrapped a robe around herself—black, soft, Will's—then padded out to the balcony. The night was crystal-clear. The moon a sliver in the sky.

She climbed the new stepladder that had been bolted to the side of the tower, used the turrets to haul herself over the top and landed with her usual lack of finesse.

And there he sat, rubbing a hand over his beard as he finessed the mighty new telescope that took up half the roof. Maia had been retired to their London pad and lived in her own custom-built glassed-in, rooftop conservatory, for ever pointing at the sky.

Will looked up at the reverberation of her landing. He pressed back into the seat and rubbed the eye that had been pressed against the lens. His voice was a familiar deep, wonderful rumble as he said, "Hey."

She couldn't hold back. She ran. And she leapt. He caught her, strong enough not to topple as she launched herself at him.

"When did you get back?" she asked, her voice muffled by the fact she was nestled into his neck.

"An hour ago."

"Why didn't you wake me?"

"You know how you are."

"Like a Labrador puppy, all energy then…deep, deep sleep; yeah, I know. How was the trip?"

Will had spent three days lecturing on his beloved Orion Nebula at Boston University, had hosted an international day of moon-viewing from the northern tip of Alaska, then had headed to London to record a voice-over for a BBC documentary. And it sat so well on him, he looked as if he'd just woken from eight perfect hours of sleep.

The man was a natural phenomenon. No wonder the whole world wanted a piece of him. Thankfully Sadie had grown up with a best friend who was a wanted man. She'd learned to be a good sharer.

"Good," he said. "Great. Some brilliant young minds out there giving me a run for my money. I might even have found the first recipient of the new and improved Templeton Grant."

"Oh, Will, that's so cool."

"Isn't it just?" Will lifted a hand to push Sadie's hair from her face.

Her heart skittered in her chest at his touch. She wondered if it always would. She figured there was a pretty good chance.

She settled on his lap, wrapped her arms about his neck and kissed him. Or he kissed her. They probably met somewhere in the middle, which seemed to be their way, and that was her last thought as sensation took over. Her body was all melting warmth, the chill of the night air a distant memory as they too made up for lost time.

Light years later they pulled apart, Sadie sighing. "Now get back to work. All that data won't record itself. I'll just sit here quietly and do my best not to disturb you." With that she sank her head against his chest.

"I'm not sure my calculations will be entirely reliable."

"No? How about if I do this?" She wriggled a little more until she was sure she was getting the reaction she was after.

Will picked her up as he stood. She laughed, and clung to his neck, as he stepped out of the chair, her voice carrying off into the night, over the top of the village that was now her home—their home—dissipating long before it reached the mountains beyond.

And out there, dark beneath the bright white caps of snow above, the palace slept.

Its story no longer her own.

"Oh?" she said, feigning surprise. "You done for the night?"

"Not even close," Will rumbled as he dropped her feet to the cold stone floor.

He chased her down the ladder and took her to bed, where he made her see stars.

* * * * *